MOONSHINE KISS

BOOTLEG SPRINGS BOOK 3

LUCY SCORE

CLAIRE KINGSLEY

That's What She Said Publishing, Inc.

The book is a work of fiction. The characters and events in this book are fictitious. Any similarity to real persons, living or dead, is purely coincidental and not intended by the author.

ISBN-13: 978-1-945631-35-1 (ebook)

ISBN-13: 978-1-945631-36-8 (paperback)

Lucyscore.com

060920

DEDICATION

To Kevin Kneupper. You know why.

1

CASSIDY

Eight years ago...

"I don't feel so good, Cass." My best friend and perpetual partner in crime, Scarlett Bodine, looked up from her hands and knees. She wiped her mouth on the sleeve of her t-shirt.

I stripped the just-in-case hair tie off my wrist and fashioned her long, dark hair into a sloppy knot. "That's 'cause you puked up half a bottle of Jack and a couple of beers, Scar," I reminded her. "You shouldn't have taken Zirkel's bet."

Wade Zirkel had stupidly bet Scarlett he could outdrink her. He was still passed out in the dirt back at the bonfire.

"I'm hungry," she moaned. "Wait, no. More puke."

As Scarlett heaved up her dinner of cheese sticks and coffee into our old Sunday school teacher Mrs. Morganson's hedgerow, I patted her shoulder and drunk dialed my choice of designated drivers.

Bowie picked up, his voice husky. "Y'all need a ride, don't you?"

Just a couple of words and I swear my heart did a swan dive into my belly full of Jack Daniels.

"Maybe I'm calling to listen to your pretty voice." My super sexy flirting was ruined by a hiccup.

"You owe me $10."

It wasn't the fee for the ride. It was the bet we'd made not four hours ago when I'd picked up Scarlett. I was home for the summer fresh off my first year of college, eager to show off my sophomore self to my best friend in the world. And maybe her older brothers. One in particular.

Bowie Bodine.

I'd been doodling that man's name on my notebooks since elementary school. My crush on him was woven into the fabric of my childhood. In kindergarten, when I'd learned to write my own name, I'd insisted on the spot that my teacher show me how to write Bowie's, too. In junior high, I'd developed an obsessive interest in the high school baseball team thanks entirely to their all-star pitcher, Bowie.

"I got your damn ten dollars, mercenary. Now, get your ass down to Mrs. Morganson's before your sister poisons her boxwoods with regurgitated bourbon."

"Ah, hell. Be there in five. I'm holding you personally responsible if Scar tosses up in my back seat again, Cass." He hung up.

I smiled and undid one extra button on my shirt.

"Fix your hair," Scarlett instructed from the ground. "Can't land a man with drunk hair."

Scarlett was aware of my friendly feelings toward her brother. We had a plan. I was going to entrap Bowie with my feminine wiles, marry the man, and then Scarlett and I would be real-life sisters.

I was calculating with a stubborn streak wider than ten miles, at least, according to my mom. With Scarlett's take-action-without-minding-the-consequences attitude in my corner, Bowie didn't stand a chance against my long game.

I'd switched up my strategy from the hand painted sign-carrying preteen at every home game to the leggy, cleavage-displaying, ambivalent college girl. I flirted lightly as if it were mere habit and pretended that I had handsomer fish to fry than Mr. Bodine.

I didn't. There was not a handsomer fish in all the water in all the world than Bowie. And I had a good feeling about this summer. I was bourbon-confident.

By the time Bowie pulled up in his SUV, I'd managed to drag Scarlett to her feet and wiped her face.

He climbed out in well-worn jeans and a clean polo. My stomach did a weird slosh. It was his casual, first-date outfit. It either hadn't gone well or I'd interrupted. Either way, he was here, and I was happy.

I'd gotten used to watching the man of my dreams date other women. Hell, *I* dated and had a damn good time doing it.

But I was confident that *someday* Bowie and I would end up together. My confidence was telling me that this summer might be that someday.

He shook his head and grinned his crooked grin that he'd been smiling at me for our entire lives as he took in our drunk and disheveled selves. "Looks like you girls are havin' a good night." He opened the back door. "Throw her on back here."

"Bow, I want pancakes!" Scarlett said, throwing her arms around her older brother's shoulders.

"Jesus, Scar. You smell like puke and hot dogs."

"Cheese sticks," I corrected, shoving Scarlett into the back seat and rolling her window all the way down. Bowie and I spent some quality time together over Christmas break cleaning Scarlett's last puke fest out of his door pocket.

"I had a corndog, too," Scarlett sang. "Junior was makin' some in the microwave."

"That's probably why you just destroyed Mrs. Morganson's shrubbery," Bowie observed.

Scarlett thought that was hilarious and laughed until she hiccupped.

"Where to, trouble?" Bowie asked, settling behind the wheel as I buckled myself into the passenger seat. Trouble was his pet name for me. It was meant ironically since I was never in trouble. I'd never be calling someone for bail money on dollar shot night at The Lookout. Not with my dad presiding as sheriff over our sweet little slice of West Virginia. I was the good girl. The smart girl. The criminal justice major who planned to come back here and serve my town. I was the best friend who got Scarlett out of her messes of trouble.

Bowie was like me. Practically a choir boy. Secretly, I thought maybe he was doing his best to make up for his parents while I was living up to mine.

Scarlett warbled a little song in the back seat.

"Let's get some food in her," I suggested, leaning back in the seat and sighing.

Bowie nodded at the waters he'd thoughtfully stashed in the cupholders. "You know the drill."

"Hydration," I twanged. I opened Scarlett's bottle for her and handed it back. "Drink up, buttercup."

Bowie opened mine for me, and I drank deeply. I wasn't much of a heavy drinker. I had better things to do than go around getting shitfaced all the time. But Scarlett sure could be persuasive when she got started.

But the fact was, I was always there to hold Scarlett's hair.

I always called Bowie, and he always came.

It was who we were.

2

CASSIDY

The 24-Hour Eats Diner was our go-to place to shove fried foods down to soak up the varieties of alcohol underage drinkers were inclined to ingest. It was far enough out of town that we didn't have to worry about running into any Sunday school teachers or father sheriffs. Best of all, it was completely empty.

I slid into the booth and was surprised when Bowie shoved in next to me, leaving Scarlett the whole other side to herself.

My heart did that familiar tap dance when he was close to me. No matter how many boys I dated, none of them ever made me feel that cocktail of nerves and anticipation that he served up for me. It was almost embarrassing how eager my body was just to be close to his.

I opened my menu and pretended to study it. In my peripheral, I gave Bowie the once over. What was it exactly about him that got me? Was it habit? Had I just loved him for so long there was no other way to feel about him?

He was tall like his brothers but leaner. Gibs and Jame were two sides of the same lumberjack coin. Flannels and facial hair. But Bowie was a little more stylish with his haircut and his clothes. Dark hair, gray eyes. That nice, almost-straight nose that had the slightest kink in it from a baseball knocked back at him after the pitch. He'd made the catch, got the out, and earned two black eyes for it.

He was leanly muscled everywhere from the line of shoulders to the tapered waist. I knew, from up close visual inspection, that he had those abs that were all the rage in Misty Lynn's mama's collection of *Playgirl* magazines that she'd charged us a buck a piece to look at in seventh grade.

But Bowie was more than a sexy-as-hell body. There was so much going on behind those sterling silver eyes. When he looked at me, I felt like he was trying to decode my DNA. Like he wanted to know *everything*. It left me breathless and the exact opposite of the apathetic, available woman I was trying to be.

He was smart. He was kind. He was quiet. He was steady. He was good. Deep down, movie star hero quality good. I'd be stupid not to love him.

I just didn't know if he loved me.

The signs pointed to a strong maybe. I'd been keeping a running tally for about three years now, every look, every comment, every stray physical contact. My instincts were telling me that the man had feelings. But I preferred a black and white, definitive answer.

"I'm havin' pancakes *and* waffles," Scarlett decided. She was lying down on the booth bench, holding her menu aloft over her face.

"You want coffee?" I asked her as our usual late-night waitress approached.

"Yes, please," Scarlett called.

"What'll it be?" Carla the rockabilly poster girl asked, peering at us through her purple cat-eye glasses. We were in here, drunk and a little disorderly at least once a quarter, yet she'd never shown us the slightest bit of recognition, forcing us to increase the percentage of her tip to astronomical realms. We'd left her fifty percent last time. I thought that would at least get a "the usual?" out of her.

"Coffee, water, pancakes, and waffles, please," Scarlett ordered from her repose.

"Water and the veggie omelet," I decided. I didn't need caffeine coursing through my system when Bowie's arm was resting on the back of the booth an inch from my shoulders.

He ordered his eggs and sausage and coffee while I tried not to think about how close that arm was to touching me.

Carla wandered off in no hurry to plug our order into the system.

"Y'all have fun tonight?" Bowie asked me.

Let's see, I'd done shots with Scarlett and three summertimers—what Bootleggers called the outsiders who flocked to our hot springs and lake every summer. Then I'd picked the cutest summertimer and showed him a two-step by the fire that had both our heads spinning. I'd gotten into a debate about recidivism with a fellow criminal justice major. And now I was sitting here with Bowie Bodine's arm almost around me.

"Yeah. It was all right," I told him. "You have a date tonight?"

He gave me one of those long, quiet looks. "Yeah."

"Have fun?" I asked, blasé as you please. *Cassidy Tucker couldn't be bothered to care about his date, no sir.*

"It was all right." He echoed my own words with a slow grin.

He shifted, taking up more space in the booth. When his knee brushed mine, I considered swooning and then decided against it. It should take more than the accidental brush of denim to impress me, I decided.

Scarlett snort-laughed at something that was only funny to her in her alcohol-addled mind, and Bowie and I shared an amused look. I was finally an adult. Nineteen years old. I'd long clung to the idea that Bowie had never made a move on me because I was too young.

It was either that or he was physically repulsed by me.

But I was pretty sure that wasn't it. I was no big-boobed, bleached-blonde Misty Lynn Prosser. I had my own long-legged, freckled-nose appeal. It was a damn shame it was taking Bowie so long to realize it.

Our food arrived, and Bowie's arm disappeared from the back of the booth. I was a little relieved seeing as how the "will he or won't he touch me" debate would have raged in my head until I'd bitten through my tongue or lip. It'd happened before. There'd come a day when I'd probably choke to death on something because I was too distracted by his presence to chew my dang food. As a safety precaution, I'd taken to eating less around Bowie.

Scarlett popped back up on the other side of the booth and gave Bowie a ten-minute, breakfast carb mouthful rundown of our evening. "Cassidy, what was that guy's name that you were dancin' with?"

Even drunk, my Scarlett was a schemer. She said it as innocent as you please, but I saw her eyes skim Bowie's face, looking for a reaction.

I reached for my water. "Blake." I was almost sure of it. Or maybe it was Nate? Hell, his name wasn't Bowie and that was that.

"Looked like you two were gettin' real cozy," she purred. My best friend was a tiny little fireball with an evil, calculating mind. I loved her to bits and pieces.

I lifted a shoulder as if my own dating exploits were too boring for comment.

Bowie was suddenly very interested in his plate of food. I didn't know what that meant, but Scarlett was grinning like a jack-o-lantern on Halloween.

3

CASSIDY

"I don't need a chauffeur," I argued.

We'd deposited Scarlett on Grumpy Gibson's couch for the night. Neither of us wanted to deliver a drunk Scarlett home to her perpetually drunk daddy. She needed someone who could help out should she decide to barf all over herself or talk her out of drawing a hopscotch board in the middle of Main Street...again.

Gibson, the oldest Bodine, drew the short straw...again.

Bowie crossed his arms. "You know the rules, Cass."

"Callie Kendall disappeared four years ago, Bow. I think we can rule it an isolated incident."

"Get in the car, trouble," he said, pushing me down the sidewalk.

I argued, just so he'd give me another little shove. I wasn't proud of it. Being this hangdog needy-in-love wasn't who I'd expected to grow up to be. But love was love, and there wasn't much point in fighting it.

"Don't make me pick you up and put you in the car," he threatened.

A really big, needy part of me wanted him to do exactly

that. But I was no giggling schemer looking for some manipulated physicality. No, I was in this for the long haul. I wanted the white dress with Bowie standing at the end of the aisle looking at me like I was the most beautiful thing in the world.

"Bowie," I said with a yawn. "I've been carrying pepper spray since I was twelve and taking self-defense classes since I was eight."

"I don't care how prepared you think you are. I'm driving your ass home."

Always the gentleman.

"I'm not telling you how prepared I am," I said sweetly. "I'm telling you what I'll do to you if you try to pick me up and cart me to your car."

It was the wrong thing to say. I was tired and still a teensy bit drunk. That was my excuse for forgetting that Bowie was a Bodine. Competition and rebellion ran in his blood. His great-granddad Jedidiah Bodine had cornered the bootlegging market in West Virginia and most of Maryland. That drive to face a challenge and stomp it into the ground still ran strong in Ol' Jedidiah's kin even generations later.

In one swift move, Bowie tossed me over his shoulder and, whistling a happy little tune, strolled toward his SUV. The sidewalk swam under me as my stomach's contents sloshed dangerously.

"Bowie!" Not above causing a scene, I hammered my fists against his back. I drew the line at kicking the love of my life in the balls, which is what I would have done to any other man who thought he could manhandle me.

He slapped me on my ass and made me squawk. My body went rigid. Bowie Bodine was *carrying* me like my 5'8" frame was child-sized. *And* he'd touched my ass. I was torn between being delighted and appalled.

"Bowie Bodine, you put me down right now or I'll make you regret this for the rest of your life!"

"Cassidy Ann Tucker, you're not walking home all by your lonesome. You know that. Now be a good girl and get in the damn car." He set me down on the sidewalk and opened the passenger side door.

Dizzy, I stumbled, and he caught me against his chest.

We'd touched before. One-armed hugs and high fives. Hair ruffles and headlocks. He'd been tossing me off of docks since I could swim. But this. This full-frontal, chest-to-chest contact was frying my circuits. I was in over my head. Every inch of him was warm and hard against me. The moonlight highlighted the clench in his jaw, and I wondered if I'd gone and pissed him off.

It hit me then in a blinding flash of understanding. Nineteen wasn't adult enough to handle all of Bowie Bodine.

"Get in the car, Cass," he said quietly.

I did as I was told, not eager to find out exactly what he'd do if I took off running in the direction of my house.

My pulse was galloping like a runaway pony when I settled into my seat. Ten inches of console separated us. I buckled my seatbelt with shaky hands. I'd dated. I'd had sex. But I was starting to realize that none of that life experience had prepared me for *him*. He wasn't a boy. He wouldn't be playing games. And I was just a kid still playing them.

I wasn't ready for Bowie Bodine.

If I was the crying type, I'd be sobbing into my sleeve right now. Instead I stewed as my hopes and dreams for the summer popped like bubbles.

"What's wrong?" he asked gruffly.

My world was rocked. I wasn't the confident, experienced grown-up I'd been peacocking around pretending to be.

"Nothin's wrong," I lied.

"Liar."

"Just tired," I said, staring out the window.

"You'd tell me, wouldn't you? If it was something that needed fixin'?"

Oh, holy damn hell. I couldn't stand him being sweet to me right now. Not when I'd gone and realized I had a hell of a lot more growing up to do.

"It's not your job to be fixin' things for me, Bow," I pointed out.

He reached out and took my hand, and I got a hell of a lot closer to bawling. "So you know, if there's anything that needs fixin' you come to me. Got it?"

I stared out the windshield, refusing to meet his gaze.

He squeezed my hand until I nodded. "Got it."

He let go of my hand and drove me the four blocks to my parents' house in silence. I sulked, and Bowie did whatever he usually did in his head.

My perfect southern gentleman put the SUV in park and turned off the engine. He was walking me to the door whether I liked it or not. We walked up the brick sidewalk to the house. It was a wide, white two-story with tall columns. "I live in the White House," I'd told Scarlett when I met her on the first day of kindergarten. It was about three times the size of Scarlett's house. And what went on within my walls was a hell of a lot different than Scarlett's. Sometimes I felt guilty that I had so much. That my parents were so good, normal.

Bowie shoved his hands in the pockets of his jeans when we reached the door.

I sighed. Just because I was devastated and all didn't mean I shouldn't thank the man for giving up his evening to come to my rescue again. I reached into my own pocket and pulled out the ten-dollar bill I'd stashed there about thirty seconds after making the bet with Bowie.

"Thanks for being there. As usual." I leaned in and pressed a quick kiss to his cheek. A kiss good-bye to my fantasy that this summer would be the summer Bowie realized he was mine.

His hands were out of his pockets and on my waist, and I was jumping out of my skin like a bullfrog hopping for the pond. He was probably only holding me up in case I went unsteady again.

I slapped the money to his chest and gave him a little push back.

"Keep it," he told me.

"I always pay my debts."

He took the bill, folded it neatly, and without taking his eyes off of mine slid it into the neck of my shirt and under the bra strap.

"Keep it, Cass."

I'd lost the power of speech. And apparently all major motor skills because when I stepped back, I tripped over the antique dang watering can my mother kept full of pussy willow branches next to the door. I caught myself with my palms against the painted brick.

"You all right there?"

I could hear the smirk in his voice.

"Peachy." I made a grab for the door handle.

"Cass?"

He stopped me with just my name.

"Yeah?"

"Glad to have you home."

4

CASSIDY

It was too hot for a bonfire, but you couldn't have a lake-front party in Bootleg without one. It added to the "rustic ambiance" as Blaine—not Blake—the cute summertimer from the other night pointed out. It also kept the dang mosquitos from eating us alive.

Blaine was in town for the month staying with his family in one of the big houses on the dog-leg end of the lake. He was a junior at one of the lesser known Ivy League colleges studying economics. And he was currently dancing up on me like we were in some nightclub with dark corners and $15 beers.

I wasn't particularly into it seeing as how I'd spotted Bowie wander by a minute ago. But Blake—I mean Blaine—was going to be my palate cleanser. I was going to make out with this whale logoed polo-wearing cutie and get Bowie Bodine out of my head.

"Tell me more about your fraternity, honey," I purred, not giving a flying crap about Kappa Papa Whatever.

While his hands wandered my waist and midriff, Blaine

launched into another story about his fraternity brothers. I tried not to notice when Bowie wandered by again, beer in hand. But his gray eyes met mine and held. I felt more from that contact than I did from Blaine's soft, smooth palms brushing my bare skin.

The bonfire flickered behind him, the music played all around us while our friends and neighbors drank and danced. All I saw was Bowie.

It wasn't fair.

Side-by-side, poor Blaine didn't stand a chance. Bowie was wearing a beloved t-shirt that molded to his chest. His jeans were slung low on his hips. He had on leather flip-flops and a battered ball cap.

Blaine was wearing pink-checkered shorts and a turquoise polo with the collar popped. He wore his sunglasses backward on his head. He hadn't asked me a single question about myself. Instead, he'd told me his entire privileged, entitled life's story.

But Bowie knew me. Bowie who was staring at me with something like disappointment on his handsome face. Why was he here? Why was he focusing in on me? Did my sudden decision to give up my crush on him throw up some kind of flag?

This wasn't me. Using one guy to get over another. *Ugh. I was going to have to do it the old-fashioned way. By feeling feelings.*

I wasn't really sure how to fall out of love with someone, but I'd figure it out. It probably involved a lot of crying and punching stuff and maybe some ice cream. Sooner or later, Bowie would be nothing but a neighbor to me.

I closed my hands over Blaine's as they skated ever closer to the underside of my breasts. "I'm gonna go get another beer," I fibbed. "I'll see you around."

"Don't be long," he said in a teasing whisper.

I turned away from him, away from Bowie, and made my way through the throng of summer fun-havers.

"Where ya headed, Cass?" Scarlett called after me. She was kicked back on a tailgate, entertaining a handful of eligible summertimer bachelors.

I waved, rather than answering and veered away toward the woods. I needed darkness and solitude.

"What in the hell am I doing?" I cursed myself as I stepped onto the path that skirted the lakefront.

"Interrupting my reading."

My big sister, June, was perched on a fallen log on the edge of the festivities. She was wearing a headlight and reading *The Wall Street Journal*.

"Juney, we didn't bring your ass to the bonfire so you could treat it like a library," I reminded her.

She looked up, blinding me with her LED forehead.

"I socialized for exactly ten minutes," she said.

Scarlett and I dragged June out for forced socializing twice a month when I was home from college. Otherwise my brainiac sister would never leave the comfort and quiet of our parents' house. It was an unspoken deal, I'd socialize Juney if she'd help me pass my math requirements. Neither one of us enjoyed it, but we both recognized the necessity.

"Exactly ten minutes?" I asked.

"I set a timer," June said, folding her paper. "Are we leaving?" My usually unemotional sister looked hopeful.

"Soon," I promised. The desire to party had evaporated. I wanted to go curl up on the couch while June watched SportsCenter and I forgot that I was a lovesick pup.

"How much longer? I'll set my timer," June decided.

"Give me five minutes, and we'll head out."

Without a word, June pulled out her phone, set a timer, and went back to her newspaper.

I sighed, wondering if June would ever pull herself out of her head long enough to connect with someone. Then I remembered my own situation. Juney was safer in her own head. Her heart would stay intact.

I slunk off down the path into the trees where I could mourn my teenage love and lament my inadequacies in peace. I could smell the lake, hear the night breeze ruffling the leaves above my head. The summer night wrapped me up in it like a humid, buggy hug.

"I need to get over him," I whispered into the dark.

"Get over who?" Scarlett demanded, scaring the bejeezus out of me.

"How can you sneak up on people in those boots?" I asked, deflecting.

Scarlett looked down at her pretty stitched cowboy boots. With her long hair and tight denim shorts that showed off tan legs, she was every country musician's wet dream.

"Your mopin' was drowning everything else out," she said. "What's goin' on? You look like you're at a funeral, not a party."

I hadn't the first clue how to explain to Scarlett what I was feeling. My attraction to her brother was the realest thing I knew, and one moment of standing a little too close, of catching a glimpse of what being with Bowie would be like, and I was scared shitless that I'd never be enough for him.

It was too much, too real. If the miracle of miracles occurred and he kissed me or pledged his undying love to me, I'd die on the spot. Disintegrate into star dust. I was still a kid, a girl with a teenage crush that I might not survive. And I might not grow up into the woman that Bowie Bodine wanted.

"Just a headache," I lied. "I think I'm going to take Juney

home. She's hit her quota of fun. Will you be okay with your brothers here?"

Scarlett and I always watched out for each other. Which is why she was giving me the squint eye right now.

"Cassidy Ann, what is going on with you?" she demanded.

"There you are." Blaine appeared on the trail behind Scarlett. The way he was listing in his spiffy boat shoes, he'd had a shot or two of the 'shine. We Bootleggers liked to test out our moonshine recipes on the summertimers before the Shine On. Were we the only little town in the country that rang in Black Friday with a moonshine tasting and drunken Christmas tree decorating? Probably.

"I'm sorry, Blake, was it?" Scarlett asked sweetly. "Me and Cassidy are havin' ourselves a private conversation right now. How about y'all come back later."

Blaine snorted. "You're so country. Wait, excuse me. Y'all are so country."

Oh boy. It was nice knowing you, Blaine.

Scarlett put her hands on her hips, and I sidled my way between them. My sheriff father wouldn't appreciate it if I allowed my best friend to commit a homicide within town limits.

"Now, listen here, you entitled shithead," Scarlett began.

Blaine peered around me at Scarlett.

"What's your friend's problem?" he muttered with scorn.

"Nobody has a problem," I said calmly. "Scarlett, why don't you go collect June for me while I say goodnight to Blake—"

"Blaine," he corrected me with a frown.

Shit. Blaine wasn't used to girls forgetting his name. But here in Bootleg Summertime, the Blaine/Blakes were a dime a dozen. Cute boys teemed the lake and swarmed the town all summer long.

"Blaine," I repeated through clenched teeth.

"I thought we were going to spend some time getting to know each other." He pouted and jabbed a finger into my neck. Depth perception was often the first thing to go with Hester Jenkins' blueberry 'shine. She'd perfected the recipe at seventeen and won Best Amateur Moonshine in the state three years running, entered under her mom's name, of course.

"Well, now, honey," I punched up the southern charm and went with "honey" to avoid any more name mix-ups. "Unfortunately, I've got myself a real bad headache. So you're gonna have to excuse me. But I'm sure I can introduce you," I offered. Misty Lynn was around. She'd be happy to take him off my hands.

He grinned at me with one eye closed, and I knew he hadn't heard a damn word I'd sugared up for him.

"C'mon," he slurred, taking me by the wrist. "Let's go for a little swim."

To be clear, at no point was I in any danger. My dad had made sure that June and I spoke self-defense like a second language. We were fluent in it. If Blaine had meant me any harm, well, that poor boy wouldn't have been able to find his balls after I was done with him.

He was just drunk and a little stupid. Thinking that he was being charming, that dumbass tossed me over his shoulder like a sack of potatoes.

Like Bowie had three nights ago. Only I wasn't amused this time. Or turned on.

"I'm not going swimming," I told him curtly, hoping that my frosty tone would be the only weapon I'd need to yield.

We were back on the fringes of the party with me grunting at every step he clumsily trod. If he dropped me on my face, I was going to kick his ass.

"Who wants to swim?" Blaine hollered. His summertimer friends raised their beers and hooted.

"Put me down," I said in no uncertain terms.

He spun me around in a dizzying circle.

"Knock it off, Blaine!"

"Put her down. Now."

5

CASSIDY

Bowie's voice snapped like a whip. And a voyeuristic crowd materialized around us.

"Ooooh. Local boy doesn't like it when we take his toy," Blaine taunted. His cronies snickered.

I kneed him in the gut, and his friends laughed harder when Blaine chucked me off his shoulder as he doubled over.

I hit the ground hard on my hip and hand.

But before I could pop up and slap the crap out of him, Bowie was on him.

He grabbed Blaine by the stupid shirt collar and hauled him up on his toes. "When a girl tells you to stop touching her, you do it. Understand?"

Blaine didn't answer fast enough, and Bowie gave him a good, hard shake.

"What's your problem, man?" Blaine shoved uselessly at Bowie's hands.

"My problem is you put your hands where they weren't wanted," Bowie said. His voice was quiet, scary.

"Bow, it's fine," I said, climbing to my feet swiping at the dirt on my legs. Scarlett appeared at my side with June on her heels.

The bonfire crackled in the silence that followed.

"What the hell is goin' on?" Scarlett demanded.

"The timer went off," June announced, walking obliviously into the circle. "We can leave now."

Bowie shot me a look, gave me the once-over. I pleaded with my eyes for him to let the moron live.

Reluctantly, Bowie released Blaine. "Watch yourself," he warned him, turning his back and heading in my direction.

Uh-oh.

Blaine straightened his shirt, and I saw the look he telegraphed to a couple of his bigger, drunker friends.

"Let's go home," Bowie said, reaching for my arm.

I don't know if he saw the attack coming or not, but there wasn't time to shout a warning. Blaine came running—or staggering real fast at him. I side-stepped Bowie and stepped in front of the charging Blaine. There were fights all the time in Bootleg Springs. Good, clean fights. But nobody attacked from behind. It just wasn't done.

It might have been a fist or an elbow or one of Blaine's stupid friends' appendages, but I took the first shot right in the chin.

"You stupid son of a bitch!" I lashed out with my foot and caught a drunk jackwagon still wearing his sunglasses right in the balls. Bowie's fist was busy plowing its way through Blaine's face. Then I heard Scarlett's legendary battle cry. Jameson and Gibson, the other two Bodine brothers, appeared and entered the melee, throwing punches indiscriminately.

It was a free-for-all as the rest of the Bootleggers present joined in good-naturedly. Some of them were throwing punches at each other just for fun.

I threw an elbow into the ribs of one of Blaine's pals and watched Hester kick a guy in the stomach.

June waded in and grabbed me. "It's time to go," she said.

"June! I don't care about the goddamn timer!"

She pointed at the flashing red and blue lights as our dad's patrol car rolled through the grass.

"Ah, hell."

There was an unspoken truce between law enforcement and the Bootleg Bonfire community. As long as no one drove home under the influence and there were no fights or property destruction, the cops pretended that these bonfires didn't exist.

I'd broken the truce.

Sheriff Tucker climbed out of his car, all long legs and silver mustache. I knew better than to call him Dad when he was on the job. He shot me a disapproving look as he hustled into the melee, a portly deputy named Bubba wading in behind him.

It took both of them and Gibson to pull Bowie and Blaine apart.

Scarlett bebopped over, fixing her hair that had gotten disheveled in the fight. "He *fought* for you, Cass," she whispered breathlessly. She had dirt smudging her chin, and the sleeve of her blouse was torn. "Y'all are one step away from diamond rings and babies."

Bowie had punched out another guy over me. Was Scarlett right? Did he do it because he cared? Or was it reflex?

"Shut up, Scar," I hissed.

"I mean, come on. He totally overreacted to that stupid jackass messing around with you—as if you couldn't handle yourself if necessary. It was like he was *claiming* you!"

I watched as my dad pointed Bowie to a picnic table before slapping restraints on Blaine.

"Why the fuck am I being cuffed and he's just sitting there?" Blaine whined like the privileged brat he was.

Bowie shot him a smirk that had Blaine fighting against his restraints.

"We're gonna give you a ride home," my dad said amiably. "And you're going to promise your parents that you aren't gonna be starting any more fights in my town. Or I'm gonna slap you with a $500 fine for disturbing the peace, underage drinking, and public drunkenness."

He handed the squirming, whining Blaine over to the deputy. My dad's gaze skated over me again and then on to Bowie. He stroked his fingers over his mustache before heading in Bowie's direction.

"Dad looks unhappy," June mused. "Did you do something to upset him?"

"You mean besides starting a fight and drinking underage?" I asked with sarcasm. "No, I can't think of a thing."

"Huh. Maybe he's constipated again." June didn't get sarcasm.

I tuned out June's erroneous observations and watched my father lay a hand on Bowie's shoulder. It looked like a deep discussion, and I wished I could hear what was being said. Bowie looked at me, his gaze connecting us across the space. His face was unreadable. He nodded at something my dad said and then looked down at his feet.

My dad clapped Bowie on the shoulder again. Bowie nodded once more and headed in the direction of the parking lot.

"Where's he going?" Scarlett wondered.

"Bowie," I called after him.

"Cassidy Ann Tucker." My dad looked even more disapproving in his uniform. His mouth was pressed into a firm line under his mustache.

I was already trying to juke my way past him to go after Bowie. "Dad, I need to talk to Bowie—"

"Leave the boy alone," he said wearily. "I think you've caused him enough trouble. Now, explain to me how you started an all-out brawl when you promised you were just going out for an hour or two to hang out with friends." His voice raised at the end of the sentence, cueing me in to the fact that my easygoing, implacable father was five seconds away from blowing a gasket.

"It was a misunderstanding," I told him, shifting gears into Downgrade Hurricane Dad. "A simple misunderstanding. Blake was just messing around."

"Blaine," June corrected me.

"Blaine was just messing around, and Bowie thought I was scared and he stepped in. That's all."

"I wonder if Blaine thought Bowie was going to prevent you from having intercourse with him?" June mused.

My father and I shot June twin looks of horror.

"June! What's the rule? What's the one rule?" I snapped.

My sister furrowed her brows, working her way through her memory banks. "Ah. Don't discuss intercourse with Dad. I forgot. Can we go home now?"

6

CASSIDY

I texted Bowie as soon as I got home. Dad and June and I struck a deal. We girls would walk home, and Dad would pretend we had nothing to do with the mess at the bonfire. We all preferred to tiptoe around Mom and her hour-long family "discussions" on responsibility and adulthood. I don't think Dad wanted to sit through another one any more than Juney and me.

It wasn't like she wouldn't find out through the grapevine, of course. But by then it would be so blown out of proportion Bootleg style—*did y'all see Bowie break that boy's leg with a spinning roundhouse kick?*—that it would be easy to write off as idle gossip.

I got no response to my text. So I called. It went straight to voicemail. Bowie *always* took my calls.

I washed the makeup off my face in the bathroom that I shared with my sister and glared at the bruise blooming on my jaw. This was all that stupid summertimer's fault. He was lucky the Bodines didn't do any serious damage.

My mind started spiraling out of control. *Did Bowie really fight for me? Did it actually finally mean something? Did I mean something to him?*

My brain clicked into spin cycle as the possibilities danced through my mind one after the other.

He's in love with me.

He thought Scarlett was in danger.

He thought I was in danger.

He hated Blaine's stupid shirt.

He has feelings for me.

Wandering into my bedroom, I flopped down on my bed and texted Scarlett, hoping for some insider information.

Me: Is Bowie okay?

She responded immediately, thank the Lord.

Scarlett: He's shitfaced. Passed out on Gibs's couch. If he thinks this means I'm sleeping on the floor, he is sorely mistaken.

I sat down on the edge of my bed. Bowie never, ever drank to excess. Jonah Bodine, their dad, was a no-good drunk. So Gibson didn't drink and Bowie moderated. Who knows what Jameson did. He was the quiet type. Scarlett was blessed with the metabolism of a linebacker and could outdrink almost anybody in the county and their brother and still show up to work the next day. But Bowie drunk? What in the hell had gone down?

Scarlett: How's your face? You took quite the wallop.

I headed back into the bathroom and snapped a picture of my black and blue glory.

Me: Is it noticeable?

Scarlett: Holy shit. That guy's lucky Bowie didn't smash his head in for pulling a stunt like that.

Me (after a good long deliberation): Why did Bowie jump in like that? There wasn't any mortal danger.

Scarlett: Someone's on a fishin expedition.

She even texted Southern.

Scarlett: He slapped the crap out of the idiot because the idiot had his hands on you. Now hurry up and get married already!

Scarlett's opinion carried weight. After all, she'd known Bowie her entire life. But why in the hell would he suddenly go and develop feelings the second I decided I wasn't ready to take the man for a test drive? Or was my mental tally correct and he'd had them all along for me?

I needed answers. I just wasn't sure I could survive them.

Flopping back on my bed, I pulled a cheery yellow pillow over my face. If I didn't suffocate by morning, I'd go and have myself a little chat with Mr. Bowie Bodine.

AGAINST MY COLLEGE STUDENT NATURE, I woke early. It had been a restless night of tossing, turning, and practicing exactly what it was I was going to say to Bowie. My phone was still annoyingly free of text messages, so I was going into this blind.

Yanking on a pair of running shorts and a sports bra, I

decided to jog over to Gibson's. Being a criminal justice major, I was starting to realize that there was something to be said for keeping my body in shape. I didn't want to be wheezing asthmatically after a perp...or a neighbor if I got my wish and got hired on here in Bootleg.

I was tugging a tank top over my bra on the way downstairs when I ran into my mom.

"Cassidy Ann Tucker, what in the hell happened to your face?"

My mother paused her descent in her blue-checkered pajama top. My dad wore the bottoms. While I made a show of pretending to barf over the grossness of it, I'd always secretly hoped that someday Bowie and I would be sharing a pair of pajamas.

Mom's hand was cool on my cheek, but her green eyes flashed. Someone had messed with her little, almost-adult girl and she didn't like it.

I may not be the adult I wanted to be, but I could lie better than my teenage self.

"Juney and I were walking home last night, and damn if I didn't run face-first into a tree branch hanging out over the sidewalk. Does it look bad?"

Just because I was a better liar than I used to be didn't mean my mom was dumber than she used to be. "I already heard about Bowie and that summertimer," she said, flicking my nose smartly.

"Well, why didn't you say so?" I asked, exasperated. Nothing got by my mother. She may still look like the beauty queen she'd been as a teenager—Miss Olamette County 1980—but motherhood had honed her instincts to a needle point. Her hair was more blonde and less dirty than my own. She kept in shape with power walking and old Jane Fonda videos. She was the apple of my father's eye and the heartbeat of our little family. She'd rip anyone who threatened any of us a brand-new asshole before church on Sunday.

"Maybe I wanted to make you squirm a bit. You'll help me with your father later?"

No one crossed Nadine Tucker. Since I was busted, I was automatically pressed into service to aide my mother's revenge plot on my father. Those were the fun kinds of family games we played.

"I guess," I sighed.

"So?" Mom looked at me expectantly.

"So what?"

"What does this mean?" she asked, poking my bruise. "With Bowie?"

"I honestly don't know, Mom. But I'm going to go get some answers now."

My mom looked like she wanted to tell me something and then changed her mind.

"What?" I demanded as we plodded down the stairs together.

"Be careful okay?" she said, studying me as she pulled the coffee supplies out of the kitchen cabinet.

"Mom, it's Bowie. What's there to be careful about?"

My mother's look spelled it out for me. There was no fooling her here either. But she was nice enough not to humiliate me by voicing the fact that I'd been in love with the man my entire life.

"Will you be back for breakfast?" she called after me as I headed toward the back door.

"I guess it depends."

~

I HATED RUNNING. I'd much rather work up a sweat in a

boxing class or pedaling like demons were chasing me on a bike. But running the six blocks to Gibson Bodine's apartment would give me a chance to shake out the jitters and get in a workout.

What if he told me he loved me?

What if he thought he was looking out for a friend?

What if I puked on his shoes and he never talked to me again?

The blocks blurred as my thoughts swirled. I almost tripped over Mona Lisa McNugget, the little free-range chick that had adopted Bootleg Springs proper as her backyard. I vaulted over the chicken, calling a quick apology over my shoulder and soldiered on.

Gibson was renting a two-bedroom shit hole over a retail space that changed hands every six months or so. It was currently a dingy card and knick-knacks store that was only patronized by summertimers.

Bowie's SUV was parked on the side street, and for a second I thought I'd keep running. But there were questions that I needed answers to.

I opened the front door and jogged up the musty staircase that led to the second floor. I could hear them inside, the easy Bodine banter. Ribbin' and rilin', Scarlett called it.

I wondered if they'd all be this close if their parents hadn't been so bad at raising a family.

The door opened before I could even raise my knuckles to knock, and Scarlett blinked at me. "Well, hey there. Holy hell. Look at your face!"

"'Zat Cassidy?" Gibson called from somewhere inside.

Jameson was sitting on the couch, a game controller in his hands. He glanced up, gave me a nod, and went back to whatever game he was playing.

I clapped a hand over my jaw. "Is Bowie here?" I asked.

Scarlett got that hopeful look on her face. "He is. Bowie

Bodine. Get your ass on out here." She stepped back from the door to make room for her brother.

He looked as rough as I felt. His hair was standing up in all directions. His eyes were redder than Moe Daily's bloodhound's. He was still in his clothes from last night.

"What do you need, Cass?" he asked, not quite meeting my eyes. There was a coolness in his tone that I wasn't used to. I couldn't say that I cared for it.

"I need to ask you something," I said quietly.

He read the importance behind my words and stepped out onto the landing with me, shutting the door behind him. He was still having trouble looking me in the eye, but he did take notice of the spectacular bruise blooming on my jaw.

"What's going on?" he asked, rubbing his eyes with one hand, and bracing the other against the wall.

"Why did you go after Blake last night?" I asked, not able to keep the words inside one more second.

"Blaine," he corrected me. "I thought he was giving you trouble. Didn't think he was being respectful."

These weren't the answers I'd wanted. Or feared.

"Bowie, you went after him like it meant something." *Like I meant something.*

He looked away. "Look, Cass. What do you want me to say? I didn't like the way he was handling you and look what happened."

Bowie reached out and angled my chin so he could get a better look at the bruise. I wanted to melt into his touch. I wanted to throw myself on his mercy, ask him to show me what love was really like. He could teach me. I was a quick study. Eventually I'd pick up the pieces of the heart he'd definitely break.

"You should pick your boyfriends more carefully," he said, his voice rough.

"He's not my boyfriend. Bow, I need to know. Is there more to it?"

I saw his jaw clench and release. "More to what?"

My swallow got stuck in my throat on the words that were wedged in there tight. "Us."

It was an energetic two-step my heart was hammering out in my chest. I'd never been more scared or hopeful in my entire life.

"Is there more to you and me?" I asked softly.

He looked me in the eyes, his gray to my green. And I saw a flash of pain and then nothing. He was so quiet I thought maybe he wasn't going to answer me. Maybe the answer was as hard for him as the question had been for me.

"Cass," he sighed. "You're like a little sister to me. That's all."

My heart cleaved in two like he'd taken an axe to it. I could feel myself bleeding out on the inside. "That's all?" I repeated.

He nodded briskly and rubbed a hand over the back of his head.

"Look. I'm sorry. I'm hungover as shit. I was concerned that he was too rough with you last night."

And yet it was Bowie who was being too rough with my delicate heart.

I'd always believed we'd end up together. When the time was right. When we were ready. How could I have been the only one with these feelings? How could I have been so wrong about his?

I turned away from him, something like a fever burning up my cheeks. But he grabbed my hand before I could race out of the building.

"Cass, it has to be enough," he said earnestly. His eyes were telegraphing something that I didn't understand. Did hurting me hurt him? Good. Then he should be on the floor in the fetal position with a pint of mint chocolate chip and a mountain of used tissues. Because that's where I was planning to be.

"Tell me you're okay," he insisted, squeezing my hand.

I didn't know what he was talking about. I was too busy trying not to hyperventilate or worse: cry. I hated that my whole body still reacted like wildfire at his touch.

"I'm fine," I said flatly. I wrenched my hand free. Fine was not the f word I would have chosen. But my pride was at stake. "See you around."

~

I RAN until I couldn't see straight. My wounded heart limped along with me as I slipped down Bathtub Gin Alley to avoid the summer crowds. I slunk and stumbled my way toward the woods. Gasping for breath, desperate for peace, for numbness, I skidded to a stop.

Of course I'd come here. It was a clearing half a mile out of town on the lakeside trail. I'd played here as a kid. Partied here as a teenager. Fell in love over and over again with Bowie.

Half-heartedly I kicked at a rotting log and then sat. Feeling my insides rot right along with this chunk of nature. I closed my eyes and took a deep breath of the air that was already thick with humidity. This was the spot where I discovered how important answers were.

Callie Kendall disappeared from Bootleg four years ago on a summer night. This was the last place anyone had ever seen her. I watched my father, my town, Callie's family, ask the same questions over and over again. But there weren't any answers. And I couldn't accept that.

Now Bowie had given me the answer I dreaded. Now I knew. I was nothing but a nuisance to him. All my needing him to help me and Scarlett out of scrapes. All my depending on him to be there. All my dreams of shared pajamas. It was over.

I needed to be glad to have the answer. I wouldn't waste any more time pining and plotting. I'd move on.

Just as soon as I mourned what I'd lost. What I'd never had.

7

BOWIE

Present Day

The text message ruined my life. It wasn't a surprise. Just confirmation that things in Bootleg were going to get rougher.

Scary Lawyer Jayme: DNA results are back. It's Callie's blood.

I swore and swung my legs over the side of the bed and let the family attorney ruin my day off. Snow fell pretty as a picture outside my bedroom window. It was a snow day. School was closed. I was going to catch up on a few hours of sleep then drink my body weight in coffee and fix some shit around the house I'd been ignoring until I noticed it all when my half-brother Jonah moved in.

Instead, I was waking up with a family crisis on my hands.

I'd been elected the Bodine point of contact for our attorney. Mainly because Gibson was an ass. Jameson "couldn't people"—and was too busy loving up on Leah Mae to be of any real use. And Scarlett would only make a heap of trouble for everyone. I debated responding. But before I could formulate a response, the phone vibrated in my hand again.

Scary Lawyer Jayme: They've had the results for a few weeks. Just keeping a lid on them.

I glared holes in the wall across from my bed. Cassidy's wall. Her bedroom was on the other side. We lived parallel lives in opposite sides of a duplex. We shared a wall, a backyard, a front porch. Given that Cassidy was my sister Scarlett's age and best friend, we shared a good long history, too.

She had to have known. The dark thought had me dragging on a pair of sweats. I stopped in the hallway and stared at the door that connected my side to her side. We'd never used the door. We didn't have a relationship like that. Not anymore.

Now, I was wondering what the hell kind of relationship we did have if she'd been sitting on the DNA results all this time without a word.

I took the stairs two at a time and yanked the front door open. In two steps I was standing at her front door, banging on it with the pent-up frustration that had been my constant companion for years. It was fucking cold, and I was barefoot, but my anger kept me warm.

Sometimes life just plain wasn't fair. The thought stuck in my mind when the door swung open.

"If you're fixin' to break down the door, by all means, go right ahead," she yawned.

Same pretty, freckled face, only a touch pale today. She had dark circles under her eyes. Her hair, that tawny blonde-brown mix, was a mess. She wore a hoodie and gym shorts that highlighted that mile of leg that I was so fond of.

Deputy Cassidy Tucker was the literal girl next door. And I never had a shot at her.

"You don't own any shirts?" she demanded, shivering at the cloud of cold air that I was letting in.

I pushed past her into the foyer that was the twin of mine. Beadboard and plaster. She'd painted hers a soft gold. Mine was still the dingy ivory it had been when I moved in. A more romantic frame of mind would have me waxing that fate had us buying opposite sides of the same house around the same time. But realistically, I knew I'd put my offer in because I wanted to be close to her.

Pathetic. Yeah, I was well aware.

"Come on in, why don't you?" she muttered, closing the door behind us. I was too riled for conversation. So I stormed down the hallway to her kitchen. Like mine, it was too small with a minuscule amount of counter space and squeaky cabinets that were born sometime during our grandparents' generation.

She always had her coffee maker set to 7 a.m. I pushed the override button and it sputtered to life. I pulled a mug out of the cabinet and then shot her a look. She was perched on a stool at the tiny island she'd squeezed in on top of the black and white tile, still yawning. Reluctantly, I pulled a second mug off the shelf.

"Late night?" I asked. I couldn't seem to quit caring when it came to her.

"Accident on Mountain Road. 2 a.m. No injuries. Just a hell of a mess."

I poured coffee into the Bootleg PD mug, keeping her favorite Cockspurs mug for myself, and put it in front of her. She could get her own damn cream and sugar. "When were you going to tell me about the DNA results?"

I saw the shadow in her green eyes come and go. I knew this woman as well as I knew anyone on this earth. At least, I had.

I swung away from her, not wanting to face her betrayal. “Goddammit, Cass.” I wanted to hurl my mug into the sink and shatter it. She was one of us. No matter what had or hadn’t gone down between us all those years ago.

She sighed. “Look, Bow. What do you want me to say? I’m a cop.”

“You’re a deputy.” If I was good and pissed, she should be, too.

“Same damn thing,” she said, coolly. It was a sign I’d landed a direct hit. Where my little sister Scarlett raged with hellfire, Cassidy froze me out until every inch of my body was frostbitten. “It doesn’t change anything anyway.”

“It’s a bloody finger pointing at my father as a murder suspect.”

“The investigators are looking at all leads—”

I took the step that brought me to her, and it pissed me off even more when she recoiled. “Don’t feed me that bullshit, Cass. You owe me more than the standard line.”

“You may not take my job seriously, but I sure as hell do,” she shot back, working up the energy to get mad.

“Apparently I take our friendship more seriously than you do.”

“That’s not fair, Bowie. I’m doing my job. Connelly says keep a lid on it, so what do you want me to do? Run blabbing all over town?”

I crossed my arms, not inclined to get out of her personal space. “No. I want you to come to me. Or Scarlett. I assume my sweet little sister doesn’t know about you holdin’ out on us since she isn’t here burning down your life.”

Now Cassidy winced. The fear of my sister was strong in all of us.

“Why, Cass? Why’d you keep this to yourself?”

She slid off her stool and paced the eight feet of tile. “What do you want me to say? That it's been eatin' me alive? That I hate being in this position between you...Bodines and the investigation? I'm not even supposed to know about the results. I'm some peon to Connelly. Someone he dumps grunt work on and orders coffee from."

That would irk her, I knew. She'd worked damn hard to stand on her own two feet and not just be seen as an extension of her father, Sheriff Tucker.

I grunted, not feeling particularly sympathetic. "You owe us all an apology." *Me. You owe me an apology.* "You chose to work in Bootleg. You chose to be a part of our family. Now deal with it."

She skidded to a stop in front of me. "I'm not apologizing for doing my job!"

"Then apologize for being a shitty friend." It was a low blow. One I wasn't particularly proud of. There wasn't a more loyal person in my life than Cassidy. She reacted as if I'd hit her. By that I mean she balled up her fist and started to wind up. I took defensive measures and pinned her up against her fridge.

"Now, Cass—"

"Don't you 'Now, Cass,' me! You come into my house, insult my job, and accuse me of being a shitty friend?" She squirmed against me, and I was pretty sure she was trying to work a leg free to knee me in the balls. I crowded her, stilling her with my hips. I'd known Cassidy her whole life, and this was the most physical contact we'd ever had. It made my day a little worse.

"I'm pissed off," I admitted, gritting my teeth. Holding her in place wasn't easy. She was trained to take down 200-pound drunk assholes. If she really wanted to, she could have already handed me my balls. "Okay? You hurt me, Cass."

She froze against me. "*I* hurt *you*? Oh, that's rich."

I felt her heart thumping in her chest against mine, felt the soft, subtle curves of her breasts pressing into my bare chest.

"What's that supposed to mean?" I needed to get some space between us right quick before my traitor dick—that didn't give a good damn what Cassidy had or hadn't done—got any harder against the flat of her belly.

Too late. I saw the second recognition flickered into her eyes. Her breath caught, her body stilled. I could see her pulse fluttering at the base of her neck.

"You gonna take a swing at me if I let you go?" I demanded, my voice was rough on the edges of the words.

She hesitated, then shook her head. I stepped back immediately, taking my chances.

What the hell was I doing? I was the good guy. I didn't barge into women's houses and pin them between appliances and hard-ons. I was polite. I said "ma'am." I walked dates to their front doors without an agenda—though to be fair, more often than not I was invited inside.

It was Cassidy, I decided, shamelessly blaming her. She drove me fucking crazy. And I wasn't about to walk through why that was. Not for the nine billionth time.

"I'm going home," I announced, shooting a glance at her. Her eyes were pinned on the front of my sweatpants. "Come find me when you figure out how to fix this mess."

I slammed her front door and then my own. Two doors between the mess of feelings I had tangled up around Cassidy. It still wasn't enough.

8

CASSIDY

The thudding on my front door was getting old, real old. It was just after 8 a.m. And I was working on my second visitor of the day.

"Cassidy Ann! You open this door right this second!"

I knew exactly who it was even before she started bellowing. Bowie was out for blood, and there was only one person he'd send my way to extract it.

I wrenched open the door, trying to fight my way out of the hoodie I'd pulled on backward.

Scarlett, my best friend, co-conspirator, and wingman, stormed inside with all the heat of a thousand Julys.

"I am so mad at you right now!"

I looked over Scarlett's shoulder to the SUV idling in front of my house. Devlin, Scarlett's live-in boyfriend, sent me a wave and mouthed "good luck" to me before pulling away from the curb.

Scarlett unwound a mile of blue and gold striped scarf from her neck and shrugged out of her parka. "You have five seconds exactly to earn my forgiveness," she said, crossing her arms the same way Bowie had barely an hour before.

I had a feeling Scarlett at least wouldn't be pushing me up against my fridge sporting hard wood.

"Coffee?" I offered. I was so damn tired.

"You're forgiven," Scarlett chirped, skipping her way back to my kitchen. She was as at home here as June or Bowie. Damn him.

Scarlett helped herself to the mug she'd made me with our high school graduation picture on it. "All right, sit 'n' spill."

In the rest of the South, it was "sit a spell." But in Bootleg Springs, where gossip flowed faster than the creeks to the lake, it was spill.

"Look," I said, "the DNA results came back a few weeks ago. Connelly's keeping everything under wraps so he could have more time with the investigation before the whole town turns into a circus over nothing."

"Over nothing?" Scarlett snorted mid sugar dump. "It's her blood."

"That's a good thing, Scar." I sat down wearily on the same stool I hadn't bothered pushing back in. "It was always going to be her blood. What's more important is what they didn't find."

"What didn't they find?"

"No DNA belonging to your dad."

She leaned against the counter and contemplated. "You still should have told us."

"I was under direct orders not to say a word. No matter what your stupid brother says about me, I take my job very seriously."

"He's real mad, Cass." Scarlett turned her back on me and began to rummage through the refrigerator that her brother had pinned me to with his very hard—I'd think about that later. No, I wouldn't. I'd refused to give Bowie more than a passing thought since I was a teenager. No siree. My brain didn't have enough room for the man. Or his morning wood.

"What are you digging for?" I asked, changing the subject. Bowie being mad at me was something new to our 27-year-old relationship. It didn't much bother me when anyone else had an axe to grind with me. But it wasn't sitting well that he was good and pissed.

She pulled out eggs and milk. "If you make me pancakes, I'll probably forgive you."

"You forgave me over the coffee," I reminded her.

"Yeah, but this way I'll doubly forgive you and I'll be inclined to share all the dirty details of what Devlin did to me last night."

My dating life was a disaster. My sex life had coasted on fumes for so long I'd forgotten what an orgasm felt like. Scarlett was my only connection to the world of pleasure...and dating men who weren't half-wits.

I yawned mightily, giving up on the idea of sleep. "Go snatch the bacon out of your brother's fridge and you've got yourself a deal."

Over crispy, pilfered bacon and fluffy pancakes, we caught up on lives that seemed to be moving faster and faster these days.

"How's living with Devlin?" I asked, swirling a piece of pancake through the river of syrup on my plate.

"Amazing and awful and everything in between," Scarlett reported cheerfully.

"Awful?"

"The man has more shoes than a Macy's! I mean, we have rolling racks for his suits in the living room."

I laughed. The suave, educated, charming Devlin McCallister had been on track for some sort of political post in Washington, D.C. when Scarlett set her sights on him. They were both miles happier with him opening up his own law practice here. Rumor had it, he might be eyeing up Ol' Judge Carwell's seat when he hit the residency requirement.

"When are y'all gonna build?" Scarlett and Devlin had bought a pretty piece of lakefront property and spent the last few months arguing over house plans and tile samples.

She rolled her eyes in the direction of my window. "Ground breaking was supposed to happen tomorrow. Thanks, Mother Nature."

I watched the fat flakes fall from the white sky. "Couple of days and it'll be gone. You'll be in your house in no time," I predicted.

"Let's hope so before I end up strangling my handsome roommate with one of his nine belts. *Nine.* Who the hell needs that many ways to hold your pants up?"

I topped off our coffees and pushed my plate away. Too little sleep, too much caffeine, and a pissed off next-door neighbor were wreaking havoc with my insides.

"Bowie said he let you have it this morning," Scarlett said, beginning her fishing expedition.

"He wasn't happy with me," I said cagily. There'd been a time in our lives when Scarlett and I had no secrets about my feelings for her brother. But those days were over. She'd stormed my bedroom two days after Bowie had told me I was basically just another sister to him and demanded to know what the hell my problem was.

I'd never told her what he said to me. But I made her pinkie swear she'd never, ever bring up me marrying Bowie ever again. I reckoned she'd gotten the hint. And true to her word, Scarlett had done what I'd asked. She was a good friend.

"He told me I was a shitty friend," I admitted. The insult bothered me more than a nest of nettles.

"He holds you to a pretty high standard," Scarlett said carefully. "Higher than most anyone else. He's taking it personally that you didn't come to him with this."

"Why in the hell would he think I would come to him? He's not my keeper. If anything, I should have shown up on your doorstep the minute I found out."

"Yes. You should have."

Dang it. Walked right into that one.

"Scarlett, my job—"

"Your loyalties are torn right down the middle. I get it. I really do. You're a law enforcement officer. And you're my best friend. I don't know what I would've done in your place, Cass. I really don't. But I think some of the reasoning behind you keeping us out of it is because you're hell-bent on doing everything yourself."

"I am not hell-bent on doing everything myself!"

"You've taken independence to a whole new level," Scarlett pointed out.

At that moment I heard the scrape of metal on concrete. Scarlett and I got up to look out the back window where Bowie Fucking Bodine was shoveling *my* walk.

"I was getting to it," I grumbled. Jesus, a girl couldn't catch a few hours of sleep after a late-night call and then shovel her own walk? It wasn't like anyone but me would be using the back door anyway.

"May it please the court? Exhibit A of Cassidy's overinflated independence."

"We need to stop watching all those lawyering shows." Scarlett and I had binge-watched our way through *Boston Legal* and now the better part of *Suits*. She wanted to get a better handle on what Devlin did for a living. I just liked the bromances.

"And you and Bowie need to work this out."

9

BOWIE

Jayme swirled into the Brunch Club in head-to-toe city black. Her spiky heels weren't snow storm appropriate. But they worked just fine for ass-kicking. Silence descended over our table in the private room. I glanced around at my family.

Scarlett leaned into her boyfriend Devlin's side. Devlin, fancy lawyer that he was, had gone and gotten us Jayme when Scarlett found Callie Kendall's sweater in our dad's house last spring. Jameson and Leah Mae had their heads together, sharing the same menu like stupid in love new couples tended to do.

Jonah, our half-brother and the newest official addition to our family, kicked back in his chair and waited for Jayme to drop whatever bomb she had stored in her big-ass pocket book. Gibson stared moodily into his coffee.

The server, a tall, pale senior from my high school, approached. He didn't make eye contact with me, which was fine with me. The whole town probably already knew we were meeting with our lawyer.

"Coffee me," Jayme ordered succinctly. She ran a practice

in Charleston and also paid us enough visits in Bootleg Springs to keep our asses out of trouble. I wondered if she was charging us double time for bringing her in on a Saturday. "Keep it coming." She sent him scurrying off.

"You're acting like I'm one of the four horsemen of the apocalypse," Jayme complained. "This isn't terrible news."

"It's Callie's blood," Gibson snapped.

"Callie's. Not your father's. And not yours or yours or yours," she said, pointing around the table at each of the male members of the Bodine clan. "You think the investigators aren't considering all possibilities? You all lived in Bootleg. You all had access to that house and the victim."

She let that sink in as the kid returned with a huge mug of steaming coffee. The rest of us shared a long look.

"Thanks," Jayme said, sticking her face in the mug.

We ordered somberly, and when the server left, Scarlett leaned in. "You're saying my brothers are suspects?"

"I'm saying they would have been. You too, Scarlett, if anyone thought you could murder someone in cold blood and keep quiet about it for years." Everyone but Gibson cracked a smile at that. If Scarlett killed someone, it would be in a fit of rage in front of the whole damn town, not in cold calculation.

"Yes. It's Callie's blood on the sweater. But there wasn't a speck of Bodine DNA found. Your dad could have found that sweater in the woods. Hell, the real killer could be a neighbor trying to frame Jonah Sr."

"That's unlikely," I said dryly. It would have been real nice if our father hadn't up and died so he could answer the questions we all had about just how he came to be in possession of the bloody sweater Callie Kendall went missing in all those years ago. And those pesky other questions about where the hell he'd disappeared to immediately after cops and reporters had turned Bootleg Springs upside down in a frantic search for the missing teenager.

"Unlikely, but if it comes down to it, if the investigators get a hard-on for one of you, I can argue that."

"Reasonable doubt," Devlin said.

"Exactly."

"So what do we do now? The news is gonna break and soon, I'm sure," I spoke up. "Maybe the cops aren't looking at us right now, but that doesn't mean the entire state won't be pointing fingers in our direction."

"You're going to keep your mouths shut. You're not going to get into a single bar fight. You aren't going to say so much as 'Hey, y'all,' to a reporter or I'll drive up here and parade you out in front of the courthouse and make you give a press conference."

Jameson visibly shuddered. None of us wanted to stand up with a dozen microphones in our faces and explain how we didn't think our dad had anything to do with the death or disappearance of Callie Kendall.

Especially since I wasn't sure which side I fell on. Was my father a killer? I didn't think it was likely that the man I'd known my entire life had committed some gruesome murder. But could he have hit her driving drunk? Hadn't he taken out an entire hedgerow at the house after a bender? I looked up and met Gibs's eyes. He was thinking along the same lines.

I didn't know. Maybe I'd never know. Maybe Callie's disappearance would never be solved and my father's memory would always be in question. *Did anyone ever really know their parents?*

"Judging by the crickets around the table, none of you want me to make good on that threat. So let's all do our best not to ruin the advantage we were just handed."

"Yes, ma'am," we all recited together like a kindergarten class.

~

WITH BELLIES full of egg white omelets, Jonah and I climbed back in his car.

"That woman is intense," he commented.

"She's terrifying. You should ask her out."

He snorted. "I'm still dealing with finding out that I have four siblings and that my biological father might be a murderer. I don't have the mental capacity to deal with dating right now." He winced. "Sorry. I didn't sleep well. I don't mean to say shit about your dad."

"Our dad," I corrected. Accepting Jonah had been easier than I thought. He didn't want a damn thing besides getting to know us. "Too much hot sausage and 'shine last night?"

Jonah took the whole healthy lifestyle to levels that even I considered unhealthy. If it was processed or greasy, it went nowhere near his plate. He probably lay in bed at night starving from his rabbit food and protein shakes.

"I was rudely awakened by my roommate's hissy fit this morning. What was with all the door slamming?" Jonah asked with a yawn.

"I was fighting with Cassidy," I sighed.

"Really?" he perked up. "What's up with that?"

"She knew about the DNA and didn't tell me. Us. Didn't say a damn word."

"Well, she is a cop," Jonah supplied.

"Whose side are you on? The next-door neighbor's or your new roommate's?"

"Depends on who's right. Does she usually talk to you about ongoing investigations?"

"No." She didn't talk to me about much of anything. She talked to people around me. "But we had a right to know."

"Maybe she was only following orders?" He was parroting Cassidy's words back at me. The walls were too thin.

"Heard a lot, didn't you?"

He shrugged and turned off the engine. "What's her deal? Is she seeing anyone?"

Cassidy and my half-brother Jonah? The half-brother my dad had right after me. I'd sit across from them at Thanksgiving as they juggled babies and side dishes. I'd stand up for Jonah at their wedding and drink myself stupid for a week afterward. The mounds of snow scooped from the walkway took on a blood-red haze.

Jonah laughed. "Relax, man. I'm messing with you. I know you're into her."

I could feel my heartbeat in my head. Now I really wanted to kick his ass.

"I'm not into her," I lied. It was easier than telling the truth, *facing* the truth.

"You're full of shit," he said as we climbed the front porch steps. "Why don't you just tell her?"

We both paused and looked at Cassidy's front door.

"It's not like that," I snapped. "We're not like that." I unlocked the front door.

"Doesn't mean you can't be," he pointed out.

That was exactly what it meant. Cassidy Tucker was off-limits. To me *and* Jonah.

10

CASSIDY

I perused my menu and tried to pretend that knuckle-cracking didn't make me want to beat the man across from me to death. Once again, I'd been suckered in by a cute picture and charming profile.

I really needed to give up on dating apps. But I'd been mopey since Bowie went all "You're a shitty friend" on me and thought I'd take one last stab at finding lasting happiness with someone. Anyone. Even this dumbass.

I smiled over the menu at him while fantasizing about dumping the hot wax from the centerpiece candle on him. Baxter was currently having a loud phone conversation with someone he called "sweetheart." He alternated between picking his teeth with a toothpick that he'd arrived at my house with and rolling his eyes at me during every pause on his end of the call.

"Listen, sweetheart. I'm busy. Now, why don't you and your sweet ass figure out how to fix it yourself? And remember. If you don't, you're fired." He gave me a slow wink, and I gagged. I grabbed my wine and inhaled it.

He hung up, cracked his knuckles, and gave me a look that

was close to a leer. "Sorry about that. That's my secretary—oh, excuse me. My *administrative assistant*," he said with another eye roll. One more of those and his eyeballs were going to dislodge themselves from their sockets.

"Problem at work?" I asked, not giving a flying fuck. I had to hang in there and be polite and get through this evening. I never should have let him insist on picking me up. Now not only did I have to survive dinner, I had to survive a thirty-minute drive home. Ugh. What had I been thinking?

That Bowie would see a date arriving and dropping me off. That's what I'd been thinking. I wasn't about to unpack that thought. Not while Mr. Misogyny was preening in front of me.

How much would it cost to Uber back to Bootleg?

I didn't date in town when it could be helped. Bootleg was my whole life, and I preferred to meet potential suitors/disasters on neutral turf. Plus, I'd dated just about every eligible man in town by now. I needed fresh meat. I had a feeling Baxter here was past his expiration date.

"She can sit there lookin' pretty as a peach, but ask her to do a simple task like make sure everyone gets paid on time while our accountant is on house arrest and she's useless. Poor gal screwed something up with the server and the payroll system went down on payday." He shrugged, not giving a damn. "Not my fault that no one told me not to turn off the backup server."

"I'm guessing not much is ever your fault," I predicted.

He plucked that damn toothpick he'd been sucking on out of his mouth and pointed it at me. "You're damn right. I knew I liked you. You know what else ain't my fault?"

I didn't, but I was afraid he was going to tell me.

"That you're so pretty I think I'm gonna hafta kiss you before the night is over."

Gross. Barf. Disgusting. I mentally ran through a list of pressure points to squeeze.

"I don't think that's going to be necessary."

Jesus, when had dating gotten so hard? I first made the mistake of joining the wrong app and getting bombarded with dick pics for a week. Not that I didn't take great pleasure in responding with a picture of my badge and an explanation of assault. Now, I had to weed out the losers and assholes based on doctored pictures and vague profiles.

Baxter here billed himself as a small business owner who enjoyed giving back to the community. He was slick and plastic-looking. His blond hair was gelled back from his too-orange-for-natural tanned face. He wore a suit and instead of a tie, accessorized with a thick patch of chest hair and a large gold cross. I guessed the only giving back to the community was the amount of money he spent on things like legal representation in sexual harassment lawsuits.

He chuckled like I'd just told a funny story that ended up with me naked with another girl. When he reached across the table and took my hand, I'd had enough.

"You know what, Baxter?"

My threat about him keeping all his fingers only if he kept them off of me was interrupted by the maître d' fussing over the chairs at the next table.

Mirabella's was a fancy Italian place where the draperies were heavy, tables were too close together, and I was scared shitless about spilling my dinner on the pristine white tablecloths. Some unlucky couple was about ready to watch me spill Baxter's guts on the table.

"Your server will be with you in a moment," the man said to the couple.

"Thank you."

Oh, holy hell in a damn handbasket. That voice.

Bowie in a goddamn suit came into my field of vision, and I nearly upended my wine glass. Bowie's gray eyes widened in surprise when they met mine. And then they dipped, reflexively, to give me the once-over.

"Shit."

His date blinked at him. "Excuse me?"

Bowie turned away from me and looked back at her. She was pretty, if you were into petite and brunette and curvy and perfect. She looked like she'd been a cheerleader in high school. I felt the flush explode on my cheeks like a brushfire.

"Nothing. Sorry." He held out her chair for her and then took the one across from her. The one with a direct line of sight to me.

"What were you saying, sugar?" Baxter asked, still holding my hand.

Bowie was back to looking at us. His gaze held on our joined hands. Because I was a "shitty friend," I didn't stab Good Ol' Baxter with my steak knife. Instead, I let him hold my hand for a moment longer. *Take that, Mr. Bodine. Not everyone found me so repulsive.*

Bowie's date was looking at me now and—damn it! I'd gone and made eye contact.

"What's going on?" the cheerleader asked. She was no dummy. She picked right up on the tension that crackled like a storm over our two little tables. You'd have to be dumber than a box of rocks not to notice that the air had suddenly taken a turn for the awkward. Baxter didn't notice.

Bowie laughed nervously. "Uh, Erin, this is my neighbor Cassidy. Small world." Neighbor? *Neighbor?* That's what I was to him?

"Hi," I said pulling my hand out of Baxter's sweaty grip to shake Erin's hand. "This is..." *My soon-to-be stabbing victim? A man about to be missing his testicles? My biggest mistake this week?* "Baxter."

"Good to meet you, Baxter," Bowie said, offering his hand to shake.

"Yeah, uh-huh," Baxter gave a limp fish shake. "Now, if y'all will excuse me. I'm in the middle of charming the pants off this little lady." He leaned forward and added in a stage whisper. "Maybe we should have that kiss now as an appetizer? I don't mind if you use tongue."

I stared at him, trying to telegraph the message: *Shut. The. Fuck. Up. Help me show Bowie that I'm no little sister or shitty friend.*

But Baxter was a dumbass and didn't get the message.

I did the only thing I could do. I laughed with an edge of hysteria that had other diners looking in our direction. That's it. I was done dating. I'd go get a cat. Two of them. I'd embrace the single lady life because I couldn't possibly deal with this one second longer. I'd never have to share the TV remote. Leftovers would always be mine. And I'd just wear both halves of the pajamas. Single wasn't bad. Single was better than Baxter.

The waiter returned with another glass of wine—thank the Lord—and took our appetizer order. Bowie and Pretty, Perfect Erin were stuck in the uncomfortable position of not having their own conversation because, by proximity, they were a part of mine and Baxter's.

"What is it you said you did again, sugar?" Baxter asked picking up his gin and knocking it back like a shot.

"I'm a cop." I hadn't told him. That tidbit of information didn't usually make it into my profile for a variety of reasons. Including but not limited to: dates trying to get me to fix speeding and parking tickets for them, questions about whether I'd ever shot anyone, or the bullshit of "girls can't be cops." I had a feeling I knew which way Baxter would lean.

"Woo wee! Girls can't be cops," he howled, slapping the table. Everything was funny to Bonehead Baxter.

I stared at him coolly. Bowie caught my eye and mouthed "What. The. Fuck?"

I didn't need him on my side. I didn't need him anywhere near my single cat lady life.

"Well, I do have a vagina, and I am a cop," I assured him.

"Prove it." He cackled lecherously, and I ground a layer of enamel off my teeth.

I could feel Erin's discomfort radiating out of her totally cute blue sheath dress.

Bowie leaned over. "You better mind those opinions or she'll tase your ass."

"I mean, come on. You're with me, man. Ain't cha? Women aren't as strong or as fast as men. Hell, I bet *I* can outshoot this pretty little thing."

I threw my napkin on the empty plate in front of me. "If you'll excuse me, I'm going to find the restroom." *And punch a few holes in the drywall. And Google cat rescues.*

Without another word, I stormed away from the table. Away from Baxter and Bowie and Bowie's perfect date.

11

CASSIDY

I shoved the restroom door open with enough force to have it rebounding back at me. So I gave it another bad-tempered push on my way in. It was one of those bathrooms that was decked out to be soothing and spa-like with caramel colored tiles all the way up the wall and a fancy sink that looked like a trough.

Peering in the mirror, I wondered how in the hell I'd sunk to this level. I was a good person. A law-abiding citizen, a squeaky-clean deputy sworn to uphold the law, an excellent daughter, a good friend...despite what *some* might say. I'd gone to college. I donated to food drives and fire station roof funds. I paid my taxes.

So what bad karma led me to this mirror in this restaurant on this shitty date where Bowie Bodine of all people got to witness my humiliation?

Something needed to change.

I'd name my cats Smokey and Bandit, I decided. I'd figure out how to cook and host elaborate dinners for friends. I'd learn Italian. I'd have strings-free sex with handsome, sexy, STD-free gentlemen. I would be the cool aunt. If June ever got over her disinterest in people. Gosh darn it, I would have a rich, full life all by myself and never again subject myself to the Baxters of the world. Or the Bowies.

The restroom door opened and closed quietly.

"Cassidy, right?" Bowie's perky, adorable date asked. She barely came to my shoulder in her cute wedge boots.

"Yeah," I said warily. Usually when female strangers approached you in the bathroom it wasn't good.

She joined me at the mirror, opening her small clutch and pulling out lipstick. "He mentioned you on our first date."

First date? They'd gone on more than one date? I hated the icy wave of pain that ran through me. He wasn't mine anymore. He had never been mine.

"I grew up with his little sister," I mumbled, making a show of washing my hands.

"Yeah, that's what he said. But here's the thing." She reapplied her already perfect lipstick and slipped it back in her bag. "It was the *way* he said it."

"What way?"

"Like you were special. Important. Who brings up a little sister's friend on a first date? Girl to girl, that man out there has some big, scary feelings for you."

"I don't understand." I dropped all pretense of washing my hands for a third time. "He told me in no uncertain terms years ago that I was nothing but another little sister to him."

Shut the fuck up, Cassidy! Mayday! Mayday!

I turned back to the mirror. "I'm sorry. You're his date. I shouldn't be saying any of this."

Erin sighed. "Look, no matter what he said, the way he looks at you says something entirely different. He looks at you like you're the center of everything."

I looked down at the soap suds in the sink. "Why are you telling me this?"

"Because I don't play second fiddle. No matter how cute the conductor is."

"Are you warning me off? Because we're next-door neighbors. It's hard to avoid each other. Believe me, I've tried."

She smiled. Damn it. She had a dimple in her right cheek. "I'm not warning you off. I'm letting you know that my date has some powerful feelings for you, and I'm going to go back out there, make an excuse, and leave you two to what should have been your date."

"I'm here on a date," I reminded her. A date from hell.

"The way Bowie was laying into Mr. Shithead when I left the table, I doubt he'll be much of an obstacle."

She started for the door, then paused. "Good luck out there."

"Why are you doing this?" I asked.

She gave me another smile, and I immediately pictured her at the top of a pyramid at a football game. "Maybe I'm a romantic at heart. Or maybe I'm just annoyed it wasn't me he was looking at that way. Either way, there's a tall, sexy drink of water at the bar I might let buy me a drink," she mused.

"I spent most of my life thinkin' I'd marry him," I confessed as she turned.

"Maybe it's time y'all get started on that." With those parting words, Erin floated out of the restroom.

I took another couple of minutes to breathe cleansing breaths and repair my armor. I didn't know if what Erin was saying was true or if I wanted it to be true. To be honest, I didn't have the energy to consider either option. I wanted to go home. Alone.

Bracing myself, I returned to the dining room and found my table empty except for the stuffed mushroom caps Baxter had ordered. Even his toothpick was gone. Bowie was staring pensively into his beer and looked up when I approached.

Erin was nowhere to be seen, and a quick peek at the bar showed that neither was the hottie she'd mentioned.

Good for her.

"Where'd Baxter go?" I asked.

"He had an emergency," Bowie said. I knew he was lying because he squinted just a little bit. The corners of his eyes crinkling up. The first time I caught that tell was when he was desperately trying to cover his slip-up about there being no Santa Claus.

I flopped down in my chair.

"He was my ride home." I guessed I was about to find out how expensive Ubering back to Bootleg was.

"I'll take you home," Bowie said.

"Where's Erin?" I asked, ignoring his offer.

"She had an emergency, too."

Liar, liar, pants on fire.

I picked up my wine and stared down at the appetizer. Everything sucked.

"Come on now. Don't look like that, Cass. You know it kills me to see you sad," Bowie coaxed.

"Oh, now you care how I feel? Even though I'm a 'shitty friend?'" I shot back.

"I was mad," he said simply.

"Yeah, well, now I'm mad."

He rose from his chair and took Baxter's vacated one. "I'm sorry, Cassidy."

I tried looking everywhere but his face.

He leaned in, helped himself to a mushroom cap. "Now, it's your turn."

"My turn for what?"

"To apologize."

I could actually feel my nostrils flare. "I'm not going to apologize for doing my job."

"No. But you could apologize for the fact that doing your job hurt us."

"I already apologized to Scarlett," I sniffed.

"You hurt me, Cass."

Crap. Crap. Crap.

"You're not gonna let this go, are you?" I asked quietly.

He rested his elbows on the table. "You live next door. You're part of my family. I'm not going to let this fester between us. We're too important to each other."

I swallowed hard and poked at a mushroom with my fork. Erin's words popped into my mind in big bold font. But I'd opened myself up once to those kinds of possibilities with Bowie and had to pick my devastated self up off the floor when the door slammed shut in my face.

He'd never know how much he hurt me that day all those years ago. I'd vowed it then and I reminded myself now. Part of that meant being cordial now. Not taking out old hurts on him.

One deep breath and I took the plunge for the good of the many. "I'm sorry that what I did hurt you," I said. I chanced a look up at him. He reached out and stroked a finger over the knuckles of my hand. It was so different from Baxter's sweaty pawing. So intimate. So stirring.

Damn it. Think about cats!

"I accept your apology," he said.

"You don't have to drive me home," I said, changing the subject. His finger was still running the mountains and valleys of my knuckles.

"We live together," he said dryly. "It would be stupid not to go home together."

"All right. But I'll pay you gas money." I wasn't about to start owing Bowie anything again.

"Since we're here, why don't we grab a bite before we go."

Not a date. Not a date. Not a date. Do not think of this as a date.

And I was hungry. Starving actually. "Since we're here."

The waiter returned and cast a baleful eye at the now abandoned second table.

"Change of plans," Bowie said.

"Musical chairs," I added.

We ordered and sat in awkward silence for several moments. The tables around us filled with happy couples and loud parties. Everyone enjoying the night except for us. I'd known this man my entire life but couldn't seem to find the words for small talk.

Bowie had never been one for small talk.

"So where did Baxter really go?" I asked.

His lips quirked, and he squinted at me.

"And before you say anything, you do know that I can tell when you're lying, don't you?"

"No you can't," he argued amicably.

"Try me," I encouraged.

"I hate oysters."

No squint. "True."

"Hm. I think football is overrated."

"False. Come on, really test me," I told him.

He paused, studying me. "I think you look real pretty tonight," he said finally.

No squint.

I shoveled a mushroom cap into my face to buy myself some time. I had fallen for this once before. Bowie being nice to me did not mean he was attracted to me. I'd learned it the hard way. Where this man was concerned, my instincts were garbage. "True. But I already knew that I looked good. Is that all you've got?"

"I think they should bring back *Buffy the Vampire Slayer*," he announced.

"Hmm. True. And I agree." I nodded my approval.

"Erin left because she thinks you and I have feelings for each other."

I wasn't sure which one of us was more surprised by the statement.

"Why did Baxter leave?" I asked again. Softly this time.

"Because he wasn't good enough for you. When are you gonna stop wasting your time on these assholes and find someone who deserves you, Cass?"

12

BOWIE

I shouldn't have said half of the things I said to Cassidy tonight, I thought to myself as I steered in the direction of Bootleg Springs. I was already kicking myself for it. Those feelings were locked down long ago and had no business being voiced.

She shifted in the seat next to me, and I tried not to think about how right all this felt. Dinner had felt like a date. But not just any date. The kind with a whole history behind it, behind us. The kind with a cozy future in front of it.

I was walking a fine line right now. I could reach out and take the hand she rested on the console between us. And that would be crossing the line. The line Cassidy didn't know about. The line I spent more time than I cared to admit wondering if it still existed.

I'd worked so damn hard trying to erase the stain of my upbringing. I was the son of an alcoholic and an emotionally unavailable mother. We'd been poor. Once in a while we'd been hungry. And that's still what some people saw when they looked at me.

Not the master's degree-earning high school vice principal. Not the community volunteer. The town council member. Or the shoveler of sidewalks, the carrier of groceries.

Cassidy had never seen me that way. But others had.

"Mighty big sigh you got there," she commented, still looking out her window.

"I thought you fell asleep."

"Nope, just running through my shopping list," she said.

"Whatcha buyin'?"

"Cat supplies."

"Cat supplies?"

"I'm adopting a cat." Her tone implied that she was daring me to have a problem with it.

We lapsed back into silence, and I found myself once again wishing that I was holding her hand.

"Sorry about Erin," she said, breaking the silence again.

"Not your fault."

"She seemed nice."

"I think she left with a guy at the bar," I told her.

I could see the corner of Cass's mouth lift. "Did she now?"

"And what's so amusing about that?" I wanted to know.

"Nothin' at all. Not a damn thing. Were you two serious?"

I shrugged and turned the radio on low. "Nah. Just a couple of dates."

"You ever been in love?" she asked, turning to look at me.

"Nope," I lied.

"Mmm." She made that skeptical-like noise she tended to when she wasn't believing the line she was being fed.

"You?" I asked.

"Never."

We rode in companionable silence, listening to the radio.

When the lights of Bootleg appeared ahead, I drummed my fingers on the steering wheel. "Still early. Want to get a drink at The Lookout?"

She glanced my way, looked at the clock. "Sure. Why not?"

The Lookout was a bar that sat high up on an outcropping of rocks that overlooked part of town and the lake. It got its name from its storied and exaggerated history as a lookout for bootleggers running their 'shine across the lake into Maryland.

Now, it served as the center of our town. A place for neighbors to catch up, games to be watched, dances danced, and fights fought.

I pulled into the gravel lot, already overflowing with cars, and together we walked toward the front door. Cassidy stumbled in her impractical heels, and I caught her elbow. "Bootleg's not gonna know what to do with you dressed like that," I told her.

Usually she was in uniform. Who knew khaki and badges could be so sexy? Her off-duty uniform was jeans. And if I were being real honest, I couldn't tell you which Cassidy I preferred. The stern deputy. The casual girl-next-door. Or this new creature in a slim-fitting dress and stilettos that Jayme would approve of.

Her eyes were smokier tonight, lips painted. I wanted to wipe the lipstick off with my mouth. I wanted her to mark me with it. *Face. Neck. Chest. Cock.*

I'd given up trying to stop the fantasies a long time ago.

And damn it. There it was. The erection that had been lurking since I sat down at the table next to hers.

I followed her into the bar, taking in the familiar sights and sounds. Nicolette was tending bar in one of her snarky t-shirts. Tonight's read *Y'all Need Jesus and Whiskey*. The lights were dim. The tables were full. And there was a band on the stage doing their best to butcher Lynyrd Skynyrd.

Our neighbors and friends crowded around the bar watching the Steelers gain ground on the field.

I pointed Cassidy in the direction of the tables skirting the dance floor and mimed getting a drink. She gave me a thumbs-up and headed off to find us seats. I ordered two drafts of Cass's favorite.

"You're lookin' spiffy tonight, Bowie," Nicolette pointed out.

"Somebody had a date," Opal Bodine, no relation, piped up. She was wearing a Cockspurs sweatshirt and nursing some moonshine concoction in a jar.

"Guessin' it didn't go well?" Nicolette asked, plopping the beers down in front of me.

I looked over to where Cassidy waved from a table in the corner. "It didn't go too bad," I told them.

Weaving my way through the crowd, I found Cassidy sharing a table with Millie Waggle, Nash Larabee, and—damn it all to hell—Amos Sheridan, Cassidy's ex four or five times over.

Cassidy had taken the chair next to Amos, and they were arguing about Zac Brown's new album. I pulled out the chair next to Millie and slid Cass's beer across the table. "Evenin', all."

"Hey, Bow. You two are looking fancy tonight," Millie said. Millie was my sister and Cassidy's age and dressed like a 70-year-old Sunday school teacher. She also baked like an angel and did the bookkeeping for the Bootleg Springs Spa.

"Yeah, y'all finally go on a date?" Nash asked.

The table erupted in laughter except for me and Cass.

"Did you know you two were voted least likely to hook up in the last town newsletter?" Amos pointed out. "See, Cassidy here is never gettin' over me."

Cassidy elbowed him in the gut with a familiarity I didn't much care for. I hated it when she dated him. Hated it when she dated anybody, but especially Amos.

"What's your name again?" Cassidy asked him sweetly batting her eyelashes. Everyone laughed again.

"What's this about the newsletter?" I pressed.

Millie giggled. "Oh, it's just silliness. Every week there's a poll. You two were voted least likely to date. Y'all beat out Misty Lynn and Rev. Duane."

I must have been making a face because Millie leaned in. "It's for fun, Bow. Nothing to get your knickers in a knot. You two are as close to brother and sister as you can get without the blood is all."

I looked across the table at Cassidy. What I felt for her wasn't even a distant relation of brotherly.

"I really need to start opening my newsletters," Cassidy joked. I could tell she felt as awkward as I did over the topic.

I sat back in my chair and forced myself to relax. We yelled over the music, and I tried not to want to punch Amos in the face when he looped his arm over the back of Cassidy's chair. When the band shifted gears into something low and slow, I went with it.

"Wanna dance, Cass?"

The table shut up right quick, and Cassidy blinked. She was a sucker for Chris Stapleton, and "Tennessee Whiskey" was one of his best.

"All right," she said slowly.

I stood and held my hand out to her. She took it after the slightest hesitation, and I led her onto the dance floor. It was crowded with bodies swaying and sliding. I pulled her into the darkest corner and thanked the sweet baby Jesus when she slid her arms around my neck.

I didn't care what anybody said. This was *right*.

We ticked and tocked with the slow beat. I'd shed my suit jacket and loosened my tie at the table. Cassidy had pulled the pins out of her hair. Here we were halfway between who we were every day and who we were on special occasions.

I thought she'd talk. Ask me why I'd asked her to dance. But she kept her eyes glued to me as we worked our way around in a lazy little circle. I felt her fingers playing with the ends of my hair and pulled her close enough that neither one of us could pretend this was a friendly dance.

Our faces were close. Cassidy's heels put her within easy kissing distance. I could feel her breath on my neck. Could see her pulse flutter at the base of her throat. I wondered what she was seeing of me up close and personal.

We'd danced before. About a hundred times over the course of our lives. But this was different. And I didn't know why. Maybe it was the clothes. Maybe it was the challenge from the newsletter. I was a Bodine after all. Tell us we can't do something and watch us do it with both middle fingers flying proudly.

"People are gonna talk," Cassidy said softly.

"About what?"

"This. Us. Showin' up here all fancy and then slow dancin'."

Her lips were that rose petal pink that I found absolutely irresistible. I stopped myself from tracing my thumb over her full lower lip.

"Does that bother you?" I asked, sliding my palm over the small of her back.

She shook her head. "Don't much care. Besides, we know the truth."

"What truth?" I asked. Every inch of her was pressed against every inch of me. I could feel the heat rising off of her.

"That I'm nothin' but your little sister's best friend."

"You've never been just my little sister's best friend, trouble."

My old nickname for her made us both smile a little.

The song was over. The band was kicking it up again with an East Coast swing. Cassidy was unwinding her arms from my neck, but I didn't want to be done touching her yet. I squeezed her slim hips with both palms, keeping her against me for just a second longer.

She brushed her hands across my chest. "Thanks for the ride and the dance, Bow."

13

CASSIDY

Minnie's Meow Meow House was indeed a house. The low wooden structure had started as a simple cabin but had been added on to in weird and wonderful ways, making it a rambling haven for homeless cats. It smelled like fresh cat litter and the special catnip potpourri Minnie Faye made especially for her charges.

Minnie Faye and her husband, Hubert, had a soft spot for strays. Together with their gigantic hearts, they'd built a rainbow of a family, first with foster and adopted children and now with fur babies.

Minnie Faye was currently in the Meow Meow House's front office scrutinizing my nine-page adoption application, my three reference letters, and credit report.

"What about that one?" Scarlett pointed at an orange ball of fluff hanging upside down from his spacious cage's ceiling. His meow was closer to a shriek.

We were in Cat Room Number Two. Each room had a different theme. This one was kitten posters. They'd plastered the green pine-paneled walls in a glossy, fluffy mural of cute.

I winced. That cat was exactly the kind of hellion Scarlett

Bodine would be attracted to. She stood there entranced, peering through the cage door. The kitten, sensing an audience, launched himself at the front door of the cage, mewling plaintively.

"I'm more in the market for a fat lump that I have to pick up to vacuum under," I told her. But Scarlett was still staring at the kitten with a mix of adulation and longing.

June sneezed and blew her nose. Though allergic to cats, my sister had insisted on helping me choose my first pet.

"Why don't *you* adopt him?" I said to Scarlett, stepping around her to stare into the next cage.

Bonded pair, read the sign.

I couldn't imagine a stranger pair. One cat was gray and black and looked to weigh about twenty pounds. He was too lazy to open both eyes to observe me. Instead, he settled for one. The other cat was a skinny, long-legged tabby that alternated between licking its own butthole and biting the tip of its tail.

"You could name the large, handsome one George," June suggested, peering over my shoulder. She sounded like she was pinching her nose closed.

"George?" I asked. The larger of the cats not obsessed with his butthole lifted his head, made eye contact with me, and yawned.

"George Thompson, more commonly known as GT Thompson, the most consistent receiver in the league." Some women crushed on shirtless models on Instagram. My sister preferred to admire a man's football stats.

I chewed on my lip and wondered if I was committing to this cat lady lifestyle too early. Maybe I should go on one more date? Or maybe I should ask Bowie for one more slow dance...

No! I couldn't spend the rest of my life thinking maybe someday.

"I'll take them," I decided. I'd given up on Bowie a long

time ago and didn't need to open that box or door or whatever the hell it was again. One dinner and a steamy slow dance did not mean a man was interested. And it sure as hell didn't mean I had to be interested either.

George was gazing at me like he could see into my soul. He sneezed, making his younger, skinnier partner freak out and jump across the cage floor. The little one shot me an accusatory look and then immediately flopped over on its back to view me from upside down.

"I can't bring a cat home," Scarlett lamented. "We don't have room for Devlin's shoe collection, let alone a whole entire cat. Where would I put his food dish?"

"Y'all want to meet any of the cats?" Maribel Schilling, a part-time volunteer at the Meow Meow House, asked, sticking her beehived head in the doorway.

"I'd like to meet these two," I told her.

"What the hell? Gimme a shot at this guy," Scarlett decided, pointing at little Lucifer, who was violently attacking his tail while sitting in his water dish.

"You want one, June Bug?" I asked.

She sneezed four times in a row. "Cats are too independent. The ideal pet is a potbellied pig."

"A pig? You're going to make a tolerant man very confused someday," I predicted.

Maribel led us into the meet and greet cat room. This room had a big bay window and a half dozen armchairs.

"Have a seat, y'all. We'll be back with your fur babies."

"Do you have any pigs?" June asked.

"Sorry, pumpkin. Just kitties here."

June blew her nose noisily and flopped down on a pink-checkered armchair. "She said 'your' to make you feel obligated to complete the adoption. She's assigning ownership. It's basic psychology." She sneezed three times in rapid succession. The tissue pile on the arm of her chair was growing rapidly.

"Why the sudden need for cats anyway?" Scarlett asked, pacing back and forth like an expectant parent.

I sighed and perched on the rolled arm of a recliner. "I'm giving up, y'all."

"Giving up on what? Not being covered in cat hair?" Scarlett asked.

"Dating. Looking for Mr. Right. Or even Mr. Semi-Okay and Tolerable," I announced.

Scarlett stopped mid-pace. "You can't give up. You're only twenty-six years old."

"Twenty-seven," I corrected. Scarlett always forgot about the few months when we were a whole birth year apart. "Twenty-seven and no closer to finding a guy I could stand for the rest of my life than when I was ten years old. I don't think it's healthy to keep looking. My life isn't that bad. Hell, it's pretty great. I love my job. I have my own house. I live near my family. I can see your weird face anytime I want. And now I'll have two furry kids that I can leave home alone for long hours and will still want to snuggle with me at night."

Scarlett stared at me like I'd announced I was turning in my gun and badge and becoming a kindergarten teacher. "This displeases me," she said finally.

June squinted her puffy red eyes at us. "I don't understand why women waste so much time looking for relationships. You could be doing so many more important things with your time. Learning foreign languages, studying the tax code, building an investment strategy."

June's apathy toward love was legendary and baffling to Scarlett and me. While we'd watched *Pretty in Pink* forty-seven times the summer between our freshman and sophomore years in high school, June had created an underground football fantasy league for our classmates.

Now, I was jumping ship, too. To Scarlett, who'd discovered the love of her life right next door—just who in the hell did that happen to anyway—it was appalling. We'd been planning weddings and great loves since elementary school. My goal was to find what my parents had and replicate it. Her goal was to do better than her parents had.

Jonah and Constance had fallen hard for each other in high school and had never grown into their relationship. Petty jealousies, mistrust, and volatile fights followed by frigid days of silence were the hallmarks of Scarlett's childhood. One night in fourth grade, Scarlett had slept over at my house after her parents indulged in a particularly nasty fight. She'd confessed to me her mama claimed she would have divorced him years ago but couldn't afford to. He'd thrown a scratch-off at her and told her to do them both a favor and get a lawyer.

That stuck with me. I'd snuck out of my room after she'd fallen asleep and tiptoed downstairs. Mom and Dad were sprawled out on the couch, Dad's head in Mom's lap. The TV on low while they both read their respective books. I'd hugged them both hard that night.

One night, a long time ago, Bowie had called my dad. He needed help breaking up an argument. It had started between Jonah and Constance. Then seventeen-year-old Gibson had gotten involved. My dad hadn't even paused to put his uniform on. He ran out of the house in his sweatpants. He'd come back an hour later with all four of the Bodine kids. The adults had calmed down, but the kids needed some soothing. My mom treated it like a big party. She made us midnight pancakes, and we all camped in the living room watching *The Sandlot*. I'd loved them even more for that night.

Scarlett had outdone her parents' relationship by finding Devlin.

And I had given up.

But when Maribel dumped twenty pounds of Handsome George into my lap, I felt a little something like love. And that was good enough for me.

I'd given up on Bowie a long time ago. Closed my heart to the man. One slow dance wasn't going to open those creaky doors again. I didn't need him to have a full, fun, interesting life.

Handsome George reached up with one paw and placed it over my heart as if to tell me that everything was going to be just fine. I believed him. Cats didn't lie.

"Oh. My. Goodness," Scarlett crooned, snuggling the devil in fur to her face. "I love you to tiny little bits."

Potential George looked up at me, and I swear that dang cat smiled. His partner in crime clawed his way up the back of the chair and perched neat as you please on my shoulder, his tail twitching against my neck. He blinked his yellow-green eyes at me slowly.

"I'm textin' Devlin," Scarlett announced. "We're gettin' a cat, y'all!"

"Wait," June said, holding out one hand while blowing her nose with the other. "I'll take your picture. It will be harder for him to say no."

Scarlett juggled cat and phone and assumed the appropriate position.

"Make your eyes wider and sadder," June ordered.

14

BOWIE

"At this time, Jonah Bodine remains a person of interest in the disappearance of Callie Kendall," Detective Connelly said, his lined face sober as photographers snapped pictures like he was a Hollywood starlet confessing to butt implants and a drug problem.

He stared into the local news station's camera with hooded eyes as a light drizzle of freezing rain fell from gray skies. Sheriff Tucker stood behind him, mouth set in a firm line under his mustache. "We are asking that anyone with any information about Callie Kendall or Jonah Bodine come forward."

"He's gonna have half of Bootleg Springs lined up to tell him their reminiscences of that summer," I muttered at the TV screen. It was six in the morning on a Monday, and I had a feeling it was going to be a shitty-ass day.

Jonah grabbed the remote and turned off the TV. It was a replay of what we'd seen breaking live yesterday in time for the five o'clock news. "I need Jayme to scare them into at least using middle initials," he said.

On cue, Jonah's cell phone rang again. We both swore.

Sharing a name with our father was not only insulting to the guy who grew up without the man but now it was a direct link for the press to exploit.

They'd descended like locusts. Journalists, bloggers, conspiracy theorists arrived in Bootleg Springs in time for last night's press conference with their noses for news and their shiny camera equipment. Ready to violate the privacy of each and every resident until they could serve up some twisted version of the truth that would sell the most advertising space.

Our landline rang so many times after the press conference that I'd unplugged the damn thing and tossed it in a closet. I decided to focus on getting to work early.

I, unlike the rest of my siblings, didn't have the luxury of working for myself. I was the high school vice principal. A job that I loved. A job I'd hate to lose over a family scandal that I hadn't at least earned.

If my father did play a role in Callie Kendall's death, would I be found guilty by association in the court of public opinion?

I honestly didn't believe my father was a murderer, but accidents could and did happen. The result was the same. Callie Kendall was gone. And the rest of the Bodines were still here.

Jonah, my roommate and half-brother, could leave. He could go back to his old life and pick up where he left off in Jetty Beach, chalking up Bootleg to an extended visit. But my entire life was here.

I couldn't help but wonder if Dad was reaching out from beyond the grave to ruin my life.

"Holy shit," Jonah muttered, peering through the front window.

"What?"

"There's a low-budget news crew setting up in front of the house."

I joined him at the window and stared in horror at the two guys setting up a tripod and running wires on the sidewalk. A third guy, in a rumpled trench coat, paced back and forth taking selfies.

Jonah made a move for the front door, and I stopped him. "What are you gonna do? Tell them to get off the public sidewalk while providing them with footage of an angry Bodine?"

"This is ridiculous," he argued, arms crossed over his chest. I think Scarlett's temper was rubbing off on him.

There was a tap on the back door, and we glanced at each other. Nothing we could do about reporters on a public street. But one climbing fences in our backyard? We could at least punch that guy in the face once or twice.

In silent agreement, we tiptoed into the kitchen. Jonah put his hand on the doorknob while I positioned myself on his right. I nodded and just as another tap sounded, Jonah hurled the door open.

"Oh my God! Y'all scared me out of my boots!" Leah Mae, my brother Jameson's girlfriend, clutched her hands to her heart.

Her long blonde hair was tucked up under a red knit cap. She wore a heavy down coat and she was indeed wearing boots. They had frogs all over them.

"We thought you were some dumbass reporter tresspassin'," I told her, pulling her into the house and shutting the door.

She slid out of her coat and hung it on the hook inside the back door. "That's why I'm here. I'm giving all you Bodines a crash course in media training."

Jonah and I looked at her like she'd started clucking like a chicken.

"We're not allowed to talk to them," Jonah reminded her.

"You're not allowed to talk to them about the investigation," Leah Mae corrected him. "I've been here before. A couple of times. I can make this easier on you by sharing my bountiful wisdom with y'all." Leah Mae had been a successful model looking to break into acting when her ex-fiancé set her up for a series of humiliating scandals to raise her profile. She was familiar with negative media attention.

"What do we do?" I asked.

She gestured at the table in the dining room and we all sat. "Let's start with the basics. You both are going to change your outgoing voicemail messages to the robotic, no-name version. You're not to answer any phone call unless you recognize the number. Do you have a landline?"

"Closet." I jerked a thumb toward the living room.

She gave me an approving nod. "Good. Keep it there. Don't answer your front door. If anyone wants to see you, they get a key to your back gate and come in that way. Or better yet, you meet them off-site. Social media, make it as private as you can or better yet, deactivate it all for now."

Jonah swore again.

"I know you have a presence for your training clients. Maybe create a private group to stay in touch with them and turn off commenting on your public accounts."

He slumped in his chair, crossing his arms over his chest. "This sucks."

"You say 'no comment' politely to any questions about anything remotely related to the investigation. If anyone gets pushy with you or crosses any lines, breaks any rules, you contact the police immediately. Do *not* retaliate." Her green eyes narrowed at us. Leah Mae was new to the family, but she was well aware of what we Bodines were capable of in a Friday night fight at The Lookout or a run of the mill rumble on the streets.

"Jayme told us not to talk to the press at all," I reminded her. No lie, Jayme scared me a little bit.

"You have to walk a fine line of being politely silent. Don't do anything to provoke them. Don't react with anything more than one of your nice-as-pie smiles. Say 'excuse me' if they're in your way. Don't go all Scarlett on them and threaten to run them over if she sees them in a crosswalk."

I hoped that was a metaphor and not an actual retelling. Though, knowing my little sister, anything was possible.

"You're playing a public relations game here," she explained. "The angrier you get, the more negative footage they blast all over the place, the guiltier your daddy looks."

She was right. I brought the heels of my hands to my eyes. "Jonah's right. This whole thing sucks."

Leah Mae nodded sympathetically. "Yes, it does. You two are going to take the brunt of the attention. Your house is accessible, your jobs are more public."

Jonah and I shared another look. He was a personal trainer with public classes all over town. And he shared a name with a potential murderer.

This *really* fucking sucked.

Leah Mae reached out to both of us, covering our hands with hers. "Y'all are gonna be just fine. Sooner or later a more salacious story will be pullin' on their attention," she promised. "Hang in until then."

"I don't suppose you'd be willing to take the attention off of us by going back on TV for us, would you, Leah Mae?" I teased. "Maybe you and Jameson could get engaged, and you could go on one of those bridezilla shows?"

She wrinkled her nose. "You're hilarious. So funny."

"How'd you get in the backyard," I asked her. "The gate's locked."

She grinned, flashing a glimpse of the gap between her front teeth. "I jumped the fence."

Jonah snickered. "We've got models climbing fences to get to us, Bow. Maybe this isn't so bad after all?"

15

BOWIE

I was cursing myself for not parking in the garage at the back of my lot last night. Now, thanks to Lazy-Ass Past Me, Present Me had to walk out my front door and back down the driveway into a small camera crew.

Jonah, being annoyingly in shape and fueled by anger, had snuck out the back and jogged across town to meet his trail running group at the lake. I debated doing the same but didn't want to spend the entire day with slush stains down the back of my Dockers. Teenagers were often assholes. As the unfortunate substitute teacher who'd accidentally sat on a chocolate pudding lid learned the hard way last year.

I gave the ragtag news crew another look through the front window. Leah Mae was right. I was the easiest to get to. None of my other siblings had houses this accessible. Hell, Gibson was tucked away on some serious acreage on a mountain. Sneaky-ass reporters wouldn't be able to get within a half-mile of his house.

Well, I sure as shit wasn't gonna let some half-assed news crew get me worked up or make me late for work.

I let myself out the front door, locked it, and kept my head down as I hurried to my SUV.

"Mr. Bodine! Did your father kill Callie Kendall?" the dumb motherfucker in the trench coat shouted at me.

My middle finger flexed anxiously, begging to be called to duty. I pretended I hadn't heard him and slid behind the wheel. I slammed the door on the idiot's questions, swearing under my breath.

The engine came to life, and I shifted into reverse. Easing down the drive came to an abrupt stop when the news crew crowded onto my driveway blocking my exit.

Leah Mae and Jayme were not going to be happy with what I was about to do. Maybe if I rearranged this guy's face news would travel and these turkey vultures would leave us alone...or at the very least, gawk at us from a respectable distance.

I rolled my window down, deciding to give them one last chance to live. "Y'all are in my way."

The guy in the trench coat with the tiny microphone took that as an invitation. He jogged up the side of my vehicle and shoved the mic in my face.

"Mr. Bodine, your father is a person of interest in the disappearance of Callie Kendall. What can you tell us about your father's involvement with Callie? Were they having an affair? Has your father hurt other girls?"

"Listen here, you piece of—"

"Stop."

I was cut off by the very authoritative voice of a very peeved deputy. Cassidy—in full uniform—strode around my SUV and got within punching distance of Mr. Lois Lane. "You're trespassing, sir. I'm going to have to ask all of you to step back onto the sidewalk and show me your IDs."

The guy with the mic was all smiles. "Officer, I'm just asking Mr. Bodine a few questions. The people have a right to know—"

"The people have a right to back out of their driveways safely without someone tryin' to crawl up their ass. Now, I'll ask you again, very nicely, to step onto the sidewalk and let Mr. Bodine pass."

"Technically, with setbacks, I'm still on the public sidewalk," the moron argued. Setbacks? Seriously? Did he think Cassidy was some redneck dummy? And was that a hairball on Cassidy's pants?

"*Technically,* you should do your research. Back about twelve years ago, when all of you press folks descended on Bootleg, a town ordinance went into effect stating that members of the media could only stand in the center of the public road and only during the hours of 11 p.m. to midnight. And only if they applied for the Press Access Permit to close said public road. Also only if they were very, very respectful and quiet. Now, I'd like to see your Press Access Permit and your ID. I won't ask nicely again."

Microphone Man goggled at her and then scrambled away from my vehicle like it was filled with snakes.

Cassidy gave me a cool glance. "Have a nice day, Mr. Bodine." She brushed the hairball off her pant leg.

God, I loved it when she was Unflappable Deputy.

"You do the same, Deputy Tucker." I threw her a salute and backed out of my driveway with a big ol' smile on my face.

I MADE it to the school without further incident and hustled in through a side door. The school hadn't changed much since I'd attended. Still had the same industrial tile floors, the same rickety lunch tables on wheels that folded up for floor polishing. The bathrooms were still full of pimple-faced, anxiety-ridden teenagers trying to get through the awkward years.

The library had seen some nice updates thanks to our fundraising. We now had e-readers the students could borrow and a huge online catalog. That, plus the air-conditioning and new reading chairs, made it a popular destination for students.

I turned left after the library and ducked into the main office. This place hadn't changed a lick since I'd been a student. The same long wooden bench squatted against one wall, waiting for kids in trouble. The wood had hosted the asses of generations of troubled students, including all of my siblings. Opposite it was a faded yellow countertop behind which two administrative assistants ran the show of getting eight hundred seventh- through twelfth-graders a decent education, hot meals, and an idea of what they were gonna do next.

Both the admins were on the phone. Maribel Schilling, with her dyed black beehive, had been holding court in Bootleg Springs High School since my parents attended. No one had any idea how old she was, and most of us were too scared to ask. She was giving someone what for on the phone.

Hung Kim was drumming a pencil on his desktop calendar as he repeatedly said "I'm sorry, no," into his phone. He worked here twenty hours a week to supplement his drumming career.

"No, you may *not* speak to Mr. Bodine, and no, we do not have a comment on the investigation. And if you use language like that with me again, I'll wash your mouth out with goat soap, which tastes significantly worse than regular soap," Maribel snapped into the phone.

My stomach sank. Reporters camped out at my house,

journalists lighting up the phones at school? I was so getting fired for this shit.

I turned for my office, intending to either order lunch and flowers for the admins or draft my resignation when Dottie Leigh poked her head out of her door. "Got a minute, Bowie?" she asked.

Ah, hell. I wasn't even going to get a chance to resign.

Dottie Leigh was the driving force behind a high school that consistently outperformed our neighboring districts. She believed in teaching methods that made learning accessible to everyone and constantly pushed our staff to be creative in their delivery of material. She suffered no fools and—despite topping out at five foot four—was an absolute shark on the basketball court.

She was good people, and I doubted I'd be able to hold her firing me against her.

"Sure, Dottie Leigh," I said, tagging along behind her like a puppy.

She gestured to one of the chairs in front of her desk. I sat and scraped my palms over my knees. "I just wanted to say that I've really enjoyed working with you here," I began.

Dottie Leigh leaned on the corner of her desk and crossed her arms, a smile quirking her lips that were painted an almost purple. "Are you quittin' on me?" she asked, amused.

"No, ma'am. Just trying to thank you for the experience before you fire me."

She rolled her eyes. "Bowie. I'm not firing you. I'm asking you how we can help you get through this."

I felt blind gratitude sweep through me. Leah Mae, Cassidy, Dottie Leigh. Each one of them had stepped up for me in a different way today, and I was grateful.

"I'll understand if I'm too much trouble," I told her,

wanting to make extra sure that she was sure. I was the good guy. I didn't cause a fuss. I didn't demand special treatment. I didn't bring my problems to work with me, ever. And I'd understand if this ugly business changed the way people saw me. If it reminded them of who I came from.

"Bowie," Dottie Leigh was exasperated now. "You're not in trouble here. Nothing your father did or didn't do is going to change your standing in this school."

That wasn't entirely correct. I'd basically sat in my own version of a chocolate pudding lid, giving every hormonal smartass in the building a real good reason to mock me.

"I appreciate that, Dottie Leigh," I said, meeting her gaze. She had brown eyes that, depending on the situation, could make a person feel all warm and fuzzy inside or terrified for their lives. It was a warm and fuzzy instance, thankfully.

"Maribel and Hung are under strict orders on the phones. No comment and nothing gets transferred to you unless it's a parent or a board member," she told me. "If there's anything you or your family need, give a holler. Okay?"

"Will do. Thank you again." I was beyond grateful.

"Good. Now get on back to work. We have a few hundred hormonal minds to influence today."

"On it."

She turned her back on me and pulled the paperwork out of her inbox. I was officially dismissed.

I paused in the doorway and looked back. "Are you sure you don't want to fire me?"

She threw a wadded-up sticky note in my direction. "Get!" she said, shooing me from her office.

"If one more blooger puts a microphone in my face—"

"What's a blooger?"

"You know. One of them there people who types stuff on the internet."

"I think they're called bloggers."

"Well, that's just stupid."

16

CASSIDY

Busting the three dumbasses camped out in front of my house this morning gave me a nice little buzz. So had the $200 fine I'd slapped them with for loitering without a permit.

It was cause for celebration. I called in an order to The Brunch Club and swung by on my way to the station. Donuts might be the preferred pastry of choice for cops across the country, but here in Bootleg our palates were more refined.

I tucked the box of fresh-from-the-oven bacon and egg pastries into the back seat of my car and cranked the volume on Mr. Garth Brooks as I cruised the two blocks to work.

News would travel and the rest of the vultures would get the message, I thought with satisfaction. We did things differently here in Bootleg Springs.

Turning the wheel, I pulled in to the back lot of the station. Dad had been sheriff for the better part of my lifetime, and the police station was as much home to me as the couch in my parents' family room.

I balanced the box of pastries and the stack of files that I'd taken home to peruse and flashed my key card under the reader. It was one of the visible signs of progress at the Bootleg PD. We were woefully behind on our technology. All case files prior to 2011 were still paper. I'd been pushing for an intern or two to tackle the scanning job. Dad was mulling it over.

"Mornin'," I greeted Fanny Sue Tomaschek, deputy sheriff and my father's right hand. Fanny could trace her family back in Olamette County five generations. She was Bootleg Springs. It made her one of the best assets our little department had. She balanced somber professionalism with the kind of public relations that only comes from knowing every single person born and raised in town for the last forty years.

She was fifty-eight, ran one marathon a year, and was the second-best shot in the department.

I was the first. And I was gunning for her job when she retired in exactly four years. Not that I'd confessed my ambitions to anyone. Some things were best kept to myself. So until then I reviewed old case files, took online classes on public administration, and was the best damn deputy I could be.

"Morning there, Cass. Heard you had some excitement this morning," she said swiveling away from her ancient computer monitor.

"News travels fast."

"Sure does, Deputy Obvious," Fanny Sue smirked. "That's $200 towards the Repave the Parking Lot fund."

"These snoopy weasels are probably gonna pay for the whole project before things blow over," I predicted.

I dumped the pastries on Fanny Sue's desk and the files on my own. It was a green metal monstrosity, a dinosaur leftover from the 70s. Two of the drawers stuck unless punched at exactly the right spot. The flat screen monitor that didn't flicker and flip had come out of my own pocket. Not having seizures or migraines was worth it in my mind.

The phone was ringing off the hook, which was to be

expected after Connelly's little show last night. Bex, our tattooed, eyebrow-pierced organizational badass, fielded calls like it was her superpower. She worked out of the property room, where evidence and confiscated property was stored. There was a sliding glass window in one wall so she could deal with walk-ins and accept dog license fees and applications.

Behind the property room, well out of public view, was the Summertimer Board. In an unofficial pool, we each identified potential troublemaking summertimers. At the end of the summer, the employee with the worst summertimer infraction won the pot. Fanny Sue—and her infallible instincts—remained undefeated.

The board was currently blank and wouldn't be filled again until June of next year.

I booted up my computer, ignored the red blinking message light on my desk phone, and plated up two pastries.

Dumping one on my own desk, I delivered the other one to Bex. She flashed me a grin and an eye-roll. "That does sound like something Detective Connelly would be interested in, Mrs. Varney," she said into the phone.

I snickered. Mrs. Varney was eighty-seven years old and dressed like every day was someone's funeral. She introduced herself as "Mrs. Varney of the Bootleg Springs Varneys." Her husband's family had been in Bootleg for four generations, and Mrs. Varney considered herself to be local royalty.

She was snooty, in a funny old-lady way. At least once a month, one of us deputies was dispatched to her home smack dab in the middle of town. Always under the guise of investigating a strange smell or sound. Every visit invariably ended with bitter tea and crunchy cookies and reminiscences of the good ol' days.

"How about I pencil you in for four o'clock today? Uh-huh. Uh-huh. Oh, no, ma'am. I don't think bringing your good pocket book would be too uppity. Great. We'll see you then."

Bex hung up and dove on the pastry.

"Mrs. Varney has a hot tip for Connelly?" I ventured.

"She feels she would be remiss if she didn't report that her little doggie, Cleveland, had a barking fit the night Callie Kendall disappeared," Bex explained through a mouthful of puff pastry. "Claims Cleveland was a good boy and never barked at anything."

"Except the mailman, the UPS truck driver, anyone who walked past the house on the sidewalk, leaves blowing across the yard, and literally anything that ever moved in his line of vision," I ticked them off on my fingers. I remembered the fluffy little bastard. He'd bitten about a hundred and fifty people in his fifteen years of ornery life. But, being four pounds two ounces, no one paid him much mind.

"Figured it wouldn't hurt to dump her on Detective Snappy Fingers."

Connelly had made the fatal error of snapping his fingers at Bex and ordering a coffee. She'd pointed him in the direction of the department's ancient coffee maker and told him to pour his own damn coffee.

I'd seen my dad's mustache twitch at that. Harlan Tucker was the most diplomatic man I knew in this life. But I could tell that even he was rubbed the wrong way by the state police detective who had elbowed his way into the case and acted like the rest of us were his maids, cooks, and personal assistants.

I did my best to follow my dad's lead and treated the man with a cool respect.

I was real good at hiding my feelings.

"Is his highness in residence today?" I asked Bex.

She nodded her head in the direction of the conference room. The door was closed.

"He's in there with the sheriff. I think your daddy dumped about sixty messages on him that came in after the press conference."

"Mmm." I had a lot of things I wanted to say about that press conference, but like a good deputy, I bit my tongue. The phone rang again, and I backed out of the property room as Bex answered with her chipper "Bootleg Springs Police Department, how can we help?"

I returned to my desk, casting a glance at the closed conference room door. Connelly had no idea the shitstorm he'd stirred up.

There was nothing Bootleggers liked better than rehashing every detail of Callie Kendall's disappearance. And what was more salacious than a break in a missing person case that had baffled authorities for twelve years? There was no way the Bodines would come out of this unscathed.

I had a sticky feeling about that press conference. We'd no sooner gotten our first reporter calling in about the DNA results than Connelly was organizing a press conference.

It was like he hadn't been the least bit surprised that the news had leaked.

My phone pinged from inside my jacket pocket. I pulled it out and unlocked the screen.

Scarlett: Potluck takeout. Pick up Bow and Jonah and meet us at the Red House tonight.

I felt something like unease skitter through my belly. With as public a stage as Bootleg had become, was it even okay for me, a law enforcement officer involved in the investigation, to be seen with the Bodines?

My phone pinged again. This time it was a different Bodine.

Bowie: Thanks again for the Stern Deputy routine this morning. I owe you one.

It was just dinner with friends, I rationalized. Of course I should go. A cop couldn't be separate from the community they served, not in a town this small. Not when I knew about every resident.

"Cassidy? You're on Mrs. Varney pickup for her very important meeting," Bex said poking her head out of the property room.

Ah, hell. With that, I got to work.

17

CASSIDY

I couldn't figure out what had Bubba Rayhill, our third full-time deputy, giggling like a junior high sleepover until I swiveled my chair around.

Bowie and Jonah had arrived at the station to pick me up. In disguise.

Thank God Connelly had bugged out. Jonah was wearing an inconspicuous black down jacket and a beret. Bowie had gone for a fedora and high school letterman's jacket.

"Is this a Halloween dinner?" I asked.

Bowie shucked the hat off his head. "You try being chased by a pack of rabid photographers for an hour after school and see how you like it."

"Sallie Mae Brickman scared them off with an umbrella and a muzzleloader. Then she gave us these disguises," Jonah explained.

I'd seen first-hand the mess the "newsies" were making all over town. They were clumping in public areas demanding interviews from every passerby. They blocked streets with news vans, surrounded citizens like they were Meltdown-in-Progress Britney Spears, and hogged up all the Wi-Fi at Yee

Haw Yarn and Coffee. It was already a nightmare, and they'd been here for only twenty-four hours.

As far as I could tell, not a single Bootlegger had stepped up to the microphone. My town might be torn over whether or not Jonah Bodine Sr. was guilty, but one thing we all could agree on was that no outsider was going to make fools of us.

"We ditched my car on Rum Runner Avenue," Bowie told me. "So you're probably gonna have to drive us unless you don't mind having a dozen reporters jogging next to you asking if any of your family members are killers."

He was having a rough day. So I cut him some slack on the snark. Besides, he looked pretty cute in that letterman's jacket.

"All right, boys. Let me get my coat. Did y'all call in the takeout orders?"

TWENTY MINUTES LATER, loaded down with Thai food and a mixed assortment of subs and two six-packs of beer, I pulled onto a long, winding drive on the outskirts of town. The Red House was on the opposite end of town from the fancy lake houses summertimers rented for a month at a time. It was also conveniently tucked away on a private lane with a scrap of lakefront beyond its front porch.

"Why are we having dinner here?" I asked, putting my car in park.

"Last minute cancellation," Bowie explained from the passenger seat. Our elbows were almost touching on the console that separated us. Scarlett was a mini real estate mogul in Bootleg Springs. She had a handful of rental properties that gave her a very nice cash flow during the spring, summer, and fall. "Scarlett figured we'd have less of a chance of attracting attention if we all met here instead of one of our houses."

It was a good plan. If all the Bodines had descended on Bowie's house, they would have attracted every journalist in town. I probably would have had to shoot someone or at least tase several of them.

We pulled around the front of the house where the rest of the Bodine vehicles were parked on the lawn. Lugging the food and beer with us, we trudged up the front steps. Bowie didn't bother knocking. He opened the door and gestured for me to enter first.

The Red House was on the tiny side. I'd thought Scarlett was crazy when she bought it two years ago. It had been a heap of rotting wood under a holey roof at the time. But she'd redone it into a cute little cottage perfect for a couple's getaway.

"There y'all are! I thought you got swallowed up by a horde of reporters," Scarlett chirped from the kitchen. She was helping Devlin arrange their contribution to the meal—pepperoni rolls and potato chips—on the counter.

Gibson was flipping channels on the TV in the living room. I guessed he was the one who brought the hot wings from The Lookout. Jameson and Leah Mae unpacked bags of paper plates and napkins, followed by a bucket of fried chicken.

Jonah added our spoils to the buffet and slapped a spring roll out of Devlin's hand. "We're adding muscle, not food bloat."

Devlin moped and moved on to the grilled chicken salad some joker had brought.

"I invited June Bug, but she's pouting over some fantasy football player's injury," Scarlett told me.

I nodded. "GT Thompson." My sister had been an avid fan

of the guy since his NFL career began ten years ago. She was taking his injury as a personal affront, claiming he'd ruined her entire season.

Gibson wandered in, big and broody. He reached over and ruffled my hair. "How's it goin', deputy?"

"Oh, you know. Another day in paradise."

Plates were distributed, and food was shoveled onto them. We crowded around the table and spilled into the living room. Bowie sat next to me on the floor. His knee was brushing mine.

"We still good?" he asked quietly. Even surrounded by his family, it still felt like we were in our own little bubble.

"Uh, sure. Yeah." I bobbed my head like one of those weird drinking bird toys. I liked being mad at Bowie better. The feelings were easier to manage, and I didn't have to worry about, you know, *talking* to him.

"So, who got asked the dumbest question today?" Leah Mae asked cheerfully.

There was a collective groan.

"One of those jackwagons caught me at the Pop In and asked me if I thought it was my daddy or my brothers who murdered Callie Kendall. Then they started in on poor Opal on account of her last name," Scarlett said.

"They caught us outside Leah Mae's storefront," Jameson said. Leah Mae had changed gears from model to shopkeeper. She was hoping to open a fashion boutique sometime in the spring with a little help from my sister the investor. At least she would if June would stop haggling the building owner to death over rent and utilities.

"Yeah, they wanted to know if I was marrying into a family of homicidal maniacs and if so, would there be a reality show?" Leah Mae chimed in.

"I had six reporters and photographers show up for the

trail run this morning," Jonah complained. He cracked a grin. "Too bad it was such a fast crew. Some of 'em are probably still trying to find their way out of the woods."

I snorted in appreciation.

"They say anything about your name?" Bowie asked.

"Just wanted to know if homicidal tendencies were genetic."

"What a bunch of dumbasses," Scarlett said succinctly.

We all grunted in general agreement.

"Cassidy got to play hero this morning," Bowie told everyone. He recounted the morning's driveway incident, and I was given an enthusiastic round of applause by all present.

"I get the feeling news organizations aren't really sending their best people," Jameson said. "These folks seem like they're a special kind of stupid."

Devlin cleared his throat. "I had a few calls and messages today from some contacts back in Annapolis and D.C. If this story gets any bigger we might be facing more than a few dozen dumbasses," he warned.

"Good Lord," I muttered. "What about you, Gibson?" I asked him.

All eyes turned to him and he glanced up from his plate.

He shrugged. "You'd be surprised at how many people leave you alone when you hang a couple of rifles in the back window of your pickup," he deadpanned.

The Bodines thought that was hilarious.

I, however, had the sinking feeling that I'd be arresting one of them before this whole mess was over.

No longer hungry, I leaned back against the couch and found Bowie's arm resting there. He didn't move and neither did I. I thought about my cats.

"Enough about this mess," Scarlett said, sliding onto Devlin's lap. She had a piece of gauze poking out of the sleeve of her flannel shirt. "Did y'all hear that Bowie and Cassidy showed up dressed all fancy at The Lookout and shared a slow dance?"

"Ooooooh!" the crowd collectively cooed.

"Very funny." I threw the heel of my bread in Scarlett's direction. "Why are you bandaged up?" I asked, trying to change the subject.

"Kitten Jedidiah was just having some fun. Anyway, as I was sayin', some folks are calling for a recount on that Least Likely To poll. Y'all might have edged out Reverend Duane and Misty Lynn," she said with a wink.

Bowie's fingers brushed my shoulder. Back and forth in a steady, soothing kind of motion. The effects of the touch were anything but soothing. Secret touches from Bowie Bodine? Had I accidentally ripped a hole in time and space, taking me back to my high school yearnings?

Cats. I was a mother to cats. I needed to remember that. I had given up. I was committed to life as a single cat lady.

"All right. Enough with the bullshitting," Gibson said. "Let's get down to why we're really here. We need to make sure we're on the same page with this investigation shitstorm."

"Party pooper," Scarlett hissed in his direction.

Bowie tensed next to me. His fingers stopped their gentle strokes. "No offense, but I don't think it's a good idea for Cassidy to be here."

Offense taken. I whipped my head around so fast my neck cracked. I felt wounded. I'd always been considered a Bodine as much as the Bodines had been considered honorary Tuckers.

Eyes were popping out of heads all over the place.

Bowie turned to me. "Cass, I don't want you feeling like you have divided loyalties over this mess. We don't want to jeopardize your job."

He was punishing me over the DNA results again.

I rose abruptly. “Yeah. Got it. I’ll go.” I was shockingly hurt. Like arrow to the chest, knife to the back hurt. *Why did I keep letting this man close enough to hurt me?*

I was going to throw the used kitty litter onto his back porch tonight.

“We can drive Jonah and Bowie back,” Jameson volunteered, giving me an apologetic look.

I nodded briskly, not making eye contact with any of them. “Yep. Thanks for dinner, y’all.”

I pushed my way out the front door to a chorus of “Cass, don’t be like that.”

I felt like the front door was slamming shut on a lifetime of friendship. I wasn’t one of them. They didn’t trust me. And that fucking hurt.

18

BOWIE

I caught her as she was yanking her car door open.

"Cass." I stopped her with a hand on her arm. She turned on me, ice in her eyes. That was Cassidy, more ice than fire when she was mad. She never lost control, always kept her emotions buttoned up.

Sometimes I wondered what would happen if she ever let that leash slip.

"What?" she asked crisply.

"It's for your own good," I told her.

"I don't need you looking out for me. I haven't in a long time."

It was my turn for pissed off. "You don't get to tell me to stop caring."

"I'm not your little sister," she snapped at me.

I was crowding her against the door of the car, but I had enough room to give her the once-over. "I'm well aware."

Her breath was coming in pants, little silvery clouds that hung in the night air between us.

"Are you?" she demanded. "I'm not your little sister and

I'm not some teenage wild child who needs you to take care of her."

"Cassidy." I was exasperated. "What do you want from me? You want to sit in on a Bodine pow-wow so we can figure out how not to let an investigation that you're helping with ruin our lives? Do you want to be in a position to have to answer questions from that outsider detective about your involvement with my family? You already made it clear your job and our friendship are separate entities. I'm tryin' to respect that."

Oh, that fire in her green eyes. It warmed me straight through, chasing the winter out of my bones.

My hand had a mind of its own, reaching out to tuck that stray lock of blonde hair behind her ear. She closed her eyes for a second as if she was melting into my touch. And then the moment was gone.

"Respect? It looks like you're trying to make a point."

"I'm a Bodine, Cass. We aren't a subtle people. If I was trying to say something, I'd say it."

She gave a humorless laugh. "That doesn't explain the decade of mixed signals."

I wished I didn't know what she was talking about. No matter how hard I tried to hide them, those true feelings bled through, staining everything.

"What are you sayin'?" I asked, knowing perfectly well exactly what she was saying.

She shook her head. "Nothing. I'm not saying anything. Neither are you. That's the way it's always been. The way it will always be."

"What the hell do you want me to do, Cassidy?" Frustration and desire were simmering beneath my words. But if she told me. If she *wanted* me, would I be able to keep the promise I'd made all those years ago? When I gave my word, I meant it.

Take it to the bank. If I said it, it was the God's honest truth. Except this.

Our relationship was a lie. Me pretending I felt nothing but brotherly love toward her.

I knew that if she said the words. If she asked me the question, I'd crumble. I'd put my hands on her like I'd longed to. I would kiss her until everything else in the world disappeared. All she had to do was give me a definitive sign. Tell me she wanted me. Ask me to show her how I really felt.

She gave me one more long look and shook her head. Was that disappointment I saw on her pretty face?

Disappointing her crushed me.

"I'll see you around, Bowie," she said in her flat, professional tone. She got in her car, feathers still ruffled, and I watched her drive away.

I wished for a lot of things in that moment. That the situation were different. That Dad hadn't once again screwed things up for us or that he could be here to answer the questions. That I was good enough for what I wanted most in this world. I picked up a rock out of the gravel driveway and hurled it into the lake. It was too dark to see it, but I heard the splash. I knew the ripples were spreading out and out and out, ruining the glassy surface.

I turned my back on the water and went inside.

"Was that absolutely necessary?" Scarlett demanded.

"Yeah. It was," I snapped.

"She's family," Scarlett argued.

"No. She's not. In this situation, Cassidy Tucker is a cop investigating our father. We can dance around it all you want, but y'all better remember that she's a cop first and a friend of the family second. She's already chosen between us once."

"Let's table that discussion for now," Devlin suggested,

slipping into attorney mode. "Leah Mae, why don't you explain what we're all doing here."

Still glaring at me, Scarlett flopped down on the chair next to Dev. I wisely chose a seat on the couch, out of punching distance.

Leah Mae stood. "Right. So, y'all are in a sticky situation and I think it's important that we have a game plan for dealing with both the investigation and the media," she began, addressing all of us. "Now, what are your objectives?"

"Talk plain, Leah Mae," Jameson teased her, looking up at her like a puppy to his master.

She winked at him. "What do you all want to get out of this situation?"

"Get rid of the reporters hounding us all day and night," Jonah said.

"Prove Dad's innocence," Scarlett chimed in.

"Do you really think he didn't have anything to do with it?" Gibson asked Scarlett. It was a source of tension in their otherwise fiercely loyal relationship. Gibson hated the fact that our sister always tried to see the best in Dad.

Gibs had it the worst out of all of us. I'd at least had a tenuous connection with the man over baseball. But Gibson had been the reason why our parents never pursued their dreams of music and travel.

"Don't start again," Scarlett cautioned him, baring her teeth.

I tossed a pillow off the couch, breaking their stare down. "We're on the same team," I reminded them.

"Bowie's right," Devlin put in. "You don't have to agree to have the same objectives. What's best for all of you is to present a united front. You need each other now more than ever."

"Fine," Scarlett said, reluctantly giving up the fight.

Gibson grunted.

"Then let's talk game plan," Jameson sighed. "What do we do about the press?"

"I put together a packet of acceptable responses and suggestions on avoiding being cornered by them," Devlin said, handed out spiral bound copies.

I felt the corner of my mouth lift. *Who would have guessed that Scarlett would fall for a law nerd?*

"I ran all of this by Jayme and she approved it. Especially the part where none of you get arrested for beating the hell out of a blogger or photographer," Devlin added.

He ran through the points one by one, and we agreed to a general strategy. Basically, don't give them anything to report.

"Remember, this only works if we don't give them a weak link," Leah Mae said pointedly.

I shot a look at Gibson.

"Why's everyone starin' at me and Gibs?" Scarlett demanded.

"Because you two are the most reactive," I told her.

"I can control my temper," Scarlett scoffed.

Gibson grunted again.

The rest of us cracked up. "Neither of you have any more control than a three-year-old comin' down from a sugar high," Jameson pointed out.

"Fuck off," Gibson shot back.

"Point proven."

"There's something else I'd like to bring up if you two can put your bitchin' aside for a minute," I told them.

They all looked at me expectantly.

"I feel like this Detective Connelly is convinced Dad did this. I don't know if we can trust him to do a thorough examination of the facts, especially if those facts don't line up with his theory."

"So what are you saying?" Gibson asked, crossing his arms. "You want us to start our own investigation?"

"Not anything officially. But we knew him, we knew Callie, and we know damn near every person in this town. Maybe there's something the police missed. Maybe there's something they overlooked. Maybe one of us holds the key to why that sweater came into his possession."

"I agree," Scarlett piped up. "I think doing some digging on our own is better than sittin' on our asses, twiddlin' our thumbs and trying not to smash a camera in a dumbass's face."

"Agreed," Jonah said. He was quiet during family gatherings. Maybe he was still finding his place with us. Or maybe it was the fact that Gibson still treated him like an outsider.

"Where should we start?" Jameson asked.

"Let's start with the week Callie disappeared. Try to figure out exactly what each of us were doing that week and maybe one of us will remember something important."

"This is bullshit," Gibson said, getting to his feet. "He did it. And you want us to speed up the process to prove it?"

"How can you be so sure?" Scarlett asked, jumping to her feet.

He glared down at her. "Because Jonah Bodine ruined everything he touched in this lifetime. The whole town knows it. Y'all might as well get on board." Without another word, he snatched his coat off the back of the chair and stormed out.

The room fell silent for a minute. We heard Gibs's truck rev and pull away with the churn of gravel.

"He does that on purpose so I have to rake the damn rocks out of the damn yard," Scarlett complained.

Ignoring my brother's typical abrupt, angry departure, I let his words echo in my head. *The whole town knows it.* "Speaking of the whole town," I began.

"No," Jameson said adamantly.

"Yes!" Scarlett insisted. "This is more than just our problem. It's affecting the whole dang town."

"It has to be done," I said.

"What are we cryptically arguing about?" Jonah asked.

19

CASSIDY

The reporters were taking over the town like a hoard of zombies. They clogged up the streets with their news vans, took all the available stools at the diner, and generally made asses of themselves as they chased residents down the sidewalks demanding answers to their questions. The high school had to set up a line of sawhorses in front of the building to keep the no-good, nosy snoopers away from the faculty and students.

Bootleggers weren't happy. I could feel the rebellion building like the *Jaws* theme song. Ugliness was inevitable.

My father called two of our summertime deputies back into service to manage the mess. Now our budget was shot to hell. Forget repaving the parking lot, we had fat payroll expenses to deal with.

Detective Connelly seemed to not give two shits that Bootleg was on the verge of a mutiny. He was still residing in the police station's musty conference room like a spider in a web.

We generally used the space as a lunch room when we did potlucks or for the monthly staff meetings that also involved food. There weren't a lot of open investigations that required us to gather 'round that table. But it was the principle of the matter. He could have taken an empty desk, but Connelly preferred to be separate from it all.

The river of citizens lining up to recount their exact whereabouts and recollections of the night Callie Kendall disappeared had trickled to a stop after a day or two of him acting like a low-down snake in the grass to every single person who walked in the door.

Connelly made it clear he didn't have time for small-town gossip and he made no bones about being quite the dick about it.

And after more than a few veiled "someone's gonna have to talk to him about how we do things around here" mutters around the station, I realized it was gonna have to be me. My dad, while a lovely, fair, and just human being, couldn't communicate worth dog crap. His conversations with my mother consisted entirely of "uh-huhs" and "yes, dears". And that was over where they'd go to dinner. Throw in a topic with some conflict, and my dad clammed up like an inanimate object.

It was after one particularly annoying incident in which a blogger from *WV Tattle Tales* jumped in line in front of Bernie O'Dell at Yee Haw Yarn and Coffee and snagged the last fresh cup of coffee that did it, resulting in a shoving match that I had to break up. I lost my own damn coffee in the melee. Someone needed to do something, and I was going to be that someone. These visitors needed to be reminded of their place. They were visitors here and should be behaving respectfully, not mowing down townspeople like a stampede of gassy, entitled bison.

I knocked briskly on the open conference door. Connelly

didn't bother looking up from the screen of his laptop that he was frowning fiercely at.

I waited, schooling my face into blank professionalism. It was a power play, I thought, as the seconds ticked by. But everything the man did was, and I was willing to play if it meant my town could shake these idiots loose. He was probably scrolling Facebook like a jerk.

"What is it, deputy?" he asked, finally looking up.

"The press is causing disturbances around town," I reported. "How would you like us to handle it?"

He stared at me for a long minute. "Comes with the territory. I'm sure you and your neighbors will adapt."

I wondered if his wife had ever pepper sprayed him for his holier-than-thou attitude. I could imagine him sitting down to a home-cooked meal and instructing his wife on how she could do her job better. Then BAM! Face full of pepper spray.

"We're familiar with media attention, sir. We lived through plenty of it after the disappearance," I reminded him.

He grunted, still studying me with those watery blue eyes. If he thought the stern silent treatment would scare me, he had another thing coming. I'd made it my personal mission in life to never let the cracks show. Connelly would have to up his game big time to get a rise out of me.

"If you're so well-versed in dealing with media attention, then I'm sure you can find an appropriate way to handle the situation," he said.

Subtext: You annoy me with your pissant questions.

"After the disappearance, the sheriff's department enacted a few town ordinances to protect citizens' privacy," I said, soldiering on. "Are you comfortable with us enforcing those ordinances?"

"It's never a good idea to piss off the media, deputy," he told me.

"Sir, some of them are toeing the harassment line pretty aggressively. Trespassing on private property, blocking traffic, surrounding vehicles." I remembered Bowie's white-hot anger the other morning being cornered in his own driveway. Even though I was still good and pissed off at him, he deserved some level of police protection. "It's not a popularity contest. It's a safety issue. They're harassing innocent people."

Apparently, it was the wrong thing to say.

"How innocent can they be if their father's a murderer? What are the odds that one of them didn't know something?" Connelly drawled.

I blinked. "Excuse me, sir?"

The accusation was made. The lines drawn. Now he was moving on. "Deputy, I suggest you and your *kin*," his eyes skated to the glass window where my father was talking football with Bex, "treat visitors with the utmost respect lest they decide to paint you as a gun-toting, uneducated redneck."

"Hillbilly, sir," I corrected.

"Excuse me?" His eyes iced over.

"'Round here we prefer the term hillbilly."

His thin lips twisted in what might have been a smile. "Hillbillies then."

"We'll do our best to be respectful," I told him. *Yeah, right. Bootleg Springs had a hive mind, and if their police department wasn't stepping up to protect them, they'd take matters into their own hands. It was gonna be a real mess.*

I turned to leave and then paused in the doorway. Something had been bothering me since that press release. "You sure are organized, sir."

He looked up from his laptop again.

"We no sooner got the call that someone had leaked the DNA results and you had a whole press conference organized."

"If you want to accuse me of something, deputy, man up and say it."

It was my turn to give him that long, cool stare. "No, sir."

There was a simmering pissed-offness cooking away under his cool surface. "Maybe you're not used to how investigations work," he suggested grimly. "But right now the more attention on this case, the more information we'll dig up. People can't hide in the spotlight. Someone somewhere is gonna remember something that your daddy missed the first time around."

I kept my face cool and neutral.

I'd known it in my gut. Connelly had been the leak. And then he'd gone and lectured us on keepin' our gums from flappin'.

I turned to leave.

"One more thing, deputy. You might want to decide where your loyalty lies. With this department or somewhere else." He turned his laptop around so I could see the screen.

It was an article with a picture of me glaring down the loafer-wearing moron in Bowie's driveway.

Live-in cop girlfriend defends suspect's son, threatens press.

Well, hell. It looked like things were about to get real messy.

20

CASSIDY

It had been a long, shitty week. Not only were the assorted "journalists"—and I used that term very loosely—wreaking havoc on my town, but Detective Connelly had decided the only way I could prove my loyalty to the department was by becoming the perfect lackey. He had me scanning, faxing, and general paper pushing all the days of my life.

My dang papercuts had papercuts.

Meanwhile, he and my father had been sitting down with every witness interviewed in the original investigation looking for any information that may have been overlooked. Connelly didn't come right out and say it, but his attitude made it clear that he thought Bootleg was a bunch of ignorant rednecks policed by a smaller group of even more ignorant rednecks.

I couldn't say that I much cared for his barely veiled contempt. Neither did Mrs. Varney, who said the man was slicker than owl shit. Or Fanny Sue, who'd been berated by the man over a misunderstood message. Fanny Sue was so mad, when she spotted a drunk Otto Holt mid-piss on Connelly's front tire, she just turned around and went whistling on her way.

It was an hour from the end of my shift tonight. An hour before I could go home and smush my fur friends. And I was relishing the fact that the Man Who Shall Not Be Named had left on some vague, urgent, "nobody questions a homicide detective" business. He probably had to poop or kick a nest of baby squirrels.

I used the opportunity to grab one of the ancient cruisers in the parking lot.

It was a Thursday night on the cusp of winter and Thanksgiving. Dark. Cold. Quiet.

Very quiet.

The only people on the streets were press. You could tell them from everyone else by their shoes—usually loafers—and the tech gadgets permanently affixed to their hands. Where were my neighbors? I cruised up the hill to The Lookout. The parking lot should have been full but there were only a handful of vehicles parked up against the building.

I looped around and drove back into the heart of town.

Storefronts were dark, which wasn't unusual for 9 p.m. on a Thursday. But what *was* unusual was the fact that the apartments above Bootleg's retail spaces and the houses were dark, too. Where in the hell would my entire town have gone?

On a hunch, I pointed the car east. Bootleg Springs depended on tourism, but that didn't mean that we didn't get good and sick of the tourist crowd every once in a while. While most of the rental properties were on the western end of town, doglegging the lake, Bootleg had reclaimed a few places to the east.

The secret hot springs were there. Protected by No Trespassing Signs and solemn vows that Bootleggers would never reveal to outsiders the existence of the springs. We'd long ago ceded the regular springs in the lakeside park to the crowds of travelers that descended every year. But the secret springs, we kept those to ourselves.

There was also a crescent moon-shaped beach tucked between tall rock outcroppings, accessible only by boat or what was affectionately known as a goat path. Everyone headed there the weekend after Labor Day for a beach BBQ that lasted into the early hours, celebrating another successful summer.

My nose for trouble didn't give me anything to sniff at near the springs so I continued on. The weather had warmed enough for some serious snow melt. I noticed what looked like a whole mess of wet tire tracks leading off of the main road and onto Still Lane, a twisty, turny mountain road. There was nothing up there but a handful of private properties and an army of potholes that could swallow a Mini Cooper.

Curious, I turned onto the road. I bumped along slowly, wondering if something really was wrong or if I was imagining things. I liked to think I had good instincts, but they'd let me down before. Case in point: Bowie Bodine. Maybe I was one of those people who thinks they're really good at singing when they're actually just really annoying and warbly. And convinced of their talent, they go around singing in the grocery store just waiting to impress passers-by. When in reality, they're scaring everyone off. Like "Oh, no! Here comes that dang crooning third-grade teacher again. Will someone please tell her she doesn't have to sing her to-go order to me?"

I shoved my concerns out of the way when I spotted it.

Old Jefferson Waverly's property was lit up like a Christmas party. There was a veritable sea of vehicles parked in his north pasture. Light spilled from the cracks between the planks of his picture-pretty picnic barn.

I spotted Rocky Tobias's souped-up pickup parked next to

EmmaLeigh's VW Bug. Reverend Duane's decades-old sedan was parked in front of Granny Louisa's El Camino. It looked to me that every dang Bootleg resident was in attendance. Was there some hoedown that I'd forgotten to RSVP to?

I spotted Bowie's SUV toward the back of the field on one side of Wade Zirkel's flashy extended cab. Gibson's Charger was on the other side. They were parked right up against Wade's truck. I rolled my eyes.

The Bodines didn't feel kindly toward Wade Zirkel after he cheated on Scarlett. Never mind that she shouldn't have been dumb enough to date him again in the first place.

I parked my cruiser near the barn and climbed out. The low murmur of a sizeable crowd reached out and beckoned from the barn. *Something was definitely afoot.*

Picking my way over the uneven ground, I came up on the side door to the barn and stopped to listen.

"All right. All right. Let's call this meeting to order," I heard Mayor Augustus "Auggie" Hornsbladt call.

What in the hell was going on?

My curiosity got the best of me, and I pulled the heavy wood door open. Yep. All of Bootleg Springs was crammed inside on lawn chairs and wooden benches. Mayor Auggie was standing up at the front on a milk crate talking into a wireless microphone.

Not wanting to announce my presence quite yet, I decided to get inconspicuous. Zadie Rummerfield was sitting on the end of a bench at the back of the barn. I nudged her over. She shot me a guilty look as she scooted.

Uh-huh. So this was an event I wasn't invited to.

I noticed that my father wasn't in attendance. Either it was something against me and my family, which I doubted, or this was something Bootleg wasn't keen on advertising to the law.

"Thank y'all for coming," Auggie said into the mic. He was

wearing his usual uniform, a cowboy hat and bib overalls. "As you're all aware, we've got ourselves a problem."

I crossed my arms and kicked my legs out. Someone poked me in the shoulder, and I looked up.

Bowie.

"Move down," he whispered to me.

Reluctantly, I scooched closer to Zadie who was, by now, all but falling into Jimmy Bob Prosser's lap.

Bowie sat next to me, shoulders touching, knees rubbing. "What are you doing here?" he demanded in a low whisper.

"My job," I said flatly. "You think the Bootleg PD wouldn't notice when the entire town goes missing?"

"It's not what you think, Cass."

"What do I think it is?" I seriously had no idea. But it was yet another thing I'd been cut out of. I wondered if I should get another cat.

"You're not gonna like what you hear," he predicted.

"I think I'll survive," I hissed dryly. I didn't need him deciding what I should and shouldn't hear. *I didn't need him period.*

The crowd was rumbling again over whatever their shared problem was. I had a feeling I knew what it was.

"They set up shop in my cafe," Annie called from the middle of the crowd. Annie ran the Yee Haw Yarn and Coffee. "They buy one cup of coffee and suck up the Wi-Fi for the whole day."

"They've been blocking my driveway for a week straight now," Lula complained from somewhere on my right. Lula owned and operated Bootleg Springs Spa. She also lived two blocks over from me. I'd been shooing reporters away from the neighbors, but I'd have to expand my reign of terror.

"They're littering."

"One of them almost ran over Bex when she was crossing the street the other day!"

"They called us all uneducated slow-talkers in their paper!"

"They're sitting in front of the high school offering students money for information!"

"I heard one of them call Reverend Duane, Reverend Redneck!"

"One of them tried to kick Mona Lisa McNugget!"

A collective gasp rose up in the barn.

"I hear y'all and I'm in agreement. We gotta get rid of these here reporters," Auggie announced. "Now, who's got a plan?'

Oh, Lordy.

21

CASSIDY

As it turned out, every damn body in the barn had a plan. Otto Holt and Jimmy Bob Prosser wanted to confine the press to a paddock-like area. Old Judge Carwell suggested enacting Title 57 in the town's charter that allowed a majority of white, land-owning males to ban groups of people from Bootleg Springs boundaries. It was completely illegal, but no one had gotten around to scrubbing the law from the books.

I made a mental note to talk to Devlin about that one.

Clarabell, the beloved owner of Moonshine Diner, showed her frustrations by suggesting that some food poisoning might encourage the undesirables to go the hell home.

I was about ready to announce my presence and put an end to the foolishness when Bowie put his hand on my leg.

"Hang on a second," he told me quietly.

I was too busy reeling from the physicality to remember to jump to my feet and call my fellow townsfolk dumbasses. I suddenly wished I'd just gone on home to George and Eddie.

"Y'all, my daughter has an idea that I think would work fine."

"Is that *my mother*?" I hissed.

Bowie squeezed my thigh again.

Yep. Sure enough, Nadine Tucker stood up in the third row and hauled my sneaky-ass sister to her feet.

"Go ahead, June," my mom said encouragingly.

My sister shoved her hands in her jeans. "A reporter's primary responsibility is to search out and disseminate facts from fallacies," she began.

"English, Juney," Cheyenne Hastings called out from across the aisle.

I could feel my sister rolling her eyes. "If a reporter is only divulging easily refutable lies, their perceived usefulness would come to a swift and unceremonious end." As usual, June's dumbing it down had the opposite effect.

I could hear crickets chirping in the barn while Bootleg Springs tried to translate.

"What she's saying is if we use these reporters to spread absolute bullshit, they'll get recalled to whatever rock they crawled out from under," my mom translated.

The crowd began to murmur, and the enthusiasm warmed.

"It's a misinformation campaign. Just like Jedidiah Bodine did during the 'shine running years," Mrs. Varney cackled.

Mayor Hornsbladt stroked his silver beard like a cartoon villain. "Why, June Tucker. I think that's a mighty fine idea."

"Yes. I know that," June stated.

Mom elbowed her in the side.

"I mean, thank you," June reluctantly corrected herself.

The buzzing of the crowd hit deafening levels, and the mayor had to smack a clawfoot hammer on the crate under his feet. He hit it too hard and it collapsed, spilling him onto the floor.

He sprang back up and hammered the wall for a minute

until everyone quieted down again. “Y’all, we gotta keep this orderly. Now, let’s strategize all strategic-like. Who’s got an idea?”

Hands shot up all over the barn, and the chatter returned.

“I can’t sit here and let them obstruct a police investigation,” I told Bowie. His hand was still on my knee.

“They’re not obstructing the police. They’re obstructing a bunch of disrespectful outsiders who think we’re all stupid, toothless hillbillies. There’s nothing illegal about not being truthful to a reporter,” he insisted.

I gritted my teeth. This whole thing was chapping my procedural ass. “How often do y’all call secret meetings?” I asked him.

“Only when absolutely necessary,” he said evasively.

“And are my mom and sister usually in attendance?”

He smirked at me. “They’re usually the ones callin’ the meetings.”

“You’re shitting me.”

“Remember when your dad couldn’t prove that Donna Tarper’s husband was knocking her around?” Bowie asked.

My eyes narrowed. “Yeah.” My dad had a big, squishy heart. He couldn’t stand to see anyone or anything hurt. Knowing that one of his citizens was getting the crap beat out of her on the regular never sat well with him. But Donna had refused to press charges.

“Remember how the husband suddenly attacked his neighbor Pete? And that mysterious video footage of the fight just happened to show up at the station?”

I closed my eyes. “You can’t be serious.”

Bowie nodded solemnly. “Your mama called that meeting and made us put our heads together to figure out how to catch the sonofabitch and make sure he got locked up.”

I rubbed a finger between my eyebrows where a headache was sprouting.

"Feelin' left out?" Bowie asked.

"Yeah. A little."

"Now you know how it feels," he said smugly.

"Are we back to that again?" I was starting to get my hackles up.

"No, Cass. We're not. But there are some things it's better if law enforcement doesn't know about. Who's gonna get hurt if we run these idiots out of town by telling them a couple of tall tales?"

"That's not the point, Bowie. Right is right and wrong is wrong."

"Honey, sometimes there's a whole lot of something in between right and wrong."

I didn't like that one bit. Law and order kept people safe. It defined exactly what was good and what was bad. It gave people answers, truthful ones. The law made the consequences of our actions clear.

If you stole your neighbor's cable, you paid a $500 fine. You laundered money, you spent up to a year in jail. Blowing up shit that's not yours on the 4th of July could have you serving up to two years and shelling out a cool $10,000.

We had rules.

"You know I have to tell my dad about this," I told him.

"No, you don't," Bowie countered. He pointed up to where my mom was sitting. "That's on her. Not you."

I opened my mouth and then closed it again. He may have a point.

"Look, if it's bothering you, I can tell you that nothing real illegal has ever come out of any of these meetings," he told me.

"Define 'real illegal.'"

"I'd prefer not to." He winked at me.

"Imma tell that shithead in the corduroy pants that I have evidence that Big Foot took Callie Kendall," Wade Zirkel called out, catching my attention.

I snorted. I couldn't help it. The idea of Wade Zirkel strutting up to *The Charlottesburg Post* claiming a sasquatch had carried off Callie was laughable.

"Hang on, y'all. We gotta be careful and make sure that definitely we're spreading bad info," Sonny Fullson, the shaggy-haired owner of Build a Shine—Bootleg's answer to the popular Build A Bear chain—said, coming to his feet.

"Are you saying you think it's possible that Harry from *Harry and the Hendersons* walked on into Bootleg and carried a girl off?" the mayor asked, appalled.

Sonny shook his head. "No, sir. I'm asking whether we're leading them to or away from Jonah Bodine, Sr.? May he rest in peace."

It was Bowie's turn to scowl. He crossed his arms over his chest and looked like he wanted to hit Sonny with Mayor Hornsbladt's hammer.

"My daddy, may he rest in peace, did not have anything to do with Callie Kendall's disappearance," Scarlett said, climbing up on her bench and glaring daggers at the crowd.

"How'd he end up with her bloody sweater then? May he rest in peace," someone yelled.

I slapped my hand on Bowie's leg when I felt him tense next to me. He was coiled to strike.

"Easy, tiger," I said quietly.

"Y'all know she's not dead. She ran off with some guy."

"If she were still alive why ain't no one heard from her since?"

"She's definitely dead."

"But do we know that Jonah Bodine did it? I mean, the

man was a drunk, but does that mean he's a murderer? May he rest in peace."

Devlin plucked Scarlett off the bench and motioned for the mayor's microphone. "I think it's important that everyone understands that this plan can only move forward if it doesn't interfere with the ongoing police investigation."

Finally. A voice of reason.

Bowie was still vibrating with pissed-offness next to me.

"We can come up with a solution that doesn't require us to try Jonah Bodine, Sr.—uh, may he rest in peace—in the court of popular opinion," Devlin answered.

"Huh?" someone grunted nearby.

Devlin straightened his tie. "What I'm saying is let's come up with a story or stories that won't derail the police investigation. It's their job to find out who did what. So let's make it our job to get these loafer-wearing, name-calling vultures out of our town."

It started as a slow clap and built until people were stomping their boots and whistling through their fingers. Devlin McCallister didn't know it, but he'd just given his first campaign speech.

At least I could count on him to keep things as legal as possible.

Now was a good time to leave, before I learned anything that definitely had to end up on my dad's desk. "Looks like you all have things under control around here. I'm gonna get back to town and make sure no one else is undermining the legal community's authority."

I half-rose, half-scurried around Bowie into the aisle, not wanting to draw any more attention to myself. I for sure didn't want my mom and June to see me. That was a conversation I wasn't eager to have.

Gee, Mom, how long have you been running secret operations behind Dad's back?

And June? How could my own sister keep this shit from me?

That headache was blooming like a damn fried onion at a steak place.

I ducked out the door and back into the crisp night, leaving the warmth of community at my back.

Looking around at the army of parked cars, I shoved my hands into the pockets of my coat. I sighed long and hard, watching my breath cloud up the ink-black sky above me. Their methods might be insane. But one thing I was sure of, Bootleg Springs was the best place in the whole wide world to live.

"You're not telling your daddy, are you?" Bowie's voice was quiet behind me.

I kicked at the frosted grass under my feet. "No. I won't tell him," I said finally.

He came up behind me and put his hands on my shoulders. When he turned me around to face him, I thought that it was finally happening. That Bowie Bodine was going to kiss the cold out of me under this sliver of moon.

And then he did.

His lips brushed my cheek. And then his thumb brushed the spot where his mouth had touched. "Thanks, Cass."

I was still standing there when he went back inside.

Police overlook suspect in Bootleg Springs disappearance

Who is Bartholomew Jaques?

Local police a laughing stock when new suspect identified in Kendall disappearance

22

BOWIE

Bartholomew—after Mrs. McClintock's no-good nephew—Jacques—for the Parisian hotel clerk that had been quite rude to Nash Larabee's mama—was a suspected murderer.

Specifically of Callie Kendall. But Bootleg Springs was open to giving him credit for more.

Yep. Ol' Bartholomew had drifted into town in a disreputable rusted out pickup truck and stirred up trouble for the six months he'd been in town. He bounced around from job to job, with his gold tooth—courtesy of Trent McCulty—and his scraggly hair, credit to Millie Waggle.

Rhett Ginsler suggested that Bartholomew walked with a limp from a bar fight he'd started in his younger days. Those reporters ate it up.

His alleged ties to the Indiana mafia—also a work of fiction—made him untouchable by local law enforcement. And that's how the squirrely, slimy, no-good Bartholomew escaped prosecution.

I enjoyed the hell out of watching the manufactured drama play out. On Monday, Maribel reported seeing Mrs.

Varney cozied up with a blogger from *West Virginia Needs to Know* at the Pop In. This particular blogger had artlessly referred to us Bootleggers as "the grammatically incorrect, poor cousins of respectable hillbillies".

On Tuesday, Mayor Hornsbladt invited the reporter from *The Middlebury Courier* into his office for a one-on-one.

Wednesday, when the crowd of press at the foot of my driveway asked, I told them I had no comment on Bartholomew Jacques.

Everyone who spoke to the press did so on the condition of anonymity.

By Thursday, there were headlines all across the state from media outlets that were too busy to do any real fact-checking questioning why law enforcement was ignoring a suspect. It was a real treat to see the pictures of Wade Zirkel in a Halloween costume circulating as the mysterious and potentially dangerous Bartholomew. Sierra Hayes had hit the fake social media profiles out of the park.

State police ignore vital lead in Kendall disappearance

Small town too scared to pursue murder suspect

Tiny town faces mob retaliation in Kendall killing

Hillbillies vs. The Mob: Who killed Callie Kendall?

Clarabell slid a plate of scrambled eggs with a small mountain of bacon in front of me and an egg white omelet with tomatoes and peppers in front of Jonah. We were celebrating the ridding of our town with a pre-work breakfast at Moonshine Diner.

"Ya see, everyone's been scared to death of mob retaliation," Clarabell recited to me as she topped off our coffees. "That's exactly what I told the dumbass from the *Perrinville Times*."

My driveway and the street in front of my house were blissfully empty this morning thanks to the backlash that had been just as swift as the viral spread of Bartholomew Jacques.

It was their own damn fault. Jonah handed his phone over, cueing up another video of a disgraced journalist jogging down the street with a crowd of his peers shoving cameras and phones in his face. The harassers had become the harassees. "How did an entire West Virginian town concoct a fake murder suspect and convince you to write about it?" the reporters wanted to know.

"No comment," the man in question snapped, pulling the hood of his coat up and speeding his jog to a near sprint.

Detective Connelly's derisive press conference questioning the irresponsibility of the press had been toasted by half the town watching at The Lookout. We'd all also shot the TV the middle finger when the asshole called us out for making a mockery of his investigation. Callie Kendall was ours more than she'd ever be his. The only thing we'd made a mockery of was a few dozen morons too aggressive to do their jobs properly.

Yep. We Bootleggers considered the entire situation a win. Nicolette had doled out shots of whiskey like it was a holiday when the news vans packed up. And June was quietly being lauded a town hero.

"Mornin', Bowie. Jonah."

I glanced up from the phone to see Sheriff Harlan Tucker sliding into the booth next to Jonah.

"Morning, sheriff," I greeted him warily, feeling the familiar knots tie themselves together in my stomach. We'd been close once. He'd taken me to get my driver's license, and

I'd spent every Thanksgiving at his table since I could remember. Still did. But it was different now.

Clarabell reappeared with a mug and a coffee pot. "Breakfast today, sheriff?" She was all business now. None of us were keen on the idea of letting him know about our involvement. Our lips were zipped.

"Just coffee. Thanks," he told Clarabell.

The sheriff took a sip, taking his time to warm up to his point.

"Cold one today," he said.

"Yessir," I agreed. Winter had indeed gotten her hooks into Bootleg early this year.

"Sure is," Jonah said, shooting *what the fuck* eye daggers in my direction.

"You boys know anything about this Bartholomew Jacques business?" Sheriff Tucker asked real casual like. As if all he were after was a little early morning conversation.

We knew better.

"I always count on you to be honest with me, son," he told me.

Ah, hell. That knife twisted nice and neat in my chest, exactly like he'd meant it to.

Jonah shoved a huge bite of omelet into his face so he couldn't be counted on to reply.

Sheriff Tucker brushed his fingers over his mustache. It was whiter now than it had been during our last serious conversation. We were all getting older. Yet I still felt like a No-Good Bodine Boy around him.

"Seems like the Bartholomew business cleared up our little infestation problem," I observed, not answering his question directly.

The mustache twitched.

"Seems like," he agreed. "How about you, Jonah? You settling in all right?"

Jonah had just shoveled another forkful into his mouth. "Yesh-her," he said.

Sheriff Tucker grunted. He was watching me like he was expecting me to spill my guts.

"Hey, sheriff. You hear about that armed robbery in Perrinville?" Clarabell appeared at our table, swooping in to save the day.

Jonah and I shared a look across the table. I didn't much like lying. Even if it was only by omission. But there was no way in hell that I was telling the man that his daughter was the diabolical genius behind scaring off the press.

Clarabell and the sheriff shot the shit for a few minutes before she puttered off to serve up carbs and gossip for the rest of the breakfast crowd.

"Well, boys. I'd better be on my way," he told us, sliding back out of the booth.

"Have a good one," I said, giving him a nod that I hoped didn't say *sorry about helping orchestrate a town-wide mutiny*.

Jonah slumped back against the booth when the front door jingled, signaling his departure.

"I feel like I just narrowly avoided getting called to the principal's office," he said. "No offense."

Grimly I pushed my plate aside and pulled out my phone.

Me: Your daddy's on a fishin expedition.

Cassidy responded immediately.

Cassidy: If you tell him I had any involvement, I'm going to become the worst next-door neighbor you've ever had.

I smirked.

"Man, when are you going to ask her out?" Jonah asked.

I put my phone away. "Shut up."

It was Jonah's turn to smirk. "Anyone in the family come up with anything about the week Callie disappeared?" he asked.

I shook my head. "You ever tried to remember anything that happened twelve years ago? I remember finding out she was missing. I remember the mess with police and reporters and search teams afterward. That's all etched in my brain."

I pushed my eggs around my plate, no longer feeling like celebrating the eviction of the press.

"But everything else?" I continued. "Dad leaving? Mom sending us to stay with Gibs that night? I've got nothing. Scar says she's comin' up empty, too. Who knows about Jameson and Gibs? Gibs didn't have much to do with Mom and Dad after he moved out, so I doubt he's got anything to add."

"Someone will remember something," Jonah said.

"You get a side of Pollyanna with your egg whites?"

"Nah. Secrets don't keep. Sooner or later someone remembers something."

23

CASSIDY

George and Sir Edmund Hillary—named for his enjoyment of climbing literally everything in my house—had settled in nicely. The litter boxes were in my mudroom off the back porch. Their scratching post was in the front window. And their fur was everywhere else.

I'd stepped up my vacuuming game to every other day to keep up with the hairballs that accumulated all over the damn place and tried not to think about the hairless pigs Juney kept harping on about. I liked having them around. They were good nap buddies. They meowed back to me when I talked to them. The three of us had spent hours playing with feathers on a stick and catnip-stuffed mice.

I wished I hadn't pulled the trigger on those store-bought Christmas cards in August so I could have dressed the cats up in Santa hats and done one of those pet picture cards.

Next year.

Yep. I was embracing being a cat lady.

I was on-call today. One of those rare Sundays when I could mostly pretend to be a regular person. But other than handling a nuisance complaint or two, the day was mine. I'd slept in, with George cuddled to my back and Eddie sprawled on the empty pillow next to me, then made myself a beef stew that would feed me for a week straight.

The cooking was done. The cleaning complete. The cats were napping.

I didn't know what to do with myself.

Normally, I'd be scrolling through a dating app or flipping through old case files. I was a deputy now, but that wasn't the end of the road for me. Someday, I'd be sheriff. But I had to earn it. Not be handed it because of my last name. So, I studied those case files and I audited the occasional public administration class online. But that was just the beginning of the job. In Bootleg, the sheriff's department was sewn right into the fabric of our little, weird society. Our job wasn't only to police and protect, but to communicate and help, to educate and sometimes even entertain.

I followed in my father's footsteps, taking an active interest in every single person in my town.

But today, I kind of wanted to be a regular human.

George snored from his perch on the windowsill in the dining room, and I whipped out my phone to record the adorableness.

I wondered if being a crazy cat lady would hinder me in my pursuit of the office of sheriff?

I heard a noise out the back and poked my head outside. Jonah was hauling a bag of trash to the bin Bowie kept along the back fence. Our yards were divided by a useless, hip-height fence that had seen better days.

Bowie had once suggested tearing it down and opening up the whole space to us both, but I preferred that physical barrier. Just like the door between our two halves. Barriers were essential when it came to dealing with the man that had broken my teenage heart.

"Howdy, neighbor," I called out.

Jonah tipped his chin. "Hey, Cass. Got any trash that needs hauling?" he asked.

"Nope," I called back.

Why couldn't it be Jonah? I wondered. Why couldn't that particular Bodine brother make my blood sing? He was a pleasant sort, easy on the eyes, too. And being a personal trainer, he'd keep my ass in shape. He already lived next door. Convenient for booty calls.

I considered the situation for a moment before remembering my recent decision to give up on the male gender entirely. Besides, did I really want to settle down with someone who would put me at the Bodine table every holiday? No siree. It was bad enough seeing Bowie in my parents' kitchen every Thanksgiving.

"I'm headin' over to the Pop In," Jonah said, zipping up the vest he wore instead of a coat. "Need anything?"

The Pop In was the Bootleg Springs version of a gas station and general store. "Popcorn!" I'd have myself a cozy movie night tonight. Maybe *Dirty Dancing* or *Sixteen Candles*. Or better yet, an action movie where nobody fell in love with anybody and they all still had a damn good time.

He gave me the thumbs-up. "On it. I'll deliver."

"Thanks, Jonah!"

I was still watching him, wondering why his denim-clad ass didn't hypnotize me the way his roommate's did, when the ass I was comparing it to walked out the back door.

"Hey," Bowie said, from his side of the back porch.

"Hey," I said back. He was wearing low-slung sweats and a long sleeve thermal shirt. He was tall, lean, a little scruffy, and every other damn thing that I liked in a man's body.

Yep, I pretty much hated him in that moment.

I was a split second away from finishing up my ogling and

making an excuse to go back inside when Sir Edmund Hillary decided it was a fine time for an adventure. The skinny little bastard streaked between my feet and dashed across the porch.

"No!" I yelled. It was winter, and the cats were new to me and my house. I hadn't let them explore the backyard yet in fear that this exact thing would happen. "Eddie, come back!"

Barefoot, I took off after him, ignoring the icy concrete of the walk beneath the soles of my feet.

He stopped six feet ahead of me and blinked like he was gonna let me catch him.

Cautiously, I approached. The little bastard let me get within a foot of him, and when I swooped down to make my move, he skirted out of my range.

"Holy shit! When did you get a cat!" Bowie called from his side of the fence.

"When I gave up on men."

Eddie changed course and ran straight for the fence.

"Stop!" I suddenly and viscerally empathized with every parent who ever put their child on a leash.

Eddie launched himself at the peeling wood. His little feet scrambled for purchase and then he was up and over.

Bowie dove like a receiver stretching for the game-winning touchdown pass. He landed hard with an "ooof."

I tiptoed through the residual snow and peered over the fence.

"Got 'im." Bowie held Eddie up triumphantly by the scruff of the neck. Eddie's front feet stretched out in front of him uselessly. He looked thoroughly disgruntled. Bowie was wet and muddy down the entire left side of his body.

I couldn't help it. They made a ridiculous picture. The laugh escaped before I could pull it back.

"Happy to entertain," Bowie smirked, cuddling Eddie to

his chest. Eddie's ears were down, and his tail twitched, but he submitted to the head scruffing Bowie doled out. I didn't blame him. Bowie's hands always did look so...competent.

We met at the fence.

"Gave up on men, huh?" Bowie asked as I leaned in to take the cat from him.

Our hands got tangled up as Eddie tried to squirm his way loose and those competent hands were smashed right up against my breasts. Why hadn't I put on a bra? Bowie's jaw was clenched, his eyes on the struggling cat pinned between us. The rough edge of the fence dug into my stomach. The ground was freezing under my naked feet. I had at least eight cat claws embedded in my skin and all I could feel was Bowie's hands.

"Sorry," he muttered to me as we wrestled.

Oh, holy hell. All those years of adolescent fantasies and *this* was how Bowie Bodine first touched my boobs. And he apologized. Real life was stupid and unfair. In desperation, I grappled my stupid, unfair cat out of Bowie's arms and stepped back. I slipped on an icy chunk of slush and almost went down, but I recovered just as he reached over the fence to grab me.

"I'm good. I'm good," I said, taking another hasty step backward.

My face had to be six shades of tomato judging by how hot my cheeks felt.

"You sure?" Bowie asked, stuffing his hands into the pockets of his sweat pants. Was it my imagination or was that a very clear penis impression in his pants?

Oh, Lord. I was seven shades of tomato now. I looked like Merl's farm stand in July.

"Yep. Good. Thanks." I ran for my back porch with numb feet and flaming face.

George was sitting neat as you please in the open back door. His tail was curled around his feet, the tip flicking to an unheard beat. He yawned as I stumbled up the porch steps.

"Don't you even think about it," I grumbled to him, shoving both cats inside and slamming the door on Bowie's gaze.

24

BOWIE

She'd given up on men. I should be popping a bottle of champagne right now in celebration. I'd never have to watch her climb into some guy's car all dolled up for a night out again. Never overhear her talking about dates with Scarlett. I wouldn't have to deal with hearing the sounds of a happy relationship through the thin walls that separated us.

But giving up on men included me, too. Sure, I'd taken myself out of that game a long time ago. But there was a part of me—a big part—that had hoped Cass would find a way to put it back on the table someday.

I wondered what it was exactly that had sent her into cat lady exploration. The dinner, the dance we'd shared, had been...nice.

My damn traitor of a cock stirred under the sheets remembering the feel of Cassidy pressed against me. I lost count of the thousands of hard-ons I'd gotten thanks to her. It was unnatural, the way one woman could turn me to granite in seconds all without ever really touching me.

I yawned, scrubbed my hands over my face, and prayed for

sleep. Sleepless nights due to my next-door neighbor were an unfortunate and common occurrence.

The shriek brought me rocketing out of bed. I was still groggy when my feet hit the cold floor. But the adrenaline coursing through my body was shouting its message: Cassidy was in danger.

If that fucker with the toothpick from dinner the other night showed up at her house I was gonna—

She screamed again, and I heard a thud. I vaulted over my bed and sprinted for the hallway. The door that separated our spaces didn't stand a chance. I don't know if I kicked it in or how I managed it, but I found myself staggering through an open door and into Cassidy's bedroom.

We faced each other on opposite sides of her rumpled bed. Her eyes were wild, her hair a disaster. And she was completely fucking naked.

I didn't think it was possible, not with the fight instinct firing my every synapse, but I went stone hard so fast I almost passed out.

"Bowie!" she screeched, and something flappy dive-bombed me.

It headed in Cassidy's direction, and she dropped to the floor, pulling the bedside lamp with her.

Cassidy Tucker was fearless. She'd hauled two-hundred-pound belligerent drunks into jail cells. She'd responded alone to plenty of domestic disturbance calls. Hell, *she* was the one Scarlett called whenever a lonely garter snake tried to hole up in her house.

But there was one thing that scared Cassidy down to her boots: *bats.*

The damn thing swooped my way again, and I ducked, not keen on flying biters with potential rabies.

"Catch it, Bowie!" Naked Terrified Cassidy could have

begged me to stick my fingers in a light socket and dance the Macarena and I'd have done it. The disoriented bat came back at me and fluttered its way to the headboard of Cass's bed.

Thinking fast, I snatched up her gym bag from the floor and dumped the contents. Cassidy peered over the edge of the bed, eyes wary.

"Come on, buddy. You and me have some business to attend to," I said, approaching cautiously. One foot in front of the other. It wasn't so hideous up close. More like a weird looking rat puppy with wings. I took a deep breath and deftly dropped the bag over the bat, using the flap to coax it inside.

I felt it flop around and quickly zipped the bag closed.

"Is it gone?" Cassidy whispered from the other side of the bed. I could only see the top of her head.

"It's all right, Cass," I promised her. I should be carting the bat out, averting my eyes. But instead, I put the bag on the floor and rounded the bed.

I shouldn't be pulling the naked object of my affection to her feet and running my hands over her arms. But here I was doing exactly that.

Cassidy leaned into me, her forehead resting on my chest. "That fucker scared the crap out of me. I almost shot him."

I spotted her service weapon on the nightstand and breathed a sigh of relief.

I was sporting morning wood at 2 a.m. I was so hard, if she moved one little muscle I might go off like a gun. "Cass, honey. You're not wearing any clothes." I reminded her, pushing her back enough to give my aching, throbbing, pulsing hard-on a little bit of breathing room.

She looked down. So did I.

I'd dreamed about this moment for a long-ass time and I wasn't about to ruin it by being a gentleman and looking away. Not when she was *naked* and *in my arms*. She had gentle curves, like the backroads that meandered around the lake. Her legs went on for fucking ever. Her breasts were perfect teardrops that looked like my hands were made to hold them. I loved every damn inch of her. The muscled shoulders, the subtle nip of her waist. The scar on her right hip from a fish hook that I personally removed when she was eleven.

I swallowed hard and tried to remind myself why I'd never touched her.

But she was still looking down, staring at me. Or my cock that was trying to fight its way out of the boxer briefs I'd slept in.

"Like a little sister, huh?" she asked, throwing that lie back in my face.

Fuck. I had her back against the wall before she could say another word.

I pinned her against the drywall and held her in place with my hips. My cock throbbed against her belly. Her breasts were flattened against my chest so hard I could feel her heartbeat. Instead of trying to kick me in the balls—which is what she had every right to do—she sank her teeth into my shoulder and then ran the tip of her tongue over my skin.

I went ahead and lost my damn mind. I held her by the throat, her pulse skittering under my fingers, and I let myself do what I'd spent years thinking about doing.

The second my lips found hers, everything changed. She wasn't scared anymore, she was starving. For me. And I was drowning in her. I kissed those lips that had smiled at me, frowned, smirked. A lifetime of expressions and we were finally discovering one more together.

She sank her teeth into my bottom lip, and then we were nothing but teeth and tongue and razor-sharp lust. When she bucked her hips against me, I ground my hard-on into her. The only barrier between us was the thin cotton of my underwear that I would gladly shred with my bare hands if it meant I got to bury myself in her.

I lifted her up, and she eagerly wrapped her legs around my waist. The head of my dick nestled between her silky thighs like it knew where its home was. I could feel her heat through the cotton.

"Yes, Bowie. Yes."

It was my undoing. My name, breathed from Cassidy's lips, was my salvation and damnation.

"Oh, God, Cass."

Her hands were everywhere. Stroking, squeezing, tempting, teasing. I kissed her like she was the center of my world, tasting her. I cupped her breast and reveled in the feel of her nipple pebbling against my palm. Our bodies recognized each other. Recognized that connection, the physical craving that only the other could satisfy.

She shoved a hand between us, and I was scared that she was coming to her senses. But those long fingers wrapped around my shaft, and I couldn't feel anything but need anymore. She freed me from the briefs and lined up the head of my dick against her. Wet and hot, the evidence of Cassidy's need was kissing the crown of my cock. I shifted, gave a shallow thrust, testing us both.

Oh, fuck. Just the tip buried in Cassidy's core was better than anything I'd ever experienced in my life. Including orgasms. The giving and receiving. This torturous inch of pleasure was better and more and everything.

"Oh, my God, Bowie. Yes, please. Please. Please," she gasped into my mouth.

I could feel her pulsing around me already. Greedy, needy, and so fucking perfect. Through the haze of lust, the crushing need to drive into her, our eyes met. Those moss green eyes pulled my soul from my body. I saw us in those eyes. Our past, present, and future all wrapped up in the hope and need in Cassidy Ann Tucker's beautiful green eyes.

"Are you sure, baby?" I gritted out.

"Bowie!" She squeezed me everywhere, milking the head of my cock.

I drew my hips back, ready to finally take what I'd wanted for so damn long.

"Everything all right?"

Jonah Bodine was a dead man.

25

CASSIDY

The half-asleep Jonah spun around so fast I thought whiplash was a possibility. He missed the open doorway and walked smartly into the doorframe.

"Ouch! Holy shit. Sorry!" he sputtered, holding his face.

"Get out, Jonah!" Bowie growled, lowering me gently to the floor.

I yanked the sheet off the bed and wrapped myself mummy-style while Bowie pulled his underwear back into place and stood between me and his brother's view.

My body was in full-on overdrive. The adrenaline from the flying vampire rat and the almost sex had my heart thumping in my head. *Almost. Almost. Almost.*

"You might want to—I don't know—close the damn door next time?" Jonah offered.

"There was a bat! We weren't—"

"We were about to," Bowie interrupted.

"Hey," Jonah said, holding up his hands. "Whatever you're into. None of my business."

I threw a shoe at him. "Hilarious. Get out."

My gym bag shivered on the floor.

"What the hell?" Jonah stared at the bag like it was possessed.

"It's the damn bat!"

My work phone rang on the nightstand. *Shit.* It was after midnight. I was no longer on call.

Bowie and Jonah were still yelling at each other.

"Would y'all shut the hell up for a minute?" I screeched. "Lo?"

"Cassidy." For a shitty communicator, my dad's voice sent a clear message. He needed a favor.

"What do you need, Dad?"

Bowie and Jonah shut up.

"I hate to bother you this late but I have a little situation and I could use your help," he told me.

"I have a little situation of my own," I said, eyeing Bowie's still hard dick through his underwear. He and Jonah were taking turns looking at me and the gym bag.

"Ya see, it's your grandmother."

It was a short list, the things that scared my father. Losing me and Juney, Black Friday shopping, my mom's mad face, and Gram-Gram. Gram-Gram was my mom's mother. Most of us found her to be a hoot and a half. The woman packed a hell of a lot of energy and attitude into a four-foot ten-inch body.

"What did she do now?" I asked, moving around the bed to my closet and grabbing my uniform shirt. I pointed at the bag and the door. Bowie and Jonah stared at me like I was insane.

Covering the phone, I mouthed "get out" to them both. When Bowie hesitated, I pointed at the door. Our beautiful, shining moment of uncontrolled lust had been ruined by his brother, my father, and now my damn grandmother. I wanted to cry and kick something. George wandered in and curled up on my pillow. Apparently my cats weren't bat hunters.

"She's in a little scuffle at The Lookout."

"Damn it," I muttered. Bowie and Jonah carried my gym bag out of the room like it was an explosive. Bowie's eyes met mine on the way out, and I could already see him rebuilding those walls that had always existed between us. *Damn it.*

"I hate to ask you, Cass. But you know I can't arrest her again," Dad said. The Christmas after Dad arrested his mother-in-law for vandalizing the church's nativity scene would go down in Tucker family history. Gram-Gram had refused to speak to him and then handed him a gift bag with an "I'm a narc" t-shirt in it.

I ducked into the bathroom clutching my uniform to my chest. "I'll go. Let me get dressed."

"Just go as you are," Dad suggested. "It sounds like it's gettin' a little out of hand."

Me showing up in a sheet toga with almost-fucked hair wouldn't settle any situation.

"I'll be there in five. But I'm definitely callin' in a favor on this," I warned him.

"Name it and it's yours," he said, breathing a sigh of relief.

I dressed quickly and was scraping my hair back in a bun as I jogged down the stairs. Jonah and Bowie were coming in the back door. Bowie was still wearing only underwear. I had to turn my back on him so I wouldn't weep with unrealized lust. *So close. So damn close.*

"Where are you going?" he asked.

"Fight at The Lookout," I said, grabbing my coat and keys.

"You aren't on call," Bowie pointed out. I didn't want to know how he was so intimately acquainted with my schedule. There wasn't time to ask.

"It's Gram-Gram," I told him.

"Oh." He got it. Of course he did. Bowie knew everything there was to know about me. Including the fact that my crazy little grandmother scared the shit out of my father and terrorized other senior citizens when the moonshine flowed a little too freely.

"Is your grandma okay?" Jonah asked, looking confused.

"I'll fill him in," Bowie promised.

"Great." I pushed past them both and headed out into the cold night air. "Thanks for taking care of the bat," I called over my shoulder.

I jumped into my car and was dialing Scarlett before I even got it in reverse.

"'Lo?" she said sleepily through the car speakers.

"I don't know if I just had sex with your brother," I announced, steering the car in the direction of the bar and flooring it.

"WHAT?"

Scarlett was now wide awake.

"Which brother? How do you not know if you had sex? Are you drunk? Is he drunk? Which brother is it?"

She fired off questions like bullets. *Pew. Pew. Pew.*

"Bowie and it's a long story. But I need to know if I need to update my list of sexual partners." If that was my one and only sexual experience with Bowie...well, hell. I didn't know what I'd do. All those years of closing off and keeping my distance had just imploded, resulting in one or two inches of the most intense sexual experience of my life.

"Bowie! Bowie Bodine? Good guy? Next-door neighbor Bowie? 'Never ask me about Bowie again' Bowie?"

"That's the one," I said accelerating up the steep hill to The Lookout.

While the rest of town was asleep on this frosty winter night, The Lookout's lights were blazing, and the parking lot was half-full.

"How do you not know if you had sex with Bowie?" Scarlett demanded. "I'm coming over. This is a face-to-face discussion. Ouch! Jedidiah! Stop clawing the shit out of me!"

"It's a technical Tab A Slot B question," I told her. "And I'm just pulling into The Lookout for a disturbance."

"If you don't call me tomorrow I will hunt you down and—ouch! Stop biting!"

"George and Eddie never bite me," I teased, throwing the car into park and climbing out. At least the fight hadn't spilled out into the parking lot.

"That was Dev biting me, not the cat," Scarlett said smugly.

A barstool exploded through The Lookout's plate glass window and landed with a metallic thunk on the sidewalk. It rolled back and forth over crystals of glass.

"Shit. I gotta go."

"Tell Gram-Gram I said hi."

26

CASSIDY

My grandmother was a woman of contradiction. She went to church twice a month, baked an exquisite lemon cake with homemade icing for my birthday every year, and was currently wielding a pool stick at Myrt Crabapple.

Myrt had a good seven inches and fifty pounds on my grandmother. But her glass eye and arthritis evened the odds. She was trying to break a beer bottle off of the bar. *Thwack. Thwack. Thwack.*

Nicolette was calmly filling a pitcher of ice water to dump on them.

"Gram-Gram!" My voice snapped with authority. Unlike my father, Gram-Gram could usually forgive me for playing cop.

My grandmother dropped the pool cue.

"Shit. It's the po-po," Myrt yelled. Myrt thought she was whispering, but without her hearing aids she couldn't hear a damn thing.

"Cassidy, sweetie! What are you doing here?" Gram-Gram

asked sweetly. She was wearing her Bootleg Bingo sweatshirt, and judging from the bingo cards and overturned tables everywhere, the games hadn't gone someone's way.

"Who threw the stool?" I asked calmly.

Nicolette placed the pitcher on the bar and nodded to me. Bootleg senior citizens were an unruly bunch, but a good dousing was usually all it took to break up any altercations. They didn't much care for their polyester outfits to get wet.

"What stool?" my grandma asked innocently.

"The one spinning around like a top in front of Trent McCulty's pickup truck."

"She did it," Myrt hollered, pointing a gnarled finger at Gram.

The crowd around us erupted as everyone tried to explain all at once. I looked at them. White hair and crooked glasses. Flannel and ugly sweaters. A shoving match broke out between Old Jefferson Waverly and Marvin Lloyd. Granny Louisa and Estelle were trying to look innocent over by the jukebox.

"Knock it off, y'all," I shouted over the din, reaching for the pitcher of water.

I could have given it another minute. Neither man had much energy and they were both already huffing and puffing like steam engines. But I'd had a rough night and I just wanted to go home and figure out whether or not Bowie and I had sex and what, if anything, that meant.

I threw the water in their faces and then tossed the pitcher on the ground. "Everybody better get real orderly or I will drag every single one of you downtown, and y'all know how uncomfortable the cots are in that cell."

We had one official jail cell in town. And most of these fine citizens had spent at least a night in it at some point.

They all shut up real fast.

"Now, tell me who threw the stool so we can get on with it." Bootleg Justice required the instigators of bar fights to participate in the clean-up as well as paying for any property damage.

"I'm tellin' you! It was Gert!" Myrt shouted.

"I was mindin' my own business, trying to climb up on that stool and it slipped right out from under me," Gram-Gram insisted.

"It slipped out from under you through a plate glass window and into the parking lot?" I asked wishing to God it had been my father who responded to the call.

"Between you and me," Gram-Gram said in a stage whisper, "the floors in here are real greasy. Just like the food. I'm surprised it doesn't happen more often."

"Hey, now!" Nicolette said, taking offense.

Gram-Gram shot her a beaming smile. This was part of her street cred, lying to the authorities—usually her family—about whatever mess she'd stirred up.

"Okay, this is how it's gonna go. Y'all are going to clean up every bingo card and broken shard of glass. Gram-Gram, since the floor is so slippery, you're gonna mop it and then reimburse Nicolette here for the window. Then I'm going to drive you home and decide what kind of fine I'm gonna slap you with."

Gram-Gram pouted prettily, adjusting her pink frame glasses.

"Anyone have any problems with that?" I demanded.

"No, ma'am," they barked in unison.

"Good."

The soggy and chastised elderly of Bootleg Springs hopped to, pulling out brooms and dustpans, righting tables, and straightening chairs. Nicolette handed my grandmother a mop. "You know where the bucket is."

An hour later, with The Lookout sparkling clean, the window boarded up, and the geriatric population on its way home to bed, I plunked Gram-Gram in my back seat. It wasn't a police cruiser, but she still had a reputation to uphold.

"When are you gonna stop causing trouble on Bingo Night?" I asked.

"When are you gonna start having something to do instead of fixin' trouble on Bingo Night?" she countered.

"Tonight."

She hmm-ed knowingly. "I thought you looked a little hot and bothered. Did you swipe right on a hot one?" she asked.

"We're not discussing this."

"Did he have a man bun?" Gram asked. "I love a good man bun! I wish Marvin could have one but his combover won't reach."

"It wasn't a man," I lied. "It was a bat. It flopped my face."

Gram shifted gears into caring grandparent. "Poor sweetie! I hope it didn't bite you."

I turned onto Spirits Lane. "No. Bowie caught it in my gym bag and he and Jonah released it into the wild."

"Bowie, huh?" Gram mused pointedly. "When are you two gonna quit dancin' around it and get naked already?" Gram-Gram had two boyfriends and another in the hopper in case one of the other two became defective or up and died.

I DROPPED Gram off at her cute little brick-front row home. She waved to me from her front step like I'd chauffeured her to and from church.

Suddenly irretrievably exhausted, I headed home. I squeezed my car into the garage and trudged up the walkway toward my back porch.

"Everything okay at Bingo Night?" Bowie was leaning on a porch post on his side of the railing.

I paused on the step and climbed up to his level.

"Your door wasn't locked," he told me, crossing his arms over his chest.

"What door?" This was Bootleg Springs. My back door was never locked.

"The one between us." His face was shadowed in the soft glow of the porch light.

I was tired. Too tired to play any more games. "It's never been locked, Bowie."

He swore quietly and toed one of the spindles between us. I knew that to him, tonight had been a mistake. One he didn't want to repeat.

"So, that's it then? That's all it's gonna be?" I pressed. I wanted him to say the words. "You're just gonna go back to thinking about me as a little sister."

We both knew there was nothing little sisterly about what had happened a few short hours ago. But I wanted him to lie to my face. To give me something to hate him for. A reason to give up on him again.

He didn't answer me, so I stepped closer until the railing pressed against my hips. I grabbed him by the front of the sweatshirt he wore to ward off the chill.

He brought his hands to my shoulders, squeezed. "Cass, honey. We can't."

I was tired. That's why I dropped my head to his chest. That's why my heart did that stupid tumble when he rested his chin on top of my head. I'd been in his arms twice tonight.

And both times had been thoroughly unsatisfying. I wanted more and I hated myself for it.

"I promised," he said quietly.

"You promised what to who?" I demanded. *Whom? Whatever.*

"Ask your dad," he said wearily.

27

CASSIDY

"Girl, what are you doing here this morning?" Bex asked as I trudged into the station the next morning. "I thought you'd be sleeping off Gram-Gram's shit-show at The Lookout."

I'd intended to catch up on some sleep. Instead, I'd sprawled out on my bed, staring up at the ceiling, thinking about the man on the other side of the plaster and studs. My room was marked by him now. I kept picturing him, bursting into my bedroom, fists closed and ready for a fight. The wall that he pushed me up against, almost shoving himself into me.

It felt like fate. Like it was something that had been written in the stars before either of us were gleams in anyone's eyes. Destiny. Right.

Ask your dad.

Those words sent my guts to churning. I had a question for my father all right. And I was going to get an answer.

"Sheriff in?" I asked her, ignoring her question.

"In his office." Bex nodded toward the shoebox my father called an office. My gaze slid to the conference room.

"Connelly's out today," she said, reading my mind.

Good. I had a feeling a little family drama was about to play out and I didn't much care for any outsider audiences.

I headed for Dad's office and nodded at Bubba, who was watching an epic fail video on YouTube and combing his mustache.

My father was hunting and pecking on his keyboard, his readers perched on the end of his nose.

"Mornin' sunshine," he said, taking in the bags under my eyes.

I closed the door and flopped down in the rickety chair in front of his desk. "How's the Kendall investigation going?" I asked. You couldn't just ask a direct question to my father. You had to ease him into talking. Get him used to the flow of words leaving his mouth. Warm him up with a topic he was comfortable with.

"Not a whole lot of new information. The blood on the sweater was hers, but they didn't find any DNA evidence in or around Jonah's house. Cadaver dogs didn't catch a whiff of anything on the property either. So far Connelly's comin' up with squat on the speeding ticket. There's nothing in that area that ties to Jonah Bodine, Sr.," he recapped.

I nodded. Nothing new there. "Anything interesting come up in any of the new interviews?" I hated to think that Connelly had brought in the press and pissed off our entire town for nothing.

Dad's mustache quirked. "Nope. Nothing new. Which didn't please His Highness. He could've gotten the same info reading the old case files, but he seems to think we dropped the ball somewhere along the way and let the suspect get away with murder."

He said it without malice. My dad was a peacemaker at

heart, and even with an opinionated bigwig breathing down his neck, nothing much ruffled his feathers.

"What do you think about it all? Do you think Jonah did it?" I asked.

"What do you think?" He'd always done that. Ever since I announced that I was going to be a cop, he'd talk shop with me. He taught me to trust my instincts. There was only one area of my life that they'd let me down: Bowie.

I kicked back in the chair and thought it through. "I can't see it. Maybe it's because I grew up with his kids. Jonah Bodine was an asshole at times, but I don't see murderer."

"Then how'd he get that sweater?" Dad pressed, warming to the topic.

"Found it maybe. Hell, what if he didn't even find it? What if Connie found it and worried he'd had something to do with it?"

"Why wouldn't she destroy it? If she thought it was evidence, she and Jonah didn't have the warmest relationship."

I thought back to that night when a shadow-eyed, teenaged Bowie had walked into my living room with the rest of his siblings. I'd walked right on up to him and hugged him hard. I wanted to share my family with him. I wanted him to feel like he belonged somewhere safe.

"Blackmail?" I suggested. But that didn't sit right either. "Proof maybe? In case he was accused?" We were missing too many pieces.

"What if it wasn't murder?" Dad asked, picking up his mug of now cold coffee.

"An accident?" That seemed a hell of a lot more likely to me than Jonah Sr. running out and committing cold-blooded murder.

Dad's shoulder hitched. "The man liked to drink. Occasionally he drove."

I walked through it in my head. Callie leaving the lake, walking in the direction of town, of home. The roads were windy and dark. Someone could have hit her.

"Hit and run. Under the influence. The charges would have added up to some serious jail time."

Dad nodded. "He was the primary breadwinner for a big family. They would have lost everything."

"What did he do with the body?" I asked, considering. "Would he have driven the corpse of a teenage girl to New York state where he didn't know every inch of the woods, every mountain road?" That didn't make a lick of sense to me. He'd be too exposed.

"Let's back up from this. Besides Jonah Bodine. There are two theories that everyone keeps comin' back to," Dad said, leaning back in his chair. "One."

"That she harmed herself somehow," I answered by rote. It was the official family line. The fact that there'd been no body was really what had punctured the faith in the theory. That and now a bloody sweater. "Judge and Mrs. Kendall still maintain that their daughter suffered from mental issues and hurt herself regularly."

Dad's head bobbed. "And two?"

"That there was a boy. He either ran off with her or he killed her," I filled in.

"You ever see her with someone special?" Dad asked. We'd been through this on our own a few thousand times since Callie's disappearance. I'd known her. And I wanted answers just like everyone else. But somewhere deep inside, I was scared that I had a key that would unlock everything. That I had forgotten something that would answer every question.

I shook my head. "No more than usual. She was sixteen.

But didn't seem overly interested in any boys, summertimers or otherwise."

"Where was she when she wasn't hanging out with y'all?" Dad asked.

I closed my eyes and opened up those mental files from that summer. I felt like the entire season was burned into my brain because of the disappearance, the investigations, the questions never answered. "Home. I assume. We weren't close. Friendly, but not friends. She was older. A little reserved maybe?"

I thought about those sweaters, *that* sweater. Always, even in the August swelter.

"Did her parents ever have any proof that she was hurting herself?" I asked.

"Gave us the name of Callie's therapist, as I recall," my dad said, stroking a hand over his mustache.

I decided I'd take the case files home for another review over the next few days. Anything to keep my mind off the man next door.

"I hate having all these questions," I admitted.

"The answers are there," Dad said. "Maybe we haven't asked the right questions yet."

"Speaking of, I need to ask you something," I said.

"If it's why your grandmother is a hellion hell-bent on driving me insane, I don't have an answer for you," he told me, taking off his glasses and stuffing them in his shirt pocket. "Thank you again for taking care of her last night."

"It's about Bowie."

I watched his face carefully looking for some hint of something. But my dad just looked perplexed.

"Is he all right?"

Genuine concern. Huh. Had Bowie been messing with

me? Was this just another fake lead, a red herring, in the dissection of why Bowie Bodine didn't want me?

"We had a...moment last night."

"Ah, come on, Cass. You know I hate it when you and your sister talk about your '*moments*.'"

June spoke only in very clinical terms of her sex life. And I only mentioned things in front of Dad to annoy him.

"Anyway, after this moment he said we couldn't have any more moments."

Dad looked puzzled. "Why in the hell not? You two are perfect for each other."

"He said to ask you."

I waited a beat.

Dad's brows furrowed and then his wispy eyebrows winged up his forehead. "Uh-oh."

"Dad, what did you do?"

28

BOWIE

Eight years earlier

The knuckles on my right hand stung, and my jaw ached where that Blaine asshole had gotten in a lucky shot with his elbow. I was still vibrating with barely controlled rage. The dumbass was howling about lawsuits and holding paper towels to his still bleeding nose while the bonfire crowd had thinned to just lookie-loos.

Cassidy was standing near the fire, rubbing her arms with her hands and talking with Scarlett and June. I wanted to go check on her. Make sure she was okay. But Sheriff Tucker was headed in my direction and he didn't look too happy.

"Bowie," he said.

"Sir."

"Things get a little out of hand tonight?" he asked.

We had a nice little arrangement going. We partiers kept our bonfires civil and made everyone walk home. Then the police didn't have to get involved with checking everyone's IDs and arresting people. Now I'd gone and ruined it. Technically, the jackwagon with the busted nose had ruined it. But he'd get to go home to his regular life, and I'd be stuck here in Bootleg.

Would this mess cost me my job in the fall? Had I disappointed Sheriff Tucker?

Why was it that I couldn't keep my head on straight around Cassidy Tucker? It was not an appropriate question to ask her father.

"A little, sir," I agreed.

"You wanna tell me your side of it or should I go with his version where you jumped out of the dark at him and tried to mug him?"

I smirked, and it hurt my lip. "He was getting handsy with one of the girls, threatening to throw her in the lake. She said no. He didn't listen."

"One of the girls?" the sheriff asked.

We both knew who I was talking about, but he was going to make me say her name anyway.

"Cassidy, sir."

He stroked his finger and thumb over the corners of his mustache. "Am I going to have to give my daughter a refresher course on self-defense?"

I shook my head, covering a smile. "No, sir. I think she can handle herself."

"But you stepped in."

The man had me there. Why did I have the feeling the confession he was trying to get out of me wasn't about an assault?

"I was...angry that he wasn't being respectful."

Sheriff Tucker nodded in understanding. "I appreciate you looking out for my daughter. I really do. You're a good man, Bowie."

Something warmed inside me. "Thank you, sir."

He wiped his palms over the knees of his pants and sighed like he had the weight of the world sitting on his chest. "Son, I hate to do this. But I'm gonna need to ask you to give Cassidy some space. She doesn't seem to be capable of giving you any. So it falls to you. She's young. She's still in school. You've got your hands full with your family and now your job. I don't want something derailing you both."

The something warm iced over into a chunk of ice in my gut.

"Sir, I didn't mean to be disrespectful—"

"Bowie, you're the most respectful person in this whole damn town. I know you've got strong feelings for her. And I know it's not fair, but I'm asking you not to act on those feelings. Things happen. People make mistakes. They get hitched up to the wrong people at the wrong time—"

"I understand," I said, cutting him off. My heart limped in my chest. The man I'd spent my entire life looking up to, the one who'd driven me to take my driver's license test and taken me out for pizza to celebrate afterward because my own father had been too drunk to do it, didn't think I was good enough for his daughter.

Something hot and hard lodged itself in my throat. Despair. An anger so white-hot I wondered why it didn't burn its way out.

No matter what degree I had, no matter how hard I worked, I was still Jonah Bodine's son.

29

BOWIE

Johnny Johnson kicked back in the chair across from me, arms crossed defiantly over his skinny chest. He was Bootleg's version of a punk. Black, ripped jeans, white t-shirt despite the thirty-degree temperatures outside. Eyebrow ring. A haircut that made him look like his little brother had cut it with safety scissors.

Troubled family, his file said.

We all handled our troubled families differently. I'd gone off and tried to distance myself from my unhappy upbringing with education and good deeds.

Johnny here was heading down the Gibson path of acting out. By the time Gibs had graduated high school, he'd had a desk dedicated to him in detention. He'd carved his initials into it with a knife that got confiscated and landed him another week of detention.

"I get the whole discipline problem thing," I told Johnny. "You're not a terrible human being. You're just in a terrible situation." Johnny's dad had gone off to serve his second stint in jail for identity theft, and his mother had moved in a new boyfriend over the weekend.

His eyes flicked to the photos on top of my army green filing cabinet. Front and center was a shot of me, my dad, and Cassidy's dad. They had their arms slung over my shoulders, grins on all our faces. It had been taken after I threw the last strike in the state championships. "That's my son," my dad had bellowed at the top of his lungs pushing his way through the crowd to get to me. He'd stayed sober for my games, the ones we'd won, giving me a few precious hours of having a real father. But Sheriff Tucker was as constant and dependable as they come. He was there for me, win or lose.

"No offense, man, but why should I take any advice from you? Your dad's a murderer."

Punk-ass kid.

"That's exactly why you should take advice from me," I said, fighting the urge to defend my father. "I've been where you are. And I don't want you to make a choice that will stick with you for the rest of your life. Don't do something stupid when you're this close to being an actual adult and making your own decisions. You don't have to be happy about what's going on with your parents," I reminded him. "But don't let you being pissed off at them ruin the rest of your life."

Johnny dropped his head back against the chair. "God, you sound like an after school-special."

If only slapping students weren't illegal. "Let's cut to the chase. You're fishin' for detention so you don't have to go home and make nice with your mom's boyfriend." I'd had sports and jobs to fill my time after school. Johnny here had nothing to keep him out of the house or juvie.

He lifted a shoulder to his ear, dropped it. The smirk faded from his face.

"How about we do this instead. You apologize sincerely to Mrs. Plunkett and I'll set you up as the student rep on the 3D printer lab. We'd need you an hour or two every afternoon.

Maybe even some time on the weekends when we're closer to opening the lab."

He perked up. The kid might have been a punk, but he was a tech nerd punk.

"Yeah?" he asked.

"Yeah. But that apology has to convince her," I reminded him.

Johnny snorted, but the hope remained in his eyes. "I'm like totally convincing."

"We'll see," I said dryly. "Go on. Get out of here."

I shooed him out the door and turned my attention to the inbox of new emails when someone else crossed my threshold.

"Mornin', Bowie," Sheriff Tucker said, rocking back on his heels, hands in his pockets.

"Mornin', sheriff." There were only two reasons why he'd be in my office during the school day. Either there was a break in the Callie Kendall case or he'd somehow found out that I'd had my hands and every other body part all over his daughter last night.

"I talked to Cassidy this morning," he began.

Fuck.

"Mind if I sit down?" he asked, gesturing to the chair still warm from Johnny's punk-ass.

"Sure," I said, trying not to freak the fuck out. It was ridiculous. I was just shy of thirty-one years of age and I was still scared to death of losing this man's approval.

"Y'all got any coffee around here?" he asked, taking a seat.

"Yeah, sure," I said getting up and punching buttons on the coffeemaker. I was making the man a triple espresso for all I knew. Panic was stampeding through my system.

"Think we'll see snow again this weekend," he predicted.

"Uh-huh. Maybe," I agreed. *Was I having a heart attack? Or a panic attack?* I needed to calm the hell down. I was an adult, and for all I knew the sheriff here was stopping by to talk about Thanksgiving.

"I think you and I may have had a miscommunication," he said when I handed over the coffee and sat back down.

Fuck. This was definitely not holiday chat. It had nothing to do with my father being a murder suspect. This was about Cassidy and me.

"It was a momentary lapse, sir," I blurted out my confession. "It won't happen again."

Sheriff Tucker set his mug on the desk and rubbed his hands over his face. "Christ, son, why the hell not? Do you know how horrific it is to watch my daughter date jackass after jackass? It's like she's picking dumbasses just to drive me into my grave early. For the love of all that's holy, when are you going to ask her out?"

I blinked. "Wait. What?"

"You two have had feelings for each other since forever," he pointed out.

I heard a weird buzzing in my ears and wondered if I was hallucinating or having a stroke. I reached up and felt my mouth. "Is my mouth drooping?" I asked him.

"Huh?"

"Which arm goes numb in a stroke? Or is that a heart attack?" I demanded, flapping both my arms up and down, testing for weakness.

"Are you tryin' to take flight, son?" Sheriff Tucker asked incredulously.

"I'm tryin' to figure out if I'm having some kind of medical emergency. You told me to stay away from Cassidy. You told me people get hitched up to the wrong people."

"Ah, hell. Bowie! I didn't mean forever and I was talking about your parents. I didn't want you and Cassidy gettin' together when she was too young to be smart. Y'all would have gotten knocked up or she would have hated being apart from you and dropped out of school. Or you would have given up the job you wanted so bad to be close to her at college."

He wasn't speaking English. The words weren't recognizable.

"I never meant for you to stay away from her forever. I just wanted her to have a chance to grow up first. I've been waitin' on you to finally make your damn move for years, son."

"You think I'm good enough for Cassidy?" I asked, trying desperately to clarify exactly what he was trying to tell me.

"Yes!" he bellowed.

"But you told me to stay away from her!"

"Bowie, I'm not the best communicator in the world. So maybe the words didn't come out right. I wanted you two to get yourselves where you needed to be before diving into those big feelings."

He'd been trying to protect me. He didn't think I was a bad seed or not good enough for his daughter.

I pressed my fingers to my eyes. "All this time I thought you were telling me I wasn't good enough."

"Ah, hell. Nadine is gonna kill me deader than a hammer over this," he groaned. "Bowie, I never, ever meant to make you feel that way. You're one of the good ones. Always have been. Even your daddy said so."

My eyes flicked to the picture on the file cabinet.

"So if I want to court Cassidy?" I began, wanting it spelled out loud and clear. No misunderstandings this time.

"You have my blessing. Hell, I'm begging you. You want to put a ring on the girl? I'm a thousand percent in favor. For the love of God, Bowie. Don't let me sit down at my dinner table with an asshole from one of them there dating applications!"

A weight I'd been carrying for eight long years lifted right off my chest.

I stood up, my chair smacking into the wall behind me.

"Before you go runnin' off," Sheriff Tucker said, "I should warn you that she's madder than a puffed toad. Some of that might spill over on you."

"I can handle it," I promised. There was nothing in this world that was going to stand between me and Cassidy Tucker now.

30

CASSIDY

Eddie didn't care that I was good and pissed off or that he'd just had breakfast two hours ago. He wanted food now. He expressed this desire by winding his way in and out of my feet as I warmed up a bowl of stew that I was too mad to eat.

"You want more food? Well, I wanted my dad to keep his big fat nose out of my life. Guess neither one of us is gettin' what we want," I told the cat. He was young. But he needed to learn that life wasn't always fair.

I couldn't believe my father had sabotaged my chances with Bowie back then. Bowie had felt something for me, and I'd spent the last thousand years questioning my instincts and wondering what was wrong with me. I slammed the utensil drawer shut.

George padded into the kitchen to add his two cents to the lack of food issue.

"You're already borderline overweight," I told him.

I'd stormed out of the station, middle fingers mentally flying, and decided to take a little PTO to stew in my rage. Better to do it at home than anywhere near Connelly should he come back to the station. I wished I could be like Scarlett and throw a fit, get it out of my system. But I had the icier kind of temper, freezing people out with my chilly politeness.

My phone rang on the counter. I planned to ignore it, but I saw Scarlett on the screen and picked up.

"Okay, it's tomorrow," she said by way of a greeting. "I need to know how you may or may not have had sex with Bowie and why the whole town's talking about you screaming at your daddy and then him showing up in Bowie's office, hat in hand."

"If those two do any more colluding behind my back I'm going to..." I trailed off. I didn't even know how to threaten people.

"You're going to turn your best friend loose on them to make them rue the day they were ever born," Scarlett filled in for me. Her loyal vindictiveness was one of the many things I loved about her.

"Yes! That's exactly what I'm going to do."

"I already have the perfect place picked out for their bodies," she continued on. "All you have to do is tell me exactly what happened."

I sat down in a kitchen chair and proceeded to do exactly that.

When I was done, Scarlett was real quiet. Too quiet.

"Well?" I demanded.

"I'm tryin' to remember where I put that second blue tarp. I don't think we can fit both bodies in one."

"So I'm not crazy for being madder than a wet hen?"

"Your daddy steps in to interfere with your love life and the guy of your dreams decides not to fight for you? I'd be bustin' down the wall between your houses so you can steal all of Bowie's shit. Then drive it over to your daddy's house and throw it on the lawn. If those two are so cozy they might as well live together!"

"I spent years thinkin' there was something wrong with me for him not wanting me," I confessed.

"Oh, sweetie. The only thing wrong with this situation is those two dumbasses shoving their heads up each other's butts. I get where your daddy was coming from. He saw the way you two were lookin' at each other, all smoldery like. He didn't want you making him a pappy too early and ruining your life like my mama."

"I know how birth control works," I pointed out.

"And amen to that. But what your daddy stupidly did was out of love. Stupidity and love. So hang on to that. You can and should be mad at him for a while. But Cass, Harlan loves you. He made one mistake."

"A big one."

"Yeah, but one big mistake is better than 36,000 small to mid-sized ones."

I got what she was trying to tell me. It was okay to be mad, but I shouldn't be forgetting how lucky I was to grow up with a Harlan Tucker instead of a Jonah Bodine. "I'm still going to stay mad at him for a good long while."

"As you should," Scarlett said, loyally. "Now, what about Bowie? And I want best friend points for not immediately dusting off my Bowie and Cassidy's wedding scrapbook from seventh grade."

"Burn it," I told her. "He made his choice. He would rather have my father's approval than me. There's no way I'm forgiving him for that."

"I can't burn it," she argued. "It has your junior high vows that you wrote about always letting him have the top thumb in hand-holding."

"If you don't burn that thing, I'm coming over right now and doing it for you!"

"Okay. Okay," she relented. "Let's talk about the almost sex."

"Almost sex," I repeated. "So it wasn't actual sex, right?" For some reason, I'd been in a panic thinking that my first sexual experience with Bowie had gone unfinished. *First and last experience,* I decided vehemently.

"For it to count as sex, you have to have at least fifty-one percent of the penis," Scarlett instructed.

I heard a knock at my front door and headed in that direction. "Fifty-one percent, huh?" I opened the door to a riotous bouquet of flowers. "What the—"

"What? What's happening?" Scarlett asked from the phone.

The flowers lowered to reveal Bowie's face.

"I'll call you back, Scarlett. I have to murder your brother."

"Wait! Do you need the tarp?" she asked.

I started to shut the door in his flowery face, but Bowie stuck his foot out and cheerfully shoved his way inside.

"Now listen here, Bowie Bodine—" I started.

With careful precision, he set the vase down on the floor and turned to me. He slid his hands into my hair, thumbs resting on my jaw. Before I could yell any profanities at all, he was kissing me.

Gentle and slow like he had all the time in the world. Like he was reassuring us both that this was exactly right. I felt the thawing, like a hair dryer on sidewalk ice. Parts of me were puddling up nicely.

He applied just the right amount of pressure that had me opening my mouth like I was under a spell. When his tongue danced into mine, I let out a whimper. He kissed me long and soft, and my entire body came to life. I couldn't quite remember why I shouldn't be letting him do this. I was too busy scrambling to remember what underwear I was wearing and if I'd remembered to shave my legs last night.

Then I heard a voice coming to me from the phone I hadn't hung up. "What's happening? Are y'all neckin'? Did you murder him?"

Bowie's little sister.

My brain grabbed hold of that. Scarlett was Bowie's little sister, and he'd once lied to my face and told me he saw me as nothing but the same.

I pressed my palms to that crisp dress shirt he was wearing and shoved.

"Hold your horses! There's not gonna be any more kissing!" I told him.

He grinned down at me looking like he hadn't a care in the dang world.

"Cass, honey, kissing isn't the only thing I'm after."

I looked down at his crotch, and sure enough it looked like Bowie Bodine, Jr. was *very* happy to see me.

"I can still hear y'all," Scarlett chirped through the phone.

He plucked it out of my hand and disconnected the call. I realized I was still plastered up against his chest like a bug on a windshield.

"We're not having sex. Not ever, Bowie," I said taking a big step back. "You picked my father over me."

"I did no such thing," he argued, advancing on me. I found myself pinned up against the back of the couch and his long, lean body. Sir Edmund Hillary dashed across the top of the cushions. Bowie skimmed his hands from my shoulders to my wrists in one long stroke. "I wanted to be good enough for you, Cass."

"You backed off of me because my father asked you to."

"I thought he was saying I wasn't good enough for you."

"You told me you didn't have feelings for me, Bowie!" It was like we were having two different conversations.

"I lied," he said simply. "I've had big feelings for you for as long as I can remember."

A panic was welling up inside me. He was saying all the things I'd wanted to hear for so damn long. And now they weren't enough.

He released my wrists and threaded his fingers into my hair again, moving in on me in slow motion. His lips found mine, and it was like my body was hypnotized into accepting the pleasure he was offering. I kissed him back like my life depended on it. It wasn't so slow and leisurely now because there was a fire growing between us.

Why did this feel so good? So right?

"Nope. No. Not happening," I said, pushing him back and then dug my fingers into his shirt to hold him in place.

"I'm gettin' some mixed messages here, Cass," Bowie said with that damned boyish grin.

"I'm furious with you."

He traced a finger down my nose. "I'm gonna make you forgive me, Cassidy. Then I'm gonna spend about a year kissing you to make up for lost time."

I shook my head. "I'm not forgiving you, Bowie Bodine. You broke my heart." *Stop admitting things, Cassidy, you damn moron!*

He cupped my face in his hands. "I broke mine, too. Now I'm gonna put them both back together and you and I are gonna spend the rest of our lives together."

"Did you confiscate some hallucinogenic drugs today from a student? Do you even know what you're sayin'?"

"I sure do. I'm saying I'm gonna marry you so you might as well hurry up and forgive me so we can move on to the good stuff."

"You've lost your damn mind. I just got cats. Cats, Bowie! I've committed to the cat lady lifestyle and now you come runnin' and expect me to marry you? You are the damnedest man on the planet!"

~

"Did y'all see that bouquet Bowie Bodine bought for Cassidy Tucker? It's about damn time!"

"I had a feelin' puttin' them in that newspaper poll would stir things up!"

"Did y'all see her throw him out of her house?"

"And the smile on his face? That girl just waved a red flag in front of a bull. He's a Bodine. You can't tell them not to do something."

"They'll be married by spring."

31

CASSIDY

The station smelled like bad coffee and good pastries when I entered the next morning.

"Your boyfriend is my favorite person right now," Bubba announced, cheerfully wiping crumbs off his uniform shirt and tie.

"Boyfriend? I don't have a boyfriend." I was still in a mood from the Bowie-Dad situation. Also, the Bowie kissing the crap out of me situation.

"Your beau then," Fanny Sue said, handing me a paper plate with an assortment of delicate pastries on it. "He's the best thing to happen to us all year."

Confused, I took the plate. "What the hell are y'all talking about?" I demanded.

"Bowie brought us goodies. And he left this for you," Bex announced, handing over an envelope and giving me an expectant smirk.

"Your eyebrow gets any higher and that ring is gonna get stuck in your hair," I warned her with a grumble.

I took the envelope and the pastries over to my desk making a show of being here to work. Booting up my computer, I pointedly ignored the card.

"I don't think she's gonna open it," Bubba hissed.

"She'll open it," Bex predicted, unconcerned with the fact that I could hear them.

The station's front door opened, and my father strolled in. He shed his winter coat and his hat on the rack next to the bookcase that held all of our public safety brochures.

"Mornin'." He said it to everyone but looked directly at me. I was far too engrossed in staring at my login screen to pay him any mind.

Everyone else called out their greetings. Out of the corner of my eye, I watched Dad's shoulders slump and I staved off the guilt. He'd earned my wrath. He deserved to know that I was unhappy with him.

"What's all this?" Connelly asked appearing at Bubba's desk, eyeing up the pastries.

Oh, hell. The last thing I needed was Mr. Where's Your Loyalty knowing a Bodine was trying to get into my pants.

"Cassidy's bein' courted," Fanny Sue explained. "Isn't it romantic?" I shot her a death glare telegraphing the fact that she should shut her trap immediately.

Connelly took another look at the spread and rolled his eyes. He muttered something that sounded an awful lot like "hillbillies" before heading on into the conference room.

Bex snickered when the door slammed behind him. "Maybe if he were a better investigator he could solve this case and get out of this hillbilly town," she said before heading back into the property room to answer the ringing phone.

Relief coursed through me, and I flopped back in my chair. "Jesus, Fanny Sue. He can't know about Bowie making an ass of himself. He already thinks I'm too involved with the family," I told her.

Fanny Sue snorted indignantly. "What the hell are you

supposed to do? Stay away from everyone in town who's ever committed a crime or been related to someone suspected of committing a crime?"

The idiocy of it didn't make my job more secure. I was determined to ignore the card that was burning a hot hole in my consciousness. I made it a whole six more minutes before I quietly ripped open the envelope.

It was a card with a glittery red heart on it.

Cassidy,

You've had my heart for longer than you know. Say yes.

Yours always,

Bowie

Say yes? Yes to what? Forgiving him? Dating him? Getting naked with him? Marrying him? Or all of it?

The station door opened and one of the baristas from Yee Haw Yarn and Coffee strolled in, yanking earbuds out of her ears.

"Got a delivery for y'all," she announced, hefting a tray of to-go coffees.

"Woo wee!" Fanny Sue was a sucker for Yee Haw's coffee. It beat the station sludge hands down.

"It's from Bowie Bodine," the barista announced shimmying her shoulders. "He wanted to make sure his girl *Cassidy* got the good stuff today." She cracked her gum and wiggled her eyebrows.

I whipped my head around to make sure the conference room door was still shut tight.

"Keep the Bowie part zipped around Mr. Sunshine," Fanny Sue advised, jerking a thumb toward the conference room. "It's on the down low."

"More like low down," I muttered.

"What was that you were saying about not having a boyfriend?" Bex asked wickedly, reaching for a cup of coffee.

"Shut. Up. We're not dating. In fact, he's the last man on the planet I'd date."

"You've got red glitter all over your face," Fanny Sue pointed out.

"I told you she'd open the card," Bex said.

"I hate you all," I said. I still took one of the cups of coffee. But only because it would be a sin to dump Yee Haw coffee down the drain. And I had those pastries on my desk. Ill-gotten pastries, of course. I should throw them in the trash. Or better yet, save them until tonight and then go next door and smash them in Bowie's face.

But he'd just try and kiss me again, and my body would do that thing where it wouldn't stop him because it was too busy trying to get naked.

Damn it. I needed back-up.

~

"THANKS FOR MEETING ME, JUNEY," I said, sliding into the booth across from her at Moonshine.

"Why do they keep changing the specials?" June asked, staring at her menu. "I like having the open-faced turkey on Tuesdays. Turkey Tuesdays. Now, it's a meatball sub."

"You like meatball subs," I pointed out.

"On Saturday nights. Not on Turkey Tuesdays."

"Why would it taste any different on a Tuesday?" I asked, not necessarily wanting the June version.

"I have my dietary needs carefully mapped out throughout the week to optimize my nutritional intake. I'm getting my period Sunday so I need red meat on Saturday to increase my iron levels."

I was already sorry I had asked. "Get the turkey then."

"It's not on special," June argued.

"Juney, you make more money than half the people in this town combined. Spend the extra two bucks and quit complaining." June was an actuary, and though none of us knew exactly what that meant, I knew that she worked with numbers and made a lot of money. My sister had always had a brain for numbers. Her investment portfolio made her the Bootleg Springs version of Richard Branson. She had a finger in just about everything.

"I'm not *com*plaining. I'm *ex*plaining. You asked. I answered."

I was beginning to think I'd made a big mistake coming to June for advice on my love life.

"Hey, y'all." Leah Mae looking fashionable in an oversized pumpkin-colored sweater and leggings chirped. "Mind if I join you?"

"Sure," I said, sliding in so she could take a seat.

June folded her menu neatly and slid it to the edge of the booth. "I spoke to the landlord yesterday. She came down another hundred dollars on the rent," she told Leah Mae.

"That's great! When do we sign?" Leah Mae asked.

"I'm holding out for another hundred. Cheaper rent gives you more breathing room on your profit and loss," June said.

June was partnering with Leah Mae on her clothing boutique. Leah Mae was bringing the creativity and the products. June was bringing the cash and the negotiating skills.

Leah Mae blew out a nervous breath. "Do you think she'll drop it again? I think I can swing the rent as is."

"We'll hold out," June said firmly.

"No one knows business in this town better than June," I promised Leah Mae. "You'll get your cheaper rent and be open before you know it."

She chewed on her lip. "Okay. Okay. Ooh. Meatball sub!"

"Ugh," June grumbled.

"Don't you like meatball subs?" Leah Mae asked.

"Don't get her started," I begged. "Let's talk about something else."

"How about the fact that you're dating Bowie Bodine?" Leah Mae suggested, brightening.

"Let's go back to the meatball sub," I suggested.

"You and Bowie?" June asked.

"We're not dating. We had a moment and now I'm furious with him and never forgiving him," I explained lamely.

"I'd like to hear about this moment," Leah Mae prodded.

"I'd like to hear solutions on how to get rid of a man that I don't want to date."

"I'd like to know why there aren't any turkey sandwiches on special today," June muttered.

"You look stressed," Leah Mae said to me.

"I feel like I'm five seconds away from losing my damn mind," I confessed.

"You know what you need?" Leah Mae asked.

"A turkey sandwich?" June suggested.

I picked up my menu and smacked June on the head with it.

"Girls Night Out," Leah Mae said.

32

CASSIDY

I was absolutely crazy for being here, I decided, easing down the drive to the rambling, cedar-shingled house on the lake's edge. Yes siree. I'd done gone and lost all my marbles. I was mad at my dad, pissed off at Bowie, annoyed with my sister, and the only thing I could control was work.

I'd been on patrol, cruising through Bootleg, hoping that I could get some air and settle my thoughts. And get away from those damn pastries.

When I'd swung down Speakeasy Drive to look in on some of the bigger lake estates and spotted a car in the Kendalls' driveway, I'd pulled right on in.

The Kendalls were here. And I had questions.

When Callie disappeared, I'd been a kid. When Scarlett found the sweater, Detective Connelly had been pulled in quick, fast, and in a hurry. So I'd never actually had a professional conversation with the Kendalls about their daughter.

Sure, I'd seen them around town. Made small talk here and there. They were fixtures here during the summer, a couple of weekends in the spring and fall. They even did

Christmas here every other year. Everyone always looked forward to the tree they'd put up in the second-floor window. All silver and tinseled.

The house was wood and stone with graying cedar shingles and multi-level decks off the back, taking advantage of the lakefront view. I'd never been inside. I wondered if any of Callie's friends had. She'd never brought anyone to Bootleg with her for the summer. It was always just the three Kendalls.

And now it was only two.

I had a feeling Connelly wouldn't take kindly to my pitstop, but odds were I wouldn't dig up anything of interest. What harm could it do?

I pressed the doorbell, heard it echo inside.

I waited long enough to start to second and third guess myself before the door opened. "Oh. I'm sorry. I wasn't expecting anyone, Deputy..." Mrs. Kendall glanced down at my name tag. Her hair, a soft, silvery blonde, was pulled back in a sleek bun, and she was wearing black slacks and a black cowlneck sweater. She was barefoot.

"Tucker," I supplied. "Cassidy Tucker."

"Do you have...news?" she asked, reaching up to touch the gold cross she wore around her neck.

"Oh, no, ma'am. I had a few questions, if you've got a minute?"

"Certainly. Of course. Please come in," she said, standing back from the door. "Can I get you some coffee or tea?"

"No thank you, Mrs. Kendall. I'll be out of your hair in a minute."

Mrs. Kendall led the way inside to a sunken living room with tall windows overlooking the lake. There was a two-story stone fireplace that divided the living space from the kitchen. An eclectic collection of art adorned the wood-paneled walls. It was a little outdated and a lot ornate. Kind of like Frank

Lloyd Wright on a lake vacation with Rich Grandma's heavy furniture and brocade sofas. No family photos, no throw pillows, no homey touches.

But Mrs. Kendall was barefoot, so it must be home.

"My husband isn't here. Is this something I can help you with or would you prefer to wait for him?" Mrs. Kendall asked, perching on the edge of a green settee.

I took a seat on a silk covered couch across from her and took the plunge. "I was reviewing the original case files of the disappearance and wondered if you could tell me about Callie hurting herself."

The woman across from me sucked in a tiny breath, and I wondered just how much pain she'd endured over the years. Would it ever end?

She knotted her hands in her lap. "I must say, I'm relieved that law enforcement is finally taking this seriously. You must understand, deputy, Callie's father and I never believed there was any foul play. This fiasco with the Bodines is unnecessarily dragging another family into our pain. Callie was sick. Callie hurt herself." The words burst forth like water over a dam.

Outwardly, I stayed calm. But on the inside, excitement bubbled. *She knew something.* "How did she hurt herself?"

"They call it cutting. She'd take knives or other sharp objects and slice at her wrists. Long shallow cuts," Mrs. Kendall said. She was looking out the window with a faraway gaze. "I failed her. As a mother, I failed my child. Nothing I did helped her, fixed her."

"Was she ever hospitalized?" I pressed. Were there medical records we didn't know about?

Mrs. Kendall shook her head. "Callie and my husband, well, neither of them wanted the attention. We arranged for her to see a private therapist. He prescribed medications, but she often went off of them. She was fine for weeks and months at a time. Such a lovely girl. Sweet and pretty. But then the cloud would come again. She'd lose interest in school and friends. She wouldn't eat or get out of bed."

"What did her therapist say?"

"I'm sure you have all of his files on Callie," Mrs. Kendall said flatly, still staring through the windows at the winter scene. Bare branches, icy gray skies. "He felt she was depressed, unstable. She had such a happy childhood, but once she hit her teen years the happiness never lasted. I learned to treasure those times when things were good for her, for all of us."

"Mrs. Kendall, I'm sorry to ask this. But do you have any proof that Callie was cutting herself? Since there aren't any medical records maybe there's something else?"

Her jaw trembled. "There may be something," she said, finally.

I waited. There were times to push and times for space.

"No one's ever asked me for proof before," she said quietly. "All they've done is run rampant with ridiculous murder or runaway theories. No one is interested in the truth."

I'd long wondered how insulated the Kendalls had been from the conspiracy theories that were still part of daily conversation in Bootleg.

"I don't know why I took the pictures," she said, rising gracefully from the settee. "I don't know what made me do it. Maybe I wanted to show them to Callie when she was better. To remind her that there weren't any answers in the dark, that she needed to fight whatever monsters plagued her."

"What pictures, Mrs. Kendall?" I was feeling the buzz in my blood again.

She crossed to the wall of built-ins near the windows.

"I know my daughter did this to herself. I know in my

heart of hearts that she hurt herself one last time. I knew it when she didn't come home by curfew. No one believed me. Until you." She gave me a long look before leaning over and unlocking a file cabinet.

She pulled out a file. "Maybe they'll listen to you."

My hands wanted to tremble when I reached for the folder. There were answers inside. And with those answers, probably more questions.

I opened the file, and now my hands shook. I recognized the arms in the photos. Callie, the girl I knew, had thin arms and long, slim fingers. There was the sterling silver thumb ring she'd always worn. I stared at the pretty, familiar fingers before letting my eyes take in the gore.

Those lovely arms were stretched palm up on what looked like this house's kitchen counter.

Blood seeped from angry cuts from wrist to elbow. It ran red and pooled on the countertop beneath. Vicious, shallow, mean slices carving through lovely skin. There were scars, some white and some pink, up and down the inside of the arms.

"That's what she'd do to herself. She said this kind of pain was better than what she felt in her head and heart. Once, she went too deep and I didn't think I'd be able to stop the bleeding." Mrs. Kendall's voice broke.

I closed the folder.

"Why didn't you ever show these to investigators?" I asked her.

She raised her blue eyes to mine. Calm. Determined. Unwavering. "Because no one believed us. A murder was more salacious, more interesting. If they were going to waste their time searching for a murderer that didn't exist, it was their own fault. I've talked to so many detectives and investigators over the years. Not one of them believes what I know. My daughter is dead, deputy. She did it to herself."

Again, she laid a hand over the cross. Her eyes remained cool, but the fingers that touched the necklace trembled.

"And I'm relieved," she confessed.

I blinked.

"I know it's terrible. I'm a horrible mother. But I couldn't take her suffering like that. There was no hope for her. Because I would have found it. I did everything I could. Her father and I watched her like a hawk, locked up the knives, checked on her every hour throughout the night. It still wasn't enough. She still suffered. Until she finally stopped. My daughter is dead, deputy. And I won't let her ruin another family over it. Please, take the photos."

33

CASSIDY

"Dad." I burst into his office without knocking and came up short when I realized Detective Connelly was making himself at home in my dad's visitor chair. It was an hour past the end of my shift. I was supposed to be getting ready for Girls Night Out.

But I had Callie Kendall's photos.

"Excuse me for interrupting," I said, trying to decide if the photos burning a hole in that file were worth me demanding they give me some time right now. It didn't prove anything definitively, but it gave weight to the ignored suicide theory.

"Do you need something, deputy?" Connelly asked coolly.

What the hell. I'd done my investigative duty and turned up something that no one else had in twelve years. "I have some new information on the Kendall case," I said.

"You?" Connelly asked. "Did your boyfriend confess?"

I wanted to kick his chair out from under him and watch that smug expression fall off his face. "No, sir," I said crisply. "I spoke to Mrs. Kendall and she provided me with photographic evidence that Callie was harming herself." To be a bit of an asshole, I handed the folder over to my father instead of Connelly.

My father stared at the photos, his face impassive. But his mustache twitched. He slid the folder across the desk, and Connelly gave it a cursory glance.

"Deputy, why were you talking to the victim's mother?" Connelly asked. There was an edge in his voice. But I hadn't done anything wrong. I was an officer of the law involved in an investigation. I'd investigated.

"I saw a vehicle in the driveway when I was doing my patrol and had a couple of questions."

Connelly closed the folder and set it on the edge of my father's desk.

"It's not your job to have questions. Not unless I tell you you're allowed to have them. Your job is to support me and my investigation."

"That's what I was doing, sir." If my jaw got any tighter I was going to crack a few teeth.

Connelly rose from his chair and gave me that icy stare. "I don't give a shit how things were done around here before me. What you two need to grasp is there is an ongoing murder investigation that requires a certain level of professionalism."

"Disappearance, sir." I probably shouldn't have corrected him. But he was already in my space talking down to me, so what the hell. Which one of us wasn't professional now?

"Excuse me?"

"We don't know for sure that Callie Kendall was murdered and those photographs, if they can be verified, cast more doubt on that theory."

Connelly clearly didn't like to be educated. His face turned a mottled red, and a vein throbbed in his neck.

"You know what I think, deputy?"

"No, sir." *But I'm sure your rat face is all excited to tell me.*

"I think that you know your boyfriend's family was involved. I think you know that maybe it wasn't just the father who had something to do with it. And I think that you're doing your damnedest to protect them."

"Are you accusing me of impeding an investigation, sir?" And the Bodines of conspiring to murder a teenage girl? I may be good and pissed at Bowie Bodine but nobody, *nobody* could call his character into question. The damn fool got in trouble for being too good, too careful.

"I'm accusing you of not having an impartial bone in your body. I can't trust you. And if I can't trust you, I don't want you to be part of this team."

My nostrils were flaring, and I think I felt a filling give way.

My father cleared his throat. "Detective, I think you need to remember that this is a very small town. My officers know the people we serve. It's impossible to exist in a vacuum here," he said. He looked calm. But the way his mustache was twitching to the left meant he had a full head of steam worked up.

"I don't care if this is Bumfuck, West Virginia, we have a job to do. Find out what happened to Callie Kendall."

"And that's exactly what Deputy Tucker was doing," Dad said, his voice deceptively calm.

"I don't trust your daughter's judgment," Connelly said, glaring at me. "She's too busy playing house with the son of a suspect. Perhaps even an accomplice."

"Every one of them Bodine boys was alibied solid." Technically that was a lie. All of the Bodine boys except Gibson had an alibi. Gibson's alibi for the night was that he'd had pizza delivered to his apartment around 9 p.m. and his siblings showed up around midnight. I knew the case files inside out.

"Fact is, so was Jonah Bodine," my dad continued. "You

may not like how we do business here in Bootleg. But we know our town, our people."

Connelly glared back and forth between us. "I don't want her anywhere near this investigation. Deputy, from now on, your contribution will be to scan files, fax memos, and get me coffee." He stormed out, pushing his chair out of the way with enough force that it tipped over backward.

I watched him go and squashed the need to flip him the bird.

"You did good, kid," Dad said gruffly.

"Good? I just got demoted."

"Those pictures are the biggest find in this case since the sweater. You found them, not Connelly."

"So he's throwing a temper tantrum and taking my job away from me? What is his damn problem?" I was getting more and more worked up by the second. I wasn't sure if I'd be able to control myself. There was only so much I could take before I boiled over or imploded like a still.

"Let it sit a spell. Things will calm down," my father said confidently.

"I'm supposed to play personal assistant? That's not what I went to school for. That's not why I'm here. Why don't I just resign right now?"

Dad sighed. "Cassidy. I need you here. We need you here. Don't let some outsider with a God complex chase you off."

I kicked at the overturned chair with the toe of my boot before righting it and pushing it back into place.

My father sat back down behind his desk. "You did the right thing. He's holdin' up a mirror right now. Connelly came in here already convinced that Jonah Bodine was guilty. He's the one who's having trouble with impartiality. Not you."

"Yeah, well he's the one in the position of power and I'm the one at the bottom of the totem pole."

"Hang in there," Dad advised. "He's tryin' to scare you off. Be professional. Do your duties. It'll drive him nuts."

I puffed out a breath and nodded. "Fine."

"What's the order of your Top Three right now?" Dad asked.

"Top Three?"

"Which one of us are you most mad at?"

"It's a three-way tie at this point."

34

BOWIE

"You're trying too hard," Jonah observed as I scrolled through another page on the website. He was steaming broccoli while I searched for exactly the right set of pajamas.

"Cassidy loves these things," I said, remembering the matching Strawberry Shortcake pajamas Nadine Tucker had given Cassidy and Scarlett for Christmas one year. Every time Cassidy slept over, she had on a different set of pajamas.

I imagined a cozy pair of pajamas would be a smart start to worming my way back into her good graces. I could see her lounging around in soft purple thermals while we curled up on the couch to watch one of those eighties movies she was obsessed with.

I was in this for the long haul. Cassidy Tucker was meant for me, and I wasn't letting her slip away a second time.

"She didn't seem to be wearing any pajamas the other night," Jonah noted.

"Don't make me drown you in boiling broccoli water," I said mildly.

He grinned, checking the chicken breasts roasting in the oven.

Having Jonah as a roommate was all right in my book. He did most of the cooking, slapped baked goods out of my hand, and was, in general, the easiest Bodine brother to talk to.

"How are things going for you?" I asked him, adding a red satin short and cami set to my shopping cart.

He shut the oven door with his hip and reached for his water bottle. "Good," he said with a roll of his shoulders. "Business is pretty steady for the off-season." He'd started some group exercise classes during the week that had a huge and primarily female following. But Jonah didn't seem to notice the adoring attention.

"How about everything else? It's gotta be weird to share not just DNA but a name with our dad."

It was the vice principal in me, checking in, testing the waters.

"Everything's weird as far as I'm concerned. I try not to worry about it much," he said.

"I noticed reporters are trickling back into town," I said. "Any of them giving you any trouble?"

"They're a bit more respectful than the last bunch."

The school was only fielding about six or seven calls a day from journalists looking for a story. There hadn't been any more newsworthy breaks in the case since the sweater, and interest seemed to be tapering off.

Jonah looked like he wanted to say something else.

"What?" I asked.

"What was he like? Your father. To you, I mean. Scarlett's told me some. Jameson, too. But it seems like you all had different relationships."

"First of all, it's y'all."

"I'm not an official Bootlegger yet. I don't think I can appropriate your language."

"You're kin," I said in my thickest West Virginia drawl. "Round these parts you can y'all anyone and anything y'all want to."

He chuckled, knowing full well I was stalling. He pulled two beers out of the fridge and popped the tops. I accepted the one he offered.

"I had a complicated relationship with my dad," I told him.

Jonah waited while I took a long pull on the beer and collected my thoughts.

"He wasn't as hard on me as he was Gibs. But he didn't love me like he loved Scarlett. We had a bond, a tenuous one, around baseball. He played in high school and so did I. In fact, I think the only reason I played was because he liked that I played." I hadn't really thought it out like that before. The other reason I'd kept coming back to the diamond was the fact that Sheriff Tucker was the coach.

I waited for the sharp edge of shame that always poked out when I thought about Sheriff Tucker and realized that I didn't have to feel it anymore. That I'd never needed to feel it. He'd never thought I wasn't good enough.

"What's happening? You look like you're having some epiphany right now."

"Since when are personal trainers the new bartender therapist?" I shot back.

Jonah slung a dish towel over his shoulder and crossed his arms.

"We won the state championships my senior year," I told him, getting back on track. "Dad was over the moon. He'd been a star on his team in his time, but like his music, he never got the chance to reach for any dreams. Mom got pregnant. They got married. He got a job."

"Did he want you to make a career out of it?"

I shook my head. "It was more like he thought baseball should be my ticket out of here. Gibs never went to college. So Dad set his sights on me to live out the dreams he never got to."

"Did you?"

"I played ball until my junior year. Got hurt. And never went back. Dad didn't think a degree in school administration was nearly as interesting as a baseball career. He wanted adventure for us that he never got, I guess." And all I'd wanted was a happy home. A place to plant roots. A real family, not just one held together by blood and scotch tape.

"Was he always a drinker?" Jonah asked.

I shook my head. "No. Mostly he was pissed off at the world in general. I remember him being grumpy all through my childhood. The drinking really ramped up in my late teens." I thought back to those days. "Mom died in a car accident. Took us all by surprise. I think as much as he was unhappy in that relationship they really did have a bond."

Jonah picked up the pot and dumped the steaming contents into a colander in the sink. "What was your mom like?"

"She was...different. She made an effort with all of us. But you could tell that her heart wasn't in it some days. She blew hot and cold. None of us ever knew which Mom we were coming home to. When she was happy we were all happy. We'd roast hot dogs over the fire outside and make a party of it. But when she was down, it was like there was a cloud over this house. She loved us. But she wasn't capable of any kind of consistency. It was like her highs burned her out until we started to dread them as much as the lows. What about your mom?"

"She's great," Jonah said with a small smile. "Toughest woman I know. But not like hard, you know?"

"Yeah."

"She raised me single-handedly. Made sure I brushed my teeth and could throw a ball and do laundry. She always tells me she was training me for a nice girl someday."

"You haven't been datin' much," I pointed out.

"I don't think someday is right now. Not when I share the name of a man under investigation for murder and I'm only starting to get to know the half-siblings I didn't know I had. Do you think he did it?"

I looked up from the screen.

"Kill Callie?"

He nodded.

"I think it's unlikely. I don't know how that sweater got there. Our father was no angel. But he never lifted a hand to any of us. If he had anything to do with it, it wasn't murder. And if it was an accident, like a hit-and-run, I don't think he'd be able to cover his tracks."

"Good to know," Jonah said, pulling plates out of the cabinet.

I didn't know if he liked the pieces he was getting of our father or if he was relieved the man had never been in his life.

"So what should the gift receipt say?" I asked, changing the subject. "For our own sleepover?"

Jonah winced. "Too creepy."

"Yeah, definitely creepy."

"How about *'For sweet dreams on winter nights.'*?"

"Much better," I agreed.

Jonah looked up at the flash of headlights through the back window. "Looks like the object of your affections is home."

I hit the Order button and hustled out onto the back porch.

"Evenin', Cass," I called to her as she stalked up the porch steps.

"I'm not talking to you," she told me with a fierce frown.

"That's all right. I'll just talk to you. You look real pretty tonight." She was still in her uniform, her hair pulled back in that tight bun that always made me want to loosen it and let it spill down into my hands.

She reached for her door and then paused, rounding on me. We were separated by that slim strip of railing that I was going to take down one of these days. No more barriers. Nothing keeping us apart.

"I don't appreciate you insinuating yourself and playing Courtin' Fairy all over my job." She stabbed a finger into my chest, and I relished the physical contact.

I grabbed her hand and brought it to my lips.

"Honey, I'm gonna be insinuating myself all over your life," I promised.

"I have never wanted to slap someone so hard in my entire life," she hissed. There was fire under the iciness in her eyes. That's what I loved about her. You always knew where you stood with Cassidy Tucker. She didn't play games, didn't hide behind the silent treatment, didn't go out of her way to throw a temper tantrum. She told you exactly what she felt.

"Try it," I teased her. "I'd have to defend myself by wrestling you to the ground and kissing you until you can't breathe."

Her breath hitched, and I saw that spark of desire fire to life in her eyes. "You're lucky I have plans tonight or I'd be seriously thinkin' about kickin' your ass," she told me.

"Plans?" If she had a date, I would ruin it. I'd stood on the sidelines long enough. I would answer her front door buck naked if it meant chasing off a man who mistakenly thought he belonged in my spot next to her.

"Girls night out so I can complain about how much I. Do. Not. Like. You," Cassidy snipped.

"You could have told me it was a date. Tortured me with it."

"I've dated with your knowledge before," she pointed out, eyes narrowed.

I reached out, knowing that I was pressing my not-getting-slapped luck, and pulled her a step closer. "That was before I made my intentions crystal clear."

"Your intentions?"

"You're it for me, Cass. You can waste time being mad, but that doesn't change the fact that I have every intention of living happily ever after with you."

"You can't just suddenly decide to get married because my dad says it's okay! You should have fought for me."

"I should have," I agreed. "And I'm willing to spend the next eight years wearing you down to make up for the time we lost."

35

CASSIDY

"Men are stupid stupid faces!" I slurred, raising my glass.

"The stupidest," Scarlett obliged. "No offense, babe." Devlin was our designated driver.

"None taken," he promised, elegant and gorgeous in navy slacks and a cashmere sweater with tiny threads loose around the cuffs. Kitten Jedidiah, named for Scarlett's moonshine-making bootlegging great-grandad, was hellbent on destroying everything the happy couple owned.

"Would you like to talk about it?" Devlin offered.

I certainly would. I launched into my sixteenth explanation of exactly why Bowie made me so damn mad, except this time I couldn't quite remember the specifics. Thankfully, I had enough wits about me not to bring up the clusterfuck with Connelly at work. And the pictures. I shuddered. I couldn't stop thinking about the pictures. There was something so... dark about them.

I knew the Bodines would want to know about the pictures. But I didn't want them to get their hopes up. With Connelly running the show someone could produce a notarized suicide note from Callie and he'd still try for an arrest warrant on a Bodine.

So instead of talking about it, I drank.

We'd started at The Lookout and then made our way to a bar called The Still farther west. It was easier to get shit-faced in a place where you wouldn't be as likely to have to arrest someone in a week.

The Still was a little shabbier than The Lookout. The floors were stickier, the darts were sharper, but the drinks were poured with heavier hands. Drunk was I. But not too far gone to forget to hydrate regularly and stuff fried food down on top of the liquor.

"June Bug, come take a selfie," my mom screeched. Nadine Tucker didn't let her hair down often, but when she did, she could rival Scarlett in party antics. I'd spilled my guts to her this afternoon about the Dad and Bowie situation, and in solidarity she'd left my father home with a frozen TV dinner.

June, mourning the career-ending injury of her fantasy football receiver and the lack of a Turkey Tuesday, came along to mope alongside me. Leah Mae and Scarlett were the only chipper ones in the group. But their good moods buoyed mine enough to keep me from thinking too hard about Connelly.

"Lula!" Scarlett shouted over the country twang of the band on the stage. The band was horrible, but the drinks were cheap, and that's how I was blitzed out of my gourd before 9 p.m.

I swiveled on my stool and slid right off. Devlin, kind gentleman that he was, helped me back up. "Luuuuuu-laaaaaa," I crooned. "You're so pretty!"

Lula was a massage therapist who ran the Bootleg Springs Spa. She was annoyingly beautiful with her flawless dark skin and fabulous thick hair. She was wearing a plaid shirt knotted above the top of her probably size four jeans.

I magnanimously chose not to hold that against her.

"I'm here to get the dirt on you and Bowie," she told me.

"Bowie is a stupid face and you need a drink to hear why," I insisted.

I leaned over the bar and shouted "Yoo-hoo" at the bartender. He shot Devlin a "control your ladies" look, and Devlin gave an amicable shrug.

"Hey! Stop that," I said, poking him in his arm.

Devlin looked at me. "Stop what?"

"Stop the tele-path-ic male communication," I told him being careful to enunciate each word so no one would realize how drunk I was. Deserving of an Emmy, that's how good my performance as a sober woman was.

He grinned at me, and I wondered if Scarlett lived her life in constant mid-swoon. He was terribly good-looking. Selflessly, I decided not to hold it against him.

Lula ordered a vodka tonic and took the stool next to mine. "Spill, sister," she ordered.

I was too happy to comply. "So, a hundred years ago, my dad told Bowie to leave me alone because I was too young to get tangled up in a relationship."

Lula nodded, listening intently. "And?"

"And. He. Did." I drilled a finger into Lula's shoulder with every word. One of my eyes closed so I could focus in on the Lula in the middle.

"Wow," Lula said, sipping her drink. "So who are you more mad at?"

"Bowie!" I spat his name out like it was Brussels sprouts flavored. "Not only did he listen to my father and back off, but as soon as Sheriff Stupid Face announces he only meant to it to be temporary, Bowie Dumb Jerk decides now he can tell me he intends to marry me!"

"Marry you?" Scarlett spun me around so fast I slipped right off the stool again and landed on her.

We got tangled up in legs, bar stool ones and human ones.

"Bowie says he wants to marry you?" Scarlett shouted in my face.

Something cold and wet was working its way through my jeans.

"Did you just pee on me?" I asked her.

"It's your moonshine, dumbass," she told me as Devlin picked her up off of me and set her back on her feet. He helped me to my feet and propped me against the bar as I swayed.

"We're gonna need some coffees, waters, and three more orders of chicken strips," Devlin told the bartender, sliding a hundred dollar bill across the bar.

Leah Mae skipped over to me. "Can I design your wedding dress?" she asked, listing to the right. Leah Mae had only recently moved back to Bootleg so her alcohol tolerance was nowhere near as good as a native Bootlegger.

"I'm not marrying that good-for-nothing sheriff's boy. He chose my father over me! And now that my nosy, interfering father gives him the thumbs-up Bowie acts like it's off to the races."

Lula thought about it, lips pursed. "Cassidy's right. She has the right to be supremely pissed at both of them for at least a week or two."

"Two," I decided firmly.

"To Bootleg justice," my mom said, wiggling into our circle holding her bourbon and Coke aloft. Half of it spilled down her arm, and I felt a little bit bad about how sticky we were going to make the interior of Devlin's SUV.

"To Bootleg justice," we all echoed, clinking glasses and sending an enthusiastic shower of beverages down our arms.

"You're totally going to marry him though, aren't you?" Leah Mae asked. "Because I see you in this fabulous lace dress with little cap sleeves. Cowboy boots. Some flowers in your hair."

While Scarlett, Leah Mae, and Lula began to debate my bridal look, I looked to June for help.

She was frowning at her phone.

"Whatsamatter, Bune Jug? Why the face?" *Did I just say Bune Jug? Good Lord, I needed chicken fingers stat.*

"George Thompson is the reason for my face," she said flatly.

"My cat?" I asked her, closing my other eye to bring her into focus.

"The receiver. The most consistent player in the league. His injury is most likely career-ending."

"I'm very sorry to hear that," I said. I was. I was a good little sister. I cared when my weird sister was upset over weird things. "Did I tell you why I'm upset?" I asked, eager to repeat all the reasons that I wanted to tie Bowie up and stuff him in the trunk of a car and drive it into the lake.

"You've spoken incessantly about it since we got here."

"Do you want to tell me in-chest-antly about George?" I offered.

She gave a mopey shrug. "I could always depend on him for my fantasy team."

"And you feel like he let you down?" I filled in the blanks. Juney came by her shit-tastic communication honestly.

"It's stupid. He's stupid. I'm stupid," June said.

In elementary school, the guidance counselor had pulled my sister out of class to test her to see if she was weirdly gifted or just weird. Her IQ hovered somewhere around 141, putting her in the genius category.

The bartender plopped down a steaming basket of deep-fried chicken in front of me.

"Wanna eat your feelings with me?" I asked, offering her a chicken tender.

"I fail to see how eating trans fats will improve my overall mood."

I snorted. "Honey mustard sauce is a proven mood enhancer."

June narrowed her eyes at the grease-soaked, paper-lined basket. "I'd like to review the evidence for that statement."

"Eat your fat and grease. It's all the evidence you need."

"Well, well, well. If it isn't Bootleg Night Out."

I swiveled around on my stool and came face-to-face with the fried blonde hair and perpetually over-tanned face of Misty Lynn Prosser.

She was flanked by two carbon copies in ripped up, too-tight jeans, with crispy hair and low-cut tank tops.

"It's thirty-one degrees outside," my mother interjected. "Shouldn't you girls be wearing more layers?"

Misty Lynn smirked. "It's a crime to cover all this up." She hefted her giant fake tits with her hands. "Ain't it, girls?"

Sidekick #1 mirrored Misty Lynn's movements with the B cups that were barely concealed behind an I'm Too Sexy tank. Sidekick #2 was too busy drooling over Devlin to play along.

"What brings y'all out?" Misty Lynn asked. "I hear that Bowie Bodine's been paying you a little extra attention."

"Lemme tell you about Bowie Bodine," I began, but Scarlett cut me off.

"Why don't y'all do yourselves a favor and go play Venus fly trap someplace else?" Scarlett hated Misty Lynn and the feeling was very mutual. Misty Lynn had wormed her way into Gibson's bed years ago and then had cheated on him when their mother died. Scarlett had broken her nose over it a few years back, and the bad blood still ran strong.

Especially since Misty Lynn kept trying to wriggle her ass back into Gibson's good graces. When she wasn't busy breaking up marriages or shoplifting the morning after pill.

"I was bein' neighborly," Misty Lynn drawled. She took a cigarette out of her blue leopard clutch. "Maybe I should go be neighborly with Bowie, since y'all are so busy ignoring him."

"I don't think that's wise," Devlin interjected calmly before I could choke on my chicken tender.

"You stay away from my brothers, you gonorrhea-spreadin', no-good shithead!" Scarlett squalled.

"Gonorrhea?" I asked Sidekick #1. "Is that true?"

"I thought it was just crabs," she said.

"Shut up, Belinda," Misty Lynn snapped. "As I was sayin', maybe I'll pop on by Bowie's house and see if he needs some *attention*. Seein' as how Cassidy is too high and mighty to give it to him."

I knew she was saying it to get a rise out of Scarlett. Just as I knew Bowie wouldn't let the woman cross his threshold given the fact that she was such a shitty human being. But despite all this knowledge, the moonshine in my belly overruled my sensibilities.

The noise that drew every eye in the bar was coming out of my mouth as I threw myself off of my stool in Misty Lynn's direction.

36

BOWIE

"Yeah?" I rasped into the phone.

It was after midnight, and I'd been involved in a very detailed dream re-enacting the other night with Cassidy. Only this time it wasn't Jonah interrupting us. It was Devlin.

"Bowie, I could use a favor," Devlin announced crisply in my ear.

"Now?" I asked, staring blearily at the clock.

"It can't really wait."

"'Kay." I came to a seated position.

"I need you to drive over to my place and grab the billfold out of Scarlett's underwear drawer."

"Don't go diggin' around in there!" I heard my sister shout in the background.

"Billfold. Underwear drawer," I repeated, pulling on a pair of jeans from my dresser.

"Then I'm going to need you to drive down here to the police station."

"You've got to be shitting me."

"I assure you. I'm not shitting you. There was a little altercation tonight—"

"I told you. Did I not tell you to watch those girls?" I was wide awake now, grabbing a sweatshirt and sneakers on my way out the bedroom door.

"What the hell's going on?" Jonah demanded from his doorway. "Why does shit always happen in the middle of the night in this house?"

"Girls got arrested," I filled him in.

Jonah perked up. "Lemme grab my shoes. I'll come with you."

"Thanks, Bowie. Appreciate it," Devlin said.

"That's what family's for."

I did the math and told Jonah to drive separately.

DEPUTY BUBBA RAYHILL was pacing the sidewalk in front of the police station when I pulled up. "How's it goin', Bubba?" I called, sliding out from behind the wheel. Jonah hopped out of his vehicle and joined us on the sidewalk.

"Thank god you're here. We gotta get this mess cleared up before Sheriff Tucker gets wind that I had to arrest his wife and daughters," Bubba said, wringing his hands.

"I've got the cash," I said, waving Dev's billfold like a Willy Wonka golden ticket.

"Thank you, sweet Jesus," Bubba said throwing up a prayer to the winter sky.

Jonah and I followed him into the station, and it took all of half a second to know why the man had been waiting on the sidewalk for us.

The noises coming from the holding cell were an unholy cacophony.

"Y'all started it!"

"No, you all started it!"

"Girls, I don't care who started it because I'm gonna end it by dunking all your heads in this toilet." That last one came from Nadine Tucker, who was standing between Cassidy and Misty Lynn. The cell was so crowded that Devlin was pressed up against the bars in the corner, holding Scarlett around the waist as she tried to join the fight.

"If this is how eating my feelings ends, I'm never attempting it again," June grumbled from the cot. Two women I didn't recognize were taking turns wailing and blowing their noses.

Lula looked unruffled, pressed up against the stainless-steel sink mounted to the wall. She was admiring her nails as if she were contemplating a manicure color.

"Ladies…and Devlin," I said.

They all launched themselves at the bars, talking at once and pointing fingers.

Cassidy was flush-faced and was glaring pitchforks at Misty Lynn, who was reaching for me through the steel bars. "Hey there, Bowie. Nice of you to come down and see me," she purred.

"That's it! You keep your hands off of the Bodines, you herped harpy." Cassidy grabbed Misty Lynn by the bleached-blonde hair and pulled.

Devlin waded in as the women rolled around on the cement floor.

"We've been through this, ladies," he said, prying them apart. Unsupervised, my sister climbed up on the cot like it was the ropes of a wrestling ring.

She hurled herself down on top of Misty Lynn, and the fighting began again.

"I'm so gettin' fired for this," Bubba muttered under his

breath as he fumbled with the door keys. "Y'all stop that, right now!"

June scooted over two inches to avoid the hair extension that Scarlett threw in her direction.

Bubba hurried inside and made a grab for Misty Lynn, knowing better than to try to go for Scarlett. She was a biter in close quarters.

I sighed and followed him inside. I wasn't afraid of Scarlett's canines. Not after having grown up with her. Hell, we'd taught her all her fight moves. It made it easier for me to anticipate the elbow she threw at my jaw.

"Chill the fuck out, Scar," I growled at her. Cassidy was trying to kick at Misty Lynn while Devlin picked her up off the ground.

"Trade me," I shouted. We swapped the women we were wrangling, and I got Cassidy cornered up against the cinder block wall. "Hey there, Cass."

She stopped squirming against me and hiccuped. Drunk Cassidy made very few public appearances. It was usually my sister drinking to excess, and Cassidy playing the responsible one. I had to admit, she was one hell of an adorable drunk.

"Hey, yourself," she responded, tilting her head until her ear touched her shoulder.

"Whatcha doin'?" I asked, ignoring the commotion behind us.

"You're really, really good-looking," she announced, her eyes wide.

"Why, thank you."

She frowned at me. "I think I'm forgettin' something."

"What kind of something."

"Something that has to do with you," she said, closing one eye and tilting her head to the other side. She brought her finger up to my nose and poked me probably harder than she meant to. "I like your nose."

"I like all of you, Cass."

She brightened and then her face immediately changed to a fierce frown. "I know what it is! I'm mad at you! Very, very mad." She poked my nose again.

"Why's that?" I asked, grinning at her.

"I don't know, but when I remember, you're gonna be in b-i-g trouble."

"Well, I'm sure I deserve it."

She nodded fiercely. "Yep. You definitely do. So, what are you doin' here?"

"I came to get my girl," I told her.

"Your girl isn't Misty Lynn, is it?" Cassidy demanded. "Because she's a stupid face and a terrible human being."

"You're my girl, Cassidy Ann."

"I am?" She grinned at me like I'd given an entire orphanage Christmas presents.

I nodded. "You sure are."

She frowned again, trying to do some figuring. "Was I always your girl? 'Cause this feels kinda new."

"Oh, Cass," I sighed, stroking a thumb over her lower lip. "Always. You've always been my girl."

"Misty Lynn said she was gonna show up on your doorstep and be neighborly."

"She did now?" Fucking Misty Lynn. Her two main superpowers were seducing stupid men and pissing off anyone with lady parts.

"She didn't show up, did she?" Cassidy asked very seriously.

"No, honey. She didn't. She's trying to kick my sister's teeth out right now."

"Oh! Good! That's really good," Cassidy breathed a sigh of

relief that smelled like blueberry moonshine. I made a mental note to keep her away from open flames for the next hour or two.

"Cass, honey, can you stand right here and not move while I help Jonah and Bubba and Devlin?"

She looked at me like a cartoon deer, all big eyes and sweetness. "I sure can," she promised chipperly. "Question: Do you think you'll kiss me again tonight? 'Cause I really, really like it when you do that. Asking for a friend."

I was definitely enjoying this momentary amnesia. I wanted to bundle her up and take her home and let her pass out on me. "Cassidy, I promise to kiss you every chance I get."

"Yay!"

I propped her against the wall and went to work separating Misty Lynn's henchwomen, who'd started arguing about God knows what. Bubba had scratch marks on his neck. Devlin had tossed Scarlett over his shoulder and was spinning her around until she was too dizzy to fight anymore.

Jonah had cornered Misty Lynn who—enjoying the attention—flashed him her tits.

"Look away, Jonah!" Scarlett screeched. "Look away! She'll hypnotize you with them and then cut your dick off!"

"Fuck you, Scarlett!" Misty Lynn hollered.

"I'd say fuck you, Misty Lynn, but just about everyone in this town has had their turn already," Scarlett shot back.

"What do we do?" Bubba demanded, picking the second henchwoman up off the floor and leaning her against the bars.

"Okay, this here's what we're gonna do," I announced, adopting my best vice principal tone.

37

CASSIDY

There was a goddamn woodpecker trying to peck his way out of my brain. I was face down on flannel sheets, and the contents of my stomach were having a raging debate over whether or not they wanted to come back up.

Wait a minute. Flannel sheets? I hadn't gotten mine out yet. I was still hanging on to the hope of a warm snap with my cotton bedding. I opened one eye.

"Well, shit."

This wasn't my bed or my bedroom.

"Please be Scarlett's," I whispered to myself through cracked lips and a mouth as dry as all the deserts in the world.

"Nope. Guess again," a cheery voice announced.

I opened my other eye, wondered why it hurt, and then focused in on the nightstand. There was a bottle of aspirin, a sports drink, and a plate of dry toast.

"Mornin'." Bowie Bodine, looking fresh as a daisy, was sitting on the foot of the mattress looking at me like he hadn't a care in the world. He was dressed for work and putting on shoes.

A few details from the night before floated up into my consciousness. I was in Bowie's bedroom. "Oh, God."

"Drink your orange electrolytes like a good girl," he told me, patting my ass.

I buried my face in the pillow that I now realized smelled like him.

"Why am I here?" I groaned, not sure if I was asking the existential version of the question or the literal one.

"You insisted on coming in last night when I brought you home."

"Where did you bring me home from?" I asked.

"Jail," he said cheerfully.

"Oh, God. Do I still have a job?" I croaked. I remembered moonshine. A whole vat of it. Me telling Devlin all about my problems. Misty Lynn being downright ugly. It got kinda blurry after that.

"Of course you still have a job. You think I'd let anything happen to you?" he teased.

I lifted my head from the pillow and peered under the sheets. I was fully dressed, but not in my own clothes. I was wearing a Bootleg Springs High School hoodie and a pair of sweats that were a good four sizes too big. Bowie's clothes.

I was in Bowie's bed, wearing his clothes.

"Where did you sleep?" I demanded.

"On the couch."

I flopped back down on the pillow and reached blindly for the aspirin.

"You don't need to look so relieved about it," he teased.

"I'm mad at you," I told him.

"So we're back to that?" He took the aspirin from me, thumbed open the bottle, and dumped the caplets in my hand. Efficiently, he opened the sports drink for me and handed it over.

"*Back* to that? I never stopped being mad at you!"

"Last night you asked me to kiss you again because you really, really like it when I do that."

I was definitely going to throw up. The memory burbled to the surface. Yep. Jail cell. Misty Lynn's hair extensions. Bowie backing me up against a wall and being sweet.

I swore.

He stroked a hand over my hair, and I didn't care for how much I liked it.

"Why am I in your clothes?"

"Well, you came in here after Bubba released y'all and told Jonah to make you pancakes. Then you took your clothes off on the stairs and helped yourself to my closet."

This was why I never let Drunk Cassidy out to play. She was a dumbass.

"You took advantage of me while I was drunk!"

"I did no such thing, Cassidy Ann," he shot back, appalled at the idea.

I rolled my eyes and then felt like I was going to puke. *Note to self: Don't roll eyes while hungover.*

"I mean, you let me be nice to you when I was drunk. Even though I'm clearly still furious with you!"

He crossed his arms and smiled at me like I was making a fool out of myself.

"Are you mad at me or Drunk Cassidy?" he asked.

"Both!"

He laughed.

"What happened last night and how do I still have a job?" I asked, closing my eyes. I pulled the hood of the sweatshirt up over my head, tying the strings real tight to block out the morning light.

"Well, apparently, y'all got into some kind of confrontation with Misty Lynn and her sidekicks. Bartender called the station and Bubba responded. With the help of a patron with a minivan, he drove you all back. He didn't think the sheriff would take kindly to him arresting his wife and two daughters. And as it turns out, Misty Lynn has one more drunk and disorderly left on her rap sheet before she looks at a weekend in jail. So we fixed it so no one got in any official trouble."

"You brokered a truce?"

I vaguely remembered Devlin and Bowie making me shake Misty Lynn's stupid hand that had probably touched sixty percent of the penises in town.

"Dev paid off the bartender to cover the damages and the tabs. No charges were pressed, and y'all went home."

"Except I came here."

"Yep."

"Oh, shit! The cats. I have to feed them." I sat upright and immediately regretted it.

"Taken care of. I fed them this morning and chased them around with that feather on a stick thing."

"Thank you," I whispered, flopping back down into his pillow. I should get up. *Get up and storm out...and thank Jonah for the pancakes that in my foggy memory were pretty fantastic.*

"I'd do anything for you, Cass."

"Anything?"

He perked up expecting me to ask him for something he could give.

"You can just go back to pretending I don't exist," I told him.

"I can't do that," he answered, amused.

"Why don't you give it a try? You might surprise yourself."

He slipped his hand under the hem of the sweatshirt and stroked my back. It felt like heaven. "Honey, you're gonna have to get it through your thick head that I'm not going anywhere. I'm not stopping until you agree to a date."

"One date?" I loosened the hood so I could peek out at him.

"That's all I need to make you fall for me," he said with a wink.

"You're an idiot," I told him.

"I'm your idiot."

"Is it safe to come in?" Jonah asked, covering his eyes in the doorway.

"She's fully clothed," Bowie reported.

"I saw a lot of boobs last night," Jonah told me with a grin. He set down a glass with something purple and lumpy in it.

I groaned, and Bowie punched him half-heartedly in the shoulder.

"Ow!"

"What's this?" I asked, eyeing the glass.

"Hangover cure," Jonah said. "Drink it up as fast as you can and be prepared to feel a hundred times better."

I'd settle for one time better at this point.

"Got yourself a bit of a shiner there," Bowie observed, looking at my ouchy eye as I sat up and started chugging. That dang Misty Lynn and her pointy-ass elbows.

It tasted like seaweed and vinegar. I wanted to stop, but Jonah tipped the bottom of the glass up.

"Now what?" Bowie asked, taking the empty glass from me.

"Now we wait," Jonah said eyeing me.

They didn't have long to wait. "Oh, God." I bolted out of bed and ran for the bathroom.

I didn't even bother slamming the door shut before I was kneeling before the porcelain throne and heaving up a whole mess of stuff.

"Works like a charm every time," Jonah said from the doorway.

I heard water running and felt a wet rag on the back of my neck. My hair was pulled back from my face and held lightly at the base of my neck.

"Get it all out, honey," Bowie's voice was soft. That big hand was at my back again stroking my clammy flesh.

I did as prescribed. And after collapsing on the cool tile floor and laying there for a few minutes with Bowie mopping my forehead and playing with my hair, I did indeed feel better.

I'd yell at him later, go back to mad once I was back on my feet, I decided.

"I have to go to work," I whispered.

"Jonah's getting your care package ready. Ginger ale, coffee, and a breakfast sandwich."

That all sounded pretty damn good.

I worked my way up to a seated position, pleased that my head hadn't snapped right off my neck. With the aide of the vanity and Bowie's helping hands, I made it to my feet.

"I'm gonna go," I announced, walking gingerly toward the door. I made it into the hall and decided to try the door that divided our sides of the double. Bowie's side was unlocked. *Damn it. How was I ever going to sleep again knowing that the door that separated us was unlocked?*

"Oh, hey, Cass?" Bowie called after me.

"Huh?" I grunted.

"Make sure you return the socks to Jonah. They're his."

38

CASSIDY

I arrived at the station five minutes early and very hungover. Thanks to Jonah's magic cure and breakfast care package, I was at least capable of functioning. Though I fully expected to walk in and be asked to leave.

What kind of a police officer could I be if I couldn't even be a law-abiding citizen?

I couldn't believe I'd basically handed Connelly a legitimate reason to fire me. I wanted to blame Bowie or Connelly or someone. But I'd been the one to pour half a gallon of moonshine down my throat last night. I had no one to blame but me.

Bubba refused to meet my gaze when I entered.

"Mornin'," I croaked.

"Mornin'," he said, busying himself by shutting down his desktop.

There was a tall stack of files on my desk. The sticky note on top said Scan. I fought the urge to shove them off my desk and make it rain decades-old police reports. At least it wasn't a friendly "You're Fired" note. I owed Bubba big time.

The conference room was empty this morning. He was

probably off digging up Jonah Bodine's corpse, trying to get a confession out of it.

"Mornin, all," my dad called as he strolled through the front door. "Any trouble last night?"

Bubba glanced my way.

"Not a lick of trouble, sheriff," he said finally.

I didn't know how long Bootleg Springs could hold on to the juicy nugget of the sheriff's wife and two daughters getting hauled downtown along with half of the rest of town for a brawl. But I was grateful for today at least.

Dad looked in my direction, and I looked everywhere but his face. I was okay at lying, but my defenses were down, swamped in hangover stew.

My desk phone rang, and I pounced on it, eager to put off any interaction with my father until much, much later.

"Bootleg Springs PD, Deputy Tucker speaking," I said in my most professional tone.

"Is your father giving you any long, broody looks today?" my mom asked on the other end of the call.

I glanced his way. "Sure is, ma'am."

She blew out a breath. "That sneaky son of a bitch has instincts. I'll give him that. He must have asked me twenty times how last night went. You don't think Bubba told him, do you?" She was talking about two decibels lower than usual. Which meant Nadine Tucker was traveling with me on this delightful hungover journey.

My father wandered into his office, and I slumped back in my chair.

"Bubba didn't say anything to him. Dad's just suspicious and as long as we don't give him anything to verify those suspicions we'll be fine."

"I threw up twice this morning," Mom groaned. "I haven't done that in so long. At least a year."

I snickered and stopped when it hurt my head. "I threw up once. Jonah made me this disgusting hangover cure. I kept it down for about ten seconds."

"That was nice of him to deliver it to you next door," Mom mused. My dad wasn't the only one with finely tuned instincts.

"I was already there. Apparently I decided to stay at Bowie's last night."

"Did you now?" Mom said mildly.

"It doesn't mean anything," I said quickly before she could get any ideas in her head.

"Cassidy Ann, you do know that man is in love with you, don't you?"

"Mom!" I hissed into the phone.

"I'm just tellin' it like it is. The way he looks at you, all soft and sweet. Real deal, my darlin'. What are you gonna do about it?"

I rubbed a hand over my aching head. "I don't know, Mom," I finally admitted. "There was a time when I thought Bowie Bodine hung the stars in the sky. Then I find out all it took was one conversation with Dad to scare him off. I don't want a man that shies away that easily. I want steady. I want a man I know is in my corner. Someone who won't shake."

"He was young and dumb, honey. Sometimes they do grow up."

I thought back to that summer when I realized that my feelings for Bowie would lead to nowhere but heartache. *Had I grown up? Or was I still the same scared girl?*

"How's Juney today?"

"Ugh. Your genius sister is fine. She worked out her protein and electrolyte ratios ahead of time and was up bright and early this morning."

"If I didn't love her so much I'd hate her just a little," I laughed.

"Same here," Nadine agreed. "Well, I'm going to head to the grocery store so I can make your father's second least favorite meal tonight."

"What? Why?"

"If I make him any of his favorites he'll know it's because I feel guilty. In fact, I should probably invite Gram-Gram over too just to make it very clear I have nothing to feel guilty about," her mother mused.

My mother was a plotter, a maneuverer, a strategist. It was slightly terrifying.

"I hope you never have to use your powers against me," I told her.

When she only laughed I felt a nervous tickle in my belly, but I was too dang hungover to pursue the topic any further.

"Well, good luck with Dad tonight. I'm going to go pretend to be a functioning adult."

"Good luck with Bowie," Mom said.

I hung up and opened up a report I'd been planning to finish yesterday. Being a small town, our police reports were a bit more entertaining than other departments. I'd pulled over drunk as a skunk Rhett Ginsler on his lawn mower as he cut a lopsided circle through the wildflower bed at Gin Rickey Park. He was upset over something or someone Misty Lynn had done.

Ugh. Misty Lynn. I hoped she'd be smart enough to keep her mouth shut about last night.

"Package for you, Cass," Bex said, dumping a thick envelope on my desk.

"Bowie?" I asked.

"A teenage messenger. So most likely."

I rolled my eyes. Only in Bootleg would a vice principal send students on personal errands and no one have a problem with it.

Bex looked at me expectantly. "Well, ain't ya gonna open it?"

"I don't need an audience."

"Sheesh. Someone's grumpy today. Also, you smell like liquor is leaking from your pores," Bex said sweetly.

I sniffed at my uniform collar and swore. I should have taken more than a two-minute shower this morning.

Once Bex was back at her desk I ripped into the envelope.

There was a second smaller envelope inside. On the back, scrawled in Bowie's handwriting was: *A night to remember. One date and these photos will never see the light of day.*

I frowned and flipped through the first few photos and snarled. Bowie Bodine was a dead man.

39

BOWIE

I'd been back in my office from the morning pep rally for all of thirty seconds before I was interrupted. The woman storming through my office door under a full head of steam was not the ninth grader that started yesterday's food fight. Cassidy leaned over my desk and tossed the envelope at me. "You are lucky I don't shoot you on the spot," she snapped.

"I'll close this for y'all," Maribel announced shrilly, her eyes wide behind her glasses. *Good luck,* she mouthed to me.

"Cassidy it was just a joke," I told her.

"My *job* is not a joke. Do you even realize how close I am to being asked to resign?"

"Your father would never—"

"Jesus, Bowie. I'm not talking about my dad. I'm talking about Connelly. The man who banned me from any involvement in the Kendall investigation and spelled it out real clear that I'm to steer clear of you and your family, too. I'm already stuck on desk duty scanning a hundred million old case files. Pictures like that get out and he'll boot my ass quicker than two shakes of a sheep's tail!"

I sat up straighter. "Why are you supposed to steer clear of me?"

"Because your father is Connelly's primary suspect. Because I'm supposed to be an objective investigator. And because he's basically a dick."

She was breathing heavy, eyes flashing. It took a lot to rile Cassidy and my little joke—a dozen pictures from my phone and Jonah's from last night—had been the straw that broke her.

"Okay," I said pushing out from behind my desk. "Let's sit and talk this through."

"Don't you use that principal voice on me, Bowie Bodine!"

"Sorry. Force of habit. Sit down. Please. Coffee or water?"

She rubbed her forehead and then flopped down in the chair in front of my desk. "Both."

I dug in my drawer and pulled out a bottle of aspirin and a roll of antacids. I programmed the coffeemaker and handed over my water bottle. I wanted to sit next to her, but she was carrying her service weapon and a taser, so I figured the edge of my desk was safer.

We sat in silence while the coffee sputtered into a mug.

"Connelly realizes that this isn't some big city, doesn't he?" I finally asked, setting the mug in front of her. "Can he honestly expect you to maintain some kind of distance from me? From us? We share a wall, for christ's sake."

"Preachin' to the choir, Bow. But the man has it out for me ever since those reporters started squatting in your driveway. He thinks I can't be impartial and after I talked to Mrs. Kendall and asked her a few questions yesterday, he lost his shit. Now all I'm allowed to do is scan files and pull over Rhett Ginsler when he's gassed up."

"Why didn't you say something, Cass?"

"Why are you acting like we're in a relationship?" she shot

back at me.

"Honey, whether you want to admit it or not, we are. Now, whether that relationship is a friendship or something a hell of a lot more is up to you. You know where I stand. But either way, you can't keep trying to do everything yourself. You can't keep shutting me out, Cass."

She ignored me and picked up the water. She downed the aspirin and chugged a gulp of water.

"I don't know what to do," she said, leaning back in the chair and closing her eyes.

"Let me help you," I told her.

"Bowie, you hurt me," she said, opening her eyes and staring at me. "Really hurt me. Yes, I was only nineteen and yes, you were probably a dumbass, but that doesn't mean that it didn't hurt. I thought we were meant to be and you telling me that you had no feelings for me devastated me."

"I'm so sorry, Cass. I thought I was doing the right thing."

"Now, all these years later, I come to find out that you did have feelings for me but you walked away because my father asked you to. Then he gives his blessing and you're off to the races. It seems to me that your relationship with my father was more important to you than your feelings for me."

I rubbed my palms on my thighs. "It's complicated," I told her.

"Try me. Explain it to me. Tell me how I'm supposed to trust that you aren't going to crush me again because you get scared or you want to do the right thing. You taught me something all those years ago, Bowie. You taught me that I need to take care of myself because I can't count on someone else to do it."

"Your dad was more of a father to me than mine ever was," I said, plucking the picture off of my file cabinet and handing it over. "That picture is in here because of your dad, not mine.

I looked up to him. He was the kind of man I wanted to be. But I didn't know if I could because of who my father was."

She studied the picture carefully, running a finger around the edge of the frame.

"So when your dad asked me to back off, when it sounded to me like he was saying I wasn't good enough for you, for your family..." I scratched the back of my head trying to find the words. "I was devastated, Cass. I wanted so badly to be good enough. To be more than just a no-good Bodine."

"No one ever thought of any of you that way," Cassidy argued. "Except maybe Gibs, but that's because he's so pissy."

"It doesn't matter if they did or didn't. I thought it. Sheriff Tucker telling me to leave his little girl be took the breath right out of me. I'd gotten a degree and a good job. I came back here to make myself an upstanding member of this community in hopes that someday your dad would come to me and tell me that I was finally good enough."

"Dammit, Bowie." She stood up and stepped between my legs, hugging me hard.

"I broke your heart back then and I'm so very sorry, Cassidy. But you weren't the only one who got broken."

She gave a shuddering breath. "I'm sorry you got hurt."

I hugged her back and breathed her in.

This was not my finest moment. When courting a girl, it was always better to impress. Here I was confessing my vulnerabilities and fishing for pity hugs.

"You know he didn't mean that, right?" Cassidy asked, pulling back.

I nodded. "Wish I would have known a long time ago. But do you get how much I looked up to him? He was my coach. He and your mom were there for me every time I needed it. Hell, your parents gave me and my brothers 'the talk' in high school."

"They did not!" Cassidy gasped, drawing back.

I wasn't done holding her. I pulled her back in and stroked her back. "They most certainly did. Your dad bought us all condoms and your mom lectured us on consent. You remember when my dad threw his back out that one winter and times were tight?"

She nodded against my shoulder.

"I'd outgrown my winter coat or probably shredded it doin' something stupid. I was wearing one of my dad's old fleeces. Your dad was waiting for me after school one day and gave me a new ski jacket and gloves."

"The blue one," she said, remembering.

I'd worn that jacket every winter until it fell apart.

"I owe your dad a whole hell of a lot and the only thing he ever asked of me was to leave you alone."

She was silent for a beat. "I'm still mad," she said finally. "At both of you. But maybe a little less mad."

"I'm real sorry about the pictures," I said, stroking a hand up to her neck and down her spine. "I thought it would be funny."

"I really liked the one of me trying to kick Misty Lynn in the face," she admitted.

"Me, too. Think you'll be able to forgive me?" I asked.

Her sigh was long and heavy. "Probably. Just maybe not right this second. I've got a lot of figuring to do, Bowie. I don't want to make another mistake. I'm all mixed up and makin' stupid decisions left and right. It's not just about you. My job means everything to me."

"I know it does, honey. But look what happened when I let someone else get between us."

She pulled back and studied me. "It's not the same thing."

"It is. It's higher stakes now."

40

BOWIE

"Is this even legal?" Devlin asked as we stepped inside the darkened interior of Bootleg Distillery.

It was 11 p.m. on a Sunday night. The distillery was quiet as a church on Monday.

"Almost entirely," I promised, turning on the lights. "Besides, it's tradition."

Jameson propped the back door open with a cinderblock, and Jonah waved Gibson's pickup truck up to the building.

Gibs hopped out and, with a flourish, yanked the tarp off the bed of the truck.

"I really feel like this is illegal," Devlin said, eyeing the six five-gallon glass carboys fitted into a custom wooden divider.

Gibson slapped him on the shoulder. "Relax. We're not the ones distilling it. We provide the mash."

"Great-granddaddy Jedidiah's recipe," Jameson said, picking up the thread of the story and lowering the tailgate.

"Ya see here, gentlemen," I said in my best Southern drawl. "We Bodines mix up Pappy Jedididah's corn mash recipe, deliver it under the cover of night to the distillery, and then

Sonny Fullson's uncle Remus turns it into a big ol' batch of moonshine for Bootleggers to flavor up for the contest."

"What contest?" Jonah asked. Jonah and Devlin were gearing up for their very first Thanksgiving in Bootleg Springs.

Gibson hopped up into the bed of the truck and hefted the first bottle. "Black Friday Moonshine Tasting Contest," he said.

Devlin and Jonah shared a look that very clearly said "What the fuck?".

Jameson took the carboy from Gibson and headed into the distillery.

"We don't have a license to distill," I explained, reaching for the next bottle. "So we deliver the mash by darkness and let the distillery make it up all legal like. Then the contestants buy it, doctor it up, and we have ourselves a midnight tasting contest on Black Friday."

Devlin looked relieved. "And we're not breaking and entering, correct?"

Gibson jingled the keys cheerfully. He was always happiest just skirting the legal side of things.

"We Bodines have a reputation to uphold," I told him solemnly. "Pappy Jedidiah would have a fit if we rolled up in broad daylight and made a legal delivery. We're honoring our heritage."

"And now you're one of us," Gibson said, shoving a five-gallon jug into Devlin's chest.

"Ooof." Devlin stumbled under the weight before recovering.

"Inside with the rest of 'em," Gibs directed.

We unloaded the jugs and lined them up in front of the still, a modern marvel compared to the copper monstrosity Great-grandad Jedidiah had used in his day.

In keeping with tradition, Remus had lined up mugs on the bar for each of us, and I was pleased to see he'd included enough for Devlin and Jonah. That was the thing about Bootleg Springs. You always knew you belonged.

Gibson ducked behind the slab of live edge cherry to play bartender.

"How was Cassidy feeling after Girls Night?" Devlin asked, accepting the crisp lager Gibson poured for him.

I grinned. "Rough around the edges. Jonah here poisoned her with some hangover cure that made her puke her guts up for ten minutes straight."

Jonah flashed us a smile. "Happy to help."

Gibs finished doling out beers and pulled a root beer for himself.

"Did she enjoy the pictures?" Devlin asked.

"No. No, she did not."

"Y'all are movin' in slow motion," Jameson complained.

"Through no fault of my own this time," I argued. "She's more stubborn than Scarlett when she puts her mind to something."

"And she's put her mind to not datin' you?" Gibson asked.

"I'm lucky if she'll say dog to me. Frankly at this point, I don't know if I should wind my ass or scratch my watch. Not only is she pissed at me, that detective is riding herd on her for being tight with us."

"That's bullshit," Jonah argued.

"He took her off the investigation, telling her he can't trust her objectivity."

"I take it Scarlett doesn't know since the detective is still among the living?" Devlin asked.

"Let's go kick his ass," Gibson suggested.

"Been awhile since I punched anyone in the face," Jameson mused.

My brothers were mostly kidding.

"I don't know what to do. If I keep forcing the idea of dating, I'm basically asking her to give up her career for me."

"And why should she trust you to do that?" Jonah filled in.

"Exactly." I nodded into my beer. "I'm torn in two. I don't want to put her in some situation where she might lose her job. But I've already wasted a good long time. If we keep waiting on the right opportunity, it might never come."

"Connelly's not gonna be here forever," Devlin pointed out. "Sooner or later the case will either break or go cold again."

I sat there with that. What would it do to me and Cass if the case broke and Jonah Bodine, Sr. was found responsible for Callie's disappearance? I could feel my brothers thinking along the same lines.

"When are you gettin' Leah Mae a ring?" I asked Jameson, trying to lighten the mood. "Maybe if I got one for Cass she'd finally give me the time of day."

"Christ. Bow. You don't propose to a woman to get her to like you," Gibson pointed out.

"Like you would know, Mr. Nothing More Serious Than a Quick Roll After Closing Time."

Gibson leveled me with a look. "I don't tell you shitheads everything."

We oohed and ahhed him good-naturedly.

"Alls I'm sayin' is there are ways to get a girl to notice you."

"I've tried every other thing under the sun. I've tried gifts. I've tried bein' nice. I bailed her out of jail. Hell, I even tried some friendly blackmail, thinkin' it would at least get a rise out of her. She says she needs time to think about it."

"Sounds like it's time to call in the big guns," Gibson said. My permanently single brother was suddenly the Oprah of relationships.

"Big guns?" Jonah asked cautiously.

"Not like gun guns. Psychological warfare," Jameson explained.

"When is she most vulnerable?" Gibson asked.

A slow grin stretched across my face. "When I'm kissin' her."

"Then keep kissin' her. Every opportunity you get. Reach out and touch her every couple of minutes." Gibson demonstrated by stroking his arm down Devlin's.

"Dating here is very different than where I'm from," Devlin observed, taking a big swallow of beer. "In Annapolis, you ask a woman out, take her to dinner, or an event. Talk about whether you're compatible."

"And that worked so well for you with Johanna," Jonah said dryly.

Johanna was Devlin's ex-wife who'd set her sights on higher aspirations and cheated her way out of their marriage. Scarlett had nearly come to blows with the woman and her string of pearls when she'd strolled into town demanding a second chance.

Devlin gave a shudder. "Okay, your way is definitely better. So how do we get Bowie and Cassidy together without costing her her job?"

"I'm all ears."

Everyone shut up and drank, wheels turning.

"Cass wants to end up like her parents. Meanwhile, I can't think of anything worse than ending up like ours," I said, breaking the silence.

"You ever miss Mom?" Jameson asked quietly.

"Sometimes. Like when the leaves start changing. Remember how much she loved fall? She'd be in a good mood for as long as the leaves were changing."

"Apple cider and hot dogs over the campfire for dinner,"

Gibson said. I didn't know my brother had any good memories of our childhood.

"Remember that time that Dad built the slingshot and we spent a whole weekend chucking pumpkins into the lake?" I asked.

"It wasn't all bad," Jameson said.

"It should have been a hell of a lot better," Gibson said bitterly.

Sensing the turn in the mood, Jonah piped up. "Hey, what if you convinced Cass to secretly date you?"

I frowned. "What?"

"If no one knows you two are seeing each other then she can't get canned for seeing you, can she?" he spelled it out.

"Jonah, you've been here a few months. How in the hell is anyone supposed to keep any secret 'round here?" Jameson asked.

"Think about it, they already practically live together," Jonah argued.

"And if you were hellbent on the dinner and a movie crap you could take her out of town," Gibson added, stroking a hand over his chin.

"Isn't sneaking around kind of high school?" I asked. "And I want more."

"Do you love the girl?" Gibson asked.

I nodded.

"Are you stupid in love with the girl?" he asked.

"Yeah." I was, and it felt damn good to say it.

"Then get her to say yes."

41

CASSIDY

"Heard you pulled the short straw earlier this week," Fanny Sue grinned when I walked into the station.

I rolled my eyes to the heavens. "I swear every time Misty Lynn does somethin' stupid, Rhett Ginsler runs out and tries to top her."

Fanny Sue flipped open the file. "Driving a lawn mower under the influence," she recited from my report. Rumor had it Misty Lynn had been caught making eyes at Freddy Sleeth over a round of beer pong, and Rhett had taken offense. "That's a new one."

"Did you confiscate the mower?" Bex asked, filling her bottle from the water cooler.

"I paid Rhett's 9-year-old nephew to drive it home and park it in the garage."

"Shoulda kept it. We could have put a plow on it and used it for the sidewalks," Fanny Sue quipped.

"Thought about it but it's one of those zero turn ones. No place for a plow."

"Dang it."

"Maybe Rhett should hop back on and do a 180 in the opposite direction of Misty Lynn," Bex suggested.

"Amen to that sister." I raised my coffee cup in her direction.

"Ladies, perhaps if you were less concerned about the reputation of your neighbors and more worried about enforcing the law, maybe you wouldn't have an entire town disrespecting your department." Connelly's voice was ice cold with an extra shot of disapproval.

He was standing in front of the coffee pot, a thick stack of files under one arm. I wondered if he'd make me scan them.

Fanny Sue hitched up her duty belt and gave him a cool stare. "I think we're doing just fine in Bootleg. But thanks for the helpful observation."

Oh, he didn't like that one bit.

"You have a sheriff who's run unopposed in the last four elections who hired his daughter to one of the only full-time deputy positions in the department. And when she's not going easy on townsfolk or cooking up fake fines for visitors to this town, she spends her time gossiping. You tell me if that's 'doin' just fine.'"

Fanny Sue looked like she was about to climb over her desk and give him what for.

Bex looked like she couldn't decide if she wanted Fanny Sue to clock him or bite her tongue. I was praying hard for option number two. Because I wanted the first shot at him.

Deciding he'd spread enough of his douchebaggery, Connelly turned his back on us and walked into the conference room.

I was hot on his heels.

I closed the door firmly behind me, cutting off Bex's quiet "Ohhhhhh, shit."

"If you have a problem with my job performance, I'd

appreciate it if you'd share it privately with me, *sir*." I put some stank on the word sir. I may be young and female and the sheriff's daughter, but that didn't mean I hadn't earned my place in this department.

He sat, crossing his arms and studying me without bothering to disguise his disgust. "You are everything that's wrong with these small-town police departments. You don't deserve to be here. You haven't earned a place here. You're underqualified, inexperienced, and you're more interested in your neighbors' business than whether they're on the wrong side of the law."

"What exactly am I doing wrong in your opinion, sir?" This guy had a beef with me, and I was starting to think it went deeper than the fact that I happened to be in possession of lady parts.

"The only reason you're here is because of your DNA," he snapped. "You're involved with the family of a murder suspect. You cut personal friends breaks and then crack down on unsuspecting visitors because you're riding some small-time, pathetic power trip."

Connelly had no idea how lucky he was that I'd spent years learning to bury my feelings deep. There was something gratifying about remaining icy calm when someone else was losing their shit. Because if I weren't so busy being the supreme goddess of keeping my cool right now, this guy would have my taser contacts attached to his balls.

"I proudly serve this town the best I can. If you have an issue with my performance perhaps you should take it up with my boss."

"You mean, your daddy," Connelly corrected me. "If it were up to you and your daddy I wouldn't even be pursuing Jonah Bodine as a suspect."

"I'm not involved in the investigation," I pointed out. I

wanted to ask him if he'd even talked to the Kendalls about the photos. But I was mad, not stupid. "I wasn't aware that Callie's disappearance was ruled a homicide." Okay. Maybe I was a little stupid. It hadn't officially been ruled a homicide. A bloody sweater wasn't a body or a murder weapon.

Connelly took offense. "Mark my words, deputy. Someone in this town killed that girl and your father let them get away with it. Now, you're here throwing up smoke screens trying to protect the Bodines. If the trail goes cold this time, it's on your head. Not mine."

I leaned over the conference table, putting my fingertips on it. "I don't know where you're from, but around here we like to believe that everyone is innocent until proven guilty and that the sins of the father don't automatically get handed down to the next generation."

He rose from his chair and mirrored my stance. "Think about how old those Bodine boys were when she disappeared. What's to say they didn't know what their father was up to? Or what's to say it wasn't one of them? Any one of them could have come across her on her way home that night. Maybe their father didn't do it. Maybe his alibi was real. Maybe it was one of those boys that decided to have a little fun with a pretty girl. You should think real hard about how well you think you know them. 'Cause to me, the apple usually doesn't fall far from the tree."

The conference room door opened. My dad was dressed in what I thought of as his civilian uniform of jeans and flannel with a ballcap. It was his day off. Through the window, I saw Bex wringing her hands near the water cooler and Fanny Sue pretending to be engrossed in the screen saver on her monitor.

"There a problem?" my father asked, cool as a bucket of ice water.

Connelly shot me a smug look. *Look whose daddy came to bail her out.*

"No, sir," I said.

I gave Connelly a curt nod and walked out of the conference room.

I wanted to punch something. Something like Connelly's face. But I wouldn't give that turd in the punchbowl the satisfaction of seeing me in a temper. Nope. I was cold as the iceberg that sunk the *Titanic*. He'd accused me of being a nepotistic moron incapable of doing her job and insinuated that any one of the Bodines could have made Callie disappear.

What was I supposed to do? Report him to my supervisor? I'd just be proving his point.

The man made it clear. He was going to take great pleasure in ruining my career.

I needed to steer very clear of Bowie.

42

CASSIDY

"Knock knock," I called, elbowing my way through my parents' front door. I was lugging a slow cooker full of creamed corn. All I wanted tonight was some good food and some relaxing time with my family so I could forget about the clusterfuck that was my life.

My father and I had gradually made a tentative peace. In all honesty, I only had so much anger to go around. And right now, Connelly was sucking it all up quicker than I could manufacture it.

"Back here," my mother called from the kitchen.

Every other weekend we gathered around my parent's table for a home-cooked meal and catch up conversation. I wasn't keen on catching anyone up on my current status. I didn't want to tell Mom and June about my problems at work. I sure as hell couldn't tell Dad about the night of debauchery earlier this week that ended with his wife and two daughters behind bars. And there was no way I'd talk to any of them about Bowie. The less I said that man's name, the better. I didn't need any connections between me and him or else Connelly would have my badge.

I would talk about my cats, I decided. Cats were cute. Funny. A safe topic of conversation.

The kitchen smelled like pot roast and horseradish, and my stomach growled in anticipation.

June was frowning down at the carrots she was dicing with surgical precision, and my mother was pouring wine. "Want a glass?" she offered.

My stomach lurched, this week's hangover still fresh in my memory. "No, thanks. I'm still—"

Dad strolled into the kitchen and pressed a kiss to my mom's cheek. "Smells good in here," he said, popping the top on a beer and grabbing the spaghetti squash halves out of the refrigerator. My father's contribution to the dinner table was always something grilled. Burgers. Portobellos. Vegetables.

He was an expert outdoor cooker. But put him in the kitchen and he couldn't work the can opener.

"Y'all want to set the table?" Mom asked, shoving plates at me and utensils at June.

"I'm busy dicing," June said.

"You gave me an extra," I told Mom.

"Hmm?" Mom hummed, looking extra innocent. "Oh, we have another guest coming."

Ugh. I'd been looking forward to family time. You know, burp after the meal, make inappropriate jokes about cutting cheese family time. I couldn't do that around non-family.

In a snit, I doled out the plates around the lace-covered table. It must be some town bigwig to rate an actual tablecloth, I noted. That made me even more mad at the mystery guest. I must have one bad case of the karma the way things were going this week.

The doorbell rang.

"Cass, can you get that?" Mom called.

Reluctantly, I headed to the front door, masking my disappointment with a polite expression. Until I realized who was on the other side.

"What in the hell are you doing here?" I hissed.

Bowie peered at me over an ostentatious bouquet of dahlias—my mother's favorite. "I was invited," he said, stepping across the threshold and dropping a kiss on my cheek as if it were the most normal thing in the word.

I stood there staring at the empty doorway wondering what I'd done in a past life that had been so terrible.

"Bowie!" My mom squealed. "Oh, you shouldn't have."

"Good to see you, son," Dad said, poking his head in from the back deck.

"Why is he here?" June asked, coming up behind me with a stack of cloth napkins.

"Good question."

~

BOWIE WAS HERE to ruin my life. With my parents' blessing.

"I think you're so sweet to give poor Johnny Johnson the responsibility," my traitor mother was cooing. "I mean, that boy just can't catch a break in life."

I pushed a potato around my plate and pretended not to listen.

"Cassidy, don't you think Bowie does a great job at the school?" Mom prodded.

I stabbed the potato with my fork. "Yeah. Great."

"How's the baseball team shapin' up for next season?" my dad asked him.

Bowie swallowed his bite of pot roast. "Real good. Should see the semi-finals," he predicted. "Mrs. Tucker, this roast is delicious."

I made a gagging noise. I couldn't help it. My parents had

set me up. Now, I had to add my mother to the Pissed Off At list. *Was it too much to ask for people to stop pissing me off all the time?*

Bowie reached over and stroked the base of my neck. I dropped my fork with a clatter at his touch.

"Can I go watch *SportsCenter*?" June asked, bored and annoyed with the social requirements of the evening.

"No," Mom the Traitor said firmly. "Don't you want to join in the conversation?"

June stuck her chin out like she was going to throw a hissy fit and then relented. My sister never threw hissy fits. "Fine. Bowie, you had an impressive batting average in high school and you excelled at pitching." She sounded like a robot trying to give a compliment. *I was going to give that robot a talking-to about sisterly loyalty.*

"Thanks, Juney," Bowie said, hiding his smile.

"*Now*, can I go watch TV?" June asked.

"Bowie, would you like another beer?" my dad asked, getting up from the table. My father who damn well knew what Connelly was threatening me with had willingly brought this man to my table. Okay, his table. But I was sitting at it.

"No, sir. One's good enough for me," Bowie said.

"One's good enough for me," I mimicked under my breath. He was always such a damn Boy Scout.

"What's that, Cass?" Bowie asked sweetly.

"Can I talk to you outside?" I snapped.

"Me?" June asked. "It's cold. And I'd rather watch TV."

"Not you. *You*," I said, drilling a finger into Bowie's shoulder.

I didn't wait to see if he'd follow. I pushed my way outside onto the deck off the kitchen. It was dark now and cold, but my seething anger kept me warm.

"Cass, honey, you're gonna freeze to death out here," Bowie said, sliding the door closed behind him.

"What are you *doing here*?" I demanded.

He took me in his arms and pulled me up against his chest. "There, that's better," he said, whispering against my hair.

I hated how much better it was. He was so warm and steady. Dang it. Teenage Cassidy would have melted into a puddle over this. But I was Late-Twenties Cassidy, and she was made of sterner stuff.

"Bowie," I said, in a warning tone. "What are you doing here?"

"I'm showing you how nice it would be if we were together."

"What are you talking about?"

We were swaying side to side as if slow dancing to music that no one else could hear.

"All we have is a past of what-ifs. I'm trying to show you what it'll be like if you'll just say yes."

"Dinner with my parents?" I asked.

"I'm showing you how well I get on with my future in-laws."

I stepped on his foot.

"You aren't letting me catch my breath," I told him. "And you sure as hell aren't taking my concerns about being connected to you seriously!"

He pulled back a bit to look at me. "I know it's not fair. I know I'm pressuring you after years of nothing but space. And I know it seems like I'm asking you to choose me over your job. But that's not the case. I haven't proven myself yet. All I'm asking is for a chance to prove that I will be good to you. That I'll be the partner in life you want. That I won't let you down."

"How?" I asked stubbornly. "How can I give you your shot

and still keep my job? How can we date and not have the entire town know every damn thing?" *How can I trust you?*

"Same way your Dad doesn't know we host secret town meetings. We may be a town of blabbermouths, but we know when to keep our mouths shut. You think anyone here feels any loyalty to that clown Connelly?"

I shook my head. "It's too big of a risk. He's throwing accusations at me like impeding an investigation."

"What if we keep it secret?" Bowie asked.

"How in the hell would we do that?" *It was ridiculous. Appalling. And yet...*

"We live in the same house," he said with that boyish grin. "I think we can come up with a way to make it work. I'm asking for a chance, not a choice. Not yet. I'd never ask you to give up your career, Cass. I hope you know that."

His gray eyes were earnest, and Late-Twenties Cassidy was dumb enough to believe him.

"Why is everything such a mess right now?" I demanded. "Why doesn't anything make sense?"

"I'll tell you one thing that does make sense," Bowie said, lowering his lips to mine.

Oh, Lordy. That sparked a fire in me all right. My cheeks were cold, and my mouth was being consumed by flames. I didn't have the ability to do anything but kiss him back. I pressed myself up against him, and he held me tight as we ravaged each other's mouths.

It was too much. And not enough.

I could feel a pulse between my legs as he hardened against my stomach.

My feelings for him were so complicated. But one thing was always crystal clear. I wanted Bowie naked and sweating and growling my name in my ear. *Could I give myself that and not lose anything? My job? My heart?*

His hands skimmed down my sides, stroking over the curves of my breasts.

"I want you, Cass. Let me prove to you that I'm right for you. Let me." His thumbs skimmed over my nipples that were already fritzing out from the cold and the kiss.

I shivered against him. "Damn it all to hell, Bowie."

"Do you want pie or can I have your pieces? I want to try eating my feelings again." June asked from the back door.

43

BOWIE

She insisted on sneaking out the back into my garage under the cover of darkness. A ninja in suede boots and a wool coat.

"You better be keeping a lid on things," Cassidy told me, climbing into the passenger seat and crossing her arms over her chest. "I'm not putting my career on the line for a date." She smelled like lemons. I liked it.

It was a *first* date, not just *a* date, I reassured myself, backing out of the garage. A cantankerous one, seein' as how it had taken me thirty minutes to convince her to ride with me.

"Cass, honey, I swear there isn't a soul in the world that knows about tonight." Now wasn't the time to tell her that my brothers knew I was planning on courting her. Besides, they didn't know the specifics. And tonight, Jonah was out teaching some fitness class somewhere. So technically no one knew that tonight was our first date.

"I can't believe you talked me into this," she said.

I was used to my dates being a little more enthusiastic about things. I turned on the radio low for some background noise. "Technically, I kissed you into it," I told her.

"Your mouth was very convincing," she complained.

I laughed. I couldn't help it. Reaching across the console, I took her hand in mine. "We're heading forty-five minutes out of town for dinner in a restaurant ninety-nine percent of Bootleg would never consider stepping foot in," I told her. "We're safe. You're beautiful. And I'm already itching to kiss you again. Let's have some fun tonight."

She gave me a long look and let out a breath. "I want to make sure you're taking this secrecy thing seriously, Bow. The ground can't get any shakier under my feet at work."

"Can he actually fire you?" I asked.

"I don't know if he can with jurisdictions being what they are. But that doesn't mean he won't try. He's making my life miserable as it is."

"What's his deal?" I asked. "It seems like it's more than you being friends with me and my family."

She looked at me, relief on her pretty features. "It does, doesn't it? It's been niggling at me. It's not because I'm a woman—at least not just because I am. But he's singled me out for some reason. I feel like he's playing a game that I don't get to read the rules to."

"Ever think about doin' some digging on him?" I suggested.

She gave me another long, quiet look. "I might do that. By the way, I got a package today."

"Did you now?"

"Pajamas. Isn't that a little forward for our first date?" she teased.

First date. Cassidy might not know it yet, but she and I were on the same page. We both knew that tonight was the beginning. This was our first date. The night that would lay the groundwork for our future. Dating. Marriage. Kids. Grandkids. It all started here, tonight.

"Do you like 'em?" I asked.

She grinned, looking straight ahead, and I felt her grip on my hand tighten a little bit. "Yeah."

"I CAN'T BELIEVE you brought me back here," Cassidy laughed, looking around the dining room. She looked incredible in a dark green dress that dipped low in the front and floated out at the waist. Her hair was down in honey blonde waves, and my fingers were itching to dive in. The heels on her boots brought her within easy kissing distance of my mouth.

I was having trouble remembering my usual first date moves because I just wanted to strip her naked and kiss every golden inch of her body.

Ever since I'd seen her—felt her—naked that night, I'd thought of little else. *More.* I wanted it with Cassidy. And I was prepared to earn it, one careful step at a time.

Much as I wanted to find out exactly what she had on under that dress, I wasn't going to find out tonight. I'd be the gentleman she deserved, attentive, respectful. Hopefully, there'd be a goodnight kiss that we'd both remember forever.

Long game, I cautioned myself, as a vision of tangled sheets and Cassidy writhing on top of them popped into my mind. *Nope. Get out of my head naked goddess Cassidy.* I was determined to make this night perfect.

"What's going on in that brain of yours?" Cassidy asked as the host led us through the dining room.

"You really don't want to know."

She was scanning the room, seemingly in cop mode, picking up and storing details of the other diners.

"You're looking for Baxter, aren't you?" I teased.

She made a gagging noise that had the host glancing over his shoulder.

"She's fine," I promised him.

The host pretended we were just another pair of polite diners and showed us to the table. *Our* table.

"The same table?" she asked, eyeing me with suspicion.

If Cassidy didn't know that I was a romantic at heart, well, she was gonna have to get used to it right quick.

I pulled her chair out with a flourish. "Welcome to our first, official date."

She sat and tucked the cloth napkin into her lap. I could tell by the tension in her shoulders that she was nervous as a cat in a rocking chair store. "Relax, Cass. I don't bite," I said, taking the chair across from her.

"Before we get to the biting, I think we need to talk business first," Cassidy said, scoping out the other diners.

"I'm fine if we skip to the biting." *Down, boy! Charming, not horndoggy.*

"How is this supposed to work?" she asked. It was a big, fat, loaded question.

But I was prepared for it.

"First things first," I said, reaching for my water glass. I wet my whistle. "I've been thinking romantic thoughts about you since you were sixteen years old." Honestly, it was probably closer to fifteen, but I felt like that might be skirting a little too close to the creepy old guy line.

"You had a damn funny way of showin' it," Cassidy said.

I could tell by the set of her jaw she wasn't gonna take it easy on me tonight. "You were my little sister's best friend. And during the teenage years, an age difference like ours is a serious deal."

"And then my father opened his trap and you fell in line like a good boy." Cassidy crossed her arms.

"What do you suppose would have happened if I hadn't listened to the sheriff?" I asked her. "What if instead of lying to you when you came to Gibson's the next morning, I did what I really wanted to instead?"

She leaned in almost imperceptibly. I knew I had her hooked. "What did you want to do?"

"Welcome. May I offer you a beverage tonight?" Our waiter, a ten-foot-tall man with a ponytail and a hooked nose, hovered over our table.

"Jesus, man! Give us a minute," Cassidy yelped.

I gave him an apologetic smile as he scampered off.

"You were sayin'?" she demanded.

Reaching forward, testing my luck, I covered her hand with mine. I stroked my thumb over the ridges and valleys of her knuckles. I knew she felt it too, that electroshock charge every time we touched.

"I wanted to push you up against that wall and kiss you senseless. I wanted to tell you that you were done messing around with summertimers and jerks your own age. Because you were mine and it was high time you realized it."

Cassidy didn't move a muscle. She was staring at me with the slightest frown tugging on her pink lips. "Damn it, Bowie. You could have taken the most humiliating moment of my life and turned it into the most exciting, romantic, delirious teenage fantasy."

"And then one of us would have done somethin' stupid and screwed the whole thing up, ruining our shot."

"What makes you say that?"

"You were nineteen! I was twenty-three. What the hell did we even know then?"

"I'm not so sure we know much more now." She reached for her water glass with her free hand.

"I know that I'm not willing to go back to being just neighbors."

"Bowie," she said my name on an exhalation of frustration. "You're only saying that because my daddy gave you permission."

"Your daddy didn't give me permission to pin you up against your bedroom wall naked and taste you."

Her cheeks flushed, and I felt my own internal temperature rising at the very vivid, very visceral memories.

"There is no chance I would have been able to go back to staying away from you after that night, Cass."

"I seem to recall you giving me the brushoff after I came back."

"You think that would have lasted? Now that I know what you feel like under my hands. Now that I know what those sexy little whimpers in the back of your throat sound like. Do you honestly think I could leave you alone?" This was not the argument I had crafted to convince the sane, logical Cassidy Tucker to put her faith in me. This was a waterfall of unplanned, sincere honesty. We were both going over it in a barrel made for two.

She put her head down on the table and groaned. "You're makin' it real hard to stay furious with you."

"Uh, would anyone care to put in a drink—"

Cassidy lifted her head. "Sir, I will give you twenty bucks right now to grab us two beers, put them on our table without saying a word, and giving us ten whole minutes of solitude."

The waiter blinked. Cassidy pulled her hand out from under mine and fished a hand into her bra. She pulled out a folded-up bill and slid it across the table. "Go on now. Scoot."

He grabbed the twenty and disappeared without a word.

I couldn't stop staring at her cleavage.

"Emergency boob twenties come in handy," she said.

"What else you got in there?"

She arched an eyebrow. "Wouldn't you like to know?"

"I sure would, but I'm not gonna find out tonight, Cass. I'm serious about us. I'm after a hell of a lot more than one date and a night of sex. And I really need you to be okay with that."

"You bein' good sure gets in the way of us having a whole lot of fun."

44

CASSIDY

He was saying all the right things and looking all the right kinds of handsome. In that damn navy blue suit minus the tie. His shirt was unbuttoned at the collar. Casual and sexy. Lickable. Part of me kept pinching myself under the table to make sure I wasn't dreaming all this. I was on a date with Bowie, and he was pulling out every romantic stop.

I'd finally allowed the waiter to come back and take our orders and had worked my way through a very fine steak. Bowie had given me my hand back so we could use our utensils like civilized folk, and my mind cleared up a bit without the physical contact.

I picked up my beer and sipped. "So, say I do agree to date you." *I wanted to date him right on home and upstairs into my bed.*

He leaned in, looking stupidly handsome like every naughty daydream I'd ever had of the man.

Testing him, I nudged my boot up his pant leg. He reacted by jumping so hard his knee hit the bottom of the table. *How cute.* "How exactly do I date you and keep my job?" I asked, acting as if I wasn't climbing his leg with my foot.

"Uh. Um. Well, I think we could keep things under wraps around town. I mean, we live next door to each other. We have back door access—"

"Back. Door. Access." I repeated, skating my foot over his knee.

He slipped a hand under the table and grabbed my boot, halting my progress.

He turned an adorable shade of raspberry. "What I mean to say is no one needs to know that we're seeing each other at home. If we go out, we can stick to non-local venues."

"Hmm. What if we're both at The Lookout and a sexy, slow song comes on?"

His nostrils flared, and I knew he was thinking about our slow dance.

"Should I dance with someone else?" I asked innocently. "You know, keep everyone bamboozled?"

"No, you should not," he said.

"So you say secret. But what about Jonah, who has seen us very nearly doing the deed? And Scarlett, who I may have called and asked if that counted as doing the deed? It didn't, by the way."

"It most certainly did not count," Bowie agreed. "When it does count you won't have to phone a friend to be sure."

His eyes were on my mouth, and I did my best slow lick and hoped it looked as sexy as it did on TV. The grip on my foot tightened, so I figured I was doing just fine. I was a cat toying with a very attractive mouse.

"I repeat my question. What about Jonah—who you live with—and Scarlett, who is probably at this very moment flipping through her Cassidy and Bowie Wedding scrapbook?"

"You're the one with the secrecy caveat. What do you want to do?"

The only other secret I'd kept from Scarlett was exactly

what Bowie said the day after he punched the dumbass summertimer in the face for me. But I didn't have many secrets, and Scarlett had a very large mouth. Would she forgive me for hiding an actual relationship from her? What kind of a tangled web was I weaving?

"Let's tell them that the timing isn't right for us right now," I decided. It wasn't exactly a lie.

"To be clear. You're asking me to lie to my family about us."

"Temporarily. I'm willing to make it worth your while. The less people who know, the better."

Bowie grunted.

He wasn't happy with the arrangement. But it was all I could offer right now. I wasn't about to toss aside the job I loved for the man who'd lied to me and proceeded to keep his distance for the better part of a decade.

"How long are you willing to remain tight-lipped about our little relationship?" I asked, enunciating *tight* and *lipped*.

I watched his Adam's apple work. If I could drive the man to sex, I felt like I'd win back a piece for my damaged teen heart. And also probably have an excellent orgasm. Or two. I remembered Scarlett oversharing on the reality of multiple orgasms and wondered if Bowie here could dole out multiples.

Yeah. The man was pumping off barely restrained testosterone like he bottled it and was spritzing people with samples at the mall.

"After all, given our unique position as such good friends, we could do some damage to both families if this little trial of ours flames out." Thanksgiving would be awkward. Hell, everyday life would be unbearable. Running into each other at the Pop In. Sitting at the same table at The Lookout. Being invited to each other's weddings. If this went to hell, I wanted to make sure no one was any the wiser.

"A month," he said, the words coming out rough.

"Two," I countered. There was no way Connelly would be

wrapping his investigation before the new year. Not if he was hellbent on ignoring the photographic proof of Callie's injuries. I needed enough time to prove to the man that I was an asset to the department, not a lovesick family legacy.

"Six weeks," Bowie offered. "Don't ask for more, Cass. Because otherwise people will be real shocked when I propose to you on what they think is our first date."

And now it was my turn to turn a shade of pink only seen on sunburnt summertimers. *Touché, Mr. Sexypants.* "You want to propose to me in six weeks?" I hissed.

"I'd rather do it in a month," he said, flashing that Bodine smile that ladies had been swooning over since his kindergarten school picture.

"Six weeks of secrecy, subject to renegotiation. You will *not* propose. And we will have sex tonight," I ticked off my terms. A sexually aggressive woman had taken over my brain. One who kept reminding me how it had felt to have Bowie almost inside me, his lean, hard body pressed up against mine.

That woman was not going home unsatisfied.

"Six weeks. Potential proposal after two months. And we are *not*."

"Bowie, Bowie, Bowie." I flexed my foot in his hand and gained two inches up his thigh. His gray eyes sharpened. I should stop playing. I was smarter and more experienced than I'd been at nineteen, but there was still a lingering doubt that I couldn't handle the man. "If you want to make a go of this then don't you think it's important to find out how compatible we are in all areas?" I scraped the heel of my boot against his inner thigh and was rewarded with the flaring of his nostrils. We were staring each other down, waiting for one to cave.

Our waiter returned, took one look at our staring contest, and hurried away.

"I plan to give you everything you want, Cass, for the rest of my life. Just not tonight."

"Why the hell not?"

45

CASSIDY

"We're *not* having sex on the first date," Bowie reminded me, palming my very happy breasts under my sweater. He'd unhooked my bra one-handed like a champion lady undresser about four seconds after he'd pulled into the garage and three after he dragged me over into his lap.

His SUV windows were steamed up, and I couldn't be sure, but we were generating enough heat to steam up the garage windows, too.

"I'm tired of you thinking you get to call all the shots," I told him, biting his lower lip hard enough that he gasped in a breath.

"When I tell our grandkids about our first date, it's not going to end with 'and then your grandma put out.'"

"That's a sexist statement. Why's it bad if Grandma puts out, but not if Grandpa does?"

"Point taken," he said, licking his way into my mouth and dazzling me with a kiss akin to fireworks. "I've waited a long time for you, Cassidy Tucker. I don't mind waitin' a little longer so you can make sure."

"I'm sure I want you inside me," I told him, biting at his jawline and neck.

He made a strangled noise.

"You okay?" I asked.

"Can a man die from not having sex with you?" Bowie wondered, fisting the long tail of my hair in his hand.

"What about after the second date?" I demanded, thrusting my hips against him so I could ride the ridge of his erection. "We could go for coffee right now. Boom. Second date."

"You are fucking killing me, woman."

"That's a lot of years of pent-up frustration talking there," I said, sliding my hand under his shirt and stroking it across the ridges of his abs. When my fingers dipped lower toward the waistband of his pants, he stopped me.

"Cassidy Ann. We're waiting."

"I'm tired of waiting."

"I want you to be sure I'm the one for you."

"We're talking about sex here, Bow. Not a lifetime commitment." I shifted against him again and watched his pupils dilate.

"It's the same thing this time, Cass. I want a lifetime commitment out of you first."

"How incredibly old-fashioned of you." I rocked into him, and he groaned.

He squeezed my hips and kissed me until I couldn't figure out where my mouth ended and his began.

"How about now?" I asked, leaning back against the steering wheel and opening the wrap tie of my dress.

"Oh, fuck." His hands were on my bare breasts followed immediately by his mouth. I bucked against him as he licked and sucked and stroked. It was freezing cold outside, but in the car it was a tropical rainforest of lust.

"Come inside with me, Bowie," I demanded.

He took another long pull on my nipple, and I nearly went over the edge right then and there. And then he did the unthinkable. He pulled my dress back in place and opened his door.

"I'm walking you to your door and then you're going inside. When you're sure that this is it for you, then we'll see about the rest of it."

"You are blackmailing me with sex!"

"I'm incentivizing you," Bowie corrected. "It's positive reinforcement."

"You're lucky I don't have my service weapon with me or I'd positive reinforcement you right in the balls."

He pressed a chaste kiss to my mouth and plopped me on the ground. "I swear to you I'll make it worth your while," he said, sliding out after me.

He adjusted himself to a more comfortable position in his pants. "You are so damn stubborn," I complained. "We could be having orgasms right now!"

Bowie leaned in close enough for me to feel his hard-on against my belly. "I love you, Cassidy Ann. I fully intend to be the last man you sleep with. But I need you to be ready for that."

My hormones were begging me to agree to anything if it meant that gorgeous man would plow himself into me raining orgasms down like a sex Tinker bell.

He loved me. Bowie Bodine admitted to loving me.

"What did you just say?" I whispered.

"You heard me. I love you." He threaded his fingers into my hair and kissed me again until my insides were warm like caramel. "Always have. And you know when we make love, there's no goin' back."

I most certainly did not know it. Sure, it would change our

relationship. But we'd been friends for a decade or two. That wouldn't go away just because we had sex and broke up. *Would it?* I took offense to him putting caveats like "forever" and "lifetime" on something that was so immediate. Not when we'd agreed to a six-week secret trial. I wanted him *now*. But he was rejecting me again.

"Then I guess this is goodnight," I said stubbornly.

He leaned down and kissed the tip of my nose. "Goodnight, Cass. I love you."

I wanted to punch him, to storm into my house and never speak to him again. I wanted to say it back.

"Goodnight," I said and pushed out the garage door into the backyard. I jogged up the steps to my back door and let myself in without looking back.

HORNY, frustrated, and grumpy, I listened to Bowie moving around in his bedroom on the other side of the wall. Imagining him stripping out of his clothes, standing there naked and staring at my wall.

I didn't like how out of control he made me feel. I wanted to get it back. To hold the power.

I heard his shower come on and biting my lip, reached for my phone.

Me: There's no shower cold enough.

He responded quickly.

Bowie: Agreed.

Me: There's an easy solution to your predicament.

Bowie: What's that?

I was a law enforcement officer. I had never sexted anyone in my life. There were too many ways it could go horribly wrong. But this was Bowie. I lay down on the bed and slid my free hand up the skirt of my dress. I snapped the picture and sent it.

I heard a thump on the other side of the wall and hoped he was hitting his head in frustration.

Bowie: Christ, Cass. Do you know how many times I thought of you while I touched myself?

Me: Tell me.

Bowie: Every time. Every fucking time. It's always you.

Me: I'm one door away from you. The real thing. Waiting for you.

The water turned off next door, and I held my breath.

Bowie: I need this to be special for us. Not just some hormone-fueled fuck.

I got off the bed, slipped out of my dress, and struck my sexiest selfie pose in the mirror.

Me: So close. At least I can give you a visual to work with.

I attached the picture and sent it.

I heard another thump next door followed by footsteps. They stopped on the other side of the door that divided our places. I crossed to my side and waited.

"Go to bed, Cass," he said quietly through the door.

"I don't want perfect or forever. I want you, now," I whispered.

"Baby, don't do this to me," he pleaded.

"Are you touching yourself?" I asked, hoping to God Jonah's bedroom door at the front of the house was shut tight.

"Yes," Bowie hissed.

He groaned low.

I couldn't stand it. I couldn't stand not seeing him, not watching him. I flung the door open and there was Bowie. Fisting the cock he'd freed from his sweat pants. His eyes were hooded, his neck and jaw were tight. And that tight fist was moving up and down his shaft.

46

BOWIE

Her eyes were wide and glassy. She was naked, needy, those subtle curves begging for my hands.

"I'm tryin' to do the right thing, Cass," I rasped. But I couldn't stop fucking my hand and wishing it was her.

She didn't say a word to me. Just slowly sank to her knees in front of me in the doorway.

She made the sexiest picture I'd ever seen in my entire life. Kneeling in front of me, offering herself to me.

"Cass," I hissed at her. I wanted it to be perfect for her. Wine and candlelight and soft music.

But looking at her on her knees in front of me, those lips opening. I'd been stupid to think I could wait.

I needed her. I needed to be inside her. To know her. To possess her. To worship her.

"You said you'd give me anything," she said quietly.

I nodded wordlessly. Yes, I had definitely said that. Who was I to deny Cassidy my dick when it was what she wanted? I was rationalizing, desperately, lightheadedly. But right now I couldn't quite remember why it was important to wait.

Then she leaned forward and slicked her tongue over the tip, and I was a goner.

I shoved my hands into her hair and holding her on my cock, I crossed the threshold, shutting the door behind me.

I'd crossed the line, committed the crime. I couldn't say no to her.

I gripped her hair, those long, honey tresses that I'd obsessed over for years, and guided her down my shaft.

Groaning, I leaned back against the door.

Her mouth. Her fucking mouth. It was paradise.

She worked me wet and eager, taking me to the back of her throat like this had been a fantasy for her, too.

I could feel it building already and knew I was in danger of losing all control. I'd fuck her mouth and then I'd come, releasing it all over her lips, her neck, her breasts. I'd mark her as mine. If she couldn't give me the words yet, I'd find another way to claim her.

God. I stopped her. Holding her head still as my cock throbbed in her mouth.

I was one second away from coming and as appealing as that visual was, the first time I came with Cassidy was going to be buried deep inside her.

Pulling her gently by the hair, I backed her mouth off of my erection.

She whimpered in protest, and I fucking loved that sound. I wanted to take her to the bed, to lay her across that mattress and seduce every damn inch of her. But I wouldn't survive the ten feet. Instead, I lowered myself to her, half collapsing on her.

"Touch me," she begged. "Please, Bowie."

I'd imagined her saying those exact words in that exact tone for more years than was healthy. It broke me. My fantasy colliding with my reality. I didn't have any control anymore. I couldn't stop myself as I shoved her back down on the floor and buried my face between her legs. I couldn't not taste her.

I slid my tongue through her folds, and her entire body tensed. It was her turn to grip my hair. She tasted like something I'd never have enough of no matter how many times I sampled her.

"Open your legs," I ordered. When she let her knees fall open to the side, I rewarded her with two fingers plunged deep into her center.

She bucked up off the floor, her stomach muscles tense. I didn't give her a second to relax and get used to it. Using my tongue and mouth, I licked at her. Finding that sensitive bud, I lavished it with attention.

Cassidy's fingers yanked at my hair, stinging my scalp, and I fucking loved it.

"Bowie, I'm—"

She lit up from the inside out as an orgasm snuck up on her and dragged her under the surface. Her walls closed rhythmically around my fingers, and I realized I'd never felt anything sexier in my life. Making Cassidy come. It was my new mission in life.

I fucked her with my mouth and fingers through the orgasm. She sobbed my name over and over again. And I knew she loved me. It had never been like this for me. There'd never been a connection, an obsession like this before.

I wanted to do it again and again, all night long until dawn broke.

But more, I wanted the words from her. We'd loved each other since forever, and I needed to hear her say it. Needed her to recognize what it meant. That this was it. Us. Together. Forever.

With her tremors fading, I climbed back up her body and found her breasts.

"How do you know how to touch me?" she whispered, trembling beneath me.

The floor was hard under her, and I wished I'd picked a softer place to fuck her senseless.

"I know you, Cassidy. I love you."

"How do you know?" she demanded.

I sucked her nipple into my mouth and worshipped it with long pulls.

She bucked her hips against me, begging for more. My cock pleaded with me to take her.

"Because I've never not loved you," I told her, nuzzling her breast.

"I need you, Bowie."

"I know, baby. But I need you to say the words first." I abandoned her breasts and used my leverage to my advantage.

She was pinned beneath me, legs open. My dick throbbed against her very center. We'd been here before and I was determined that before we went any further I'd get what I needed.

"I'm scared."

Her words froze me in place, one thrust away from everything I'd ever wanted.

"Baby, look at me."

Reluctantly she obliged.

"Cass, honey. You've been it for me since you were about sixteen years old. There's never been anyone else in my heart. I'm not going to hurt you. Let me love you."

"What if—"

"What if it doesn't work out? What if we fall out of love? What if one of us changes and the other doesn't catch up?"

She nodded, eyes serious as her body thrummed under mine.

"What if we don't try?" I countered.

She closed her eyes.

"Cass, we have to give ourselves this shot. Have you ever felt this way about anyone else?"

She shook her head back and forth on the floor, and my hips gave a slight thrust. Two inches into her perfection.

"You're not playing fair, Bowie."

"I know it."

She took a long shaky breath and opened her eyes. "I love you, Bowie Bodine."

Another fantasy come to life and again, it was better than I'd ever imagined. My Cassidy. My girl. The woman I was going to marry and spend my life with. Saying the words I'd dreamed of hearing from those lips.

"You're not saying that so I'll have sex with you, are you?" I teased.

She cupped my face in her hands. "No, Bowie." And then she kissed me hard on the mouth. I thrust into her, buried to the hilt, and swallowed her cries.

"Yes, yes, yes," she chanted.

Finally, the blood pounding in my head shouted. It was better and more and everything. My dreams, my fantasies were pale replicas of a reality so fierce I'd never go back to the way things were before I'd been inside of her.

I was where I was meant to be. Joined with Cassidy. I held there, fully sheathed, memorizing the feel of her. Feeling the rightness of it all.

And when I started to move, when she joined me, it was like we'd been doing this dance since forever.

Her breasts were flattened against my chest. I dug my toes into the hardwood beneath us, driving myself into her slowly, surely.

She wrapped her legs around my waist, taking everything I could give her. Her hips met me thrust for thrust. I relished the feel of her nails carving crescents into my shoulders. She buried her face in my neck.

We'd been meant for each other. And I had a lot of lost time to make up for.

I drove into her, each thrust harder, faster until we were sweating and gasping for breath. My orgasm hovered at the base of my spine, and I tried to wish it away. I wasn't ready to stop, to finish. I wanted this time to last forever.

"Bowie," she gasped against my neck. "Bowie, you're making me—ah!"

I felt her close around me. Felt her slick walls tremble over my own flesh. Better than the fantasy. Better than I ever imagined. So much more.

My release rocketed up from my balls through my shaft, and I pinned her to the floor as I poured the first jet of come into her. We came together. I emptied myself into her like I was sacrificing my soul. She took it all, sobbing those words over and over again in my ear, as her body throbbed around me.

I love you. I love you. I love you.

Cassidy Ann Tucker was mine now. Forever.

47

BOWIE

Something hot and furry was sitting on my chest. And something sharp was poking me in the face. I opened a bleary eye to find a yellowish one staring back at me. It was early. Very early. I didn't have to be at school for another two hours.

"Meow?" the fat tub of cat said, again bringing his paw to my face.

When I didn't immediately respond to whatever he was asking, the fucker stabbed me in the face with a pawful of nails.

I asked you nicely, fucker, his grumpy face seemed to say.

"Ouch!"

"Mmm, George. No stabbing." Cassidy was curled up against my side, her back to me. She was naked and not entirely awake.

Yep. Cassidy Ann Tucker was in bed with me. Today was officially the best day of my entire life.

George celebrated with me with another stab to my face.

"Ouch! Ooof!" The breath was pushed out of me when another warm, furry bulk landed on my stomach. Sir Edmund

Hillary had decided to throw his hat into the ring for most annoying wake-up ever.

He peered over his brother, looking quizzically at me.

"They're not used to two bodies in bed," Cassidy yawned, wiggling her backside up against me. I dumped both cats on to the mattress and rolled onto my side, spooning her.

"They better get used to it," I told her, burying my face in her hair.

I was hard. Throbbingly hard. My body was busy remembering all of the sensations from last night and insistent in its desire to re-enact every single one.

Cassidy gave out a sweet little sigh and cuddled back into me. I couldn't think of a better way to start my day.

"Was it my imagination or did you tell me you loved me about eight times last night?" I asked, pressing a kiss to the nape of her neck.

"Definitely your imagination."

I could hear the smile in her voice.

"Was it my imagination or did you say we weren't going to have sex last night?"

I bit her on the shoulder. "Definitely your imagination."

Eight sets of claws sank into my hip and shoulder as two cats scrambled to perch like freaking parrots on the highest points of my body.

"Son of a—"

"They want breakfast," Cassidy said, burying her face in her pillow.

The fat one was poking me in the face again.

"Fine. You win, feral furballs," I muttered. I tried to roll carefully so as not to startle them, but it was to no avail. They knew breakfast was on the line here. George dug his back claws into me and slid down my bicep. Eddie followed suit by clinging to my flesh through the sheet until he rolled off of me.

They tried to kill me on the stairs.

George stopped short in front of me while Eddie snaked his way through my legs. While I grabbed the handrail and missed four or five steps, they resumed their race to the kitchen.

"You okay?" Cassidy called out sleepily.

"Peachy," I called back. Two murderous felines were not going to ruin the best day of my life.

I checked my phone and found a text from Jonah. *Oops.*

I probably should have told him I wasn't coming home last night.

Jonah: How long do you wait before you report someone missing? Unrelated can I have your blender if you're dead in a ditch somewhere? It makes great smoothies.

I fired off a response as the cats meowed in an obnoxious duet at my feet.

Me: Sorry. All is well. I'm willing to discuss blender custody. Be home soon.

I wasn't a fan of lying or omitting. Technically I was home. I was under my home's roof. But I'd made a deal with Cass, and I wasn't going to give her reason to regret it less than twelve hours later.

"You already have food," I said accusingly, pointing at the matching cat bowls piled high with dried food.

The cats looked at my finger and blinked.

"Look. This is food." I reached into one dish and stirred the kibble with my fingers.

That was good enough for George. He attacked the bowl like his last meal had been a week ago. Eddie was still skeptical. I stirred the food in the other bowl. Eddie sniffed.

My phone pinged.

Jonah: You're not rotting in jail because Devlin is out of bail money?

Me: All is well. Be home soon.

That should be enough to curb any more questions. Bodine men, even the one who hadn't grown up with the rest of us, didn't much care to get too personally involved in things like where our brothers spent the night.

Jonah: We're out of coffee. Pick some up on your way home?

Well, shit. I glanced toward Cassidy's coffeemaker. She was the prepared type. She probably had to go cups around here somewhere.

Me: No problem. See you in a bit.

I made a move toward the coffeemaker when the smaller cat darted in front of me. I tripped over him and knocked over a dining chair.

"Eddie, you fuckwit!"

Both cats, ears back, flew out of the room.

"Everything okay?" Cassidy called down on a yawn.

"Just fine," I yelled back.

Jonah: You know I can hear you over there, right?

"Damn it."

There was a tap on the door in the hallway by the kitchen. Reluctantly, I opened it a crack.

Jonah was standing there, smugly drinking a cup of coffee.

"I thought we were out of coffee."

"I thought you were dead in a ditch."

"I thought we were keeping this quiet," Cassidy said, grumpily from the stairs.

"Morning, Cass," Jonah said. "Sleep well?"

"You better swear him to secrecy, Bowie Bodine," Cassidy said moving past me to stab buttons on the coffeemaker.

"So here's the thing, Jonah," I began.

48

CASSIDY

Thanksgiving morning arrived with me in a post-orgasmic bliss coma with Bowie's warm body wrapped around mine. We'd had sex eight times, gone on two dates, and had enjoyed one very satisfying Netflix and chill. I still had a job. And no one—besides Jonah—was any the wiser.

My smugness was replaced with the realization that it was one thing hiding a relationship behind closed doors. It was quite another to get through an entire Thanksgiving afternoon with both our families and come out unscathed.

Reluctantly, I wiggled out of Bowie's grasp and moved to the edge of the bed. I studied him. That thick dark hair, tousled from sleep and my hands. The straight nose, firm lips. He had a subtle hollow under the high Bodine cheekbones and above the strong jawline.

The man was something to look at. And he was mine. Unable to help myself, I reached out and skimmed my hand over his bicep. I loved the feel of his skin against mine. My heart did that odd little pitter pat. I loved *him*. How exactly did I think I was going to hide this from my mother? Or Scarlett?

Or Gram-Gram? Or any of the other two dozen people who'd be downing carbs and shouting at football players through the TV screen?

One last look, one last stroke and I grabbed my pajamas off the floor and headed out. I needed to strategize.

Strategizing got the coffee brewed, two pumpkin pies in Bowie's oven, and a broccoli casserole in my own. The cats were fed and enjoying their first round of morning naps. My kitchen looked like a cooking war zone with dirty dishes everywhere and a neat stack of food storage containers hopeful for leftovers.

The small scanner whirred away on my kitchen table kicking out old case files like it was in a watermelon seed spitting contest. The digital files neatly organizing themselves on my laptop.

I peeked out the back door and took in the view of my top secret boyfriend grilling up fresh vegetables Jonah had shoved at him before heading out for the Turkey Trot 5k. Suede moccasins, sweat pants slung low on narrow hips, and a thermal shirt that fit him just right. Bowie was prettier than a picture. I had no idea how I was going to get through an entire afternoon without looking like I wanted to devour the man instead of the feast.

As if he sensed me, Bowie looked up from the grill. He shot me that good guy grin and my insides went to goop. Warm wonderful goop. I ducked back inside and tried to focus. Secrets. Keeping them from the people who knew me the best in the world. If I could hide my relationship with Bowie from them, then keeping it from Connelly for the next five weeks should be a cake walk. It should be enough time to prove to the man that I wasn't some lame duck. I was a cop and a good one.

The scanner beeped, telling me it was time to feed it some more documents. I'd paid for it out of my own pocket when I realized that technology had advanced beyond the ancient dinosaur that practically hand drew recreations of documents at the station. I one-clicked this puppy faster than a pair of 50-percent-off Uggs.

I let Connelly think he was forcing me into overtime with the menial task, when in reality I took the stack of files home every night and wrapped it up in an hour. Handy. And totally worth the look on his scowly face every morning when the files were neatly stacked on the conference table.

Not only could I write off the expense, I could finally go through Gram-Gram's photo albums and get everyone digital copies of our sordid family tree. I poured a second cup of coffee, propped my feet up on the table, and considered it a win. It was a wonder what a night of lovemaking and a day off did to the optimism.

The next file was a thicker one. I opened it wondering what Bootleg lore awaited me.

My feet hit the floor.

It was an accident report. One fatality. Weather-related.

Constance Bodine, age 40.

The memories hit me one after the other like hammers.

Dad coming home ashen-faced, soaked to the bone. Mom wrapping him up in a hard hug not minding his sopping rain slicker.

Scarlett sobbing into my shoulder while June made tea that no one wanted.

Bowie in a suit staring down at the cheap pine coffin in the cemetery.

Jonah Sr. had been too drunk to attend his own wife's funeral. So it was the Bodine kids who stood for their mother.

Bad luck. That's what everyone had said when word spread. *Nothing but bad luck for the Bodine family.* Scarlett and her brothers had propped each other up that day and from then on. The four of them—five now with Jonah—were a unit.

I paged through, finding my father's handwritten report on the scene. Low visibility. Foggy. The skies had held off long enough before opening up on the first responders. Connie had gone through a guardrail halfway down Winding Hill Road, a mountainous stretch of serpent curves and steep drop-offs. She'd had some kind of appointment in Perrinville. No one had bothered to ask her what it was about. No one had the chance to.

The coroner's report was included. Blunt force trauma. The car had smashed through the guardrail and tumbled thirty feet down the embankment into a tree. She'd been dead when officers arrived on the scene.

Someone, my father most likely, had neatly clipped the obituary from the newspaper. They'd run it with her high school senior picture. Connie had been full of big dreams that she'd never realized. She'd shouldered the disappointment of young motherhood, of never having enough, with sheer stubbornness. I often got the feeling she was holding out hope that her lot in life would change someday. But it hadn't. It had simply ended.

There were a handful of pictures of the road, the guardrail, the car. Grainy with the flash of a cheap camera trying to cut through the wet, dark night. Growing up, I'd spent as much time in Connie's sedan as I had my mother's Jeep Cherokee.

I wondered if they'd been close, my mother and Scarlett's.

Something nagged at me, and I went through the pictures again one at a time, willing it to the surface. But nothing materialized. Just a lingering sadness at what felt like a life wasted. She'd lived her days unhappy and overextended. And she'd died too young. She'd never see Scarlett finally get engaged to the debonair Devlin. Never bounce Jameson and Leah Mae's babies on her lap. She'd never dance while Gibson sang at The Lookout. Never meet Jonah. Never see Bowie get married.

There was a knock on my back door, and Bowie waved tongs in the window before letting himself in. I slammed the folder shut and stuffed it under my laptop.

He gave me a look.

"Police business," I told him, jumping up from my chair and meeting him in the middle of the kitchen. I didn't know how Bowie would take it if he knew I was combing over his mother's fatal accident report.

"Jonah's veggies are done and I heard the oven timer for the pies," he said, jerking his thumb toward his side of the house.

I yelped and jogged through the downstairs door into Bowie's kitchen. He followed me, and when I leaned down to pull the pie from the oven, he ran his hands down my sides to my hips.

I jumped and nearly bobbled the pie.

"You okay?" he asked, amused.

I felt guilty, like I'd been caught doing something wrong. Maybe I had been.

"Fine. Great," I chirped. I got the pies out of the oven and onto the stove top.

Bowie closed the oven and turned me around carefully. "I know what's goin' on," he told me.

"You do?"

"You're nervous about our first Thanksgiving together."

"I am?" I cleared my throat. "I mean, I guess I am." We'd spent every Thanksgiving together since the year Connie died.

Our families deep-fried turkeys and swapped pie recipes and shouted obscenities at the football game on TV together. I couldn't imagine a Thanksgiving without the Bodines bellied up next to me. "I hope you're a good actor because you're gonna have to be if we're going to keep everyone from finding out that we've been spending our nights naked together."

"Everyone's gonna be too busy stuffin' their faces to notice when I sneak you out to the garage to make out with you," he teased.

"I was thinking about your parents," I admitted. "This is your first Thanksgiving without your dad."

Bowie blew out a breath. "Yeah."

"How do you feel about that? Do you miss them?" I pressed.

He busied himself digging through a drawer for aluminum foil. "Sometimes. I mean, not my dad from the last years. But sometimes I miss them when we were all younger. When we all had...hope."

It was my turn to approach him. I laid my cheek on his back and wrapped my arms around his waist. "I wish it would have worked out differently for them."

He turned in my arms and wrapped me in a hug. "I do, too. But it didn't. So all I can do is make sure it turns out differently for me. You're part of that."

My heart did a little tap dance in my chest. It wasn't quite as scary now. The idea of a future. Bowie was already in my bed and at my parents' table.

"What do you think about kids?" I asked him. "And before you get any ideas in your head, I'm asking for far into the future purposes."

He laughed and slipped his hands into my hair. "I like kids. I'd like some with you."

"How many?"

"Five or six."

"Five or six? Do you want my uterus to fall out when I'm chasin' down Rhett Ginsler on his damn lawn mower?"

"With five or six one of 'em is bound to turn out right," Bowie said with a straight face.

"You are an insane person. Is this why you've never had a relationship that lasted longer than three months?"

"No, Cass. That's because I was holding out for you."

Mr. Charming. I swooned internally.

"Jeez. Are you guys just constantly making out?" Jonah groaned, looking pained from the doorway. He was sweating and dressed as a turkey. The turkey head was tucked under his arm.

"What the hell happened to you?" Bowie demanded.

"It's a Turkey Trot, man. You have to have a turkey."

49

CASSIDY

"Ugh. How can you be going back for thirds?" I asked Jameson as he heaped a small mountain of mashed potatoes onto his plate.

"If your mama learns to start makin' lumpy potatoes from a box then I promise to cut down on my helpings," he winked, sliding back in between Leah Mae and Devlin's mom, Geneva McCallister.

We had a lot of extra faces around the extended table this year. Not only was there the new and improved Jonah Bodine, as Bowie called him, we also made room for Devlin, his parents, Leah Mae, Leah Mae's daddy, Clay, and her future step-mama, Betsy.

We were an army in number, and I didn't even want to imagine the hours of dishes that would be waiting for us after the feast. If any of us could move.

My parents had put all the leaves in the dining table and popped up three extra folding tables in the living room, dining room, and kitchen. Bowie and I were cozied up to a card table in the kitchen with Gibson, Gram-Gram, and June. Above the table, we were playing it cool. Beneath, my leg was hooked over his and his hand was squeezing my knee.

"What's the score now?" Gram-Gram stage-whispered to Gibson.

My mother had a very strict "no football rule" while we ate. June, Gibs, and Gram-Gram always secluded themselves at the table farthest from my mother so they could check their phones.

"Nine to six," Gibson said, surreptitiously checking his phone.

"Saints?" Gram-Gram whispered.

He nodded. "You got action?"

"Fifty on the Saints."

"Would you be interested in a side wager?" June asked.

Someone in the dining room barked out a laugh and someone else moaned about too many carbs. Jonah was lecturing Scarlett on how to mix her protein and carb ratios so she wouldn't feel like a parade float.

This was Thanksgiving. This was family. And damn if it wasn't just about perfect.

I squeezed Bowie's leg under the table. "Wanna go upstairs to my old room and make out?" I whispered so no one else could hear me.

"As many times as I've had that particular fantasy, you're gonna have to give me about an hour so I can definitely be sure that I won't throw up on you," he teased.

"Always a gentleman," I said, batting my eyelashes at him.

"Get you another beer, Bow?" My dad laid a hand on Bowie's shoulder, and I jumped away from him like I'd been caught with forbidden candy in my bedroom.

They both looked at me like I'd lost my dang mind, and I turned my attention back to my mashed potatoes. As nice as it would be to tell everyone that Bowie and I were seeing each other, to celebrate with everyone, the secrecy was vital. I wanted it all. My job, Bowie, Connelly's respect. And I had to be strategic about getting it.

So for now, to all eyes and ears, I was Bowie's next-door neighbor.

"Psst, Gibs. What's the score?" Dad asked, leaning over the table.

"What are you doin' in there, Harlan Tucker?" my mother called from the dining room.

"Just takin' drink orders, my pearl."

DURING THE HALF-TIME we took between meal and dessert, I headed out to the garage to help my dad bring a new case of beer inside. Alcohol was required for appropriate digestion on Thanksgiving. We needed to prime our systems for the Moonshine Tasting tonight.

I was halfway between back porch and garage when I heard the next-door neighbor back out of his driveway in his very shiny Corvette—a thirty-year anniversary gift from his wife—and peeled out on the street. I shook my head as I picked my way to the garage. The dumbass never went anywhere under the speed limit. Fanny Sue had doled out three points on his last ticket as an incentive to slow the hell down.

I froze mid-step. And then ran around to the driveway. There were tire tracks in a swervy little line pointing down the street.

That's what I'd been missing.

Dad was in the garage digging into a fresh case of beer.

"Connie Bodine's accident," I said without preamble.

I saw the guarded look come over his face when he closed

the refrigerator door. "What about it?" Connie's entire family —including the man I was sleeping with—was a few dozen feet away, and here I was bringing up the accident that killed her. But I had questions.

"I had the file to scan into the database. And something was bothering me about the pictures. Was it raining when she crashed?" I asked, already knowing the answer.

"Far as I know, the rains came after," Dad said carefully.

"Then where were the skid marks? She was going what? Thirty-five maybe? Why wasn't there any evidence of her braking hard, swerving?"

Dad looked like he'd rather be anywhere but here having this conversation with me. "Because she didn't," he said finally.

"You think she did it on purpose?" I asked, leaning against the hood of Mom's SUV, mulling it over.

"Could have. Could have been an accident. It's a tough road on a sunny day. The fog was probably a factor. Maybe she was distracted?"

"But you don't think so." I connected the dots. "Why would Connie have killed herself?"

"Didn't say she did. What I do know is those kids did not need a mother who decided to abandon them. Jonah was a full-fledged drunk by then. Money was tight. They didn't need a mom who gave up, too."

"Say it wasn't an accident. Why then?" I asked. Something was bubbling up and it scared me. "It was almost a year after Callie disappeared."

My dad's mustache twitched.

"You don't think Jonah had something to do with it and Connie found out? Do you?" I was aghast. In my heart of hearts, I'd never believed that Jonah Bodine had killed Callie.

"You can't be jumping to conclusions like that, Cassidy,"

my dad said wearily. "Your job is to fit the pieces together, not make up an answer and try to prove it."

"The pieces don't make any sense. Mrs. Kendall is adamant that Callie killed herself. But Jonah disappeared for four days after Callie went missing and no one knows where he went except for knowing that he wasn't where he said he'd be. *Now*, we've got an accident that could have been a suicide. Nothing fits."

My dad sighed, his shoulders slumping with the breath. "I don't think Jonah Bodine killed Callie Kendall," he said finally.

"Why?" I felt the same way, but I didn't have any facts backing it up. "What do you know that isn't in any report?"

Dad put the beer down on the pristine workbench behind him and crossed his arms. "Connie was his alibi. He'd gotten himself shit-faced drunk the night Callie disappeared. Passed out cold on the couch."

"Could Connie have been lying?"

"Could have been. But why? Jonah was no homicidal maniac. He was an alcoholic son of an alcoholic. He wasn't the best father or husband in the world. But he was never physical. It didn't fit that he'd go wandering out into the night and murder some girl."

"Okay, and I do agree with you. But what if it wasn't murder? What if it was vehicular manslaughter?" *What if it was Connie and not Jonah who had hit Callie on some dark road that night?* It would have meant jail time. An investigation. Most likely a lawsuit. It would have ruined the Bodines.

Dad nodded slowly. "A better possibility. One I considered seriously and discarded for two reasons. The day after Callie disappeared, I stopped by the Bodine house. I did a walkaround of both their vehicles. No new dents, scratches, broken headlights. Jonah was alibied tight. And then there was the lamp post incident."

"What lamp post incident?" I asked.

"A year or two before Callie Kendall disappeared, Jonah Bodine showed up at the station hungover and shameful. Seems he'd decided to drive himself home drunk as a skunk. Took out a lamp post over on the far end of town. He came clean, was willing to take his lumps for it."

"That's not in his file," I pointed out.

My dad gave a little shrug. "We worked it out. He did a couple of odd jobs at the station, did a little maintenance for the library, and vowed never to get behind the wheel like that again," he said. "Far as I know, he never did again."

"And you believe that? Even after the sweater, you don't think he killed her?"

Dad shook his head. "If you're askin' the sheriff, I can't afford to close my mind to any theory. But if you're asking your dad, no. I don't believe that Jonah would have hurt the Kendall girl intentionally. And if it had been an accident, he would have fessed up right quick. I'm about as sure as I can be on that."

Frustrated, I paced the concrete floor. "Nothing about this case feels right."

"Sometimes we don't get the answers we want, Cass," Dad said.

"How are we supposed to live with that?" I asked. How were we supposed to live with the unknown, accept that we'd never know everything we needed to? Hell, I'd become a cop because it was a job that demanded the truth be discovered.

He picked up the beer and pointed it toward the door where half a dozen people were laughing loud and long in the backyard. "Family. Friends. Food. We put one foot in front of the other and stay thankful for the answers we do have."

The conversation was officially over. Though my feelings about it were anything but resolved.

It was ironic. One family in Bootleg Springs that desperately wanted to believe their daughter chose to leave. Another was comforted by believing their mother had been taken.

50

BOWIE

Thomas and Geneva McCallister were wasted on pumpkin pie moonshine along with the better part of Bootleg Springs.

The Annual Bootleg Moonshine Tasting was in full swing in the town square. We had twenty-six bootleggers who had set up their folding tables on the sidewalk in front of the courthouse to peddle their doctored concoctions.

The Banjo Trio, made up of Mrs. Morganson, Mayor Hornsbladt, and Sheriff Tucker, were stirring things up with a rousing rendition of "Dear Ol' Dixie" with guest star Gibson Bodine on guitar. People were alternately dancing and drinking, some both at the same time. The cold that had gripped us seemed to dissipate for the night. Though that might be due to the alcohol everyone was indulging in.

I was pacing myself, as always. Devlin was covering his laughter with a coughing fit as Thomas and Geneva treated Sierra Hayes's Cinnamon Blueberry Shine like a high-end cabernet at a tasting. Except they should have been doing a lot more spitting.

Bootleggers trained all year for the Moonshine Tasting, and we all still felt like shit the next day. But it was worth it.

"What am I looking at?" Jonah asked, closing one eye and tilting his head. Health food junkies were notorious lightweights and succumbed quickly to the 'shine.

"That would be the Bootleg Seniors table," I explained. Gram-Gram, Devlin's Granny Louisa, and her girlfriend Estelle, were manning a table lined with shots of dark purple liquid.

Jonah picked up a glass and sniffed.

"Mystery 'Shine, sonny," Granny Louisa said before returning her attention to her knitting.

"Smells like cough syrup," Jonah frowned.

"It's mostly just for the color," Gram-Gram assured him. "This here's medicinal moonshine."

I winced as Jonah downed his grape flavored cough suppressant.

"This town is pretty great," he said, picking up another sample off Wade Zirkel's table.

"Maybe we better visit the pepperoni roll stand," I suggested, leading my inebriated half-brother in the direction of the carbs he'd disapprove of in the morning. "You're still doing that Black Friday boot camp at the high school right?"

"Shyeah. It'll be awesome. Burn those calories," he said, pumping his arms like he was running. "Am I going anywhere?"

"Uh. No. But eat this pepperoni roll. Otherwise you won't get out of bed for your boot camp."

Jonah obliged, shoving half of it in his mouth. "Umm. Carbs. They get a bad rap, you know?"

At least. That's what I thought he said. His mouth was too full to be sure.

"Hey, where's Cass-i-deee?" he sang.

I shoved another pepperoni roll in his mouth. "Keep it quiet on the Deputy Tucker questions," I warned him. "We're playing it cool. No one's supposed to know that we're dating. Remember?"

Jonah snorted. "Like you could keep a secret in this town."

"We're gonna try. That Detective Connelly doesn't take kindly to Cassidy fraternizing with murder suspects' families."

"That's bullshit. That's sexist bullshit. Bet he's not sayin' that to Sheriff Tucker or Bubba," Jonah pointed out.

"Moonshine makes you wise," I quipped. Sexist bullshit or not, I didn't want Cassidy to suffer for dating me. How would I get the girl to marry me if just fraternizing with me cost her the job she'd been dreaming about since she was fourteen?

"Psst." Cassidy strolled past me, pretty in a garnet sweater and navy vest. "Meet me by Mona Lisa's coop in ten." Her lips didn't move, and she wasn't making eye contact. She took the secrecy part of our relationship to extremes, like she was a teenager sneaking out of the house to meet her boyfriend.

I had to admit. It was hot.

"Hi, Deputy Tucker," Jonah shouted.

Cassidy turned around and grinned. "Ten minutes," she mouthed.

I needed to ditch Jonah immediately.

Gibson was still playing. Scarlett was babysitting Devlin's parents and didn't need another drunkard to run herd on. That left Jameson and Leah Mae. They were canoodled up against one of the outdoor heaters, starin' into each other's eyes like they were glued at the face. I grabbed a bottle of water and another pepperoni roll and towed Jonah in their direction.

"Jonah bet that he could do more push-ups than you," I told Jameson.

I handed the food and water over to Leah Mae. "Feed him and water him."

"Where are you going?" Jameson asked as Jonah obligingly dropped down to the sidewalk and started busting out push-ups.

"One. Two. Four..."

"Important vice principal business," I lied. Jameson caught my drift and gave me the thumbs-up.

I was early and eager. But I'd thought about nothing but touching her all day long.

I paced back and forth in front of the chicken condo and wondered if Mona Lisa was in residence or if she was out enjoying the festivities.

I heard footsteps, and when I saw that flash of red sweater, I reached out and grabbed her.

Cassidy let out a little gasp of surprise that I devoured with my mouth. I'd been so close to her all day. Elbow-to-elbow and yet I couldn't touch her the way I wanted to. We'd make up for it here in this cozy alley.

I pressed her against the cold brick of the building and kissed her like a man obsessed. She tasted like peach moonshine and starlight, and I wanted more.

Her hands were in my hair, running under my jacket, streaking under my shirt, seeking skin, contact. We'd been deprived for so long. And now we were loved. Whole. Real.

"I love you," I murmured against her mouth.

"I'm starting to believe you," she breathed before dragging me down for another kiss.

I leaned into her, holding her against the brick with my hips.

"This is my new favorite position," she said on a laugh and a sigh.

"Mine, too. Whatever position you're in is my favorite."

I shoved my hands under her sweater and found her skin warm and welcoming. She was so smooth and soft. I had trouble believing she was real.

"I used to dream that you'd do this. That I'd walk by and you'd reach out and grab me. Drag me into the dark. Have your way with me," she whispered.

"Honey, believe me. I thought about it more than a time or two," I confessed, pressing a kiss to her neck.

I wanted to bite her, taste her, mark her.

"Don't you dare leave a hickey," she hissed, reading my mind.

We'd known each other for so long, sometimes I couldn't separate her thoughts from mine.

She kissed me again with a desperation that drove me insane. So familiar and so new.

"What do you say we go on home?" Cassidy asked, her eyes glassy with need.

"You don't mind missing the tree decorating?"

She snickered. The Moonshine Tasting always ended with tasters drunkenly decorating the bottom six feet of the twenty-foot spruce on the square in front of the bank. Tomorrow town maintenance workers would undo the mess and decorate it the right way. But for one shining night, Bootleg Springs proudly wore its mess.

"I think I can skip a year," Cassidy said, pressing a kiss to the corner of my mouth before pulling on my bottom lip with her teeth.

"If you don't walk away right now, we won't make it home. It'll be in an alley with a chicken as a witness," I warned her.

I was so hard I was going to have a zipper imprint on my dick.

Her eyes sparkled at me, and I realized I'd never seen a

prettier girl in all my life. Lust and love coiled deep in my gut and bloomed like a fucking rose. With Cassidy, I had it all.

"Let's go home," she said, taking my hand and pulling me toward the mouth of the alley.

"Oh, excuse me. Sorry!" Cassidy stopped suddenly, and I rammed into her back, knocking her right into Judge Kendall's arms.

51

BOWIE

I could feel Cassidy's panic when she jumped back, yanking her hand free from mine. Judge and Mrs. Kendall looked back and forth between us. It was odd knowing that both our families were so tied up in each other. But given the circumstances, both sides had done their best to avoid each other since the news of the sweater broke.

"Mr. Bodine," Judge Kendall said formally. "It's nice to see you."

"You too, sir," I said, offering my hand for a shake.

"And Deputy Tucker." His gaze flicked back to Cassidy. Calculating as if distantly interested. "My wife told me she shared those photos with you."

Cassidy swallowed audibly. "Yes, sir."

"I certainly hope you'll be able to finally put this ugliness behind us. I'm sure Mr. Bodine and the rest of his family would agree."

What in the hell was going on?

"The investigating officer was very interested in the photos," Cassidy said. The tips of her ears were bright pink, but she managed a professional tone.

Mrs. Kendall let out a shuddery breath. "It's time we let this matter rest. Mr. Bodine," she said, addressing me. "Bowie. I'm truly sorry for the pain and suffering the selfish actions of my daughter caused your family. I don't believe I ever met either of your parents. But I feel as though I owe them an apology as well."

I had no idea what to say to that. The parents of the girl my father was suspected of murdering were telling me no hard feelings. Our lawyer Jayme would murder me if she caught wind of me talking to the Kendalls.

"Thank you for the kind words," I said lamely.

Judge Kendall cleared his throat as if he were about to make a big speech. "I think both our families are ready for a fresh start," he said. "And we'd both be served best by a swift resolution to this baseless investigation."

"Yes, sir." I had no idea what in the hell the man was talking about. But in West Virginia, you just nodded real polite and sir-ed or ma'am-ed your way out of the conversation.

"Deputy, I hope we can count on you to do what's necessary, what's best for both the Kendalls and the Bodines," Judge Kendall said. The look he gave her seemed like it carried a message with it. But it was indecipherable to me.

Cassidy made some noise about telling them to enjoy their evening. The Kendalls turned away from the festivities and walked on into the night.

"Shit. Shit. Shit." She paced the mouth of the alley.

"What's going on?" I asked her.

"What are the odds the Kendalls *aren't* going to tell Detective Connelly the next time he pays them a visit that they saw me making out with you?"

"Cassidy, this is Bootleg Springs. If the cops recused themselves from every case involving someone they know there'd be no one left to investigate anything."

"I know that and you know that. But Connelly doesn't know that!"

"The judge mentioned pictures. What was that about?" I asked.

"It doesn't matter," she said. "It's not public knowledge."

"Does it affect me and my family?" I pressed, getting the distinct impression that my girlfriend was hiding behind her badge again.

"Bowie, I can't share case details with you. We have bigger fish to fry!"

"Do we, Cassidy?"

It wasn't exactly fair of me to compare her worries about her job with the effects her investigation was having on my family. But I didn't like that we were days into our trial relationship and Cassidy was right back where she started, keeping things from me.

"The judge brought the pictures up. Obviously he wants me to know about them," I pointed out.

"Yeah, and I don't like it," Cassidy said, pacing back and forth in front of me.

I grabbed her wrist and held her still. "I don't like having a conversation with three people who keep hinting at something that I should know. When you're ready to trust me, come find me," I said. I turned to walk away. She was still determined to handle everything on her own. Still punishing me for what I'd done.

"Bowie Bodine, I let you shut a door in my face once. I will *not* let you do it again." She grabbed my arm and spun me around. Temper snapped off of her like electricity.

"This isn't just investigation shit, Cassidy. I need you to

trust me," I reminded her. "You can't keep your life separate from mine."

She dropped her hold on me. "Those pictures were of wounds on Callie Kendall's arms. Cuts. Scars from much older wounds. Mrs. Kendall gave them to me when I went to talk to her," she said flatly.

"Cuts?"

"Mrs. Kendall claims Callie was a cutter. Self-harming behavior. The pictures certainly lend credence. And when I turned the photos over to Connelly he demoted me to desk duty."

My mind was racing. "Why?" I asked.

"How the hell should I know? He's an asshole who got pissed off because I turned up a piece of evidence that he didn't find. Maybe I made him look bad?"

"Is he pursuing it?" I asked. Was it possible that Callie Kendall really had killed herself? I couldn't quite see the bright shiny girl who wowed the crowd with backflips over Rusty Reef on the lake just giving up like that.

But then again, a lot happened behind closed doors.

I didn't want to be the son of a murderer. But I also wasn't keen on the only other answer being that Callie Kendall killed herself.

"I don't know. I'm not part of the investigation! I barely have a job at this point!"

Cassidy was good and pissed.

"Why didn't you tell me about the photos?" I knew damn well why she didn't, and it wasn't because of some code of conduct. At least, not entirely. Cassidy had held back bits and pieces of herself since the day I'd broken her heart. I got it. I understood. It was a survival mechanism for her, proving that she didn't need me or anything. That she could handle everything all by herself.

But that shit wasn't going to fly if we were going to have a real shot at forever.

Cassidy threw her arms up in the air and gave a groan of frustration. "I swear to God, Bowie, you drive me insane. It's evidence in an ongoing investigation. There are rules! I'm already this close to losing my job!"

"And you don't trust me," I said.

"What are you talking about?" she asked, her shoulders slumping. "Honestly, I can't be scared the Kendalls are going to tell Connelly about us and be pissed off at you at the same time. I don't have the emotional capacity."

"Then stew on it for a while. You feel like you have to do everything yourself. And that's not how a relationship works." At least, I didn't think so. I didn't exactly have the best examples in my life, what with my parents mostly hating each other and all.

She pinched the bridge of her nose and leaned back against the brick wall. "Look. I'm new at this relationship thing. Very new. I don't think I've ever actually been in a 'let's see where this goes' relationship. So I'm gonna screw up. But damn it, Bowie, you're screwing up, too. I need you to understand how important my job is to me. I need you not to get in the way of my ability to do that job."

"All I'm asking," I said, approaching her slowly, "is that you give us a real chance. That means trusting me. I understand that you aren't going to give me photocopies of all those fancy police reports. And I wouldn't ask you for them. But when something happens like Detective Connelly taking you off a case because you were doing your job a little too well, I want to know."

I put my hands on either side of her head.

"I don't know how to balance all of this," she admitted. "I

want to do right by everybody but I can't make heads or tails of being bad at my job or bad at our relationship."

"Let's figure it out. Together." I leaned down and kissed the tip of her nose.

"I don't like failing, Bowie," she said, her tone serious.

"Then I won't let you, Deputy Do Right."

She looked sad and tired. The energy and excitement from our make-out session had dissipated. "How about we go hang some tinsel on that tree?" I suggested. "Christmas decorating always makes you feel better."

"We're supposed to be keeping things quiet," she reminded me.

"I promise not to kiss you or do anything else that could be considered boyfriendly," I promised.

"Do you think the Kendalls will tell Connelly about us?"

"All they saw was us walking out of an alley laughing. They don't strike me as the gossipy type." Maybe it was because they'd endured so many years of whispers, of pitying looks. But the Kendalls looked like they could keep a secret.

52

BOWIE

We all showed up in the high school gym the next morning to watch Jonah struggle through a boot camp hangover. Even Gibs was here, peopling on purpose. Of course, Gibson was never hungover. He never drank. Our father drank, therefore Gibs never did.

I admired his fortitude but sometimes wondered if not doing something because someone else did it was as bad as doing something just because someone else did it.

"Okay, let's get started with some high knee jogs," Jonah rasped, gesturing at us to split into lines. He looked a little green around the gills.

Truth be told, most of us did. There were thirty of us, a range of ages, sizes, and shapes. I'd be willing to bet that a good fifty percent was hungover.

As if the universe bade it, Cassidy lined up next to me and we jogged down the gym floor to half court together. She'd insisted on coming alone and being aloof.

"How are you feelin' today?" I asked, trying not to huff and puff. Maybe I needed to give Jonah a little bit more of my time.

She didn't look at me. "Fine."

She'd given me a cursory peck on the cheek last night and gone right on inside, shutting the door behind her.

I could take a hint.

This relationship thing was new. We were both bound to make some missteps. It wasn't fair of me to ask her to share confidential information. Somewhere around the middle of the night while I was staring up at my ceiling, I realized that what bothered me most was that she hadn't *wanted* to share anything. The DNA results, the photos of Callie's wounds. It hadn't even occurred to her that I'd want to know. There'd been no internal moral battle between her loyalty to her job and her loyalty to me.

Her job, the law, had always been there for her. And I hadn't.

Of course, it hadn't occurred to Cassidy to *want* to share. She was a rule-follower, a by-the-booker, and that was part of what I loved about her. That steadiness. That constancy. I could depend on her to be solid. Unlike my mother, who changed moods quicker than a spring breeze.

I'd debated for a good hour before falling asleep whether or not I should call Jayme and let her know about the pictures. I finally decided to leave it be for now. If our attorney started asking Connelly questions about those pictures, he'd know exactly where the information came from. I needed to trust the law. For now.

"Cass," I said when we hit half court. *What was Jonah trying to do? Kill us with the warm-up?* "I'm sorry. I shouldn't have expected you to break your code. That wasn't fair."

She tripped and recovered, catching up with me.

"I don't know what to say," she admitted.

"How about, 'You sure look handsome this morning, Bowie,'" I suggested.

She shot me a look that ended with a small smile. "I'm not really upset with you," she said.

We made it back to our starting point, and I stepped across the line, not ready to be done with the conversation.

"Bowie," she hissed warningly, glancing around us at the sweaty, hungover crowd.

"Cass, we've had nine million conversations over the years. It's only weird now if we make it weird."

She took her time retying her ponytail. "I'm mad at myself. My job is the one on the line. I should be taking better precautions. Hell, I shouldn't even be mixing it up with you."

I didn't like that. "Don't you think we've let enough people come between us?"

She hit me in the chest and then glanced around making sure no one was paying attention. "You're only saying it because it's not you and my dad causing the problem this time around!"

I rubbed absently at the spot she'd slapped. She may have had the slimmest of points.

The woman had reluctantly cut me eight years of slack. I had a responsibility to be patient.

"Let's talk later," she suggested, eyes flicking to a pretty brunette nearby that I'd never seen before. She, unlike most of the rest of us, was perky and eager to follow Jonah's pained instructions.

"Later," I agreed.

"WELL, THAT WAS HORRIBLE." Gibson was guzzling water while I bent in half and sucked wind.

"I took it easy on everyone," Jonah said, opening his bottle and chugging something green and lumpy.

"That's not your magic hangover cure, is it?" I asked, eyeing it with suspicion.

"Nope, rebalancing shake," he wheezed.

"Looks like most of the town could use some rebalancing," Cassidy said, joining us.

There were bodies everywhere. Some curled in the fetal position. Some flat on their backs staring up at the gym ceiling.

"Anyone want breakfast?" Devlin asked. He was sweaty, but in a healthy, used to it kind of way. Scarlett was sprawled at his feet muttering about oxygen and the lack of it.

"I could do breakfast," I said. No school until next Wednesday. I was looking forward to the break.

Gibson grunted his assent.

"Can't. I have work," Cassidy said, mopping at her brow with the hem of her t-shirt. I was momentarily transfixed by the flash of her stomach, the peek of pink from her sports bra.

Down, boy. I was used to hiding my feelings for her. But now that I'd finally had a taste of her, I felt like my facade was crumbling.

"Don't you know the boss man or something?" Scarlett teased from the floor, tugging on Cassidy's shoelaces. "Can't you ask him for an extra hour so you can fuel up for your day of crime-fightin'?"

"I don't get special treatment because of who my father is," Cassidy said, her jaw tight. "Y'all have a nice day."

Scarlett clawed her way up Devlin's leg until he leaned down to pick her up. "Geez. What crawled into her knickers?" she demanded.

"My guess is Bowie," Gibson said.

Shit.

Jonah looked up at one of the lights hanging from the ceiling like it was absolutely fascinating.

I stared at the floor and scratched the back of my head. I couldn't remember how I'd brushed off comments about Cassidy before. How had I played it off like there was nothing there? Like my feelings weren't real? Right now I was standing here looking guilty.

"See?" Gibs said smugly. "Told you."

Scarlett was working her way into an excited lather. "Oh. My. God."

"Hold your horses," I hissed. "Keep it down. No one's supposed to know."

"Why not?" Scarlett was bouncing on her toes.

"That Connelly character who's investigating Dad thinks she's too close to us. If he knew we were—" I looked left and right, making sure no one else was eavesdropping "—seein' each other, he'd have her badge."

Devlin frowned. "I don't know if he can do that. I'd need to check on the jurisdictional—"

"I love it when you talk lawyerly," Scarlett breathed, leaning into him.

"He's already taken her off the investigation." If I was gonna air Cassidy's dirty laundry, then I was going to hang it all out to dry. "She's only allowed to scan old files and drive patrol."

"That's bullshit!" Scarlett snapped. "Dev, I want you to sue him or disbar him or whatever."

Gibson echoed her sentiment.

"Needless to say, none of you are allowed to breathe a word of this to anyone or I will sign y'all up as prom chaperones," I threatened.

"What are you gonna do about it?" Jonah asked. He was warming up to the way things worked around here. Bootleg Justice had a special kind of appeal.

"Nothing right now. It's better if she handles it," I told them.

"Excuse me?" That brunette from earlier was poking her head into our circle. "Jonah, was it?"

Jonah looked mildly flustered, and I wondered if it was because she was inordinately pretty or just a stranger. We'd all been a little careful around strangers the past few weeks. Especially since the press had tip-toed back into town.

"Uh. Yeah. That's me," he said.

"It was a great class," she said, beaming at him.

At least someone had enough energy to beam. The rest of us just got sweaty and wheezy.

"Thanks," Jonah said, putting his hands on his hips then deciding to cross his arms over his chest.

Scarlett was watching with a twinkle in her eye, and I made a mental note to warn Jonah. When Scarlett got an idea, everyone generally got out of the way and let her have whatever she wanted. It was easier than trying to survive the consequences.

"I'm Shelby, by the way." She held out a hand, and Jonah hesitated too long before finally shaking it.

"Are you new in town, Shelby?" Scarlett asked, the picture of innocence.

Gibson rolled his eyes. "Watch your back," he whispered to Jonah out of the corner of his mouth.

"I'm in town for the holidays," Shelby said, turning her warm smile on Scarlett.

"Well, you'll probably see all us Bodines around," Scarlett predicted.

"I bet I will."

53

CASSIDY

Dating Bowie was easy. I'd already dedicated a large portion of my mental function over the years to him—Where was he? What was he doing? Why did he smell so good? Was he watching me walk away?—and he'd been such a strong physical presence, that all this felt...natural.

Well, besides the secret part. And the could lose my job part. We'd called a truce on the topic of the pictures because there wasn't much else we could do. Neither one of us agreed with the other's priorities, me and my job and him and his family. So we ignored it and hoped it would go away on its own.

We had dinner with Jonah every night, the three of us catching up on our days. Every night, Bowie would come into my bed and we'd live out the fantasies we'd each carried with us over the years.

In public, we played it cool as cucumbers.

Except for that time that Bernie O'Dell caught a glimpse of us making out in The Lookout parking lot. Bowie covered and said I was just checking his tire for nails. Or the time that Carolina Rae Carwell maybe might have seen us holding hands walking home in the dark from the Yee Haw Yarn and Coffee Christmas Carol Singalong.

The whole town was decked out for ol' St. Nick in a few thousand strands of lights and a forest of handmade wreaths. The storefront windows were painted with holiday scenes. My cats were cuddly, entertaining roommates that only tried to kill Bowie once every few days. The only fights Bowie and I were having were over how to load the dishwasher properly and who was the better kisser.

Spoiler alert: my way and me.

Kidding. Bowie was a far superior kisser, but I was catching up quick with hours of dedicated practice.

Yeah, life was pretty damn perfect. My only problem was what did I get the man for Christmas? We'd only just started dating, and secretly at that. However, I'd known him my whole life. And our secret six weeks of dating would be wrapping up around then.

I was under pressure to find him something good. Really good.

My laptop signaled an incoming email from Connelly with another dozen item list of ridiculous administrative tasks that required my attention that afternoon when I came in for my shift.

Okay, so everything *else* was great. But work was still crap.

Since the pictures of Callie Kendall, Connelly had made one snide remark after another about me and my ability to do my job. I took pride in how well my blank cop face hid the creative and illegal ideas I had for revenge. I stood, or sat, stoically while he made barbed comments that bordered on harassment.

My dad was a go along to get along kind of guy and even his patience was wearing thin. But if he spoke up in my defense, it would only prove that I needed my daddy to help me muddle through my job.

If I stood up for myself, odds were Connelly would demand my gun and my badge.

I brought up a search engine and did a quick hunt to see if investigating state police detectives would have jurisdiction to fire employees of a municipal department. Hmm. The definitive answer appeared to be a confusing "maybe." I wondered if I should talk to Devlin about it?

"Hey." Bowie poked his unreasonably sexy head into my kitchen. The doors between our places now stayed open. Well, except at night so Jonah wouldn't accidentally catch sight of naked shenanigans.

"Hey yourself," I said, admiring the view. He was wearing those sweats that I personally took off of him with my teeth last night and a hoodie. "Jonah and I are putting the lights up on the front. Can you listen for the oven timer?"

Everything about him was so...cozy.

I got up and followed him into his kitchen. "What is that deliciousness I'm smelling?"

He snagged a coiled string of lights out of a plastic tote marked Christmas Shit. "Sugar cookies. My mom's recipe."

My heart did that funny little tumble thing. If I hadn't loved him for my whole life before, that's all it would have taken.

"Sugar cookies? You're baking? From scratch?" Bowls and beaters were stacked neatly in the sink, evidence of the fact that my secret boyfriend was the best secret boyfriend in the history of secret boyfriends. And it was his mama's recipe.

"Can't decorate for Christmas and not have cookies. Eight minutes," he said, dropping a kiss on my mouth and flashing that lopsided smile. "When they're done, you can put the next trays in."

I eyed up the four trays of cookies waiting for the oven. "What's in it for me?" I asked.

"We'll decorate your front porch and you can have as many cookies as you want."

Sold. Someone bang the gavel because I was definitely hanging on to this man.

He gave me another kiss, one that involved a promise of things to come after my shift tonight, and then I admired the view as he headed out the front door. Those sweatpants should be illegal. *Hmm. Maybe I could arrest him for public sexiness?*

I ducked back to my side and grabbed my laptop. I'd set up shop closer to the oven so I could taste the product for quality control purposes.

I could hear the guys talking from the front porch, calling to someone. Nosiness was in my nature so I peered through the side light on the front door. Well, well, it was that nice-looking brunette from Jonah's boot camp, looking cute as can be in a navy wool coat.

Shelby Something.

Hmm.

I was nosy *and* suspicious by nature. The fact that she'd made it a point to introduce herself after the class and just happened to be walking by on a cold as frozen over hell day made my nose twitch.

I went back over to my side and grabbed my phone.

When it came to Bootleg, I had my pick of gossipmongers. I picked Millie Waggle and fired off a text.

Me: Hey, Millie. You run into that Shelby yet? New in town. Staying for the holidays.

Approximately twenty seconds later, I had chapter and

verse on Ms. Shelby Thompson who was currently in residence in the B&B part of the Bootleg Springs Spa. Apparently she was considering moving into a rental. She wore size seven shoes. And was often seen jogging in the early mornings like a crazy person. She preferred tea over coffee and "seemed genuinely interested in everyone and everything."

My spidey senses were tingling. I did a nifty little search for Ms. Shelby Thompson, and when those results were too generic, I logged into the station's database.

Well, well, well. Hello, Shelby Thompson, 28, of Pittsburgh, Pennsylvania. Her record was squeaky clean. Not a parking ticket or traffic violation in the last five years. With the added information of her middle initial and hometown, I redid my regular search and found what I was looking for.

Little Miss Nice as Pie had graduated with a degree in journalism from West Virginia University. Oh, and lookie here. She was currently a freelance writer with credits in several newspapers, magazines, and blogs.

I thought of Jonah's dopey "she's so pretty" expression and felt a tiny bit bad that I was going to have to crush his crush. The oven timer zzz-ed to life. Both our kitchens could use a makeover, I thought, pulling the first two trays of hearts and trees out of the ancient oven and setting them on the scrap of table with cooling racks.

Imagine the space if we took the wall down and had one big kitchen.

The sizzling of my own flesh brought me back. I'd caught Bowie's forever fever, I thought, sucking my abused thumb into my mouth. It was contagious. If it weren't for my work situation, it would be real tempting to daydream a little about the future.

But what was the point with Connelly breathing down my

neck and causing a ruckus? I needed a plan where that man was concerned. A way to change his mind about me.

Because the fact was, until the Callie Kendall case heated up or cooled off I didn't have a future to plan. I popped the next two trays into the oven, reset the timer, and sat back down at my laptop, trying to ignore the sugary scents of awesomeness.

With Connelly still on my mind, I typed his name into the search engine.

"Well, I'll be damned," I breathed.

54

BOWIE

I eased into Scarlett's driveway and cursed when I didn't see a delivery vehicle there. She'd invited me for dinner tonight to "strategize," and I hoped to God that meant she wasn't cooking. My sister was a lot of things. A passable cook who probably wouldn't give her guests food poisoning was not one of them.

I let myself in the front door of the cabin and ran right into a clothing rack full of suits that was blocking the hallway. "Scarlett?"

Something smelled unpleasant in here. Like burnt meat and bad eggs. Why didn't I offer to pick something up?

"Back here, Bow," she called from the kitchen.

The house was doll-sized with one bedroom, a bath barely bigger than the tub, and a living-dining-kitchen space that was roughly the size of my living room. With its scrap of lake frontage and tree-filled yard, it suited Scarlett down to the ground. At least it had until Devlin the Clothes Horse moved in. There was a shoe rack on top of the coffee table that had been shoved up against the wall to make room for a folding table buckling under the weight of two laptops and a mess of paperwork.

"How do you like our home office?" Scarlett chirped.

She and Devlin were decked out in aprons and hot pads, trying to scrape something that looked like it could have been a meatloaf out of a pan.

"It's real homey," I lied, noting the books stacked up on the floor. Kitten Jedidiah was unraveling a very nice-looking cashmere sweater stored in one of the half-dozen laundry baskets piled together blocking the patio doors.

Devlin looked up from the burnt gray meat. "They broke ground yesterday. Another six months and we'll have some space to spread out," he said cheerfully.

I scratched the back of my head. Every flat surface was buried under things that should have had a rightful place. I guessed that's what you got when you took two independent lives and smashed them together in six hundred square feet. Now, Cassidy and I had an entire house to work with. We could take out walls and have plenty of room for rambling.

"Knock knock," Cassidy called from the front door.

"What are you up to?" I hissed at my sister.

"This is between me and your *secret* girlfriend who still hasn't told me y'all are together," Scarlett said wickedly. "In the kitchen, Cass," she sang.

Cassidy came around the corner, narrowly avoiding a stack of law books, and stopped short when she saw me. She was in uniform, and her hair was pulled back in that slick bun.

"Isn't this nice?" Scarlett asked sweetly. "I would have invited the others, but we're plum out of room."

"Cassidy, I have that thing in my car you wanted to borrow —" I began. But my sister cut me off.

"Bowie, do you mind gettin' the deviled eggs out of the

refrigerator?" she asked. There was an edge to her tone. She was warning me off. Family first.

I needed to get Cassidy alone and tell her she was walking into a Scarlett Bodine trap.

"I'm sure Devlin can handle the eggs," I said.

"Get the damn eggs, Bowie," Scarlett barked. "And don't even think about getting between me and your secret pal over there," she added so only I could hear when I wriggled my way between her and Devlin to get to the refrigerator.

I opened the door and gagged at the smell of sulfur. Devlin ducked behind it with me and pulled his sweater over his nose. "What's going on?" he asked, his voice muffled by cashmere.

"I think Scarlett's tryin' to teach Cassidy a lesson about keeping secrets."

"Well, that should be fun. Don't eat the meatloaf. She dropped it on the floor and the cat ran through it," he whispered back.

"Good to know."

"So, Cassidy, what's new with you? What's happening in your world these days?" Scarlett asked.

I straightened up and waved my hands like an air traffic controller behind Scarlett's back.

Scarlett must have felt the breeze because her head whipped around.

Innocently, I held up the tray of deviled eggs that were more orange than yellow at arm's length so the smell wouldn't contaminate me.

I could tell by Cassidy's wrinkled nose that the smell was wafting in her direction.

"Why, thank you, Bowie," Scarlett said, sweeter than a tall glass of sweet tea in August. Shit was about to go down.

She linked her arm through mine. "I'm so happy y'all are *friends* again. Isn't it great to be *friends*? Bless your heart."

"She knows," I mouthed to Cassidy.

Cassidy rolled her eyes. She was no dummy.

"Bowie told you," she said, cutting to the chase.

Nice as pie Scarlett disappeared and was replaced with violently angry Scarlett. "You're damn right he told me, which is what you should have done. We are family, Cassidy Ann Tucker. I have been planning your wedding to Bowie since the second grade. And you think it's okay to strike up a relationship and not tell me? Are you touched in the head?"

"Oh, I can trust you, can I?" Cassidy demanded, rounding on me.

"Don't you dare get mad at him for telling me something you should have," Scarlett shrilled.

Cassidy gave me a look that telegraphed the fact that we were going to have a discussion later. But she had louder, meaner fish to fry first.

"Now, Scarlett," she began in her calmest deputy voice.

"Don't you 'now Scarlett' me! What else have you been hiding from me? Did you win that big lottery six months ago that no one has claimed yet? Is your real name even Cassidy?"

"We should maybe step outside," Devlin said.

Jedidiah sprinted over and launched himself at the bookcase, scrabbling to the top shelf so he could knock a photo of Scarlett, June, and Cassidy over. I wondered if it was coincidence or if Scarlett had trained him.

"I think I need to stay inside in case things get ugly," I told Devlin.

"I can handle myself just fine." Cassidy glared at me.

"That right there is your stupid problem, you stupid jerk," Scarlett said, pointing an accusatory finger in Cassidy's direction. "I can do everything myself," she mimicked.

"I *can* do everything myself," Cassidy argued.

"Well, you don't have to, you idiot! What's with all the secrets? I cut you some slack over the DNA tests. But you're dating *my brother* and didn't think to tell me? This is your second strike, Tucker."

Devlin raised his hands peacemaker-style. "Maybe we should all sit down and discuss—"

"Get out!" Scarlett and Cassidy commanded.

"Yes, ma'ams," I said, running like hell for the patio doors.

Devlin was hot on my heels.

I left the glass door open a crack so we could eavesdrop safely and then sat down on a cushioned lounger that must have belonged to Devlin's past life.

He was pulling out his cell phone.

"You can't call the cops. One of them's already here," I joked.

"I'm calling for pizza."

55

CASSIDY

"I can't believe Bowie told you," I groused. I wanted to pace but there was no freaking room in Scarlett's stuffed house.

"I can't believe you didn't tell me! We're family!" Scarlett hollered. She was on the other side of the armchair and two laundry baskets full of Devlin's gym clothes.

"You don't know the whole story. And you're not exactly known for keeping your mouth shut!"

Her green eyes narrowed, and I knew I was entering the Danger Zone.

"You think I don't know Connelly's basically tied you to a desk and is holding your employment hostage? And do you really think Bowie came a runnin' telling tales about you? Why I'm so mad at you right now, Cassidy Ann, I could spit!"

"Bowie told you something I asked him not to." Christ. Did this mean he'd spilled the beans about the photos of Callie Kendall, too? My head was starting to hurt and only part of it was the smell from those fluorescent orange deviled eggs.

"Now you listen here, Deputy Assface," Scarlett said, climbing over the armchair and scaling the coffee table.

"Gibson guessed that you two had hooked up and Bowie did that twitchin' thing he does when he's lying so we all knew."

"All? All who?" My voice was an octave higher than usual.

"The whole damn family. Since Black Friday. I gave you two dang weeks to tell me the truth! My best friend and my brother and you don't think I deserve to know?"

I flinched. "It's not that you didn't deserve to know. It's just...complicated."

"I don't fucking care if its astrophysics! This keeping shit to yourself has got to stop." She was close enough to drill a finger into my nameplate on my uniform. "Get this straight, deputy, handling shit is one thing, but shutting people out on purpose is another thing."

I set my jaw. "Look. I'm sorry. I didn't know how serious this was gonna get and I didn't want you to get excited if we burned out and there was nothing to get excited over. Plus, Connelly doesn't want me to have anything to do with y'all. If he knew that Bowie and I are dating, he'd have my badge."

"Dev! Find out if that's a possibility," Scarlett screeched at the patio doors. "I know what you're doing. Bowie hurt you way back when and you made it your mission in life to never rely on anyone again. That's some shit for you two to work out. But I have never once in my entire life let you down."

I couldn't say the same thing to her. Not honestly.

"There are reasons. My job—"

"Your daddy's been doin' his job an awful long time without shutting people out and alienating them," she shot back.

That took the wind out of my sails a bit.

"Look," Scarlett said, crossing her arms over her chest. "I'm not saying you should be breaking laws for us. I'm saying use your discretion to not be some asshole's puppet. That Connelly sat on those DNA results until they'd make the biggest impact and then he pulled together a dog and pony show and brought the press down on us like locusts. Hell, I wouldn't be surprised if he were the one who leaked the results."

She must have seen the look on my face because Scarlett gave me a shove. "I knew it! And you didn't tell me? What the hell is your problem?"

I looked out through the glass and noted that Bowie and Devlin were staring out into the dark, pretending they couldn't hear us.

"My problem is he thinks I'm only here because my daddy gave me a job."

"Fuck. That. Why are you trying to prove yourself to a man who is obviously a ginormous fucking moron?"

"Because maybe he's right!" I shouted back.

Scarlett rolled her eyes. "Now you're being an idiot."

"What if he's right? What if I don't belong on the force? What if the only reason I got this job was because my daddy gave it to me?"

"You're letting him get in your head. You're letting some asshole stranger come in and tell you how to live your life. You're letting him wreck your job and turn your friends into enemies. Worst of all, you're letting him come between you and the guy you've loved since pre-school."

I flopped back on the couch, suddenly too tired to fight. Besides, Scarlett didn't like to hit people when they were sad.

"You keepin' secrets is you choosing Connelly over us when he's done nothing to deserve your loyalty. Stop treating us like the enemy and start treating him like one."

I was so tired of all the secrets. They were piling up left and right like firewood. Sooner or later it would all catch fire.

"Fine. I think Connelly's so tied up in this personal vendetta that he's ignoring important pieces of the investigation," I told her. "Mrs. Kendall turned in photos of Callie's self-inflicted injuries and far as I can tell, he hasn't even had a conversation with her or the judge about them."

To her credit, Scarlett didn't immediately jump all over me with questions.

"And for the record, Bowie knows about the pictures but only because the Kendalls brought them up in front of him. And if word leaks about them, Connelly's gonna know it came from me and that would be the final nail in my professional coffin."

Scarlett's wheels were turning. She was a fixer, a burn-it-downer. I couldn't tell which way she was leaning at this point.

"I've been seeing your brother since right before Thanksgiving. He agreed to a six-week trial to see if there's something real between us."

"And is there?" Scarlett asked expectantly.

"Of course there is," I looked to the glass door, wondering if he could hear me. "I love him. Always have. Worse yet, I'm *in* love with him. But we keep rubbing up against my job. I've wanted this forever, Scar. I've wanted to be a cop in Bootleg and I've always wanted to be Bowie Bodine's girl. Why can't I have both?"

"Listen up, Cass. You listen up good. Just because twenty-three-year-old Bowie hurt you, doesn't make him a bad guy. And just because this Connelly fella is the law, doesn't automatically make him a good guy."

She paced toward me and back around the debris of her newly combined life. "You've gone and let both of them influence how you feel about yourself. That's your damn problem. You keep letting other people's opinions about you influence your own. And it's none of your damn business what other people think of you. Your job is to go out there and be the best damn Cassidy Tucker you can be. Not livin' up or down to someone else's take on you."

I blinked. Several times. "Is that what I'm doing?"

Scarlett dramatically collapsed on the floor and covered her face with her hands. "Dear Lord, grant me the serenity to not murder all of my dumbass friends and family," she moaned.

"What in the hell am I supposed to do?" I asked, exasperated.

"Figure out what the hell you want. Do you want to be a deputy? Do you want to be with my brother?"

"Yes, but how—"

"Does knowing the people you're policing diminish your ability to be good at your job?"

"No, but—"

"Do you want to wake up to Bowie every Christmas morning for the rest of your life?"

Yes.

I did. I wanted a lifetime with the man. Of cookies baking in the oven, babies laughing, kisses stolen in the pantry, of quiet nights where nothing else mattered but his skin against mine.

Not trusting my voice and not really wanting Bowie to know all of this mess, I nodded.

Scarlett rolled up into a seated position. "Then stop letting other people dictate how you live your life. Stop trying to do everything all by your lonesome. Start standing up for yourself. Share. Be part of this life, not just some outsider lookin' in and keepin' secrets. And for Pete's sake, stop lying to your best friend in the whole world!"

"That is a whole lot of conflicting advice," I pointed out.

But Scarlett was done with me.

"A secret relationship?" she scoffed to herself as she

climbed to her feet. "That's the dumbest damn thing I've heard all week." She headed toward the patio doors.

"He got in my head," I admitted. Connelly had prodded the cracks that I'd developed after Bowie broke my heart. *I wasn't good enough. My instincts were off. I didn't belong here.*

"Well now, I think it's time you got in his."

"I might have something," I admitted. "I did a little internet research."

"Did you now?" Scarlett nodded her approval.

"Speaking of. That Shelby girl from boot camp? She's a journalist. I think she's trying to get to y'all through Jonah. I haven't told him yet." I thought back to his "ah, shucks" face at Shelby's compliments. The guy had to be lonely out here away from his mother and friends. But accidentally cozying up to a reporter wasn't the answer.

Scarlett's eyes narrowed. "Oh, we'll see about that."

We were silent for a beat and then another one.

"I don't want to see you fuck this all up, Cass," Scarlett confessed. "You gotta understand that obeying crooked authority isn't doing the right thing. Neither is making yourself small and your wants few. Deep down you know what's right. You know what you want out of life. So don't fuck that up just because you're scared."

I nodded again, and she reached for the patio door. Bowie and Devlin were probably frozen out there.

"Thanks, Scar," I said softly.

"Don't thank me. I'm mad at you, Cass. You're gonna have to make this disappointment up to me in a big way." She turned away from me and toward the porch. "Y'all can come back in."

"Good," Bowie said. "We're freezin' out here and the pizza'll be here in five."

56

CASSIDY

"Scarlett still mad at you?" Bowie asked as we wandered up Lake Drive.

I'd thrown caution to the wind and let him talk me into hitting the Pop In for a late-night ice cream treat. We weren't holding hands or sticking tongues down each other's throats, but we were visible. Together. An inflatable Frosty the Snowman tipped his top hat at me from Yee Haw Yarn and Coffee's patio.

We were a week out from Christmas, and I hadn't come up with any solutions to my immediate problems, which included:

How to date Bowie without getting fired?

How to get Connelly to stop treating me like dog crap?

How to apologize to Scarlett?

It was a lot of how to questions and not a lot of answers. And I hated to admit it, but I felt something stirring under the holiday calm. Something was gonna break. But I didn't know if it was the investigation, Bowie's patience, Connelly's limited self-control, or my heart.

"Yeah," I sighed, biting into my ice cream sandwich. "I haven't quite figured out how to fix that yet."

"You'll figure it out," he said, opening my car door for me.

I slid in, buckled up. Bowie climbed in behind the wheel and cranked the heater. He looked over at me, a sexy sparkle in his eyes. "You know how many times over the last few years I've wished I could take you for ice cream?"

I smiled back. Every time he confessed to a yearning that had tortured him, I felt another seam in my heart stitch itself up. "You know, I've had a few fantasies over the years, too," I confessed.

We'd worked our way through several of Bowie's winter-themed fantasies that he'd banked. The baggy sweater and nothing else under it had been quite enjoyable. So had the undressing Deputy Tucker scenario.

"Tell me," he demanded, steering my car toward home with one hand while devouring his strawberry shortcake bar.

"I used to imagine sneaking out of Scarlett's room and into yours when I slept over."

"I shared a room with Jameson," Bowie said, cracking a smile.

"That's why we'd have to be *real* quiet."

He shot me a look and made a right-hand turn.

"Where are we going?" I laughed as he turned us away from home.

"My dad's house."

"Are you serious?" I was equal parts horrified and delighted.

"It's a little different now with the renovations and all. But my old room still has two twin beds."

"It doesn't! We can't."

"Is the pretty deputy scared?" Bowie quipped.

"I'm an adult with a very nice queen-sized bed at home," I pointed out.

"Yeah, but imagine what would have happened if seventeen-year-old you had snuck into twenty-one-year-old me's bed."

"You would have been all chivalrous and kicked me out," I guessed. Which is exactly why I'd never done it. I'd made it as far as the hallway outside his door. Twice. But I'd never been brave enough to attempt it.

We were three minutes away from the Bodine homestead. And in those three minutes, I relived just about every teenage fantasy I'd ever had sleeping over at Scarlett's. I'd come out of the shower in a towel and Bowie would drag me into his room. Or he'd lead me into the woods during a bonfire and have his way with me against a tree. Or we'd run into each other in the kitchen in the middle of the night, and he'd slide me up on the counter and kiss me.

Or I'd sneak into his room and he'd hold the sheet up, welcoming me into his bed.

He bumped down the driveway to the bungalow with its wooded acre and its tidy white trim. They'd re-sided it in a dark green and re-stained the porch a rich, dark honey. It looked crisp, clean, inviting.

And not at all like the home I'd spent many a summer nights in.

Bowie brought my car to a stop. "Come on."

We unlocked the door and slipped inside. It smelled like fresh paint and carpet. They were still debating on selling it outright or renting it. There were a lot of memories tied up in these walls. Good and bad.

The paint was different, the kitchen updated, but the bones were the same. I remembered watching movies in that skinny living room and that the third step from the bottom squeaked. Important knowledge for when we snuck out of the house in our teenage years.

He took my hand and led me up the stairs. Bowie paused in the hallway and pressed me up against the wall outside the bathroom. My heart thumped its approval. *So many memories. So many wants and needs.*

"Sorry, sneaking in another little fantasy," he said, leaning into me.

"Tell me," I whispered.

"You'd be coming out of the bathroom real late. No one else is awake," he said, slipping his hands into my coat and settling them under my breasts. "You'd make the first move."

"Like this?" I asked, shifting our positions so it was Bowie against the wall and I was the one pinning him there.

"God, yes," he breathed into my mouth.

"Would I kiss you?" I asked, brushing my lips against his lightly.

Bowie nodded, and I obliged, closing my fingers in his shirt and holding him there. "I'd make it known that I wanted your hands on me."

"Yes," he hissed.

"You wouldn't have a choice. You wouldn't have to be the good guy. Because it's late and I want you."

His breath hitched, and I wondered how many fantasies we'd shared without the other knowing.

"What did I do next?" I asked.

Bowie took my hand and slid it down over his stomach to cup his hard-on through his pants.

I purred, no longer pretending to be seventeen. "Yes."

"What next," Bowie asked, caught up in the moment.

"We have to be together. You have to touch me. We need a room with a lock."

"The bathroom," he said.

"Exactly." We kissed and pawed our way to the bathroom door, shedding our coats on the fresh carpet.

"Jesus, Cass. I've waited so long for this."

"We're in the bathroom. Door's locked," I said. My hands were shaking, and my insides were going to liquid. "Now what?"

"You're wearing one of those cute pajama sets that I always loved."

I slipped my bra off under my sweater and fished it out of one sleeve. He swallowed hard, and my nipples pebbled. He helped me shuck my leggings so I wore only the sweater.

"You're wearing nothing but a pair of shorts," I told him, dragging his shirt over his head. Bowie made quick work of his jeans and stood before me in just tight boxer briefs. He was so hard that the head of his cock was escaping the waistband.

He backed me up against the vanity and settled me on the counter.

"That's better," he said, moving between my thighs.

I needed him to touch me right here, right now.

"How far do we go?" he asked me, fisting his cock.

"As far as we can get away with."

"I can't believe you were thinking about this, too," he said as I spread my legs for him. Bowie slid his hands around my ass and pulled me to the edge of the counter.

I reached down between us and closed my fingers around his shaft.

He dropped his forehead to mine as I started to stroke him, guiding his tip through my wet folds.

"What did you do when I slept over?" I asked him, hungry for pieces of him that I hadn't had.

"I always looked in on y'all," he confessed, staring down between us to where our bodies were almost joined.

"You did?" My heart picked up the pace, imagining it.

"I'd lay awake for hours listening to you two giggle and gossip. When y'all got quiet, I'd poke my head in to make sure you were asleep and not sneaking out."

"And then what?"

"And then I'd picture something exactly like this," he confessed.

I gripped him harder and reveled at the moisture that collected at his tip.

"And you'd touch yourself?" I asked, breathless.

He nodded and reached down. He lined himself up with my entrance that was all kinds of hydrated. "I'd think about how wet you'd be for me. How you'd say my name and I'd have to put my hand over your mouth to keep you quiet."

"Bowie."

With a slow, sexy grin, he closed one big hand over my mouth.

"Quiet, honey," he whispered. "We don't want to wake anybody up."

And then he was slamming himself into me. I cried out against his hand, and he growled. "This is what I thought about, Cassidy. You and me," he said as he pulled out and drove back into me.

I brought my knees up, so he could work himself in and out with ease. I was so fucking wet for him. I always was. My body had been programmed to respond to his. It was the only explanation for why I was already so close to coming.

He kept that hand over my mouth, and I clung to his shoulders while we stared into each other's eyes.

"You drive me insane, Cass. I can't think about anything else but you."

I didn't know if it was Past Bowie or Current Bowie saying it, but I sure was appreciative either way.

The feel of him driving into me, those powerful thrusts that bottomed him out inside me, drove me crazy.

"Hold tight," he ordered gruffly.

I gripped him with my arms and thighs, and he slid his free hand under my sweater.

"I'd fuck you like this, Cass. Right here. It would be our little secret. Our beautiful, dirty little secret." His thumb brushed over my nipple that had puckered to stone.

One hand on my mouth, one hand at my breast, tugging and squeezing, and I was coming. I felt my muscles milk his cock, closing around him, gripping and sliding.

"Fuck, fuck," I chanted against his palm.

"That's my girl. My beautiful girl," he said with dark pleasure glazing his eyes.

He was grunting softly now on every thrust, and I wanted him to come. I wanted to see this fantasy through, see what Teenage Cassidy was capable of doing to Bowie.

"Fuck, baby. When you come I go crazy," he growled. Then he was pulling out of me, gripping his cock hard. He stroked hard and fast until the first rope of his release shot out onto my folds. He kept stroking, kept coming, covering my stomach, my thighs, my center with his release.

It was beautiful, desperate, erotic. And I was dizzy with love.

57

BOWIE

"Scarlett is gonna murder us for using her new towels to clean up bodily fluids," Cassidy predicted as I ran the towel under the hot water.

"Honey she'd be a lot more pissed if we left this mess for her," I teased, cleaning us both up as best I could. She was beautiful with her walls down and her cheeks flushed. Happiness radiated out of her like heat from the sun.

"That was crazy hot, wasn't it? I mean, I thought it was," Cassidy said. She had a tendency to jabber after sex. A trait I found fucking adorable.

"Crazy hot," I agreed.

"What will we do after we run out of fantasies?" Cassidy asked, concerned.

I rinsed the towel out in the sink and looked down her long, lean body. "Honey, I think we'll be fine." I had a feeling I could spend a lifetime coming up with new ways to appreciate Cassidy's body.

"I can't believe we did that," she said, hopping off the counter and feeling around on the floor for her pants.

I leaned down and kissed her hard. "You're my every dream come true. When are you gonna realize that?"

She smiled up at me, and I couldn't help but gather her up and swing her around in the tight space.

I wondered if she'd known that she'd just given me my very happiest memory in this house.

"Is it weird to be here?" she asked, reading my damn mind.

I set her down on her feet and pulled my shirt over my head. She looked disappointed that I was getting dressed.

We had it bad. I doubted that I'd be able to hold off on popping the question much longer. Especially after I'd heard her confessions to Scarlett. She wanted me every Christmas morning. I wanted to give her time to get used to the idea, time to find the right solution at work. But all she had to do was look at me with those gorgeous green eyes, and I was already halfway to my knee.

It was right. We were right.

"It is," I admitted. "It's different now, but I still have all these memories popping out at me every room I step into."

We picked up our coats off the floor and, loose-limbed and smiling, started down the stairs. "I feel like any minute now your mom is gonna poke her head in the front door and tell Scarlett and me we have to unload the groceries from the car —" She broke off in mid-sentence, freezing on the stairs.

"What is it?" I asked. *Had she seen a bat? Did I have the chance to play hero again?*

"Her car."

"What car?"

"Your mom's car."

"What about it."

"She never let your dad drive it."

I recalled a few dozen arguments about my dad's driving ability. My mom drove a beat-up Pontiac bought from a cousin for a grand. It only started half the time and overheated the other half. The speakers on the right side didn't work, and the fabric on the ceiling had come loose. She kept it pinned up with sunflower safety pins. But it was her pride and joy.

I was surprised by the swift rush of memory.

"She hated the way Dad drove," I recalled. "He was a terrible driver, even before the drinking."

"Funny thing about memories," she said, sounding kind of far away. "Like walking down these steps I remember your mom pulling up out front in your dad's truck. Her honking the horn at us to come help unload. She was pissed because one of the bags fell over in the truck bed and the eggs were all broken."

A vague recollection was beginning to take shape.

"She was really upset about the eggs. Upset enough, I figured it was about something more than broken eggs," Cassidy continued quietly.

"She was upset about a lot of things," I said, not sure what Cassidy was getting at.

"We should probably head home," she said. But I got the feeling she wasn't hearing or seeing me right now. She had that look in her eye that I usually only saw during game night when she was one strategic play away from a win.

"Are you okay?" I asked.

But she didn't answer, she was already pushing her way out the front door.

I STARED down at the beer I was holding while *SportsCenter* replayed receiver GT Thompson's injury play over and over again as they discussed his career options. After gritty, raw, incredible sex, Cassidy had given me a perfunctory kiss on the back porch and marched right on into her own house. No invitation. No apology. Just a single-minded focus on something that she didn't feel like sharing.

I'd heard every damn word she and my sister exchanged the other night. And I thought Cass had taken it seriously. I had hope. But tonight was just another example of her shutting me out.

Jonah had tried to pry it out of me when I got home, but I'd brushed him off. I didn't feel like talking about how much my girlfriend had let me down. It was worse, coming on the heels of willingly going out in town together. And then baring our souls in a house that held hardly anything but sadness for me.

"Fuck," I swore. This wasn't the relationship that either one of us wanted or deserved. I didn't know what to do about it. I loved her. I belonged to her. We had a future together. But I couldn't make her trust me. I couldn't make her open up.

The knock was so soft I didn't think I'd heard it. Then it was back. Three soft taps coming from the door between our kitchens.

I pulled myself off the couch and shuffled down the hall. The door was unlocked, as always, but she was asking for permission.

I opened it. Cassidy hadn't bothered changing out of her ice cream and sex clothes. She was clutching a thin stack of papers. "Hey," she said.

"Hey."

"I'm sorry for kind of ghosting on you," she said.

I remained silent. I wasn't going to make this easy for her anymore.

"Bow, your mom never let your dad drive her car."

"What are you talking about, Cass?" I asked wearily.

"But he took her car to New York. He was in her car when he got the speeding ticket."

To give myself something to do besides feel hurt and confused, I headed into the kitchen for another beer even though I'd barely touched the one I had. Cassidy followed me.

"There was something that bothered me about your dad's speeding ticket. It was the fact that he got it in your mother's car. A car he wasn't allowed to drive. So why would she have lent it to him for a multi-state road trip?"

"I don't know. Maybe he stole it," I said.

Or maybe he needed the trunk of a car to conceal something he couldn't haul in the open bed of a pickup. The thought turned my stomach, and I put the second beer on the counter next to the first.

She was fired up. I could see her cop brain working. Excitement was crackling off of her. And I wanted to take it away from her the way she'd taken my hope away from me.

"What does it matter? My mother died in that car. It was totaled."

"And sent to Buddy Foster, Jr.'s junkyard," she said, shuffling the papers. "Buddy never gets rid of anything. There's a chance her car is still there."

If my father had used that car to cart Callie's body out of the state... "It's been more than ten years."

"But there might be something in it. Some clue."

"What could you possibly find?" I asked, not caring that I was raising my voice. "There's no way DNA evidence could survive ten years in the elements."

"We have to try, Bowie."

The woman I loved, the one I wanted to marry, was asking me to help her prove that my father was a murderer. She was, essentially, expecting me to help her ruin my family's life. Didn't she care what this would do to my family? Not just to our reputation, but how we saw ourselves. We were already the sons and daughter of a drunk. What would adding "murderer" to that description do?

"What about the pictures from the Kendalls?" I was grasping at straws.

"If we find the car and there's nothing in it, no evidence that Callie was ever in it, that could pull in favor of the theory that she hurt herself. If there's nothing to be found, that's another huge piece of evidence that Connelly can't keep ignoring."

I needed her to say it. *Did she think my father was guilty or innocent?*

Cassidy took a deep breath and blew it out again. "I've been struggling with wondering if I should tell you something or not. So I'm gonna say it. You have a right to know."

"You're starting to make me nervous," I said, picking up one of the beers.

"There's a possibility that your mom's accident wasn't an accident." She blurted the words out, and the beer went bitter on my tongue. "I talked to my dad about it and he had his suspicions."

"What? You think my dad murdered Callie and got a taste for it so he went ahead and killed my mom, too?" *It would have been laughable if it weren't my fucking life. My fucking family.*

"No. Not that kind of a not an accident," she explained gently. "There's a chance—a small one—that your mom crashed on purpose."

"Suicide? You think she went through that guardrail on purpose?"

"We both know she wasn't happy, Bowie," Cassidy began. "She had dreams much bigger than being a stay at home mom in a tiny town always worrying about money."

"They did the best they could." But even I didn't believe it.

My parents had let blame and dead dreams ruin what life they did have.

"I know, Bow. I know," she said softly. "But what if your dad had some kind of involvement and...and your mom knew?"

She was asking me what if my mom found out that my dad killed Callie and she couldn't live with it.

If Mom couldn't live with it, how was I supposed to?

"We need to go to Buddy's," she said, crossing her arms against some invisible chill.

We. She was including me in this. I almost laughed at the irony. I didn't want to be included.

I wanted to rewind to two hours ago when Cassidy had given me something beautiful to hang on to in that house. I felt sick.

She was supposed to be my future. My parents, my childhood, those were in my past. But if Cassidy had her way, she'd drag my past back out and make sure it haunted me forever.

58

CASSIDY

The rusted metal gate protested as it clanked open. The requisite junkyard dog made his leisurely appearance. Unlike his snarling, territorial brethren, Huck the bloodhound gave Bowie's pant leg a sniff and then meandered off in search of a warm bed or a biscuit.

"Mornin' there, deputy." Buddy Foster, Jr., junkyard entrepreneur extraordinaire, spat his tobacco in the direction of a 1980 Ford Granada on cinder blocks. There was a small cherry tree growing out of the engine block.

"Mornin', Buddy. Thanks for letting us come out," I said. I'd dressed casually in jeans and a heavy coat, not wanting to attract any unnecessary attention.

"Sure. Sure," Buddy said. His red-and-black checked flannel coat was older than I was. "Got a map for y'all." He handed over a hand sketched version of the junkyard that looked like Mother Nature was trying to reclaim. "It's thereabouts," he said pointing at a circle in the northwest corner.

"Appreciate it."

Bowie was quiet next to me. He'd been quiet, cold since last night. Since I'd shared.

Was he worried we'd find something?

Was I worried we wouldn't?

I didn't have high hopes that there'd be answers awaiting us here. But it was one more piece of the puzzle. Something even Connelly couldn't ignore.

Buddy waved us on and told us we could find him in the office trailer if we needed anything.

"You can wait in the car if you want," I told Bowie. It had been ten years since Connie had passed. But sometimes all it took was one memory to make those ten years disappear.

"Let's go," Bowie said briskly.

We walked the sloping, frozen ground, heading toward the area Buddy indicated. It was a crisp, cold winter morning just days before Christmas, and I was making my boyfriend check out the car his mother died in. This wasn't sharing. This was torturing.

I stopped. "You know what, maybe you should wait in the car," I said.

He didn't look at me, but he stopped walking. "I get that you feel ownership of this whole investigation, but this is *my* family. *My* mother. You don't own that."

I flinched. "Bowie, maybe this isn't such a good idea."

"I can see it from here," he said flatly, pointing ahead of us. There tucked in between the rusted-out corpses of family cars and broken-down pickup trucks was a white Pontiac 6000. Its front end was smashed all the way back to the dash. There were wispy tendrils of blue tarp fluttering in the winter wind out the broken driver side window. It was the kind of tarp we put over fatalities. I felt my blood go cold.

Days ago we'd been decorating cookies and hanging Christmas lights. He'd helped me put up a tree and chased the cats out of it the first six dozen times. And I'd marched him right on up to his mother's death.

"What are we looking for?" Bowie asked, stuffing his hands in his pockets. He was watching the tarp flutter.

"Dunno." I approached the car. It was free on the driver side, a grassy path dividing patches of wrecks from each other ran alongside it. The back door was missing. Dead weeds choked out the car all the way around. The tires were long gone. There was no way I was trying to crawl under the wreck and look at the undercarriage. That would be up to Connelly if we pulled the car for some forensics team to take a crack at. If he thought it might offer some hint at what had happened to Callie or if it was just another piece to ignore.

The quarter panel on the passenger side was missing. The rear bumper had fallen off on one side but was still attached on the other. The rear fender was scraped up. There was rust on every single surface, but the interior was remarkably intact aside from a decade of leaves and dirt and nature's debris. After snapping a few pictures of the exterior with my phone, I pulled the latex gloves out of my coat pocket and put them on. I ducked down and climbed into the back seat.

"Cassidy," Bowie warned.

"It's fine. I'll be a second," I said. My throat tightened when I saw the rusty brown stains on the driver seat. Old blood. So much blood.

I thought of my father being called to the scene and seeing Connie's lifeless body limp behind the wheel.

I thought of him keeping his concerns to himself to protect the family.

I'd known Connie. About as well as a teenager could know her best friend's mom. Suicide didn't make sense. She was stubborn, like Scarlett. I could see her deciding to live to ninety just to displease her husband. But accidents happened every damn day, stealing people away from their loved ones.

"Move over," Bowie said gruffly.

"Bow, you don't have to—"

But he was sliding in next to me.

"We used to fight over who got to ride up front," he said, patting the disintegrating blue cloth that sagged from the roof of the car. "Gibs was the tallest and needed the most leg room. But I had an inch on Jameson. Of course, then Scarlett started pretending to get carsick and got the front seat all the time."

"Diabolical, that sister of yours," I said.

Bowie gave a non-committal grunt. I patted his knee. "There's no need for you to be in here. I shouldn't have dragged you out here. It's gotta be hard for you."

He reached into the seat back pocket with more bravery than me. Who knew what kind of tarantulas or fanged, poisonous wildlife had taken up residence.

"Here." I shifted and pulled out a second pair of gloves.

Wordlessly, he snapped them on and dug back in. Not finding what he was looking for, he felt around with his feet on the floor.

"Still here," he said, reaching down into a pile of leaves and twigs and pulling out a pink-and-purple striped umbrella.

It sparked a few dozen memories. Grumpy Gibson carting groceries to the car, Connie holding the umbrella over him. Me and Scarlett trying to use it as a lightsaber while Connie drove us to a junior high dance. Jameson taking a whack at the Canadian goose that tried to take a bite out of Bowie's arm when Connie had dragged us out of the house for a rainy day walk.

"What's that still doing in here?" I asked softly.

"Dad was supposed to come clean the car out after...after she died. Looks like he never did."

There was a paper coffee cup still tucked in the cupholder. One of Scarlett's flip-flops was in the door pocket.

"She used to have a whatchamacallit...a dreamcatcher," Bowie said.

"On the rearview mirror." I remembered it.

I peered between the seats. The windshield was cracked in a few thousand spidery veins. The driver's seatbelt was still clipped, but the belt itself had been cut. The gas station coffee cup had brown spattered stains, and I wasn't sure if it was spilled coffee or long dried blood.

Something glimmered through the dried, frozen muck on the passenger side floorboard, and I reached down.

"Anything up there?" Bowie asked. He sounded numb, and I was reminded that I was a gigantic ass for bringing him here.

I pawed carefully through the dead leaves and mud coating what had once been a Tasmanian devil floor mat. "Aha!" I plucked it out of the debris. The synthetic feathers were long gone, but the silver hoop and wire were mostly intact.

I handed it over my shoulder to Bowie. It wasn't evidence. He could have this piece of his mother.

There were other things in the dirt. Bits and pieces of a life. A grocery receipt. A crushed soda bottle. I found one of Scarlett's old Bonne Bell lip glosses and a guitar pick that could have been Gibson's or Jonah's. There were no folded maps with a convenient X marking the spot where Jonah had gone after the disappearance, nothing that said Callie Kendall was here.

I peered over at the driver side. Glass glittered amongst the leaves on the floor. The seat's fabric had rotted through, and god knows what might be living in the sodden mess.

I tried the trunk release, but it didn't work. As I was pulling my hand back, a yellow piece of paper caught my eye. It was wedged in a crack in the dashboard between two molded pieces of plastic.

With a hard tug, it came free.

It was some kind of ticket, faded and hard to read.

"Are you done yet?" Bowie's voice had gone flat.

"Yeah. Yep," I said, sliding back between the seats into the back. I followed him out, stuffing the ticket into my back pocket.

If there was any evidence of Callie in this car, it was either microscopic or she hadn't ridden in it as a passenger. My eyes skated to the trunk.

It's not like there would be blood-soaked tarps in there. But if Jonah had killed Callie, there was a chance that there was something back there. And it would be better to have forensics go over it rather than having me poke around.

Bowie was standing there in silence, watching me and holding a plastic grocery bag.

"What's in there?" I asked.

"Some crap from the back seat. Family stuff."

I looked back at the trunk for a moment. If there was anything inside, Connelly and his forensics team could find it. I had put Bowie through enough already.

I glanced at the rear fender, the broken taillight and stepped in to get a closer look. It was definitely scraped. There were streaks of blue paint mixed in with the dirty white and the rust.

"What are you looking at?"

"Did your mom back into anything that you remember or get hit?"

"I don't remember, Cass." I was losing him. I'd found the end of his infinite patience. "Why?"

"This." I indicated the damage. I pulled out my phone and scrolled to the pictures I'd taken of the accident report. I found one of the drivers side of the car on the wrecker and zoomed in. It was grainy, but the car was much less rusty and the gouge was there.

"Maybe it happened during the accident."

"It's possible," I said. "But this looks like paint to me." I needed to look at the original photos again. But it looked as though some blue paint had transferred onto the Pontiac.

"Why does it matter?" Bowie asked.

"I need to run a reconstruction on the accident," I said mostly to myself.

"Why?"

"I don't want to tell tales out of school, without doing some research. But this accident might not have been an accident."

"Suicides usually aren't accidents," Bowie said bitterly.

I looked over my shoulder at him. "I mean it's possible that someone hit your mom's car."

59

CASSIDY

I drove us home and was surprised when Bowie followed me into my kitchen. I was fixing to apologize when he sat down at the kitchen table and put his head in his hands. Eddie skittered out of the room like it was on fire, but George wandered his chunky ass over to Bowie and wove his way in and out of his feet.

"Not everyone wants answers, Cass. Do you think I want to know for sure that my father murdered a sweet, beautiful teenage girl? Do you think that will help me sleep at night? To know that I have that in my blood?" He reached down and stroked a hand over the cat.

I pushed the start button on the coffee maker. "This limbo can't be good for you. Even if it turns out to be true, at least you'll know." He really believed there was a possibility that his father did it. I was surprised by that. I didn't believe it. Hell, I knew every piece of evidence we dug up would lead the blame away from Jonah.

"How would that help?" Bowie asked. "How would that not ruin everything for every single one of us? Do you want to marry the son of a man who committed cold-blooded murder? Are you okay with having your name linked to mine and my father's for forever? Do you want to have babies with me and then spend the next twenty years watching them to see if they display any homicidal tendencies?"

"Bowie, it doesn't have to be like that." I was scrambling for the thread. But it was lost to me. I felt like my father trying to carry on a conversation. Tongue-tied and misspeaking. I'd forgotten that not everyone needed answers like I did. I'd forgotten that for some answers made things much, much worse. "You're not your father any more than I am mine."

"What about my mother? My mom." His voice broke, and I died a little bit on the inside. "You say you think she might have killed herself. You think that answer would bring comfort to me? When I'd spent the last eleven years believing that she finally found her peace. It's not always about answers, Cass!"

"I'm sorry, Bowie," I said simply. I was.

"You come from good people. I come from misery, poverty, alcoholism. You don't like being judged for being your father's daughter? Imagine what it's like for me."

I shook my head. I was worried about living up to my dad. Bowie was worried about living down to his.

"Those answers you're trying so hard to find?" he said quietly. "They will ruin someone's life. Maybe my own. But you'll have what you were looking for then."

"Bowie, you aren't asking me to stop investigating a case because it involves your family, are you?" *I almost wanted him to say yes.* Because if he was making me choose between him and my job then he was the bad guy. Black and white. Uncomplicated.

"Of course I'm not," he said softly. "But you need to understand what you've done. You've taken that memory I've had of my mom and replaced it with something else. In twenty-four hours, you've taken a tragic accident that hurt us all and turned it into something even worse. A suicide? A hit-and-run? A tie to Callie Kendall?"

I felt sick. But stayed silent. Sometimes people needed to get things off their chests without someone else telling them how to feel.

"You're pushing so hard to find my father guilty and what happens if he is? Do you think I'm going to be happy to have answers? To know that my father was so much worse than I ever knew? To know that I come from that? Both of them are gone, Cassidy. All I've got left are my brothers and sister. And what you're doing is going to hurt them."

"I don't know what to do," I said, rubbing my arms against the cold that was blooming around my heart. Bowie was hurting and very politely lashing out. But not sharing my opinion was part and parcel of being a cop. Besides, what the hell good would my opinion be to him now? What if it was wrong, and I gave him false hope?

"You said your dad had his suspicions about my mother's accident," Bowie said suddenly.

"Yeah."

"But he didn't come running to us about it."

"He didn't have any proof," I said lamely.

"And maybe he was more worried about our well-being than a cause of death in an accident report."

I swallowed hard.

"You seek the truth. That's admirable, Cass. It really is. But sometimes it's important to balance truth with compassion. Your dad does it every day. He doesn't just try to solve. He's there to serve."

Emotions were bubbling up in me like a geyser. "I don't know how to do my job and not hurt you," I told him, stalking over to the coffeemaker and pouring a mug that I didn't want. None of this was fair.

"I don't know if you can," he said quietly. "And I can't ask you to choose."

"You can't give up. You can't give up on me. On us!" My voice rose.

He looked down at the floor, hands on his hips. "Look, Cass."

"Don't, Bow. Don't say it," I pleaded. It couldn't end like this.

He looked at me, his eyes blazing with pain that I'd thoughtlessly caused. "I want to be very clear. This is a fight. Not a break-up. Got it?"

I felt hot tears welling up and managed a nod. *A fight. Not a break-up.* I clung to that.

"Just a fight. But right now, I can't talk anymore about this." Bowie's voice was rough. "And I'm real sorry, but the only examples I have are my parents. So I'm either gonna throw a ton of shit at a wall and drink too much or I'm not going to talk to you for a bit. Okay?"

I handed him the salt shaker from my table. "Here. Throw it."

He set it down carefully.

Damn it. I would have felt a little better had he hauled off and chucked the squirrel into the wall.

"I know it seems like I'm asking you to choose between me and your job. And I don't want you to have to make that choice. I really don't. But right now, I can't see a good solution. So I'm gonna go home and I'm gonna think. And you're gonna stay safe and make good choices."

"I'm not one of your students," I said, nerves making me snap at him.

"I know that. But I just can't give you any more right now.

So I'm counting on you to take care of yourself for a bit until I can get my head on straight."

Damn it all the hell. He was a gentleman even in a fight.

"Are we going to survive this?" I asked, my voice barely above a whisper.

He looked down at the floor again. "I don't know, Cass," he said finally. "But we will talk. Later."

He turned and headed for the back door.

"You wanted me to share. I'm sharing. Now you're sorry I shared."

The unfairness of it, of him closing the door between us, struck me in the stomach hard enough to knock the wind out of me. I sank down to the floor and gathered George in my lap.

60

CASSIDY

Dear Bowie,

I think we both have some apologizing to do. Now, hear me out before you go and crumple this up and set it on fire and spend the next eight years ignoring me.

I'm sorry for a lot of things. Mostly, taking you to see your mom's car and spinning my theories for you. You wanted me to open up more, share more, and I did it, but not in the best way.

My thirst for answers can block me from seeing the rest of the big picture. I've always needed to know the why and the how of things. Flaw or not, it's served me well in my job. But I've never had a relationship to work my career around. You're my first. Or, you were. Since you're giving me the silent treatment, I'm not clear on the verb tense.

I became a cop because of Callie Kendall. Her disappearance still drives me to distraction. What happened? Where did she go? Is she still alive? The idea that we may never know was and still is unacceptable. How else can I pick it apart, put it in a neat little box, and then fit it onto a shelf? I never thought that doing so would hurt you so badly.

What I'm rambling on about, I guess, is that I shouldn't have assumed that answers would be as valuable to you as they are to me. I thought if I gave you closure, you could move on.

As a cop, I'm not supposed to let my opinion factor into how I do my job. But I guess I do every single day in invisible, incremental ways. So I'm sorry that I never told you that I believe your father is innocent. I never thought for a minute that he had anything to do with Callie's disappearance or murder. He may have had his flaws—his many, many flaws—but he wasn't a cold-blooded murderer. He also stood up and took responsibility for his mistakes.

You might also like to know that my father feels the same way. Ask him about the lamppost story...if you're still speaking to him that is. Even though I kind of hope you're not because that means you picked him over me again and I'm going to stop thinking about it before I get mad on top of my sad. Anyway, I'm going to Connelly today. I hope you understand. There are families, yours included, that deserve the truth.

Since this is a note and not face-to-face, I'm comfortable saying you also owe me an apology. You pushed me to share more of my work with you and when I did, you shut me out. I know, I know. I overshared in the most inappropriate and unforgivable way. I let my job stomp all over our relationship that I made you keep secret.

We need to face facts. We're both really new at this and we don't have great guidelines for what a good relationship is. Your parents sucked together. And mine are ridiculously perfect together, except for the fact that my dad can't string six words together and my mom organizes secret town meetings behind his back to do God knows what.

My point is, if we're in this, we need to find our own way. Forget your parents and mine. Forget Connelly and Callie. Please, let's find a way to make us work.

Love,

Cassidy

P.S. In case you're never speaking to me again, I didn't get a chance to tell Jonah, but that Shelby character is a journalist and I think she's angling to get close to you all through him. Steer clear.

P.P.S. Do you miss me?

P.P.P.S. It's almost Christmas so here's your gift. Spoiler alert: It's pajamas.

61

CASSIDY

"Here." I dropped the file on the conference table with an audible slap. It was early, and I hadn't slept. Bowie hadn't answered any of my texts since last night. So much had happened between us that the idea of going back to pretending he didn't exist was killing me.

Connelly looked up, annoyed. "What's this?"

"This came from the scanning you assigned to me. Connie Bodine's accident file, which I'm suggesting you consider reopening."

"That so?" he snorted, looking bored.

"There were no brake marks at the scene. No evidence that she tried to stop before she went through the guardrail. My father wondered if she might have done it on purpose. But this damage is consistent with being hit from behind." I tapped the picture with my finger.

"And how do we know that didn't happen in the ten years since that car was sitting in the junkyard?"

"Because of the original accident photos," I said, pulling out the next photo and laying them side-by-side. "Fresh damage. It would explain why she didn't try to stop. She was pushed. Which is a valid theory based on the reconstruction scenarios I ran since I have so much time on my hands these days."

"Deputy, why are you wasting my time with this?"

"Because when Jonah Bodine, Sr. left town after Callie Kendall disappeared it was in his wife's Pontiac 6000. This car." I pulled out a copy of the speeding ticket with the make and model circled. "The car was wrecked and junked less than a year later. It's still mostly intact in the yard about ten miles outside of town."

Connelly paged through the file I'd compiled and then sat back in his chair.

"I thought we had an understanding regarding the Kendall investigation," he said, coldly.

"We did. This was in the course of the administrative duties you assigned me." *You jackass.*

He steepled his fingers and looked like a movie villain. "Deputy Tucker, it's come to my attention that you disobeyed a direct order."

"Which one would that be, sir?" I'd had a long, shitty twenty-four hours and I was just doing my damn job. "I've disobeyed plenty recently so you'll have to be more specific." *God, that felt good.*

"The one where I told you to stay out of the Kendall investigation."

"I can't help if the scanning you assigned me uncovered a connection to your case."

"Don't be cute with me, deputy. You've done nothing but flaunt my authority since I arrived."

"I've done nothing but do my job to the best of my ability," I countered.

"You are dangerously disrespectful."

"I could say the same about you, sir."

"Turn in your badge, deputy. I don't have a need for you anymore," he snapped.

I leaned into my greatest fear. This man who had despised me from the beginning wanted to take the last thing I had left.

"I know why you feel this way. I know why you don't trust me and the rest of our department," I said, seething with rage. His eyes went icy.

"Your badge, deputy," he repeated.

"You're accusing me of letting my personal feelings get in the way of an investigation when it's your feelings that are a problem."

He slapped a hand down on the table between us. But I cut him off before he could begin a tirade.

"My research skills aren't limited to old case files. I know about your cousin," I told him and watched the anger bubble up inside of him. "I know she went missing when she was twenty. And while you and your family were leading search teams, the police chief was covering it up because his nephew was responsible. I'm sorry for your loss, sir. But you're making a mistake channeling that rage into this investigation. We aren't negligent. We aren't complicit. We take our job of protecting this community seriously."

"Your job is to catch criminals and prevent crime, not date suspects' sons."

All the secrecy. All the subterfuge. All for nothing. "I do my job damn well. And I'll see who I please. In the meantime, maybe you should focus less on *my* personal life and more on *your* investigation. Have you even discussed those photos with the Kendalls?" I snapped.

"That's none of your concern, since after today you'll be on the unemployment line!"

"You want my badge, Connelly? I'll turn it into my supervisor." I was dead calm.

"Get out of this office. I don't want to see your face in here again, Tucker!" He was shouting now.

I didn't take my eyes off him as he raged and I didn't turn around when the conference room door flew open.

"Detective Connelly," my father said, an edge to his voice. "If you have an issue with how I run my department, I suggest you take it up with me."

My father, the unflappable Sheriff Tucker, was about two seconds away from screaming bloody murder at Connelly. I could tell by the vein in his forehead that looked in danger of bursting.

"Your daughter is too busy fraternizing with the Bodines to do her damn job! And you either don't care or you're too ignorant to know a conflict of interest when it sits down at your dinner table."

"I trust my deputies to make their own personal decisions and do their jobs."

I put my hand on my dad's shoulder. When he looked at me, I shook my head. "Leave it be."

I didn't want or need him to fight this battle for me.

Walking through the conference room door, I took a hard right into my father's office. I was done. I was beyond done. I dropped my gun and my badge on his desk, dumped the cruiser keys into the top drawer and grabbed my coat from the rack near the back door.

"What in the ever-living fuck just happened in there?" Bex asked, pale-faced and big-eyed standing in the doorway of the property room.

"I resigned," I said flatly.

She tugged on her earlobe, nerves radiating off of her. "You did what now?"

"Apparently I can't serve the people of Bootleg Springs if I'm in love with one of them." And apparently I couldn't be in love with Bowie if I was still digging into his parents. So I had no job and no boyfriend.

It was all bullshit. My boyfriend was mad at me for doing my job and my job was mad at me for having a boyfriend.

Well, I'd gone and shown them. Yep. No job. No boyfriend. Fucking great. Oh, Lord. I couldn't breathe.

"I'm goin' in there," Fanny Sue said, putting her patrol hat on and straightening her clip-on tie.

I pushed out into the winter day feeling as numb as a block of ice. My uniform rubbed at my skin like I was suddenly allergic to it

Everywhere I looked, it was business as usual in Bootleg. We had a few tourists in town for cross-country skiing and holiday shopping. The storefronts were busy. Yee Haw Yarn and Coffee was full to bustin' with coffee seekers and the monthly knit-in.

Mona Lisa McNugget was struttin' right on down Main Street holding up both lanes of traffic.

This was my *home*. These were *my people, my family*.

I wasn't sure what the emotions were brewing in my chest. I felt lost and lonely.

62

BOWIE

I gave the signal, and Scarlett heaved the barn door closed.

"If I can get y'all's attention," I said, standing up on a milk crate at the front of the barn. If we were going to keep doing these meetings we were gonna need a stage or something.

It was a damn cold night this close to Christmas, but half of Bootleg had shown up. They were huddled up together on the benches trying to keep warm and catch up on all the gossip.

They were too busy catching up to hear me.

"Hey!" Gibson stood up. "Everybody shut up!"

It had the effect of a record scratch, and in seconds everyone was staring at me expectantly. *Oh, Lord. Where to begin?*

I brushed my hand over Cass's note tucked in my pocket and cleared my throat. "I've called you all here because we have a problem."

A hand raised in the back. "This about you and Cassidy courtin'?"

"Uh. What?"

Minnie Fae stood up in the second row in her yellow and orange cat sweater. "That's old news. Also, this is Fluffins and he's lookin' for a home," she said, holding up a cat that matched her sweater.

"Y'all better not have called a meetin' regarding old news!"

"I've known for weeks! Since Thanksgiving at least."

"Does Fluffins have all his shots?"

"How did y'all know?" I asked.

About a dozen people piped up at the same time.

"Saw you kissin' on your back porch when I was walking by at six in the morning."

"You two were holding hands under the table at the Christmas Carol Singalong!"

"There's security cameras on Mona Lisa's coop."

"Okay. All right." I held up my hands. "Yes, Cassidy and I are dating." Or, at least, we had been. We'd both screwed up. Her note yesterday had been dead-on. I'd asked too much of her without proving enough of myself. I'd asked her to step into the gray areas of her job for me without having earned it. Then, when she'd given me what I'd asked for, I turned my back on her. Oh, and then she lost her job over the whole disaster.

This damn mess was bigger than I could fix alone. And I needed the town's brain power behind me.

"What y'all probably don't know is Cassidy lost her job yesterday," I started again.

"Tell us something we don't know," Wade Zirkel hollered from the back.

"Anyone know what she said to that snake in the grass Connelly? I heard he was foamin' at the mouth when she walked out."

The crowd was getting rowdier and louder.

This was not going well. I was just making a mess of this,

too. I looked at my brothers in the front row, who looked concerned and a little annoyed. Jonah shrugged at my silent plea for help. We were all at a loss as to how to fix this.

Gram-Gram stood up on her bench. "Listen up, y'all. That hotshot yahoo detective forced my granddaughter out of her job! And we're gonna get it back for her!"

"Bootleg Justice!" someone hollered from the back of the room.

It was answered by a chorus of "hell yeahs," Bootleg Springs' rallying cry.

"Now, hang on y'all," I cautioned. "We need to do this the *legal* way. Connelly's a cop. We can't kidnap him and leave him in his skivvies with a thermos of coffee and bear spray in the woods."

"That only works once or twice," Marvin Lloyd pointed out. "We need some new material."

Mayor Hornsbladt stood up. "Can someone run through the facts of the sitchy-ation so we can put on our thinking caps?"

Nadine Tucker rose. "I got this, Bowie. Now, y'all listen up. Here's how it went down."

She ran through everything. Connelly claiming Cassidy was a shitty cop. The poorly kept secret of our relationship. The tension between us about her being part of the investigation into our father. Right on up to Cassidy and Connelly's dust-up at the station and that something she said to him had his face turning the color of a ripe eggplant.

The recap didn't make me feel any better about myself. I'd pushed Cassidy into a relationship and then basically forced her to share things she wasn't ready to share. Then I'd abandoned her. Just like I had seven years ago.

I needed to make it up to her. I needed to get her job back for her and then spend the next seven years groveling.

"Damn, son. You done shot yourself in the foot real good," Mayor Hornsbladt said, tucking his thumbs under the straps of his overalls.

"I'm well aware, sir. I need all y'all's help in fixing this."

THIRTY MINUTES LATER, after a lot of hollering and one cat adoption, we had a rough plan and all the players had their heads together on the details. I didn't know if it was the recreational moonshine refreshment being passed around, but the plan sounded plausible...and legal.

Scarlett's suggestions of breaking into Connelly's house and threatening him to be a better person were summarily scrapped. She was relegated to the official internet searcher for the town elders.

"We aren't all gonna fit in my El Camino," Granny Louisa noted.

"We'll take my van," Mrs. Varney decided. "Estelle, you've got the best eyesight out of all of us. You can drive."

Gram-Gram stood up again. "Now, let's talk about how you're gonna win her back. You need a grand gesture. A real big one."

"Like spelling out 'I love you' in pepperoni rolls."

"Have you changed your Facebook status to 'in a relationship?'"

"Maybe you should adopt a cat together!" That suggestion came from Minnie Murkle, who was holding a black cat aloft. I made a note to make a sizeable donation to the rescue's neutering program.

"Did y'all know that Cassidy told that Connelly fella that he had no right to tell her who she could and couldn't date?" Bex from the police station said from the second row.

"She did?" I asked, feeling a little lighter in my chest. "Did she say anything else?"

Bex grinned and wiggled her eyebrow ring. "Just somethin' about how it's no one's business if she loves you."

"How long ago was this?" Gram-Gram wanted to know. "Maybe she changed her mind."

63

CASSIDY

The knocking at my front door was persistent. Yet so was my determination to ignore it. It was the day before Christmas Eve. Christmas Eve Eve as I liked to call it before I was heartbroken and unemployed. Oh, and my best friend was still mad at me.

"Go away, Juney," I called from a cocoon of blankets, cats, and sadness on my couch.

"How did you know it was me?" my sister yelled through the door.

"You knock four times."

There was silence from my front porch.

The doors between my place and Bowie's were, for the first time ever, locked on my side. I'd said my piece in the very nicely written letter, and when he hadn't replied or acknowledged it, I turned off my phone and locked my doors. Even my cats were starting to avoid me. Every time I walked into a room, Eddie would sprint out, ears down, tail up as if Satan himself had strolled in.

Knock knock knock knock.

"I'm still not answering."

"Mom told me not to leave until I saw you face-to-face and spent a minimum of ten minutes attempting to assess your mental state."

"I don't think you're supposed to tell me that part."

"I'll set a timer," June offered.

I pulled the blanket over my head until the warm air made me feel like I was suffocating.

Knock knock knock knock.

My options were: 1. Wait her out. Or 2. Let her in.

June Tucker wasn't necessarily tenacious. But she was literal. If Mom told her not to leave without proof of life and ten minutes of convincing me that the world didn't suck, she would camp out on my front porch until she froze to death.

Really, I was doing my sisterly duty by saving her from frostbite. Besides, June lacked the ability to communicate empathy, so I wasn't in danger of being forcefully cheered up. I pushed blankets and cats aside but carried the sadness with me to the door.

June frowned at me. "You look disgusting," she said, taking in my rat's nest hair and my rumpled, stained sweats. When a person didn't have a job or a boyfriend, what did it matter if she spilled SpaghettiOs straight down her sweatshirt? Also what was the point of cleaning it up when there were two cats eager to eat the noodles right off the couch cushion?

"Thanks, Juney," I sighed, stepping away from the door.

"It wasn't a compliment. It was a statement of concern."

"Thank you for your concern."

"Wait. Stop talking. I want to make sure all this counts." She pulled out her phone and fiddled around. "Okay. Timer's set. How are you feeling?"

"Great."

June eyed me. "Is this one of those sarcastic jokes of yours?"

I face-planted on the couch. "What do you think?" I asked through the pillow.

Everything hurt. Especially that hole in my chest where my heart had been. I'd gone from having everything—Bowie, a great job, a bright future—to nothing but a greasy-haired, *Golden Girls* rerun-watching cat lady.

The pillow smelled like old SpaghettiOs. I sat up.

My sister glanced around the living room, noting the mound of used tissues. "From the evidence you're presenting, I feel that you are *not* great."

"You're very observant," I said dryly. "No, I'm not great. I suck. Everything sucks." I was horrified by the sudden urge to cry. How did I still have water in my tear ducts? I should have been dehydrated by now.

June frowned. "But isn't this what you wanted?"

"How is any of this what I wanted?" I blew my nose noisily.

"Didn't you want to prove that Bowie would hurt you again just like he did when you were in college? Didn't you also want to prove that Connelly could and would take your job?"

"What are you talking about?"

June nudged a shredded magazine with her foot. I'd ripped the cover off because it promised me seven ways to keep my man.

"It would appear that at least part of you wanted to be right," June said. Eddie jogged over to her and peered up at her. "Nice kitty."

"You're not making any sense," I accused her.

June looked at her phone. "You thought Bowie could still hurt you. So you proved yourself right. You thought Connelly had it out for you so you let him force you to resign. I thought you'd be happier."

I laughed. A dry, hacking, humorless cackle that had

George giving me the side-eye and waddling further down the couch.

"Do I *look* happy?"

June peered at me and shook her head. "Definitely not," she said with confidence.

She took a seat in the armchair I'd bought because it seemed so cheerful with its big blue flowers. Now I kind of hated it.

"What am I going to do, Juney?"

She blinked. "Either fix it or move on," she said, as if it were that simple.

The timer dinged, and June stood. She held her phone out at arm's length, and I heard the audible click of her camera.

"Seriously?"

"Proof for Mom."

"What? Your timer went off. You're free to go," I snapped.

"You're upset. Do you want me to make you some hot tea? Some people find hot beverages soothing."

It just about broke me. I shook my head. "Thanks, Juney," I said softly. "But I think I need some time to myself."

"See you at dinner tomorrow night." June let herself out and left me in peace.

Only now the solitude had lost its comfort.

I picked up my phone. There were text messages. Several dozen of them. Missed calls, too. But none from Bowie. None from Scarlett.

Was this it? Was this the end of my honorary Bodine membership? Had I lost my job for nothing?

June's words came back to me, chipping at my head like a woodpecker on a dead tree. Had I done this to myself?

I needed to know, and there was only one person who would tell me the truth. I picked up my phone and dialed. "Hi. I need help."

Approximately two minutes later, Scarlett burst through my front door. "It's about damn time!" she announced, lugging a cardboard box with her. "I've been circling your block for two hours waiting!"

"Waiting for what?"

"You to ask for help." She started unloading the box. The takeout food was followed by a new hoodie, fleecy pants, and two pre-packaged face masks.

"You forgive me?" I asked.

"All I wanted is for you to stop trying to do everything your damn self. You asked for help. I'm here. That's what friends are for. I love you, Cass."

"He hasn't called, Scar," I confessed, my eyes watering like I was cutting an onion. "No texts. I think this is the end."

"Neither one of you has ever done the long-term, forever and ever with someone before. There's bound to be a few bumps along the way."

"I took Bowie to the wrecked car your mom died in."

She sat on the couch and heaved George into her lap. "In the course of your investigation to prove our daddy innocent and save our family from public scrutiny," she insisted.

I dragged my hands through my hair and winced when they got stuck. *I really needed to shower.*

"It's my job to be impartial," I said stubbornly.

Scarlett rolled her eyes. "You can't be tellin' me to my face that you believe that you have to conduct yourself as a cop in your personal life. Because that, my friend, is bull-fucking-shit and you know it."

It was a cop-out—ha—and I was well aware. I'd deliberately kept my opinion from the man that I loved, an opinion that might have offered him the slightest bit of comfort. Worse, I'd done it because I hadn't trusted him or myself.

"Look, I'm not saying you didn't make a mess of things. But

so did Bow. Y'all are to blame and it's gonna take both of you to fix it."

"I don't think Bowie wants to fix it. He told me this is just a fight and that it's not a break-up, but he's shutting me out. But I don't know if he changed his mind and broke up with me without telling me."

"Let me ask you this. How important is your pride?" Scarlett asked.

I gave a hapless shrug. "I don't know if I have any left."

"You let Bowie walk away from you when you were nineteen."

I opened my mouth to argue, but Scarlett held up George's paw. "Uh-uh. You wanted him. You probably had an idea that he was lying to you. And you still let him go. Are you going to let him go this time or are you going to put it all on the line?"

"What if he doesn't want to be with me?" I asked. Nerves danced through my system, making me feel more scared than sad. Purposely putting myself out there, opening myself up to be devastated?

"Then he's a dumbass, but at least you would have put forth maximum effort. You wouldn't be living with any of those 'what ifs.' What if you tried one last time? What if you told him how you felt? What if you made him tell you how he felt? You could close the door on all of those things."

"When did you get so wise?" I asked as she tore open the to-go food containers.

"When Devlin taught me how to grow the hell up a little bit. Now, let's eat, watch some *Arrested Development*, and give ourselves facials."

"I love you, Scarlett. I may not tell you often enough. But you're the best friend a girl could have."

"And don't you forget it. Now, do you want the charcoal mask or the hologram unicorn mask?"

64

CASSIDY

It was supposed to snow today. Snow. On Christmas Eve. I was supposed to show up at my parents' house in a few hours for our annual family dinner. But that felt so monumental. And the nerves that I had bubbling up inside me.

I was meeting Scarlett, a little reluctantly, downtown for lunch. I had her Christmas present—a snazzy, custom-made tool belt with a beer bottle holder—tucked inside a cheerful holiday gift bag. She was going to help me with my speech. My "lay it all on the line and put my heart in Bowie's hands" speech.

I'd give him the words tonight, face-to-face if I had to break down the door between our halves.

My heart skipped a beat or two at the thought of putting it all out there. All on the line.

Scarlett had asked me what I wanted to save first, my job or my relationship. I'd surprised the hell out of myself by choosing Bowie. I could get another job, probably. I could be a security guard at the courthouse or maybe work with Leah

Mae at her boutique when it opened. Or I could venture outside of Bootleg and look for a law enforcement job.

But I couldn't find myself another Bowie Bodine.

I meandered down Lake Drive, scarf wrapped high around my neck, hat pulled low. I wasn't eager to see or be seen. Not yet. The station was up ahead. But I couldn't make myself look at it. It hurt too much. I'd mourn that loss and mourn it fiercely. But first things first. I needed to see if I could salvage things with Bowie. There were other jobs. Other ways to serve. But there was only one Bowie.

I'd done a lot of soul searching on how I'd come to be in this predicament. I had wanted to blame Connelly or Bowie or Misty Lynn, because—let's face it—she was a terrible human being. But I just kept coming back to all the ways I'd screwed up.

I'd let Connelly chase me out of a job I loved because, in the beginning, I was too chickenshit to stand up and demand respect. I'd let Bowie walk away from me twice now without laying it all on the line. And I'd omitted and outright lied to my best friend using the law as well as my own self-preservation as excuses.

I'd drawn a distinct line dividing my personal and professional lives and refused to tip-toe over it. And maybe that could work in a bigger city where no one knew their neighbors and cops didn't personally know the people they served. But that did not work in Bootleg Springs. That did not work for me.

Maybe I was too rigid? My father made it look easy. Mending fences, laying down the law, or bending it when the situation required it. Because he cared. He served.

He doesn't just try to solve. He's there to serve, Bowie had said. I felt the truth of it in my bones. Solving was what brought me to the law. But I was starting to realize that it was the serving part that fulfilled me. I would find a way to serve. Find a way to walk that line of personal and professional.

I glanced up and spotted someone in a blue winter coat that reminded me of Bowie's and felt the pang. I missed him, with a physical ache so acute I thought I was coming down with the flu. I'd been furious that he let someone else come between us, yet I'd done the exact same thing, allowing Connelly to call the shots. I'd been trying to protect my job, choosing it as my priority. That choice had cost me both job and man.

I looked around at the holiday bunting over shop windows, the inflatable nativity scene set up in front of the courthouse, the big red bows tied to the lamp posts. I was supposed to love this time of year. But I couldn't even muster the energy to wrap the presents I'd bought.

Would I have ignored my hunch at an accident scene to save the family heartache like my father? Or would I have investigated it, picked it apart, held it up to the light just so I could check all the right boxes in my report?

Was I more like Connelly or my father? The question seemed important more now than ever.

What was the point of protecting if I wasn't also serving?

I spotted Scarlett up ahead, cozy in a work jacket and ski cap over her dark brown hair. She raised her hand in greeting. We both heard the yell and turned in the same direction.

"Someone help!" It came from a small crowd gathering across the street at the park's entrance.

"The baby's not breathing!" someone yelled.

I was in a dead run, dodging a pickup truck carrying a bunch of snow inner tubes and freaking Mona Lisa McNugget out for her afternoon stroll.

"Cassidy! Come quick," Sallie Mae Brickman called from the circle.

I slammed my knees into the concrete so hard I thought I might have dented the sidewalk. A baby. Not breathing. I was already assessing while the crowd around us shouted information.

They'd been shopping. She was fine and then went stiff and started turning blue.

So tiny. Her perfect little cupid's bow lips were blue. Oh, God.

It was Christmas Eve.

Her name was Melinda Leigh. Melly for short. I remembered the birth announcement delivered to the police station. There was a welcome wall that we pinned all the baby pictures to. My father liked to say he and his deputies knew everyone in town from birth on.

Because they were family. We were family.

"Please! Please!" Melly's mama sobbed. Sybil Crabapple, at least she had been until she married Cody Wyatt a few years back. They'd gone through fertilization treatments for three years before being blessed with little Melly.

She couldn't be more than four months old.

"Everybody back up a step. Give Cass some room," Scarlett ordered shooing everyone back before hunkering down next to Sybil and wrapping the woman in a hard hug.

"Ambulance is six minutes out," Mrs. Morganson said, holding her phone to her ears.

"Goddammit." I shed my jacket. Six minutes was infinity when there was no oxygen. "Stay on the line with the dispatcher," I told Mrs. Morganson. "Someone call Cody for Sybil."

As quick as I could, I unzipped Melly's powder pink snowsuit. *Shout Tap.* My training kicked in as I called Melly's name and tapped her shoulder. No response. I freed one of her tiny feet from the suit and flicked it. Nothing. No breath.

Fuck. Fuck. Fuck.

Sybil was silent now, tears rolling down her cheeks, hands clasped under her chin as Scarlett rocked with her on the sidewalk.

It was up to me and the man upstairs. And I was gonna do everything in my power to make sure Melly got whatever was in her stocking from Santa. Thirty compressions. *One, two, three...*

I could feel the crowd around us growing, could hear the growing concern, but my focus was Melly and her blue lips.

Thirty.

I stopped, checked for breath. *Nothing. Nothing. Ten seconds of nothing.*

I delivered two rescue breaths. God, it was so different doing this on an actual human baby instead of the weird dolls we certified on. I was infusing her with my breath, my prayers, every fucking ounce of hope I had left in my body. *Please, Melly. Please, God.*

"You got this, Cass," someone whispered tearfully above me.

It was raining tears in this tiny circle. A half-dozen hands rested on Sybil's back and shoulders. I heard a commotion. Cody was here. But it was time to count again.

Thirty compressions. *One, two, three...* I never took my eyes off Melly's face. Nothing in this world existed but me, her, and my desire to see her take a breath. It was hard and fast. Was it too hard? Was it fast enough? *Twenty-eight. Twenty-nine. Thirty.*

I was sweating. It was running down my back. Steaming off my head.

"I'll spell you if you need it," Scarlett said. She was the calm in the center of a circle of fear.

I shook my head. "Not yet."

Two rescue breaths. Gentle. *Goddammit. Why didn't we have AEDs in storefronts?*

Wait! Was that—

"She took a breath!" someone hovering above me said, confirming what I thought I saw.

I leaned down, listening.

"Shut the hell up, everyone!" Scarlett ordered, and I swear the entire town held its breath with me.

A second later Melly gave a little gasp followed by another. In another second, she was shrieking and crying like she'd just been born. A roar went up around me, and Sybil and Cody were sobbing all over their beautiful, breathing baby girl. I could hear the sirens now, feel the pats on my back.

But all I saw were little Melly's teary brown eyes.

This was why I was here. To serve my town, my family.

I sat down on the concrete, and someone draped my coat over my shoulders. I needed a drink and a hug. A pair of boots approached me, and then someone was crouching down in front of me.

Bowie.

I don't know if he pulled me or if I climbed right in. But I was wrapped up tight in his arms, and everything felt a little bit better.

65

BOWIE

I shadowed Cassidy while she gave her report to the EMTs. Sybil climbed up into the back of the ambulance, and Cody followed behind in their car with his mama and Sybil's sister. There was another round of "nice jobs" and "real prouds" as Cassidy worked her way through the crowd.

She was exhausted. I could tell by the slump of her shoulders, the shadows under her eyes.

I took her arm and led her through the throng of people. "Are you okay?" I asked.

She rolled her shoulders. "I'll be better when we hear for sure Melly's all right." Cassidy shook her head. "That was the scariest moment of my entire life."

"You were amazing," I told her. She was. I'd come running with half of the rest of town. But while everyone was watching the baby and sending up prayers, I watched Cassidy. She was a hero. A real-life hero. Some people were made to do this job. She was one of them.

"Just doing my job," she said lightly. "Well, my ex-job. I don't have a job now."

"Cass, we need to talk."

She stopped mid-stride. "We sure do. But if you try to break up with me now, I will never, ever forgive you, Bowie Bodine. I'm amped up on adrenaline right now and I won't be held accountable for my actions. I have a speech prepared."

I slipped my arm around her waist and hauled her up against my side.

She rested her head on my chest, and for the first time in days I felt like everything was going to be okay.

"I am not breaking up with you. You're gonna have to work a hell of a lot harder to get rid of me."

"You disappeared on me," she said sadly.

"I've been real busy working on my grand apology," I told her.

She straightened away from me. "No, sir. No way. I'm apologizing first."

I laughed and reeled her back in. "Let's grab a coffee and then we'll both apologize."

She let me steer her into Yee Haw, and I relished being out in public with her. I ordered two coffees, keeping my arm tight around her waist.

"On the house for Baby Melly," the barista said. "You're a goddamn hero, Cassidy Ann Tucker." The clientele around us exploded into raucous applause, and I worried I'd pop the buttons right off my shirt with pride. My girl.

"Nice to see y'all not necking in an alley for a change," Old Judge Carwell said, tipping his hat at us as he wandered by with his chai latte.

Cass shot me a look.

"So it seems like our secret relationship wasn't very secret," I confessed.

"Even Connelly knew," she sighed. "Which reminds me." She handed me her coffee and patted her pockets until she pulled out a stack of note cards.

"What are you doing?" I asked.

"I'm apologizing." She studied the first card. "Okay. Hi, Bowie. Thanks for agreein' to see me."

"I found you on the sidewalk giving CPR to a baby."

"Shh!" she shushed me. "Don't make me lose my place." She cleared her throat, skimming the card. I steered us back outside. We had a very important place to be.

"Okay. Um. I owe you an apology. Several in fact." She flipped the card, and I tugged her down the block.

"You're doing real good, honey," I told her.

"Thanks. I'm sorry for setting us up to fail. For being too scared to get hurt to trust you fully."

"You're forgiven."

She looked up at me and scowled. "You can't forgive me yet. I'm not done apologizing."

"My apologies. Please continue."

"I'm sorry for not trusting you and then dragging you into a personally damaging situation without realizing how it would hurt you."

"That's real nice, Cass."

"Thanks! Juney helped me with it a little."

Clay Larkin, Leah Mae's daddy, spotted us and made a beeline for Cassidy.

"Cassidy Tucker, I heard about what you did for Baby Melly. Brace yourself because you're about to get hugged."

I grabbed her coffee just before Clay lifted her six inches off the sidewalk. Three notecards slipped out of her grasp and floated to the ground. His fiancée, Betsy, clapped and wiped a stray tear from her cheek.

"Honey, you made us all real proud. Real proud," Betsy said when Clay returned Cassidy to the sidewalk. She leaned in and gave her a kiss on the cheek. "And y'all are the sweetest couple. We're so happy for you."

Cassidy turned a pretty shade of pink. "Thanks. Uh. Thank you."

Betsy looked at me and surreptitiously tapped her watch. I nodded.

"C'mon, Cass. We've got places to be."

"We do?" she asked. I handed her coffee back and slipped an arm around her shoulders.

"Hang on. I've got more to say." She peered down at her cards and cleared her throat. "For not banging on Gibson's door and demanding you tell me the truth all those years ago. Huh. I think my cards got shuffled."

"Still sounds real good," I told her. She was so busy looking at her notes, she didn't notice the crowd forming around the police station's front door.

"I also owe you an apology for agreeing to be in a temporary, secret relationship with you because—what the hell is going on?"

At that moment a minivan blazed up the street and squealed to a stop in front of the station. The passenger doors opened, and the elderly of Bootleg Springs started pouring out onto the sidewalk. Walkers and oxygen tanks were handed out to their owners. Behind the wheel, Estelle slipped her driving gloves off and gave me a flirty wave.

"Uh, Bowie? What's going on?"

"You had your apology. I've got mine."

66

BOWIE

A woman significantly younger than the rest of the minivan's occupants disembarked looking a little shell-shocked. She wore a wool coat over a simple black pantsuit. No nonsense, professional.

"Right this way, lieutenant," Granny Louisa said, opening the police station door with a grand flourish.

"Lieutenant?" Cassidy hissed. "You kidnapped a state trooper?" She looked a little pale.

"We did no such felonizing," Gram-Gram snorted. "She *wanted* to come with us."

"Scout's honor," Estelle said, making an x over her heart.

"Come on," I told her and led her into the station at the end of the elderly parade. The rest of the crowd slowly filed in.

"Cass!" Bex threw herself at Cassidy and wrapped her in a tight hug. "I just heard from Sybil. She said to tell you Melly is a-okay and you're an angel."

Cassidy's shoulders sagged in relief. "Oh, thank God," she whispered.

"What the hell is going on here?" an angry voice snapped

out over the general din. Connelly, looking six shades of pissed off, poked his head out of the conference room door.

"Exactly what I'd like to know," the woman in the suit said coolly. "It's come to my attention that your investigation has been less than exemplary here."

"Lieutenant Garza," Connelly said with a nod. "There seems to be some kind of misunderstanding."

"When six members of a community you are supposed to be serving show up at my precinct with a laundry list of complaints regarding your behavior, you better hope there's a misunderstanding."

"I want to be her when I grow up," Cassidy whispered in my ear. She had hearts in her eyes.

Connelly was sputtering, and I saw Sheriff Tucker's mustache twitch as he fought a smile.

"Let's take this into the conference room," the lieutenant suggested. "Ladies and gentlemen, Detective Connelly, Sheriff Tucker, and I would be happy to listen to your complaints one at a time."

"He's turning that eggplant color again," Fanny Sue said gleefully, nodding at Connelly's face.

They trooped into the conference room and closed the door.

Dazed, Cassidy turned to me. "Did you somehow orchestrate all this?"

But her friends and fans demanded her attention. She was pulled from my arms and passed from person to person for hugs and handshakes. For congratulations on our relationship and kudos for everything from her lifesaving skills to her neat handwriting on traffic citations. There were fifty bodies squashed inside with more waiting out front.

One by one, citizens entered the conference room and

faced down Connelly, addressing their concerns and complaints. All standing for one of their own.

I loved this weird and wonderful town, and for the first time since Callie's sweater showed up, I felt like I belonged again.

"I feel dizzy," Cassidy said, wrapping her arms around my waist. She'd been passed clear around the station.

"I've got you," I promised her.

"I can't believe you did this for me," she said, her voice cracking as she looked at the line of people waiting to tell their tales on Connelly.

"We did it for you," I insisted. "You think I would have come up with the elder council kidnapping a lieutenant on my own?"

Cassidy laughed and squeezed me tighter. "I'm so happy I could burst."

I kissed the top of her head. "Me, too, Cass. Me, too."

The conference room door opened, and Connelly burst forth. His face was a mask of rage. He zeroed in on Cassidy and pushed his way through the crowd. I stood next to her, my arm around her shoulder so she knew I had her back. I wanted him to do something stupid so I could break his fucking face. It had been a long time since I'd punched anyone over Cassidy.

But he just glared, nostrils flaring. Cassidy was cooler than an ice cube under his gaze.

"That will be all, detective," Lieutenant Garza said from the conference room doorway.

One more flare, a twitch of his right eye, and he was pushing out of the station, barking at people to get out of his way.

Cassidy vibrated under my touch, and I knew her well

enough to know it was cold fury, not fear that had her clenching her hands into fists.

The lieutenant weaved her way through the crowd to us.

"Deputy, I've never known someone so young to command so much respect in their community. It would be a travesty if you weren't back at your desk immediately." She held out Cassidy's service weapon and badge. "Please accept my formal apology for Detective Connelly's behavior."

Sheriff Tucker stood behind the lieutenant, looking downright verklempt. Nadine slipped up next to him and wrapped her arm around her husband's waist. I saw what they had together decades into their partnership and I wanted it fiercely.

"Thank you, lieutenant," Cassidy said, accepting her gear like it was an autograph from a country star. "I'll be back tomorrow."

The lieutenant cracked her first smile. "Tomorrow's Christmas. Why don't you take the day? We'll see you on the twenty-sixth. I have a forensics lab to talk to about a car."

Cassidy nodded and then kept nodding. "Thank you, sir. Ma'am. Lieutenant."

"It looks like you've got some fans," the lieutenant said, nodding toward the windows.

There were faces of all ages pressed up against the glass.

"Guess I'm calling the window cleaners again," Bex joked.

"Go on, Cass," Sheriff Tucker said. "Tell 'em the good news."

Cassidy tucked her holster into the waistband of her pants and held her hand out to me. "Comin', Bow?"

I took her hand and followed her outside. The clouds were heavy with snow yet to fall, but the cold couldn't fight its way through the crowd.

Without saying a word, Cassidy held up her badge, and the crowd lost its damn mind hooting and hollering.

She looked over her shoulder at me, and I couldn't not be kissing her for another second. I pulled her to me and brought my mouth to hers. It sounded to me that the din of the crowd got even louder.

This was right where we belonged. Surrounded by Bodines and Tuckers and Bootleg. I saw my brothers and sister in the crowd celebrating right along with the rest of them. This was the beginning of something beautiful, something forever.

"I love you, Bowie. This sure beats a pair of pajamas."

I grinned down at her. "I'd do anything for you. I love you, Cassidy Ann. And someday not too far into the future I'm going to put a ring on your finger."

"I've loved you since forever, Bowie Bodine. We're gonna make one hell of a team."

The snow fell soft and quiet, and I kissed her hard and hungry.

"DID y'all see Scarlett hit that Shelby with a snowball?"

"One second we're all standing there, watching Cassidy and Bowie makin' out, and then Scarlett's yelling 'Back away Jonah! You're fraternizing with the enemy!'"

"Poor guy. That Shelby flirted him up good."

"Never would have guessed that sweet thing was a journalist. Just goes to show you, you can't trust a friendly stranger."

"Have to admit, she held up real well when Scarlett tried to scratch her eyes out."

"That Devlin's got quick reflexes when it comes to his girlfriend. He caught Scarlett mid-air."

"Rumor has it Shelby didn't move out of the B&B. In fact, she ordered room service. I think she's planning to stick around."

"Takes guts."

"Wonder where Jonah will live now since the lovebirds will probably want to spread out in their nest?"

EPILOGUE

CASSIDY

"Wait!" Bowie waved his hands in front of me as I teed up with the sledgehammer. "How do we know you're not going to hit some kind of plumbing or electrical?"

"Because your sister already did some exploratory hole poking. That's why there's a big ol' X on the wall," I explained patiently.

I eyed up Mr. Bodine. He was studying the plaster wall over his second cup of coffee. His pajama pants, a black and red-checkered lumberjack pattern, hung low on his hips. The untied drawstring was mighty distracting.

"You're not nervous, are you?" I cocked my hip, resting the sledgehammer on my shoulder.

"I just want to make sure you want a commitment in the form of a hole in the wall rather than a nice something sparkly on your ring finger," he said, giving me that heart-melting, boyish grin that had done me in when we were kids.

"Let's try this whole 'living together' thing first. What if I can't stand the way you blow your nose? Or you get all disenchanted with the way I do laundry?" It was, in small part, a bluff. Of course I wanted Bowie to get down on one knee and make a fuss about how much he loved me. I wanted to plan a wedding with him. To throw our loved ones a party that no one would forget. Make a couple of babies and complain about time flying too fast.

But first, I wanted to date the man. I wanted an honest-to-goodness relationship. Arguments over dishes, inside jokes, hand-holding in public. I wanted the whole shebang with Bowie Bodine.

A ruckus came from the stairs on Bowie's side of the double, and Jonah appeared in the open doorway. He was carting a suitcase and another cardboard box.

"You don't have to move out immediately, you know," Bowie told him.

Jonah gave us the once-over. "Y'all are sharing a set of pajamas. I know when I'm intruding. Besides, June's giving me a good deal on rent."

I still couldn't believe my sister had voluntarily opened her home to another human being. She was notoriously persnickety about, well, everything.

"Aw!" I crooned. "It's your first 'y'all'!"

He flashed me a grin. "I'm learning. Slowly."

"Don't be a stranger," I told him. "And don't let June be too weird."

"I'm gonna help Jonah carry some stuff out to the car," Bowie said, handing me his coffee and dropping a kiss on my cheek.

They trooped out the front door and left me in stillness.

It was snowing again. I was drawn to the window.

Fat flakes that floated down like feathers from the white sky. It was a new year, and I was looking forward to everything that entailed. Eddie wove himself between my feet like a snake on his way to his food dish. This was the first year I'd woken up to Bowie on Christmas morning.

We'd made the most of waking up early together and then gone to my parents' for a lazy brunch. The social obligations wrapped with an early, rowdy Bodine dinner at Jameson and Leah Mae's.

I caught a whiff of flowers. The riotous bouquet of red and white flowers and glossy green leaves had arrived Christmas evening, hand-delivered by Sybil, Clay, and baby Melly, who had made a complete recovery.

Family. Friends. And Bowie.

I was back to work and everything felt...right.

The investigation still hung over our heads. Connie Bodine's car had been hauled off to a forensics lab in Charleston, and we were once again playing a waiting game. But this time around, things would be different. I was serving the Bodines just like I was serving the Kendalls and the rest of Bootleg Springs.

I wouldn't be perfect, but I'd be better.

"Whatcha see?" Bowie asked, coming up behind me to press a kiss on the side of my neck.

"Maybe a bit of the future," I mused, turning to wrap my arms around him. I could hug and kiss Bowie Bodine anytime I wanted. That wouldn't get old anytime soon.

"Speaking of," he said reaching into his pants pocket.

"What are you after?"

"Before we put a hole in our wall, I'd like to make another commitment." He sank down on one knee.

"You better stand yourself back up, buddy," I warned him.

He produced a ring, a delicate band of interwoven diamonds and gold. "It's not an engagement ring. It's a promise."

I bit my lip and felt my heart kick up a notch. "What kind of a promise?"

"I know you're not ready for the real thing yet. But I want to make you a promise to be a solid partner to you. To have your back and be your right hand. To never give up on us. To give you my best every day. I'm in this for forever, Cass. You're who I've been waiting for my whole life."

My throat felt awfully tight all of a sudden. "It's beautiful, Bow."

"You're the sparkle to my gold, Cassidy Ann," he said sliding the ring on my finger. "And the minute you're ready for something a little more permanent, you let me know."

"How about six months?" I suggested, feeling flutters in my stomach.

He stood back up. "How about three?"

I laughed.

"I know you're the one," he said, rubbing his thumb over the band on my finger. I liked the way it looked there. Like it belonged. "There's no one else walking this earth that I'd want to share my life with."

"We *have* wasted a lot of time," I said.

He grinned down at me. "We won't be wasting any more of our time," he promised. "And that's why I've got something else for you."

I was already feeling swoony and delirious. I didn't know if I could handle much more.

He removed a folded-up piece of paper from his pocket with as much reverence as he had the ring.

"Go on," he coaxed, handing it over.

I hesitated, sensing that to Bowie whatever was on this piece of paper was somehow bigger.

There were two addresses scrawled across the notebook paper.

"What are these?"

"Those are the last two destinations recorded in my mom's old-ass GPS."

My lips quirked. "I remember when you kids gave it to her. She hated it."

Bowie gave a soft laugh. "Said she didn't need technology to tell her she wasn't going nowhere."

"But apparently she used it," I said.

He tapped the top address. "This is where she went on the day she died. And this," he said, touching the second listing, "is where my dad went after Callie disappeared. The dates line up."

My gaze whipped up to his.

"I found the GPS under the passenger seat while you were digging out the dream catcher," he said. "Didn't think anything of it. Until one night I couldn't sleep. Gibs's pickup still has a cigarette lighter, so I drove it out there yesterday."

I felt the familiar thrum in my blood. Answers. We were getting closer.

"Go ahead," Bowie said. "You can get excited. I've got the GPS bagged up for you to take to the lieutenant."

"I don't know what to say," I confessed.

Bowie tipped my chin up, so I was looking into those earnest gray eyes. "I gave you my promise. And I want one in return."

"What's that?" I'd promise him anything. I knew that. And I'd find a way to make it happen, no matter what.

"I want you to find the answers for me. What happened to my mom? What did my dad have to do with Callie Kendall's disappearance?"

I swallowed hard. "Are you sure?"

He nodded. "I want closure. And I want you to help me get it."

"Okay," I agreed.

"Thank you," he said softly.

I threw my arms around his neck. "I love you, Bowie. There's no one else I'd rather share pajamas with."

He stroked those big, capable hands down my back and breathed in the scent of my shampoo. "I love you, Cass. Always have. Now, let's put a big hole in this here wall and get to joining our halves."

I handed him the sledgehammer. "You take the first swing."

He wound up and swung. The plaster crumbled and sent up a shower of dust.

"Hmm. I wonder if Jonah's streak is about to come to an end or if he'll triumph," I mused.

"What streak?"

"Everyone he moves in with falls in love and gets paired off."

"You think Juney's up next?" Bowie asked.

I shrugged. "Stranger things have happened."

He handed me the hammer. "Your turn, trouble. Make me proud."

I swung for the fences, hitting in exactly the same spot. When I pulled the sledgehammer out, I could see light on the other side.

"I think three months might work," I told him.

Heedless of the dust and mess, Bowie caught me up in a fierce embrace, and when his mouth found mine, I had no doubts, no barriers. Just love.

AUTHOR'S NOTE TO THE READER

Dear Reader,

It is so good to be back in Bootleg Springs where the chickens are cocky, the mystery is intriguing, and everyone falls in love! Do you have a theory on what happened to Callie? You're welcome to join my Lucy Score's Spoiler Dungeon to chat conspiracy theories.

June's book, Bourbon Bliss, is up next and I promise you that Claire has written her to be as quirky and hilarious as you're hoping. You'll love her!

Did you love this latest trip back to Bootleg Springs? Drop a review on Amazon or BookBub and start throwing copies at your favorite reader friends' faces. Want to hang out with me daily? Swing by my house with tacos and coffee or join Lucy Score's Binge Readers Anonymous on Facebook. Sign up for my newsletter and never miss a new release or sale... unless my messages go to your Spam or Promo folders.

Xoxo,

Lucy

ABOUT THE AUTHOR

Lucy Score is a *Wall Street Journal* and #1 Amazon bestselling author. She grew up in a literary family who insisted that the dinner table was for reading and earned a degree in journalism. She writes full-time from the Pennsylvania home she and Mr. Lucy share with their obnoxious cat, Cleo. When not spending hours crafting heartbreaker heroes and kick-ass heroines, Lucy can be found on the couch, in the kitchen, or at the gym. She hopes to someday write from a sailboat, or oceanfront condo, or tropical island with reliable Wi-Fi.

Sign up for her newsletter and stay up on all the latest Lucy book news.
And follow her on:
Website: Lucyscore.com
Facebook at: lucyscorewrites
Instagram at: scorelucy
Twitter at: LucyScore1
Blog at: lucyscore.com/blog
Readers Group at: Lucy Score's Binge Readers Anonymous

ACKNOWLEDGMENTS

- Cassy Roop from Pink Ink Designs for Moonshine Kiss's cover artwork.

- Claire Kingsley for being an epic planning partner in crime.

- Dawn, Jessica, and Amanda for those eyeballs.

- Binge Readers Anonymous and the Lucy Score Spoiler Dungeon for always being entertaining and uplifting and taco-y.

- My Indie girls and ELOE guys for always being awesome.

- Taco Bell Mild Sauce. Some might find you not hot enough, but to me you're an effortless blend of seasonings and sauciness.

- Mr. Lucy just for being you.

- Cleo the cat. Just kidding. You were nothing but a furry hinderance. I acknowledge your hinderance.

- Artificial Christmas trees that work right out of the box.

LUCY'S TITLES

Standalone Titles

Undercover Love

Pretend You're Mine

Finally Mine

Protecting What's Mine

Mr. Fixer Upper

The Christmas Fix

Heart of Hope

The Worst Best Man

Rock Bottom Girl

The Price of Scandal

By a Thread

The Blue Moon Small Town Romance Series

No More Secrets

Fall into Temptation

The Last Second Chance

Not Part of the Plan

Holding on to Chaos

The Fine Art of Faking It

Where It All Began

Bootleg Springs Series

Whiskey Chaser

Sidecar Crush

Moonshine Kiss

Bourbon Bliss

Gin Fling

Highball Rush

Sinner and Saint

Crossing the Line

Breaking the Rules

Manufactured by Amazon.ca
Bolton, ON

38908622R00238